StrathNaver Legends

(The Loss of Lurelei)

Robert G. Makin

ISBN: 978-0-615-71095-2

Layout and interior design by Jonni Anderson:
        jonnianderson.com, starwatchcreations.com

Cover design by Robert Makin and Jonni Anderson

Sons of Aaron Publishing

Palm Coast, Florida

Acknowledgments

I wish to acknowledge and thank many friends without whose encouragement the *StrathNaver Legends* would have been impossible. I particularly want to thank Christy Saenz, Richard Mergener and Sophie Tredor whose steadfast enthusiasm for the story and the legend fueled my pen. I want to thank Denny Axlen for his simple but powerful statement to me, "Don't quit trying." Most important of all, of course is Kerry Franco, a real Gray Elf afflicted by the bite of the Geketz.

This book is dedicated to

Kerry Franco,

wherever she may be.

Contents

StrathNaver Legends

(The Loss of Lurelei)

Robert G. Makin

Foreward

Folk tales about Elf Wars have been popular throughout the ages. These stories originated in Eaolofia, the Elf homeland. They were not restricted to the British Isles, as in this narrative but eventually spread to every part of the known world.

Some say Eaolofia is located in the general vicinity of present day Bermuda. Others believe it was merely a regional moniker or nickname, never actually recorded, and the location is somewhere in northern North America. Although the concept of a race predating what is commonly known as the "Native Americans" may seem incongruous, archeological finds in the region of northern New England and the southern part of the Provinces of Quebec and New Brunswick, including western Nova Scotia, indicate the possibility of earlier settlers. A second hypothesis resulting from these digs seems to indicate that the blending of the races included and resulted in what actually became the Native American. One finds indications in Scotland and Wales of Elf traits and appearances; in fact, each region of the world seems to have inherited specific traits. Although the Elf race no longer exists per se, its legacy remains with us for all time.

This document does not hold forth upon the validity of any one hypothesis over another but focuses on the life and development of the interactivity of the races as illustrated in the extended works of Feshka, who was half Elf and half Homo Sapien. The characterizations are based in part on real characters who were contemporaries of Feshka and who were central in the ongoing conflict between the Elf peoples and a predatory race of unknown origin.

The preceding narrative is an attempt to present this important history in a format easy to read and remember.

FESHKA

Chapter Zero: Discoveries

*In Gear-Dagum, early Eighth Century C.E.,
The Valley of the Naver River*

"There he is," said Silver Leaf, staring into the meadow beyond the forest.

"But he's just a human boy," Aelronde replied with furrowed brow.

The two Elves sat perched in the highest branches of an old oak tree on the edge of the forest. Sheep grazed in the meadow beyond. Their herdsman, a boy of about ten years, flaming red hair and long legs, wore clothing made of the wool from the sheep he tended.

"So he's the one my father thinks will save us?" Aelronde asked with an expression of condescension.

"That's right," Silver Leaf replied softly. "He's the one Migalik thinks is prophesied by the weaves to lead our people to freedom from the Enemy."

Aelronde shook her long blonde hair, her eyes brightened and she began giggling. "But he's just a child, like you and me. He can barely lead his sheep. Just watch him racing around after this one then that one. Besides, no one has heard of the Enemy in many years. He'll never be back."

"All of us have that hope," said Silver Leaf. He changed to a more comfortable position on the tree limb. "But Migalik thinks differently. That is why Migalik has us watching over him to protect him, just in case he IS the one."

"But he's just a boy," Aelronde insisted.

"I said that to Migalik and he told me, 'boys grow up.'"

"My father is very wise," said Aelronde. "That is why he is King of the Naver Gray Elves and Dream Maker for those who live in this region. But he is not always right. How could he be? Everyone makes mistakes." She shook her hair again and brushed a leaf off her forest green cloak.

"I think it's a mistake that we sit in this tree in clear view. He could easily see us and we are not supposed to allow that."

Silver Leaf turned his attention from the meadow, smiling at Aelronde, "If a person refuses to believe in a thing, it is impossible for him to see it. The boy, Angus Williamson has been taught that Elves don't exist. If he looked right at us, he would deny what he saw and say instead that he saw a thick clump of leaves in the tree, or a knot on the trunk. He would not say that he had seen two Elves watching him from the forest. Neither would he believe it."

"But his own mother is one of us. How could he not know?" asked Aelronde.

"His mother is close kin to us, but not a full Elf. She bears a resemblance to our people, as does the boy, Angus. One day he will know."

Silver Leaf turned his attention back to the meadow. As he did, his face grew stern. "Look there. "In the distance, there is group of men coming up the road."

"I see them," Aelronde's smile faded. "They look tired and some of them seem injured in some way."

"My father, Guldockel, says that there are wars in the south between some of the humans and that when we see groups like this coming home from the wars, we should be very wary of them. There could be trouble."

"Do you think Angus is in danger?" asked Aelronde.

"That may be," Silver Leaf whispered. "Go and tell Migalik. I will stay here and watch. If there is trouble, maybe I can help."

⋐⋑

The sheep were restless. Angus shouted and raced after them, waving his oak stick, as if he thought that would make them pay attention. He stopped for a moment to catch his breath. It was a good thing his legs were so long; he was a fast runner for his age. His father was probably right about sheep being stupid, but they were also adventuresome, wandering everywhere, forcing Angus to chase them down and bring them back.

Lost in his own thoughts, at first Angus didn't hear the men's voices coming from the break on the other side of the hill. Checking the sheep a last time, he crept to the top of the rise to see who was coming. His breath was coming quicker as he anticipated this new adventure, some excitement to liven up a dreary day!

He didn't have to wait long to see whose voices he heard. Approaching from the south in the direction of Inverness, twenty or so raggedy looking men plodded up the path. They seemed worn out. Angus felt his throat tighten in fear. They wore the colors of the MacDonalds, the Islemen, and the MacDonalds were not particularly friendly to Clan McAodh. Angus heard wild stories about them and knew it would not be good for them to see him.

For the first time this day, he felt cold and alone. He knew his nose was running. He wiped it on his sleeve and shivered. *Why does cold weather always make my nose runny?* Trying to remain unseen, he watched them approach.

Some of them had four foot long wooden swords slung over their shoulders. Angus recognized these were like his father's iron sword. They carried several of their companions on litters. Some hobbled on crutches made from broken-off tree limbs; others wore bloody cloths wrapped around an arm or a leg. One man's makeshift head bandage covered one of his eyes. Angus winced, imagining the pain of these injuries.

His father warned him often, "If you see any from the other clans passing by, stay well clear of them, especially the Islemen."

Hostility and mistrust colored the relations with other clans except for Clan Gunn, who Angus' Mother called "sort of arm's length kinsmen."

But these are not from Clan Gunn. They are Islemen, Angus reminded himself. He held his breath, watching the men pass, afraid they would hear him breathe. He was so focused on these men, he forgot about the sheep and one of them now started down the embankment toward the MacDonalds, head down, grazing as it went.

One of the men in the lead noticed the sheep, just as Angus saw it himself. A chunk of dirt clung to its wool from where it slept in the sheep pen at home. The dirt flopped as the sheep moved. Its heavy coat grew nicely; it would be a rich shearing come spring. He couldn't lose that sheep. Angus crouched in the heather, waiting.

"Ho, what for--here's dinner, me boys!" one of the men shouted, frightening the sheep. "Let's catch it now!" He started gently toward it. The man wore a blood-spattered, gray shirt and muddy wool pants. His stringy, brown hair hung wet and dripped over his brow. The scratches on the man's face and arms chilled Angus the most. He might have got them running through a bramble patch but Angus knew it was more likely a gauntlet of swords. Angus could see those wounds were deeper than scratches. They were slashes from swords or spears. At one place on the man's left arm, just below the shoulder, a deep gash still dripped blood. Angus could see the hunger and desperation in the man's eyes as he stalked the sheep. His pale flesh and gauntness spoke clearly that he'd had no food in days. Angus knew about hunger and he knew this made them dangerous.

The MacDonald drew closer to the sheep. He drew a long black-handled dagger, his Skyne Dhu from a hidden place at his belt.

This was too much for Angus. He never feared strangers before, so why now? Striding out from his hiding place he raced down the hill toward the men. "That's our sheep, there, MacDonalds! He's ours, ye canna' have him!"

By this time, three of the MacDonalds surrounded the sheep and slowly closed in on it. Angus's shouting startled the men. The MacDonalds and the sheep turned to look in the Angus' direction. One of the Islemen took advantage of the sheep's distraction grabbing it by its wooly neck. It struggled but found itself caught fast in the MacDonald's hands.

"Nay, now!" Angus ran toward the men, but he stopped when he saw the expressions on their faces. All of them had grown quiet, intently watching him.

"He's our sheep, and no dinner of yours," Angus shouted at the men.

Two of the men started laughing. "Come closer," one said. "We can't quite hear what you're sayin." Angus heard the fatigue and the threatening tones in the man's voice more than he heard the man's words. He could see the circles under his eyes. He wondered how long they'd been traveling and if maybe he shouldn't give them that one sheep. But brazen Highland pride and fear of his father's anger kept him from that one charitable act that could have perhaps saved his life.

Angus stopped running. He squared off against the men. He put his hat in his pocket. His Mother made it for him from sheepskin and he didn't want it to fall off during whatever was about to happen. Successfully concealing how close he was to fleeing for his life, and how badly he wanted to wipe his runny nose Angus wondered if he could make it past those men to get home for help. He hoped they wouldn't notice that he was trembling.

"Aye, a bit closer, there lad," growled the man holding the sheep. The MacDonalds began edging toward him.

Angus stayed where he was, not quite sure what was happening. Then his good sense and fear took over. Slowly, he started backing away. The bloody band before him seemed suddenly larger than life, and dreadful. Thoughts of his father's stories about the lowland wars came rushing back to him. They were hungry, wounded and angry about the terrible losses they suffered. They may have been away from their families for months or years. These plundering clansmen of Alba were frustrated about crops that had been lost, fish that hadn't been caught and babies who missed fathering.

None dared stand in the way of their desperate hunger and need, and when hospitality was denied them, they had been known to sack the cottages of their fellow Highlanders. Feuds started this way that lasted more than a thousand years, feuds that make the grudges of other peoples seem petty and meaningless.

The men started toward him. "Come on now," one called out. "We won't hurtcha none. Don't run."

"Wait there, sonny," called another. "Dontcha' want some a' this fiiieene sheep for yer supper?"

Angus turned and ran. At the top of the hill he paused to look around. Four of the men pursued him at top speed, one with a crutch he didn't seem to need. Angus looked across the rise, wiping his nose on his sleeve and saw that his sheep were scattering. But he didn't have time for them now.

As the men closed in on him, he picked up a rock and heaved it with all his strength. It caught the lead MacDonald on his wounded shoulder. It must have been sore because the man clapped his hand over the wound, groaning. At least he stopped for a second, but the others continued. Angus heaved another rock, missing all of them.

Fifty yards away proved too close for Angus. He turned slightly to the left, taking off as fast has his long, lean ten-year-old legs could carry him, toward the heavy forest nearby. The path home went straight through the MacDonalds. Safety among the trees of the old forest seemed to be the quicker retreat.

The forest's thickness kept the sheep out but the bushes and trees near the edge grew too closely together. That made it difficult to find a place to enter. Once inside, the old-growth oaks and pines staggered Angus's imagination. Fallen limbs and thick tangled undergrowth made walking treacherous. No one ever came here except to cut wood, and then only in the daytime and just at the forest's edge.

Angus always feared this forest. His earliest memories echoed stories of goblins and ghouls that lived there. His grandfather could even remember the days when Baelrogs lurked in the deepest places, or so he said; *whatever a Baelrog is.*

At this moment, Angus feared the men behind him more than he feared any forest creatures his family may have invented to keep him out of there. He figured, they mainly feared he would get lost. In a matter of a few minutes, all the trees in a forest this thick can look alike, and a wanderer can easily lose his way.

Running through the heather was tricky enough, but Angus was used to that. Though as sure-footed as a goat, he knew one misstep would cause him to go head over heels. He could hear the men behind him, crashing through the bushes, swearing and calling out to him. Yet with all their awkward running and stumbling they gradually gained on him. One of them snagged a foot in a bush and fell flat on his face, but the others continued.

Then it was Angus's turn to trip, but instead of going down flat, he rolled and instantly regained to his feet. Muddy and more terrified than ever, he raced down the glen toward the forest.

As soon as he reached the first clump of bushes, he dived in. His landing was hard, but the branches broke his fall and he found himself under a grove of sheltering trees. His skin and clothing were torn, but at least he knew he was hidden. He knew he needed to keep going. It wasn't good enough to be just at the edge. Leaping to his feet, he rushed blindly forward, looking neither right nor left, not knowing which way to turn next.

Suddenly he thought he heard a soft voice in the distance, beckoning him on. What tricks a person's mind can play in a moment of panic. Angus kept running, tripping on the underbrush and scratching his face even more on low hanging twigs.

Then he stumbled again over a fallen tree. He lay there, trying not to breathe too loudly as he listened. Not far behind, he could hear the men crashing their way into the woods, looking for him. Fighting his fear and pain from the fall, Angus pulled himself to his feet. Again, he thought he heard the voice.

He was lucky to be smaller and more agile than the men. He could move through the woods faster. But this didn't keep him from tripping again, and falling even harder than before, against another tree. This time the noise of his assailants seemed farther away, but he kept going, his fear relentlessly driving him.

Finally he stopped, panting for breath. He could run no farther. He let himself fall on the ground and lay there sobbing, trying to catch his breath, covered with leaves and mud. Again he heard the men's voices, not far away.

"He went that way, dontcha' know," yelled one.

"No, he's over there, I could hear him just now," called another.

"We need to kill this one fast before he brings down his family on us," Angus heard one of them shouting.

"Come this way, quickly," a wee small voice urged him.

Angus lay as still as possible, trying to be invisible. Again he heard the soft voice. "Come here, boy, they're right behind you. Another moment and they'll be upon you!"

Angus turned his face from the soft earth and looked to his right, where the voice seemed to be coming from. He could see nothing but the gathering darkness of evening. The leaves of the bushes and trees around him were fading with the coming of night. "Come now, boy, before I change my mind!" The voice was sharper and a little higher pitched, but the voice of a male nevertheless, and it was tinged with fear.

In the brush near him, Angus seemed to see something that looked like a man. When he squinted the form became clearer. It was too small for a grown man, but the voice was too deep for a child. The man was a little taller than Angus. Painfully, Angus lifted himself from the ground for a better view.

"Hurry," the little man snapped. "Don't be stupid, boy, get over here, NOW!"

Standing tall, Angus approached the little man and saw a dimly lit doorway behind him. It seemed to be built right into the embankment, well sheltered from view by the foliage around it. He passed through the doorway to the interior, where he found a low table, chairs and what appeared to be two passages leading downward into the darkness.

"Inside... now, boy!" the little man commanded. He followed Angus inside and lowered a drape over the doorway. Angus marveled at its texture, how thick it was, yet transparent. It didn't block out the remaining light of day.

The little man turned to Angus and in his high-pitched voice continued talking rapidly, without pausing for breath. "Come in and have a seat, young Alban, It's lucky you are that I happened to live nearby. I was afraid you wouldn't hear me calling you to come this way. Those creatures chasing you would have you for an evening snack instead of the sheep they tried to steal. Hungry they are and tired from their long march out of Inverness and before that from the southern lowlands, and you're no doubt wondering who I am, you may call me Migalik, young Alban!"

Migalik's narrow face accentuated a long dark beard with strands of gray running through it. It seemed to Angus that the beard bothered him because he kept pushing it aside as he talked, as though afraid it would snag in the buttons of his vest where his stomach tapered outward in front of him. At one point, Migalik tossed it over one shoulder in frustration, and scratched at his throat under his chin.

"I know who you are. We Gray Elves know our neighbors and those who graze their sheep in our pastures, oh we don't mind you grazing your sheep there, young Human, there's plenty of pasture for all, and we do our grazing at night when no one's around."

As the Elf went on playing with his beard and talking non-stop, Angus gazed around the room in astonishment. *So there really are Elves in the forest! Just as my Aunt Elsa says!* But he looked like just a little man. The MacDonalds look different than those of Clan Gunn and Clan Gunn looks different than MacAodhs. This man must be from a clan of his own, one Angus never heard of before. One that lives underground!

Carved walnut shells and a few stones mounted among twigs and painted with quaint designs and geometric figures adorned the walls. Propped up in a corner, stood a long-handled broom with a thick grapevine handle and long wheat stalks bound together at the end. Shelves bearing bowls and pots seemed to be carved out of the bedrock. Angus was fascinated by the cleanliness of this underground dwelling. Not a spot of dirt could be seen anywhere. There were no root ends sticking out of the walls and no flakes of dirt from the ceiling.

What fascinated Angus the most were the wall hangings. He had never seen such things before. Tightly woven grasses formed huge mats, and on these mats were figures and scenes far beyond Angus' imagination. No paints had been used to form the images. Their different colors came from different shades of the grasses themselves. They were so cleverly joined, Angus could barely see the grain of the weave. Only after several moments of studying the mats did Angus realize how tall they stood and how high the ceiling reached. It seemed to fade into the darkness above, giving the impression of great height.

Of all the strange things in the room, by far, Angus thought Migalik the strangest of all. He was short but seemed tall, and slight, but seemed broad. His clothing looked like wool, but it had a finer texture than any wool Angus had seen. Strangest of all was Migalik's face, which seemed to be that of a young man, but his eyes seemed more ancient than any man Angus had known. Angus spent several minutes trying to figure out what color they were. They seemed gray at first, then black, then as Migalik turned to the light, Angus could see they were a deep blue. They were also wide, like his mother's eyes.

Embarrassed that he had been staring at Migalik, Angus rose from the seat he had taken at Migalik's table and approached the nearest of the woven mats for a closer look.

"Angeline, the mother of my mother, created these mystical weaves" continued the Elf. Before the Great Immigration, we transported them over the green seas in our hollow ships. They are the last remnants we have of our days in YeePhraWaine. Those days of happiness for all Elven Folk ended when the wars came and forced us to abandon our ancient homeland. But that was when the Earth was young," Migalik chuckled, "like you, young Human. It was before Humans lived in this part of the world. Yes, before even the ancient Pictish race that filled the land here before your people came. The weaves you look at now depict our flight on the sea and the pursuit behind us. See here," he pointed. "This one standing is Eonomel, a hero of our race, who led us to freedom, here in the Land of Alba." Migalik began laughing again, and stopped pushing his beard from one side to the other. Instead he began stroking it as he continued, "Eonomel is forgotten by Humans except for the beer he gave them which they still call by his name."

"My brother, Robert likes that beer," Angus smiled.

"I called the weaves mystical," Migalik went on, "but I speak only of history. On the far wall," he gestured, "is the end of the history foretold by Angeline. It depicts our return to YeePhraWaine, but only after another even more dreadful war than the last. This time we are to be led home by the figure you see standing in the bow of the lead ship. We know not yet who he is or whence he comes. We know not the cause of the coming encounter or who the enemy will be. We know only that the time will come for us once again to flee and to fight."

"Maybe the trip home will be one of victory," Angus exclaimed. "You know--a victorious homecoming instead of flight and defeat! Do you think it could mean that instead?"

Migalik stared at him, astonished. Angus watched Migalik's eyes change color again, this time from nearly black to light blue. Then, speaking slowly, "Angeline told us she knew not the meaning, but wove only the visions coming to her unbidden. She said also these are the stories of our exile. Perhaps your words are the true prophecy, for none have seen the vision before as your words describe it. And as you spoke, I saw the colors in the weave come together for me as never before. And the scene of the boats turned toward home ARE at the end of the story of the Exile."

Angus suddenly became aware that the darkness in the two doorways he noticed upon entering contained several pairs of eyes intently watching him. He continued to listen to the Elf but was acutely aware of the presence of other creatures. His fear and uncertainty began stirring again. Who were these creatures? What had he gotten himself into?

CRASH!

The sound came from right outside the Elf's door. Angus looked outside and saw three of the MacDonalds who had been chasing him.

"I coulda' swore I saw him fall here," one of them muttered. Two of the three men looked directly at Angus through the Elf's transparent door cover. Angus froze.

The Elf started laughing loudly, cackling even. He stopped stroking his beard, and throwing it over his shoulder. Again, he reassured Angus, "They can't see you at all, young Human. They can't even hear me laughing and talking right under their noses. All they can see are the ground and the plants. We Elves hide well, and you are as safe from them as we usually are from you. Completely hidden." Still cackling, Migalik turned to watch the men. "Do you think we'd use a door we couldn't hide behind? They can see nothing!"

How could this be? Still frightened and suspicious, Angus continued to eye the men outside the Elf dwelling, who were not quite ten feet away. Then, since Migalik reassured him that he was safe and could not be seen, he began to relax. Now his attention returned to the eyes watching him from the interior of the dwelling. Migalik continued talking rapidly and then started to sing. As he did so, two young Elves crept from the doorway, listening. They were girls and seemed to be about Angus's age. As his eyes became accustomed to the dimness behind the young Elves, he discovered a taller figure of about Migalik's height.

Angus watched the Elves creep quietly forward. He started to feel warm inside and very happy. Soon the Elf children were joining their father in the Elven song, and as they sang, having become accustomed by now to Angus' presence, they scurried about the tiny room preparing food. This is the song they were singing:

> We sing and sing
> Watch birds on wing
> And mice run in the heather
> We let them roam
> For it's their home
> In even rainy weather.

After each verse, they all laughed hilariously. Then, as though on cue, a heavy rain began falling outside. The drops were so heavy they made a pounding din above. The Elves laughed all the harder and continued singing:

> And now we bring
> This Human thing
> Into our home together
> For if we don't
> He surely won't
> Survive this nasty weather.

They all started laughing again with the exception of Migalik. His mouth had turned down in a frown because of strained rhyme in the last line of the song, and his eyes were now a dark blue.

Gray Elves are we
Our lives so free
We through the forest wander.
Oh it's our home,
This forest dome
And Elven deeds we ponder.

Hysterical giggling again. Angus was beginning to join in on the laughter, much to the delight of the children. He couldn't tell what food was being prepared, but a delicious aroma filled his nostrils, reminding him of how hungry he was.

It's Migalik,
He likes to pick
Those who are in danger
To bring them in
Protecting them
From dark and dreadful strangers.

He will soon
In full of moon
The work of our Dream Maker,
While those at rest
In deep sleep blessed
Can dream the dreams he makes there.

The Elves served the food on carved plates. The figures on the plates were of small animals and Elves. Birds, plants and all manner of things that can be found in the forest garnished their rims.

As they ate, the party continued. One sang while the others ate, and each in his turn would swallow their food and keep the rhyme going.

Cautiously Angus tasted the strong food. One dish contained something that looked like pine twigs with needles intact, but when he bit into it, as the others were doing, it had a consistency of a half-cooked vegetable with some of the crispness remaining. The taste translated into the pungent smell of the heather after a rain. Another dish contained something that looked like a potato but was orange instead of white and had a slightly sweet taste.

The strangeness of Migalik's family accentuated Migalik's own uniqueness. The girls though probably about Angus' age, were small, willowy and graceful in their movements. Their waist length hair curled in some places and waved in others. One was light blonde. The other's hair was the dark shade of red that some call auburn, the same color as Angus's. Their delicate features matched the weaves hanging on the walls and their wide eyes with that deep blue seemed so familiar to him. Then Angus realized with a shock that they were exactly like his mother, Laura's eyes. He watched intently as they laughed and sang and ate, repressing for now the obvious conclusion.

After the meal was over and everything tidied up, they gathered before a low fire set in a niche in the wall. Migalik lit a pipe and began talking. Angus at first tried to figure out where the smoke from the fire was going, since there was no chimney. Then he began watching Migalik smoking his pipe. Angus had never seen anyone smoke before. Smoking didn't exist yet on the Island. Angus watched in fascination as Migalik blew smoke rings from his mouth, then Angus found himself offended by the smell of it.

"Long before the Earth was made," Migalik began, scratching at his throat again, this time without tossing his beard aside, "Everything that is, came from the light, even the darkness. We all lived there. Even that which was to become, lived there," he smiled at Angus, "which means you, too. But there were still some places where there was no light. Creatures from those places captured some of the beings that lived in the light. Since they were light beings carried off into darkness, there was a great turmoil in the realms of darkness. It was like trying to mix water and fire. Out of this turmoil, the Earth came into being by combining the stolen light and the former darkness. The creatures that lived here then were a mixture of both the matter of darkness, and of light."

Migalik stopped talking to re-light his pipe, which went out while he talked. As he smoked, he blew more rings up toward the ceiling. "That's when we were sent here, from the Realms of Light. From the beginning, it was the job of the Elves to see that everything works out all right with the plants and trees and birds, since there is more light in them than anything else. Because they are helpless in their struggle to survive and return to the light, we watch over them. We protect their light."

Migalik paused again to tamp his pipe, then continued, every so often stroking his beard. "Humans, then, didn't have much light in them. But occasionally, one of them would marry an Elf, and the children would be half light, or half Elf and half Human. This only happened rarely throughout the many generations, but it happened enough that some Humans have more light in them than others, and they also have some of our Magic."

Angus was getting sleepy and Migalik could see this, so he hurried on. "The reason I'm telling you this, young Human, is that your mother is descended from one of these marriages and you have in you some of our light and Magic."

Angus perked up at this.

"She knows this, for she has seen us. And you know this for you have now seen us too, and you have noticed our resemblance to your mother. We keep in touch with our family and watch over them. She has always known that someday we would tell you about this. She has not mentioned this, because she fears you may be too young to understand. But we know when is the best time."

"I have Magic in me?" Angus asked, now fully alert.

"Yes," Migalik smiled. "Every Elf and descendant of Elves has some of our Magic. "Much of what is you, is from your Human ancestors. You are still young, so you have not yet found your Magic inside. But we can see it because we have Elf eyes and all Elves will know upon seeing you, that you are descended from us. If one calls you 'Elfkin', know it is because you are 'kin' to us. In some of the ancient languages this has been changed to 'Elskin', in the tongues of Humans. But they have forgotten its meaning. It means 'beloved'."

"But you can see Magic in me?" Angus's eyes were round with wonder and excitement.

"Yes." Migalik's own eyes twinkled at the boy's amazement. "It shines out to us like light in the darkness, for light is what it is. Every Elf has his own kind of Magic. My daughter, Aelronde is learning to use her ability to teach certain types of plants where to grow and how big to get." As he spoke, the little blonde Elf giggled shyly. As Angus looked at her, her eyes seemed to glow and lighten.

"My other daughter, Fierronde is being guided to develop her ability to teach streams... You call 'Straths'... to stay within their banks. All of us have our own job in keeping things together. I am the Dream Maker for all living anywhere near this place. Other places have other Dream Makers. This place, which is in the valley of the River Naver, or the Strath Naver, is our domain, until the..." He paused and his eyes lightened as they had earlier. He glanced at his daughters and his wife, making significant eye contact. Then he turned his eyes on Angus and completed his sentence, "our triumphant return to YeePhraWaine."

The family' eyes lightened as he said it, and they both looked at Angus, then curiously back to Migalik.

"My wife," Migalik went on, "who sits at my side is the teacher. Maybe someday she will be your teacher. Her beauty is only surpassed by her brilliance. She is 'Star Bright', and very wise."

Angus had been so absorbed with watching the girls and listening to their father, he had not paid much attention to Star Bright. Now Angus turned his full attention to Migalik's wife. In her face, Angus could see the features of the daughters reflected clearly. Her wide eyes were a deep brown at the moment, like the Earth in the forest. Her clothing was heavy multicolored wool. Looking at Star Bright's long dress was like lying on the floor of the forest in daylight and looking up through the thick leafy canopy at the blue sky. All the colors were present, even the hints of blue, shining past the leaves.

Star Bright blushed at her husband's compliments, Aelronde and Fierronde giggled at him. As Migalik talked on, Angus was soon nodding again, his head lolling to one side, then the other, then jerking awake. At a signal from their father, the girls stretched Angus out on the sofa, covered him with a blanket made from woven leaves of grasses and left him to sleep for the night.

And what an unusual night it was for Angus! He had dreams such as he never had before. He dreamed of Elves dancing around a fire and singing of the Strath Naver running its course from Loch Naver to the sea. They were telling of their legends, their dreams for their children's happiness, and of Elf children yet to come. On and on they danced and sang.

Suddenly they stopped, then vanished into the trees, leaving the fire twinkling away in the darkness. Then the night became not only dark, but black. The stars could no longer be seen through the branches of the trees. Even the flames of the fire grew darker and it seemed that dark tongues were dancing around dark coals. Then Angus felt the chill of fear. He started to shiver in his sleep and pulled his woven blanket closer around his neck. But the dream continued.

A huge shadow passed over him, making the blackness darker than pitch. He felt the quivering fear of the rabbit about to be snapped into the teeth of a wolf. It was like the terror of a squirrel when in the last seconds of its life, out of the corner of its eye, it sees the shadow of a hawk soaring out of the sky, swooping down on it.

Angus awoke with a start and a shout, "LOOK OUT!"

"Look out, what?" chuckled a familiar voice only a few feet away. It was Old William, his grandfather. He was seated on the ground, leaning against a tree, his legs propped up on a nearby stump. "Did you sleep well in the depths of the forest? You're lucky nothing found you. You'd make a tasty morsel for some wolf or Baelrog!"

Angus could see that Old Will was glad to have found him and that there was probably no real danger, but there could have been. "I love to sleep in the open under a pile of leaves, Grandpa. Have you ever tried it?"

"Oh, I've had my share of sleeping under the trees. You never know what you may find out here." Old Will shifted his legs and began scratching under one armpit. "What did *you* find, young Angus?"

"Well, I didn't find any sheep," Angus shook his head, grimacing. "How many did we lose? How did you find me? Did anyone...?"

Angus stopped because Old Will had started laughing. He took off his hat and ran his fingers through his hair, gazing fondly at his grandson. "Your brother Robert was bringing you some food and saw the Mac-Donalds. He fetched the rest of the family, just in case, but they were peaceful enough when your father showed up on the scene. They had already butchered the sheep. Your father gave it to them and thanked them for defending Alba. Then he gave them another one to feed them on the long journey home. So we lost two sheep. We were afraid we'd lost you too. You did well to run."

Old Will reached into a pocket of his ragged sheepskin coat and pulled out two biscuits, one for Angus and the other for himself. Angus took the biscuit and hungrily bit into it. As they chewed in silence, Angus looked around at their setting. Huge trees rose like a large wall around them. Angus had no idea where they were in relation to home. "Grandpa, how did you find me?"

William took another bite from his biscuit and looked off through the trees before absently replying, "You were never lost."

Angus didn't tell his mother what he had seen, but they exchanged knowing glances when he and Old Will arrived at his father's cottage. She knew. She hadn't even been worried because she knew.

Long after the meeting with the Elves, Angus was still thinking about it, recalling every detail. As he helped his father try to find the sheep that had scattered, Angus looked under every bush to see if maybe an Elf was watching him.

Angus' father wasn't angry at his son, but at the MacDonalds who had caused all this trouble. They recovered all but three of the flock. All was well. The MacDonalds were fed and no one harmed.

Chapter One: The Attack

In the following year, Old Will's visits to the Glen were spaced longer apart. If he had been verbose before, now he was reserved, restive, and downright taciturn. Today, his dark eyes, darker than ever, furtively glanced behind and around him as he strode through the center of the community as though he expected to be attacked at any moment; by what or whom, no one knew.

Angus, now eighteen years old, was cutting wood for the cooking fire when Old Will strode past. Without a word, Will continued on as though Angus wasn't there. Angus paused in his labor to watch, wondering what occasion had brought his grandfather down from the mountain.

Old Will disappeared into Steely Albright's cottage, not far down the path. After a moment inside, he came out again and headed back toward the home of his son William, Angus and their family. As he did so, Steely emerged behind him and headed in the opposite direction. This time, Old Will nodded to Angus and as if seeing him for the first time. He stopped. Still glancing over his shoulder and back up the hill toward the moor, he sniffed loudly, cleared his throat and spit. "Looks like a Williamson to me."

Angus looked up again from his wood-cutting to see a smiling Old Will, proudly observing his healthy grandson. Angus returned his look, equally proud of his grandfather. Old Will, though he was advanced in age, was broad of shoulder and stood as straight as any younger man. His footfall along the path and through the forest was as steady and sure as ever. Only his face revealed the ruggedness and span of his life.

Angus could see the lines around his eyes, the deep ravines down either cheek, grayness in his eyebrows and rims of gray in the darkness of his eyes. Will's clothing was mostly of animal skins, some of sheep, Angus guessed. His hair, unruly as always, was swept back out of his eyes and hanging at shoulder length, tied back with piece of leather string. Looking at him, up close like this, always reinforced his admiration for the man. His age, rather than making him look weak, added to his expression of guile.

"And it's a Williamson you now behold," Angus offered his grandfather a half smile. Old Will always greeted him this way. "And Williamsons of yours all over the Glen as well. You'd be hard put to miss a Williamson in this Glen."

"And in the next as well," Old Will chuckled over his shoulder, his eyes dancing, but cautious. "Will I find your father inside?"

"If you don't," Angus retorted, picking up on his grandfather's humor, "you'll find my mother alone, and I think I'll come in with ya' to protect her!"

As they waited for Angus's uncles whom Steely had gone to fetch, they talked about sheep and hunting, life in the forest and in the Glen.

Will Robert's cottage was a small one-room affair with a cooking fire in the middle, carefully protected from the rest of the dwelling by a stone circle. The piled rocks fit onto each other to a height of about two feet. Ventilation holes around the bottom allowed the fire to breathe. There was one wide cot where Laura and William slept, and a loft above that was growing too small for Angus's needs. He hadn't told the family yet that he was building his own cottage just beyond the edge of the forest.

Since there wasn't room enough for seven big men to seat themselves for a gathering, not to mention the half dozen or so of their offspring, many of them remained standing. Old Will stood at the home's entrance, the light behind him making him appear larger than life, forbidding as well as reassuring.

"There's trouble in the south again," Old Will began. "I've had word in the forest that it could be bad for us. I'm heading out to look into it. I can't tell you much more than that. If any would like to come along, I'd be glad for the company."

The brothers were shocked, mostly by the brevity of Old Will's speech. They waited for him to continue, but he did not. He stood there in the doorway, a pioneer of the Highlands who had nearly single-handedly populated a whole valley with his children. He was a tough old man, but none of them believed he was about to head off into new adventures at his age.

"Which way do you think you'll go, Pop?" one of them asked, but before he could answer, another interrupted, "Where he's goin' is crazy."

"What have you heard, Pop?" from another.

"We all have families here," muttered another. "Too much to do here to run off on fools' errands," two more of the sons chimed in.

They all felt Old Will was too old to go off on adventures. Others were trying to come up with excuses about how busy they were, and then everyone was talking at the same time. William stood up and called for them to be quiet, but by then, Old Will had already left. As he passed the perimeter of the community, Angus noticed him picking up a pack that he'd left under a bush. Steely Albright and Marla Henderson were outside the house and as Old Will disappeared around a bend in the hillside, they stood there silently weeping. *What do they know?* Angus wondered, racing down the path after him. But it was too late. Old Will had vanished.

Now what? Angus wondered. Somehow he had a feeling Old Will was right about trouble brewing in the forest. After all, wasn't it Old Will who found him that day, eight years ago? That experience with Migalik and the Elves was still as vivid in his mind as when it happened. Often, he wished he had someone to talk with who would understand. Surely his brother Robert would laugh and make fun of him. Seven years his elder, Robert was already a family man. Although all three Williamson men had the same physical features, the Williamson nose, long waist and straight back, that's where the resemblance stopped. Robert was a hunter and spent his time with the other young men telling hunting stories, with occasional tall tales over beer and cards, of dragons and sorcerers. No one ever believed them, of course, including Robert. But Angus did.

Angus knew of his mother's awareness about Migalik and his Elf encounter. But it was understood between the two of them that it was a subject to be left alone. There wasn't much to say about it, anyway.

Whenever he could sneak away by himself, Angus would head for the forest at the edge of the heathery moor. Sometimes he'd walk quietly, watching for the least movement that might signal their presence. He hiked deep into the forest and sat on a log or stump sometimes for hours, waiting for he knew not what.

Angus dreamed of the Elves. They were joyous recollections and embellishments of his experience. They would dance together and sing and tell stories. The Elves' poetry always delighted Angus and whenever he awoke after such a dream he always felt uplifted and happier than at any other time.

The dreams didn't come every night and as the years passed, they occurred less often. Now, however, there had been nearly a week of dreaming about the Elves every night. In these dreams Angus met a lovely visitor to Migalik. He'd begun looking forward to these dreams because he realized he had fallen in love with his fantasy.

It never occurred to Angus that this lovely creature really existed. Their fantasy romance was innocent and delightful. They would dance together, sing the rhymes of the Elves and talk of the beauty of the forest. They spent hours in each other's company, sharing their adventures.

In his last few dreams, however, she seemed to fade away to the point where he could barely see her. He thought she looked ill. Then one night he dreamed that she'd died. He had awakened shouting. "It's only a nightmare Angus--just a dream," his mother comforted him. "Dreams mean nothing!"

Angus didn't believe Laura. He went directly to the forest looking for Migalik, *the Dream Maker*. He hiked farther that day than ever before, calling out his name, but there was no answer. He would sometimes hear a squirrel running up a tree or leaping from one branch to another. Other times, all he could hear was the sound of the breezes moving through the leaves high overhead, or an acorn falling into the leaves. Finally, sad and discouraged, he headed back home. He began to wonder if even his memory was no more than a dream, like the one that had so upset him the night before.

In time, Angus gave up hope of ever seeing the Elves again, although during these eight years that had passed, he had learned to love walking in the forest. He hungered for the silence and beauty of this mysterious primeval place. He stopped calling out for Migalik, but that didn't stop him from halting and listening carefully whenever he heard a twig snap, or suddenly spotted the movement of a dried leaf. His eyes would dart in that direction, seeking the forest-green cap and figure of a little man half hidden in the foliage.

Angus wondered about Migalik's daughters, no doubt grown. What would they be like as young women? In his deepest thoughts Angus had not forgotten the lovely stranger in his dream, who seemed to be a visitor in Migalik's house. Angus hoped she was real and that one day he would meet her. But that seemed almost too good to be possible. Instead, he accepted the belief that maybe in the future he would meet a girl he liked very much. Thus far, however, that hadn't happened.

Angus had surprised himself with his change in attitude toward the fairer sex. Sometimes he would chuckle at his frustration in trying to find the Elves again and think to himself, old Migalik had better be protecting his daughters. I wonder what my own children would be like with an Elf mother!

∽Ꮽ ᏶ᐁ

One summer morning just past first light, Angus rose for his morning walk to the edge of the small sheep pen beside their home. As he turned around and headed back to the cottage, he noticed Laura seated by the side of the house on a small stool. Her hands were folded in her lap and she was quietly watching the last of the night's shadows slipping away. When she spotted her son approaching, Laura turned her face toward him briefly and smiled. Then she returned her gaze to the horizon.

"Do you ever see them, Mother?" Angus asked impulsively. Since meeting Migalik, Angus had studied Laura carefully for signs of her Elf blood. He looked for the least trace of points at the tops of her ears, that special deep distanced look in her eyes that he had seen in the eyes of Star Bright and the others and the way the colors changed with the mood. Sometimes he would indeed detect that special depth in her expression after she'd commented about something that seemed too unusual, or about an interesting coincidence.

Laura's ears were like his own. They were slender and elongated. Her hair was darker than his but still displayed the wild redness of the Highlands. It had a silkier quality than he noticed in other women, and others in his family.

It seemed to Angus that Laura was ignoring his question, or had forgotten it. "Do you ever see them?" he asked again, this time more softly. He knew his mother had heard him the first time, but apparently his question had not registered then, or now. He watched her eyes change as a new thought was stimulated by something else that had occurred to her, and then change again, by yet another thought. She had forgotten his question. When Angus asked a third time, Laura turned to him, smiling.

"Sometimes. Do you?" she returned the question, now gazing at him directly. Her eyes seemed to have lightened, but it might have been just his imagination. He perceived his mother was as mystified by the Elves as he was, and that she shared his joy in them.

"Only that once."

"You'll see them again--when they want you to. They're very private and I think maybe even a wee bit shy of us."

"Who are they? Where do they come from?" asked Angus.

"They said they came over the western sea," Laura replied, "but I have the feeling there's more they weren't telling me, or maybe they didn't know the answer to that question themselves."

"Did you see Migalik?" Angus pressed on. He didn't want to lose the opportunity to ask her these questions. It had been too difficult for him to bring up the subject.

"Ah yes. Migalik and Star Bright. Star Bright was expecting their first child. I never found out if it was a boy or a girl." She ended the sentence with a quizzical look at Angus.

"Migalik and Star Bright have two daughters. How long ago did you meet him?" Angus seated himself on the ground beside his mother. *How old are the daughters,* was the real question.

"Oh, let me think. It was not long before you were born," his mother continued. "It was Migalik who told me I was pregnant with you. He is the Dream Maker after all, or so he says. My sons were my highest and best hope for my life, my dream. Migalik knew and wanted me to be happy, so he told me as soon as he found out."

How could he have known?

"It had been a long time since your brother Robert was born--over six years--" she continued, "and William and I feared we'd have no more children. I was up on the hillside, there," she pointed, "where I was gathering berries one evening. Migalik seemed to appear out of nowhere, and then wanted to make a game of telling me. Him and his rhymes!" she chuckled.

Then his mother's mouth turned down in a frown and her eyes clouded over. "Angus, don't you be pesterin' that poor Migalik and his family. And don't you be mixin' with any of those Elvish girls, hear? Those marriages don't work. We're too different."

As she rose to go back into the cottage, Angus muttered, "Yes, Mum," hiding a smile.

⋍ᘒᘒ⋍

While soaking a fishing line in the River Naver later that morning, Angus reflected on that conversation, as he would many more times after that. The peacefulness of the day made for great fishing weather. His friend Tristan was gloating that he'd caught more fish and bigger ones than Angus. Angus didn't care. On the last fishing trip Angus caught more, and the time before as well. He was glad Tristan was having better luck this time.

Old William taught Angus to fish. They wandered up and down the Naver together many times. *And where is Old William now?* Angus wondered. It was at least two months ago since he'd stomped off into the forest. From time to time, Angus worried about his grandfather, but his father always told him, "That old man has been all over these mountains. He'll be back when he's good and ready. Think no more of it."

But Angus couldn't be pacified so easily. Old Will had never run off before and this was downright worrisome. The day after Old Will's disappearance, Angus climbed up the mountain to his Grandfather's cottage to see if he was there, but the cottage was empty.

Today, Angus and Tristan had wandered farther upstream than either had gone before. They'd set out that morning just after first light, anticipating a full day together. The two grew up together, sharing the same toys as toddlers, the same hopes and fears as juveniles, and they'd continued to spend much of their spare time together as young men. The two lads treasured their friendship, built on mutual respect and camaraderie.

It was Tristan's idea to explore the river farther upstream. They stopped when they came to a low falls and decided to fish in the pool below it. The dense foliage made their passage along the side of the river slow. They carefully planned each step over the boulders and loose gravel, making their way around thick bushes overhanging the water. One false step and one of them could easily have slipped into the icy rushing current below—and neither of the young men could swim.

Tristan, normally shy, felt totally at home with his friend Angus and talked constantly when they were together. *Just to hear the sound of his voice,* Angus chuckled to himself. It gave him pleasure to see his friend so talkative in his company, since he rarely spoke when others were present. Then, often when Tristan did speak, he stuttered. When this happened, Angus would feel embarrassed for him, as though he himself were stuttering. If any dared laugh at Tristan, Angus immediately boiled up with anger and would spare no words at defending his friend. "We all have our faults," Angus would lash out, "and you'd be lucky if yours were only as bad as that." Angus's anger embarrassed Tristan and he told Angus he wished it could just be ignored.

Angus often wondered what made Tristan so shy. He was a bright boy with a discerning eye and keen memory. He was also good at math--or at least Angus thought so, since he himself couldn't do anything with figures at all. That was his weakness... and also the fact that he was so awkward. Yes, he could become embarrassed about that.

Sometimes Tristan unknowingly showed up his friend, as he had just now, after tallying up their catch for the day. "Angus, I've got fifteen fish here and you've got five. I think between us, twenty fish is plenty. Let's go home."

The young men had intended to spend three days camping and fishing. Angus knew they had plenty of fish even though he had no way of counting them. "Ya know, Tristan, my Dad can't count above all his fingers and toes and he doesn't know the names of the numbers so he couldn't teach me. Maybe you will sometime, eh? What do you say?"

"Yeah, OK. I will. What do you think about heading home?" Angus knew Tristan was sweet on one of their cousins. Half the family was up in arms about it since they didn't allow close-in marriages like that. Agnes lived in the same valley and the families were trying to get him to move out, to find a mate from one of the other families.

"You're just hot to get back to Agnes," Angus teased.

"You know I can't do that. She's a first cousin."

"It wouldn't be the first time it happened," Angus grinned.

"Well, it's not so, it's not what you're thinkin.'"

"Tristan, if you want to go back, go ahead without me. I'd like to stay out here for a few days as we planned to do. Can't you stick it out with me a while longer?"

How sweet it is to have no more worries in the world than how many fish one can catch, and no more bother to find a mate than to wander into the next valley! Angus was not displeased that Tristan decided to go on home without him. Now he could be alone to enjoy this strange part of the forest where he had never been before.

As soon as Tristan was out of sight he pulled in his line, wrapping it around the long thin pole he was using for a fishing rod. He gathered up the few supplies he had brought with him and headed even farther upstream.

Climbing the ridge beside the falls, he paused at the top, admiring the rugged beauty of the deep ravine upstream ahead of him. Steep cliffs rose on both sides of the river with dense, plush foliage clinging to their walls. He continued to pick his way along the rushing stream for another hundred or so yards before he came to a level spot. It was dry a cove into the mountain, a small level ravine with a thin brook winding its way through the center of it, and steep mountain walls on all sides.

Delighted that he had found such a secluded spot to sleep, Angus dropped the sack containing his blanket and bread and sat down beside the place where the thin mountain stream met the Strath Naver. He unwound his fishing line again, stuck a piece of bread on the bone hook and dropped it into the deep water of the Naver.

The sound of the rushing stream was so soothing, he soon found himself dozing off and entering a delightful dream. In the dream, he thought he heard children's voices, and the rippling water sounded like birds chirping. He felt like he was one of the children, and then the children became Elves. What a wonderful dream! In the gathering of Elves, he noticed the one he had been dreaming of all week.

There she was, standing near the edge of the group, waiting for him to see her. She had characteristic Elfin pointed ears and wide almond-shaped eyes. She wore the deep forest greens, except for a scarf that looked like silk and exactly matched the shade of her deep auburn hair. As she smiled at him, Angus thought her eyes sparkled like dew drops on wild flower petals. For him, in that moment there was no one else in the world but this dainty little creature.

He knew she could probably see the look of pleasure on his face and he started to blush. This brought a bright grin to her lips, then laughter. The sound of it wakened him. Completely forgetting where he was, Angus jumped up and turned. There she stood, about a foot shorter than he, rich auburn hair, wide, sparkling, almond eyes and tinkling laughter. "Hello, Elfkin," she extended her hand toward him with a grin. Angus was so overcome with excitement, he stepped back and fell into the rushing cold water of the Strath Naver, flowing north, right behind him.

The icy water soaked through his clothing instantly. As his head disappeared beneath the surface, the last thing he saw was the horrified look on the face of the lovely Elf.

Angus watched the surface of the water draw further and further away. He saw the bubbles rising toward it with the shocked realization that those bubbles were his breath. Then the momentum of his fall ended. He began slowly rising again. Suddenly Angus became aware of just how cold that water was, freshly melted from the snows higher up. It bit into his flesh and burned his cheeks like fresh ice pressed to the skin.

Bursting with fear and the determination to not die, Angus struggled. For just a moment he reached the surface again. His head bobbed above the water. He was amazed that the current had carried him so far downstream so quickly. The cove where he napped only a moment before was already gone. Just before his head sank again beneath the raging current, he noticed the Elf of his dream running along the bank not far out of reach.

That she was keeping up with him drew his mind off his plight, and for a split second he tried to understand how she could move so easily through the thick foliage. He had only managed a snail's pace through the underbrush, yet here was the Elf racing through the forest as easily as he could run through an open field. Then she was out of sight again. He sank beneath the surface. Numb with the horror of it all, he watched the water's surface slipping away from him again.

Thoughts never race through one's mind faster than when facing immediate death. Angus remembered the steep drop of the falls up ahead. If he didn't drown first, he would be killed when he reached those falls. As the reflection of light on the water slipped away, he watched a small cluster of bubbles floating on the surface, keeping pace with him. He wondered if they could see him and what perspective they must have on his coming fate. It occurred to him that few live after seeing the river's flow from this direction.

He fought for his life trying to learn what he never had -- to cup his hands, fingers together instead of wildly spread apart for a better purchase on the water. It was too late to try to understand the best angle of attack for paddling with his hands. It was too late for lessons. He felt a submerged branch wrapping itself around him. Now he was attached to the river bottom. All hope of survival left him. He knew the end was near. His lungs burned. To relieve the pressure he let a little of his used up breath escape. The branch trapping him to the bottom of the river held him against the current. Miraculously his head was above the surface again, but only long enough to grab a new breath of air – one new breath and down again.

This time he submerged face down. Beneath his panic he felt a nudging frustration as he viewed the river bottom. Racing perceptions of his own drowning amazed him. His passive desire to explore the fascinating rocks and other objects down here amused him in the face of his fear. With that thought unfinished, the current and the branch holding him captive turned him face up again so he could no longer see the river's bottom. He found himself staring at the undulating mirror that was the surface above him, knowing his next breath, if there was to be one, was out of reach, beyond that thin veil.

From its tight sheath he drew his Skyn Dhu, the black-handled dagger that all worthy Albans carry concealed. While tumbling in the swift current, he tried to discover what was pinning him under the water. Possibly, the branch had snagged his clothing and he needed to strip them off. But that thought in water so cold was beyond his willingness. The next thought was to cut the branch, to release himself. At least with that done, he might grab another breath before going over the falls.

With his free hand, he began frantically feeling around his body, trying to find the point of attachment. Something... here... there! Ahh! He was amazed that he'd found the right spot and it turned out to be not the branch that was holding him, but more like a vine that had completely wrapped itself around his body at the waist. He frantically searched to find the point where the vine trailed down into the water. That would be the place to cut it. It was just out of reach behind him. He began twisting his body so he could take hold of the vine, but just as he did, his feet touched the river bottom and his head popped out of the water.

He had just found the point where the vine was attached to him and was about to cut it when he heard a voice loudly shout, "No! Don't cut the vine!"

At the same moment he realized the vine was not attached to the river bottom but to a huge plant whose old growth was attached to several trees at the river's edge. All that held him from the icy current was that thin span of wood and green that stretched from limbs, high above. He sheathed his Skyn Dhu and grasped the vine with both hands. Using its strength, he climbed back up onto the river's edge. There, he flopped down, shivering, not so much from the iciness of the water, but in shock at the nearness of his death.

As he sat trembling, he gazed at the leafy vine lying in a pile in the bushes beside him. What a lucky thing that it had fallen into the water, and at just the right time to rescue him! Then he remembered the Elf and quickly rose to his feet. He scanned the forest on the steep hillside, searching for her.

The sound of a person's throat being cleared startled him. Quickly he turned to his right, now facing south, up the valley of the Strath Naver. Beside him, less than three feet away, stood Star Bright, the wife of Migalik, smiling, with concern in her eyes. He was as startled as before, that someone could be so close to him in this forest wilderness without his being aware it.

"We didn't mean to startle you, Angus, and I'm very glad we were able to rescue you."

"But you didn't. It was..." and as he spoke he heard delightful peals of laughter directly beside him. It was Aelronde and another young Elf he had not met before, except in his dreams. *How could there be three people standing so close to me yet I failed to see them?*

Angus was embarrassed. Of all the moments that had occurred thus far in his lifetime, this was the one where he most desperately wanted to be at his best. Not only was he bedraggled and soaked to the skin, his whole body was still trembling with shock from having nearly drowned... all because of his own clumsiness.

"Look!" exclaimed the Elf whose name he didn't know. She was pointing at the vine that had come to his aid. Angus followed the direction of her eyes and watched as the vine rose, almost like a snake, and slowly climbed back up into its branches, to await its next rescue.

"It was Lurenne (Loor-Eena) who startled you," Star Bright told him, indicating the young beauty at her side, next to Aelronde. "It was also Lurenne who saved you. She has come to us from the Firthlands to learn and to teach. And I am sure you remember Aelrondenne (Ail-Ron-Deena), my daughter, and of course, I myself am called Star Bright. I am the wife of Migalik the Dream Maker." With this sweetly delivered introduction, all three bowed.

Angus was dumbfounded. At length he managed to stammer, "I am so pleased to meet you," and he bowed also, trying to imitate their politeness.

"Come with us, young Angus Williamson MacAodh and we shall dry you, warm you and feed you," Star Bright announced. "It's the least we can do for the trouble we've caused you," she smiled and tried to conceal more laughter. Turning south, upstream, she began walking briskly away. Aelronde, now called Aelrondenne, followed. As they departed, they vanished as though into thin air.

Lurenne, who waited behind, took his hand. "I will guide you," she smiled, "we don't want to lose you again. Come."

As they started out, Angus asked, "How did they disappear like that? How did you make the vine do what it did? How do you walk so easily through the undergrowth...?" Suddenly he realized he too was gliding over the thick matting of bushes and vines as though it was a clearly marked road. Only a short time ago, he had struggled with great difficulty to push through this underbrush!

"So, tell me, my new friend, which question would you like to have answered first?" Lurenne's laughter sounded like pealing bells, clear and delightful. She was thoroughly enjoying Angus's curiosity.

Angus suddenly realized that Lurenne was now almost the same height as he. Before, she had seemed to be very short. He glanced discreetly at her feet and realized with a shock that they were not touching the ground like his own. Then he understood why he was getting warm even through his wet clothing, while his companion seemed to be effortlessly flying beside him.

"I suppose what I'd like to know about more than anything else, is you. Tell me about you, lovely Lurenne. My only knowledge of you is from my dreams."

She stopped, without releasing his hand and turned to face him. As she did, her feet slowly settled to the ground and she was again petite. Angus thought to himself that her cheeks had not before seemed as pink, without understanding that she was blushing.

Leading him by the hand, they set off again toward Angus's earlier choice for a campsite. As they walked, Lurenne's voice was pitched a little higher than before.

"As a child I was called Lura, which in our tongue means 'laughter'. As a youth, as I am now, and learning all things so that I may some day teach like Star Bright, I am called Lurenne, which means 'the bud of the spirit of laughter'. If the time ever comes for me when I am as skilled and wise as Star Bright, or if I achieve some great deed for my people, I may then be named Lurel (Loor-El). The 'el' ending is like a title would be among your people. When it's added to my name it will mean in your tongue, 'The Spirit of Joy'. What does your name mean?"

"My mother says it means 'anger'," said Angus.

"That is interesting, my friend. Your people take strange names for themselves. Our people take names that mean happier ideas. 'Star Bright' means a certain kind of light. Aelrondenne means 'the bud of the spirit of air'."

"But are those not things? Why do you say they are ideas?"

"I can see how you might believe that light is a thing, but you are thinking of the light that is the brightness of the day. To us it is the illumination of the mind and spirit. Light is consciousness, and air is more than wind and breezes. It is that which gives us life. Without it, even for a few moments, life leaves us." Lurenne tilted her head and looked up at him quizzically, a slight smile tipping the corners of her delicate mouth upward. "What you sought most when you were under the water was not air, though you may have believed that to be true. What you sought most was your life, was it not?"

Angus never before encountered such thinking and could not respond. He nodded, politely muttering "Um-hmm". Then, before he could think of a better reply, they came upon a cleared area with a fire in the center. Star Bright sat on a mat beside it, playing a hauntingly beautiful melody on a wooden pipe. Aelrondenne tended a pot suspended over the fire. As they approached, Star Bright stopped playing and resting the instrument on the mat beside her, rose to her feet.

"Sit here beside me, Angus, and put this around you. It may be best to take off all those wet clothes and let me hang them to dry." She offered him a wool blanket and stood waiting for him to strip.

"I'll take the blanket. Thank you."

"Take off your wet clothing, Angus. You'll soon be chilled and sick."

"Do you expect me to strip right here in front of you?" asked Angus incredulously.

The girls started giggling at him. Even Star Bright had to conceal a smile. "We tend to forget how silly you Humans are about modesty! Step behind the bushes there and bring me your wet clothing when you're out of them. How will that be?"

The meal was similar to the first the Elves had shared with him many years ago. Star Bright started the singing and rhyming and the others took turns chiming in. He missed the conversation he was used to sharing at meals, but shortly he recognized this to be a style of conversation.

After his meal of millet and grains, Angus stretched out on the mat to sleep. "Oh no you don't, young Human," Star Bright exclaimed. "Tonight is for walking. Lurenne will guide you. Migalik wishes to speak with you. There is danger afoot and we must not delay."

"What danger?" asked Angus, thinking fearfully of Old Will and his premonition.

"Rise quickly. Your clothing should be dry enough by now. They're hanging on the bush beside you. Let's go!"

"But how could they dry so quickly, and what danger is there?" protested Angus. "I've slept abroad a few times and seen nothing to be alarmed about."

"Such things best remain unnamed lest they hear us. There has been trouble in the south and it is feared that our ancient enemy pursues us," Star Bright responded. "Messengers tell us that no word has come from the western islands in many months, and in these weeks, there has been no word from the Firthlands." Star Bight's expression of concern deepened. She swept a strand of hair from her face and nervously glanced toward the mountain before she continued. "Lurenne's father sent her to us more for safety than learning. Now we fear the Enemy may have sent scouts into the highlands to search us out. There have been reports of strange, cloaked creatures passing through some of the human villages, so the danger may well be nearly upon us. As soon as you're dressed, we must be off."

The concern in Star Bright's eyes and voice were more than enough to alarm Angus. He rose immediately, stepping behind the bush to dress. When he emerged, Lurenne came to him with a cup in her hands. "Drink this. It will lighten your feet for the journey. We call it 'Shekairee' (Sheck-eye-Ree). It comes from a certain bean in the Southlands."

As Angus sipped the hot beverage, he watched the Elves gathering their things. They had apparently slept the day here. He wondered why he hadn't seen them before.

The last chore before departing was given to Lurenne. "Watch this, young Human," Star bright turned to Angus. "Very few of your kind have had the opportunity to see this."

Lurenne approached the fire, now down to coals. She drew a mat out of her pack and carefully unfolded it. Then she laid it out over the fire, completely covering it. In moments the coals stopped smoking. She waited another minute and removed the covering. Then she kicked the coals apart so they were level with the ground around the spot where the fire had been. Lifting the mat, she shook off the ashes and placed it over the charred remains of the fire. Waiting another minute, she lifted the mat again. To Angus's surprise, the ground was now covered with grass, as though the fire had never been there. "We leave it as we found it, so that its beauty will greet us anew when we return," explained Star Bright. "And now we must go."

Star Bright told Angus they must travel quietly. "If our enemies are present, they will see our light passing through the darkness. They can also follow us by scent. It is probably safe for us, but to be certain, I will lead by some distance ahead." She nervously glanced over her shoulder into the forest. "The others know the way. You and Lurenne will be last. It is our belief that the enemy has no interest in Humans, but you carry our blood, so you could be in danger as well. The journey is not far. We should be there in a few hours."

Star Bright turned west at a brisk pace heading up a path on the steep hillside as easily as though she were traveling on a level field.

A moment later, Aelrondenne also departed, following her mother. He felt Lurenne beside him, taking his hand. Before they set out, he turned to face her, taking her other hand. "Lurenne, the first time I met your people it was beautiful and brief. I spent many hours afterward searching for them, but they were nowhere to be found. You, I have dreamed of for a long time and now that I've found you, I pray I will never lose sight of you. Vanish from my eyes and I will not rest even in death, until I find you again."

"Now is not the time for promises, Elfkin. Now is the time for traveling," responded Lurenne. Placing her arms loosely around his neck, she lightly kissed his lips. "But a time for promises may someday come. When it does, take care what promises you make, for you may have to keep them. Now we must go." She gave his hand a light squeeze, and Angus felt his heart skip a beat.

He was out of breath before the hike even began. Never before had he hiked in the forest at night. Objects that in daylight had colors and definite shapes now appeared as shades of gray. Angus could see obstacles in his path only as shadows and sometimes he couldn't tell what those shadows were. Once the moon finally rose, the journey became easier.

In spite of the darkness, Angus felt an inner glow that seemed to come from the hand that held his. Lurenne didn't speak again for at least an hour, but moved quickly ahead. Angus tried his best to keep up with her. The only sounds he could hear were his own footsteps. At times they would come upon small animals. Invisible in the darkness, they would startle Angus as they darted out of his way.

The first direction was straight up the hillside. Its steepness forced Angus to labor at staying by the side of the lovely Elf. She seemed to be practically floating along the path. He feared she would perceive his clumsiness as weakness. By the time they reached the top of the mountain ridge he was gasping for breath and dripping with sweat. His partner was as fresh as when they first started out.

As the path turned north, he recognized the ridge the people in his village called Dragon's Peak. It reached past his home to the west.

The path was much easier along the top of the mountain. His feet no longer slipped. The terrain became more level. In time he started to cool down and he felt his sweat-soaked clothing drying for the second time.

In the moonlight Angus could now see the brightness of the blue-white aura around Lurenne that made her seem to shine or glow. Ahead of him he noticed the other Elves had the same blue-white auras. It was this glow that he and Lurenne were following. Star Bright was right. The Elves were indeed easy to see in the darkness. Even he could see them.

Angus felt strangely exposed and vulnerable. The air was so calm and the rocky path so bare even the sound of rustling of leaves was gone. The little animals they had frightened farther down the hill seemed to avoid the mountaintop, so there were no more unidentifiable sounds in the darkness. It was deathly still. Angus could scarcely hear his feet moving on the rocky path and Lurenne seemed little more than a specter beside him.

Suddenly, something like a strong gust of icy wind knocked him off his feet. He lost his hold of Lurenne's hand and then lost sight of her. Where the wind had touched him on his right shoulder and part of his back, there was a strange sensation of cold, yet at the same time it seemed to be burning his skin.

He leaped back onto his feet and with a shout drew his Skyn Dhu from his sleeve. Although he couldn't see Lurenne, far ahead the lights of Star Bright and Aelrondenne were visible. Where was Lurenne? He ran to the other side of the path searching the hillside. There was only darkness. He ran again to the other side of the path. Ahead, a tiny light was visible but partly obscured by something dark and close to the ground. He raced toward it and found Lurenne lying in the leaves half hidden by a shadowy object. Angus couldn't focus his eyes on it. It was like a hole in the air, a shadowy entrance to a dark cave.

Lurenne spotted him and screamed, "Run! Run for your life! It's a Geketz! Go! Fast!"

Angus charged with all the speed he could summon and dived at the object, shouting at the top of his lungs, "Get off of her!"

He connected with a solid thud and rolled several feet away from Lurenne. Struggling like two wrestlers, the object tried to grasp his wrists. Angus kicked and stabbed at it, shouting at the top of his lungs. The Geketz leaned down as though to kiss him.

"Noooo!" he heard an enraged voice. Something struck the Geketz from one side and it rolled off him, coming to a stop a few feet away. He leaped to his feet and saw that it was Lurenne who had attacked it and was now at its mercy. The Geketz was about to bring its lips to hers again when Angus picked up a rock and heaved it, striking the creature on the head. But the impact didn't seem to affect the Geketz at all. It turned its face toward Angus and laughed. Then it bent down again to begin its meal. In a rage of anger and hatred, Angus dived in a flying tackle and rolled with the Geketz several feet away from Lurenne.

Hysterical rage fueled Angus's attack, adding the strength of passion to his fury. The Geketz pinned him down as before, waiting for Angus's rage to abate. As it waited, the Geketz spoke to Angus: "I thought all the Elfkin were in the valley below. Are there more on the mountain or are you the only one? No matter, only one more to kill." The voice of this creature sounded like the noise of a rock-slide, but not as loud. Angus was nauseated by the smell of its breath. It reeked with the stench of death. The words it had spoken terrified him. *Had it been in the valley earlier?* Angus feared for his family.

He could see Lurenne standing beside them, watching. He wondered why she didn't help him as before. As Angus stopped struggling in order to listen better, the Geketz moved in for the kiss of death.

At that moment Lurenne screamed again, "*Nooo!!! Get away from him!!*" and dived on the Geketz again. With a sweep of its arm, it deflected her and she was thrown aside like chaff in the wind. This further enraged Angus and he renewed his efforts to rid himself of the Geketz.

Suddenly a brilliant flash of white light like a lightning bolt streaked across the sky. The Bolt struck the Geketz on the back and threw it up and off of Angus. It rolled away and scrambled to its feet. A second Bolt struck it in the chest. It turned and fled down the hillside, careening like a wounded deer with the hunter's arrow in its throat.

Angus pulled himself into a sitting position, then fell back again on the ground. He felt faint and dizzy and his arms and legs were limp. Again he tried to sit up but could not.

Aelrondenne was running toward him. Gasping for breath, Angus motioned in the direction where he thought Lurenne was lying. Aelrondenne bent over her body and Angus felt a moment of panic, fearing Lurenne was dead. With great effort he forced himself to his feet, but as soon as he was upright, his legs gave out and he fell, rolling down beside Lurenne. The Elf's face was pale and her eyes were dark, too dark. Her light was no longer visible. He reached for her hand, but she quickly pulled back. "Touch me not, Angus, for in my touch..." Angus blacked out and heard no more.

Chapter Two: Aftermath

Angus felt himself tumbling again. He believed himself back in the Naver. He looked up and believed he saw the underside of the water's surface. Nausea rose from his gut. He looked down and saw the irregular bottom, and again he felt himself choking. He saw the rocks, just as he had in the river. They were dark and brown, covered with a dull moss. The vision sickened him more. It looked like so much brown slime. Shadows cast by the rippling surface gave the rocks an eerie appearance and caused the slime to grow lighter, then darker. He watched the silt. Sunken twigs and dead fish floated quickly past, skimming over the rocks, getting trapped in a crevasse, then freed again by the current, floating out of his range of vision. He looked up and down the river through the tunnel of water with its rocky brown floor and a shining, undulating, translucent ceiling. He felt again the frantic fear, the panic of being close to death.

His lungs burned. He remembered the relief of expelling some of his spent breath, so he tried it once more. A cluster of bubbles floated from his mouth, carried seven or eight feet downstream before bursting through the surface. In his heart he knew he was dying. He accepted it. In that acceptance, his fear floated away from him as though lifted like bubbles, the very ones he had just released. *Welcome oblivion. Welcome death. Come for me now.*

He could feel the anchoring vine wrapped around his waist but this time he knew it was connected to the bottom of the river, not to a tree growing on the bank. Lurenne was not coming to his rescue this time. She had been kissed by the Geketz. The vision of her limp, helpless body lying among the fallen leaves brought him a deep sadness he had not felt at the realization of his own death. It was a sense of loss deeper than he had ever known.

His lungs were burning worse. He released more air and realized he had only a little left. Angus turned his eyes down the long tunnel formed between the river's surface and its bottom, wishing he could once more see the lovely Elf of his dreams, just once more. Then in astonishment he thought he saw her swimming upstream toward him. She was a graceful swimmer. Her strokes were long and clean, reaching, hand over hand, palms flat, fingers tightly together as she grasped the water, pushing it behind her, reaching again, and again... Angus could no longer hold his breath. He released the last of his air.

The water's grip seemed to tighten around him, or perhaps he hadn't noticed its pressure before his lungs were empty. Idly, he wondered how long he would stay conscious, then suddenly became aware of the pain on his right side where the Geketz touched him. He simply had to breathe. All other thoughts left him. He prepared himself for choking, opened his mouth and inhaled.

Suddenly the images all around him changed. He dreamed he was lying on his loft bed at home in the glen, his mother and father asleep below. They had been trying to get him to move out, to find a wife and become independent, but he had resisted their efforts. No women in the valley or the neighboring one could compare to the lovely Elf in his dream. Angus longed for her. Where was she? Then he felt the pain again in his right shoulder and arm. His throat, where the Geketz held him, ached and burned. The nausea was constant. He retched.

His bed began to rock up and down and from side to side. He grasped both edges to hang on. The movement only increased the pain. He groaned with its persistent pressure and felt himself sinking. The vine holding him to the river's bottom pulled him deeper. Then he knew he was in a bed and it was shaking and rocking. He began crying out for help, hanging on for dear life.

The vision changed. Now he was on his back on the ground and the Geketz was on him. Its dark mouth opened. Its horrible breath covered his face. He felt like vomiting. He turned his head, so it wouldn't get it all over his face, and then heaved. The Geketz slapped him and grinned. Its mouth seemed toothless, until Angus looked closer and noticed the rows of dark protrusions. Angus managed to grasp the Geketz by the throat holding it away from him. It seemed amused at his struggle.

Then Angus saw the creature's face clearly for the first time. It was the same face as Lurenne's, deformed and twisted into a thing of pain and anguish.

"Touch me not," it cautioned him. *"For in touching me you will sure-ly find your death."*

Angus closed his eyes, clenched his fists and began screaming. The dream began again.

❧ ❧

The house of Migalik was in turmoil. This attack was the first to oc-cur so close to an Elf community since the flight from YeePhraWaine. Friends and neighbors frantically, sought guidance from him. Star Bright needed several more nights before she would fully regain the energy she spent. Angus was severely injured. He rested in Migalik's house screaming in delirium. The worst loss of all, the event that Mi-galik had the greatest difficulty accepting, was the loss of Lurenne, the daughter of his sister, Lee-eesh, and her husband, MarNosh, Migalik's closest friend from the old days.

Migalik's pride in Star Bright was boundless. Without her, they would all have been taken. She killed the Geketz but with what effort? Very few Elves had learned the secret of the Bolt--and even fewer of them had the ability to summon up two of them in such a short amount of time.

Star Bright had told Migalik it required the focusing of her full life's force to create a Bolt. Therefore it was to be used only in dire emergen-cies. Star Bright had made not one but two Bolts, without help — and without time to recover. Now Migalik feared she might not recover at all.

Aelrondenne had withdrawn to the forest without consulting him. Perhaps she was too sensitive and needed solitude. Migalik feared for her safety. The persistent vision of the faces of MarNosh and Lee-eesh, when they would hear the news of Lurenne, haunted him. *What pain I have brought them*, mourned Migalik.

Fierrondenne, Migalik's' youngest daughter was clearly unable to accept the truth of the situation. She remained to help and alternated her time between sitting with Star Bright and going to check on Angus. Soaking a cloth in cool water, she repeatedly wiped her mother's face, more giddy over her mother's accomplishment than fearful for her state of exhaustion. *TWO Bolts she had made!!* Fierrondenne kept saying to herself.

Earlier that evening, Migalik was walking in the forest, watching for the return of the three, he saw the two Bolts flash in the sky. He knew immediately what he was seeing. Sounding an alarm to bring a few oth-ers, they quickly made their way to the spot. Lurenne waited for them.

He could see that she was changing, her form fading into darkness. Only her upper body remained visible and it too was fading as they talked. Star Bright was unconscious even then.

Migalik and Aelrondenne heard Lurenne's last words as an Elf. They found her seated on a log beside where Angus was lying. She cried bitterly. "He tried to save me," she sobbed. "Then it attacked him and I only watched. It had taken too much of what I am and I was nearly part of it, one with it, when Angus struck. When it leaned down to take him, enough of me came through to resist and try to help him. Please tell my family I love them." Lurenne rose and fled into the darkness. *She had become one with it!! United with the Unspeakable!*

Migalik's mind drifted back to his own youth and a conversation he had with Migdal, his father. "What is it, father, that causes us to grow old? Some of us live for centuries and never show our age while others become gray in less than one century and others yet are gray while young."

Unwilling to continue that thought at the moment, Migalik urgently sent some of those with him to search for the other Geketz, organized several more to build litters for carrying Angus and Star Bright back to his house. He knew Aelrondenne was under great stress and was proud of her for being able to help without breaking. He himself, kept his mind busy and away from the fear by living in this present moment instead of the last one, and the next one that he knew would surely come. His own flood of tears wasn't released until he was alone and he allowed his father's answer to come to him.

"It is loss and grief, my son, that make us old."

Star Bright had made two Bolts! *And Lurenne is one with it! On my life! How could I have prevented this?* Migalik could think of little else. Upon reaching home, he sent a messenger to his cousin WarNock, King of the Sea Elves who lived in the far north, and VishNaronn, King of the Wood Elves, who lived in the Far East on the mainland. He even sent messengers to the Dwarf King BroeNann in the Southerlands. But the first message he sent was directed to the Firthlands, to the Ancient Order of the Brith Gar-Nunsum, whose headquarters were in The City of The Vision. *The Enemy is here! The Enemy is upon us! Guard yourselves! Send help!*

These messages were dispatched with runners, going in pairs for safety. Numb inside with grief and terror, Migalik stared at the weaves on the walls, his face pale, his eyes glazed.

&ᑫᕽ&

When Tristan finally reached the Glen, darkness had already fallen. His pleasure of returning with twenty average-sized fish faded quickly. The first cottage he passed was his cousin's, Ian Williamson. No light came from the windows. Tristan wanted to leave some of his fish for the family, but no one was home.

He continued down the path until he came to the cottage of his brother's wife's family, the Hendersons, who had come to be among them from Glen Hender, to the west, toward the lands of Clan Gunn. No light was in that house, either.

As Tristan continued through the Glen, passing house after house, he found no one home until he reached the cottage of Robert Williamson MacAodh, Angus's brother. Bruda, Robert's wife, was inside cooking something in a huge pot over the fire. Her twin babies were in a trundle bed in the back of the one-room cottage.

Tristan tapped on the frame of the open door, just loudly enough for her to hear. Her response startled him. "So it's you, Tristan! We thought you might be dead with the others. Thank God you're not. And where's Angus? Wasn't he with you? William said you went fishin' together."

Tristan stared at her in dismay. "Well come on boy. Don't keep me in suspense! Where's Angus? And they'll be wantin' ta know at his house too, so out with it. Where is he?"

Bruda was a big woman, as tall as Robert and after giving birth to the twins, she'd become even heavier than before. It was common knowledge that Bruda ruled her house and Robert did as he was told, but he didn't seem to mind. She was not one to be toyed with.

At the moment Bruda's flushed face was moist with perspiration. Tristan thought she looked a bit tired and for the first time he could see worry lines above her eyebrows and at the corners of her mouth. Her long, brown hair was tied behind her head. A few strands had come loose, falling over her face. Her customary long-skirt was soiled at the hem as though she had been out walking, and her apron was no longer crisp and white.

Her deep blue eyes darkened and flashed as she asked again, "Tristan! Speak slowly, now boy, and tell me, have you seen Angus?" She tried to soften her tone to keep from upsetting him. Tristan hated his stuttering and in moments like this one when someone urgently wanted information, he knew it would be even more difficult to overcome his nasty impediment. "H-h-h-h-h-eee's up th-th-th-th -th, ohhhhhh. H-h-h-h-h-he's u-u-u-u-u-u-p…"

"Bruda interrupted him with, "Do you mean he's up the river, Tristan?"

Tristan began nodding and trying to say "Uh huh," but it came out sounding more like "U-u-u-uh U-u-u."

"When did you last see him? Was it just a few hours ago?"

"Y-y-y-y-y-yup."

"I'll go and tell his father. He'll be wanting to go right off after him, or send Robert to do it. I've been putting together some soup for William and Robert and those who've gathered at the house. Would you take a pail for them?"

Tristan's head was spinning. *What was Bruda telling him? Gathered at the house?? What's happened?? Where is everyone?? It's unlikely they'd be out this late. Which house?* Numbly Tristan picked up the pail Bruda had filled with soup.

"Let me just dip some out for you, then you'd better be getting home. Your mother's very worried about you." Bruda ladled some soup into a second pail, bundled the twins into a back pack which she slipped over her shoulders, and headed off through the door saying to no one in particular, "Come now. Let's get it down there while it's still hot, what do ya' say?"

∽⌘⌒

The house of William Robert Williamson MacAodh was ablaze with lights. Candles had been placed on all the tables, and torches lit the front yard. Most of the neighbors were there with their children. As Bruda and Tristan approached, Angus's brother ran to his wife, gently scolding, "I was worried for you! I never should have left you go up there alone. God knows what might have happened. We didn't know it then, Bruda, but she's dead--and the marks at her throat--my God! *My mother is dead!*"

"Ah Robert, that sweet woman? Are ya' sure?"

Ian Williamson, Tristan's cousin who was the same age as his cousin Robert, Angus's brother, came up and took his arm, not noticing the soup. Some of it slopped out of the wooden pail and just missed burning Tristan's foot.

Tristan had never seen his family in such a state. Ian's strawberry colored hair was wind whipped and tangled as though he'd been outside most of the day and hadn't had a chance to wash for dinner. For the first time, Tristan noticed it had started to streak with gray. "Do ya' know what's happened here, young Tristan?"

Tristan shook his head.

"About an hour after sunset somethin' come through here like Hell itself. Some of them say they saw it. It come inta' one house after another, killin'. And it had a strange appetite, so it did. It didn't kill everyone about, just some here and some there. Ole Tom there, he says it was in your house but touched no one. Just sort of snorted and went on its way."

"Bring the soup into the house, Tristan," Robert called. "We'll dish some up for everybody."

Tristan's mind was practically numb in the presence of all this panic. Robert was frenzied with rage and grief. His words were terse and his movements deliberate. Both he and his father, William seemed about to explode. "And where the hell was Angus when this happened?" Robert kept demanding of anyone who would listen.

Finally William put his hand on Robert's shoulder and took him aside. "Enough now about your brother. He's lucky to have been gone. It's lucky for you too that you were in the fields late. That creature was killing Elfkin. Laura's grandmother on her mother's side was an Elf, dontcha know. And if Laura is Elfkin, then so are you and Angus, and I'll tell you this, my angry first son. I'm very fearful for your brother and still for you. I'd like to know where that thing went and what it was. If Old Will was here, he could probably tell us, but he's gone. Maybe this is some of the trouble he was afraid of."

A dozen other members of the family were gathered. Ian's wife, Carly, was there, with her long, flowing blonde hair that Tristan so loved to look at, and her sister, Madge had come with her husband and four sons. Steely Albright watched over the gathering in silence. It was Steely who had pronounced Laura dead. She acted as midwife to the community and was wise in herb lore. When someone was sick, it was Steely they turned to for help. She was an old woman, short and stooped. It was said that her snow white hair had once been as lovely and blonde as Carly Williamson's, but none of the young men believed it.

Steely Albright emerged from William Williamson's door, walking slowly with the short steps of age. She stopped at the first step outside the door and raised her eyes to look at the group crowded round. The deep wrinkles in her face belied the brilliance of her deep blue-green eyes that still reflected her lively spirit. Tristan was always astonished at how long her earlobes were, pulled down from many years of wearing heavy rings in them. As she silenced the crowd, Tristan's eyes wandered to her raised hands.

The skin on her hands gave the impression of brittle delicacy and their blue veins resembled the roots of a small plant stretching up her wrists. But though they were withered, those still commanded the silence she sought. The people gradually stopped talking and all eyes turned to her.

For effect or to make sure she had everyone's attention, Steely waited almost a full minute before speaking. "There's twelve dead in the Glen tonight," she announced finally.

A loud gasp emerged from the group, followed by a babble of exclamations as couples turned to each other, angry and shocked. Steely waited for the silence to return. Children stopped fidgeting and listened with full attention.

Steely lowered her eyes to the ground, probably to check her footing as much as to gather her thoughts. No one ever remembered her to be at a loss for words and they knew she had more to say.

"There's trouble afoot. This was no normal thing, this tonight." She raised her steely blue eyes to meet the group again and continued. "None of us know what it was. William here says it was an Elf thing but we all know Elves are things of children's tales. We do know it was an evil thing and evil things are of the darkness. Until we get to the bottom of this I think it'd be best to stay inside at night with doors and windows barred. None were hurt tonight who were barred inside."

Tristan's family was one of the few lucky ones. No one was taken from there even though their door was open. Tristan's father, also called Tristan, said he thought he had seen something moving up the Glen just after dark. He couldn't tell what it was because of its speed, but he was sure he'd actually seen it.

"I bet it was Vikings," Tristan's mother, Brenna suggested.

"There's been none a' them in a hundred years," Tristan, Sr. replied.

"Well it could've been Islemen. MacDonalds are always up to no good."

"Tweren't no Islemen neither," Tristan Sr. answered. "Islemen don't leave victims looking like that. Did you see the bruises and burns on Laura's throat? Did you see the burns on her wrists? All of 'em were like that. They had bad burns on their throats and wrists." Softly, almost under his breath he added, "and lips."

⋘⋙

The next morning, young Tristan went up the Glen to see if William was all right, hoping to learn if Angus was back yet.

"Glad to see you, young Tristan. Maybe you can take some time to tell me where Angus has gone."

Tristan laboriously explained that they had originally expected to be back late today. He described the spot by the River Naver where he left Angus in the late afternoon, yesterday.

While he was talking, William was handling an old sword that had belonged to his father and to his grandfather before him. Tristan had seen it only a few times.

"I see you're looking at the old knife. You've seen it before, haven't you?"

Tristan nodded.

"I'm not the only widower in the valley this mornin', you know. I was wonderin' if some of the others might like to join me in huntin' down whatever it was that did this to us. What do you think, Tris?"

Tristan eyed William's hard lined face. William was about forty, not all that old. His shoulders were square and thick like Old Will's probably used to be, and his arms and back were seasoned to hard work. Now, he had no one to work for, to support, and he was angry. Tristan could sense his blood lust and knew it would not be long before he heard William's voice raised in a battle cry. The excitement of it captured his fantasy and eagerly he nodded. "Y-y-y-y-es. I-i-i-'ll go t-t-t-t-t-too, if that's all r-r-r-r-r-right."

"Get you a weapon son. I'll see what kind of army I can raise in the Glen, and then we'll go trackin' if there's any tracks to be found. If you still want to go, meet me at the Long Stones at the north end of the village at first light tomorrow."

The Long Stones marked a small graveyard for the village. Most of its graves were poorly marked. The families remembered their dead with wooden stakes that often didn't stay put for long.

The Long Stones was also a gathering place where the people of the Glen met for festivals and celebrations. It was at the Long Stones where William and Laura and half the other village couples had celebrated their wedding. The name came from the ancient standing stones that formed a circle on the crest of a low hill just south of the village.

Tristan arrived long before dawn. He had packed only a few things, believing he'd be gone for perhaps a week. He had a sack with biscuits and dried mutton, and his father had given him an old wooden sword from the days of the Pictish wars. Unlike William's iron weapon, his was carved, hard-wood and good only for stabbing.

William arrived shortly after Tristan. Without uttering a word, he walked silently under the shadows of the large oaks at the edge of the clearing and took a seat on the ground to wait.

The next man to arrive was old Ingram Williamson, the woodsmith. Ingram brought some tools for carving, and the short iron sword his grandfather, like William's grandfather had stolen from the Italians in the southern wars. Ingram was heavy of frame and shorter than the others, only five feet-eight. His auburn hair, though he was the oldest, about fifty years old, had not yet begun to gray, but his beard that reached to his chest was a salt-and-pepper mixture. Ingram was a soft spoken man of stolid will, known throughout the Glen for his stubbornness and dogmatic adherence to distrust of strangers. It was his wife and daughter who had been murdered the night before. Ingram was burning quietly behind his expressionless face, but Tristan could see his eyes flashing in the twilight of morning.

Donald Hender came next to the clearing, close behind Ingram. Tristan gasped when he saw Donald because Donald's house was one he'd passed the night before on the way home, before he knew what had happened. How close had he come to the thing that had done this? He might have passed it on the path or bumped right into it in the dark forest on the last leg of his journey! He shivered at the thought.

Donald Hender, about William's age, had eight sons and six daughters from three wives. The men of the community held him in awe, and the women in fear and respect. So many children for a man so young was regarded as a respectable accomplishment. He had outlived his first two wives, Elsa and Morgan; both had died in childbirth. It was with fear and trepidation that his third wife, also named Elsa, married him. "Who could say 'no' to those big brown eyes," she laughed to her sisters on the morning of the wedding.

Hender was a large-boned man, as tall as the Williamsons but heavier of build. It was Hender, they always called on to help lift the timbers when someone was building a new cottage or replacing the walls of an old one. His dark hair disturbed the ladies of Glen Williamson. They were so used to seeing men of red, auburn or blond hair that a big black-haired man was a curiosity. It took them years to get over dropping in on their cousin Elsa for a visit, just to look at him.

Hender was of quiet disposition. None in the valley had ever heard him raise his voice, but they were well acquainted with his physical strength, and Tristan for a brief moment pitied whatever ill creature had sinned against them two nights past. Hender was filled with rage as were they all. It was a deep quiet rage, consistent with his demeanor, but his movements betrayed him to Tristan. His father, Tristan, Sr. had often said to him of Hender, "Still waters run deep, Tris. We know that man has more passion than he shows us. Just look at his fourteen children. I'd hate to see him angry." And now, Tristan did see Hender angry, with a third dead wife and the three newest of his children buried yesterday.

Hender walked over to William and sat cross-legged on the ground at his feet. They immediately began talking. Tristan moved closer so he could hear what they were saying.

It was William whose voice he heard first. "Two more said they're coming, Old Bill Scobie, cousin Janey's husband, and James MacBain, who just married Laura's sister. So we have three Williamsons, countin' Tristan, and three from other valleys, all MacAodhs."

At that moment Bill Scobie strolled into view with a copper cutlass slung over his shoulder and no pack. "An' what'll ya' be eaten, no pack or bag with ya?" Ingram broke the silence.

"We'll not be gone long," Bill reassured him.

"Could be a week or more," Hender shook his head. "We've no way 'a knowin' how long it could take."

"You'll see," Bill Scobie squared his shoulders, fingering his weapon. "Anything as dumb as this thing was, has to be asleep in the forest nearby waitin' for his next meal at the village. The rest of the men have set up a watch for the next few nights."

As he approached the small group, Bill tripped over a fallen branch that the others had stepped over easily. Scobie was known for his near-sightedness. "He'll still be good in a close fight," William said of him later.

MacBain, close behind Bill Scobie, prided himself on his stealth. He was known to be able to slip through the forest without making a sound. None present heard him approach, but William saw him coming, and when he was close enough he called out, "Hey MacBain! Good to have us all together. There are six of us."

MacBain, the tallest of the men was light of build. Younger than the others, with an age of about thirty years. His long pointed nose and thin cheeks seemed to emphasize his stature. MacBain always wore a goat skin cap to cover the naked flesh of his bald head. MacBain was the storyteller in the village, when he wasn't tending his garden or cottage. He had lost a wife and all three of his children. His wife, Merda, had been a valued resident of the Glen. Her shy beauty, sweet demeanor and skill with a needle and thread were unmatched by any of the other women.

Tristan eyed the group with misgivings. He didn't know what they were up against, none of them did, and he was afraid. MacBain named Tristan's fear with his first words. "So. Are we chasin' an army of ghosts and can a ghost be killed with these old swords?"

Chapter Three: First Contact

At the end of the second day after the attack on the village, Angus had quieted somewhat but he was still unconscious and sleeping fitfully. His dreams were less constant but still just as terrifying, with a few hours of dreamless sleep between.

Fierrondenne finally went for some rest when Aelrondenne returned from the forest. Migalik was taking his first meal of the night at the same table where he had entertained Angus as a boy. No song or rhyme delighted his ears. His meal was the famous "quick bread" that sustained his people when traveling. He was alone at his table for the first time he could remember, since first joining with Star Bright.

Some of his initial panic had passed. He settled into a mood of gloom and bitterness. A pall of fear hovered over the entire community. Silence replaced the usual happy chattering and domestic sounds of an active life that was the norm among Migalik's neighbors. Some volunteered to stand watch in shifts. That practice had been discarded long ago, even before Migalik was born.

Reports of the presence of another Geketz had come back to him. So far, it had attacked no Elves or Elfkin but the bodies of small animals had been found in the night. Instead of feeding on Elves, the Geketz was killing their animal friends. Migalik felt sure the Geketz that was feeding on animals was Lurenne. Her body was not found two nights ago when he retrieved Angus, his daughter and wife.

He was nearly as offended at the deaths of the animals as he was when Elves and men were attacked, but inwardly relieved that Lurenne's new transformation had not yet caused her to become an enemy of her own kind.

Migalik knew of the Geketzim from legend only, but he believed these legends. "Legend is the only means our ancient fathers have of warning us and saving us," his old teachers had lectured. "The problem we have with them is gleaning the truths from the myths."

His old friend VelMud of the southern valley ridges, the highest part of the highlands, had come down from his lonely mountain retreat. His arrival near first light yesterday was met with awe and surprise. VelMud now entered Migalik's home through the magic veil that Angus found so fascinating during his first visit.

On the day of VelMud's arrival at the community of the Naver Grays, he had not spoken except for polite greetings. His brooding silence frightened some and offended others, but Migalik knew VelMud was waiting until he was certain of his surroundings. Always been reclusive and silent, Velmud today seemed unusually taciturn. Most Elves thought this was what led him to his self-imposed exile on the high ridge of the Strath Naver's southern valley, but there was more to it than that. Migalik knew.

VelMud and Migalik were rivals for the hand of Star Bright. When she committed finally to Migalik, VelMud withdrew in anger. He had not been seen since. Over the years, reports of the location of VelMud's retreat were delivered to Migalik.

When VelMud entered, Migalik did not speak. He knew of VelMud's preference for silence and respected it. Rising from his chair, he removed a wooden mug from one of the shelves and poured a drink for VelMud from a stone pitcher that Star Bright's family gave to them at their wedding. The pitcher was engraved with images of dancing Elves and others seated at a long table, feasting on the harvest of wild seeds and grapes and other fruits.

When he saw the pitcher, VelMud's eyes that had been dark with foreboding, filled with delight. "I had forgotten the Wine Well," he grinned. "I can see that you've not got to its bottom yet. Do you think you ever will?"

"You know better than that, old friend," Migalik's eyes sparkled. "Here's something you don't know. Star Bright has learned the secret of it and now makes such pitchers as gifts to newlyweds."

"She'll drown us all in wine then," VelMud chuckled. "Is that the idea?"

VelMud seated himself at the table directly across from Migalik. He was there, before Migalik's wedding when the pitcher was presented. Old BarrenNock, Star Bright's father had presented it as an "eternal fountain." None of them believed it. They thought it was a trick, that it poured and poured and never seemed to be more than half full, or less than half empty.

"I tried to empty it once to see what would happen," Migalik began." I filled three small barrels before I grew weary of the experiment." Migalik could see that VelMud had no interest in the story. His eyes had grown dark again.

VelMud's eyes were wider than a typical Elf's eyes and instead of tapering to a point, completing the almond shape, they were more rounded at the outside corners. This was why VelMud's appearance frightened other Elves. He was also much stockier than most of the rest of them, almost like a Dwarf in build. His flaming red hair reminded them of the Williamson clan that lived nearby, and he was almost as broad-shouldered as the Humans. But the pointed ears were a dead give-away of his Elvish lineage. That and the darkness of his eyes were the sure mark of the Grays. Few still lived who knew that VelMud's distant lineage included a Dwarf. This explained the unusual eyes and broad stature.

VelMud's eyes darkened even more. His brow furrowed and his hand trembled as he took a sip of the spring wine Migalik had given him. When he spoke, his voice was deeper than a moment before and Migalik could see the anger burying the deep fear VelMud was suppressing. "It would seem that our old Enemy has found us."

"One of his has been here," Migalik said softly, afraid to enunciate the word.

"I have seen Flying Shadows," VelMud informed Migalik. "It seemed that my mountains were the northernmost reach of their search, but if they have also sent a Geketz, then he will know where we are. We must flee again."

"You saw a Flying Shadow?" Migalik eyed VelMud intently.

"Yes. It was circling on the southern side of the peak as though looking for something. I'm not sure if it saw me. If it did, I thought it would come closer. It simply circled a few times, then dived out of sight, toward the south."

"It has always been so for our people. He drove us from the stars, then from the clouds of YeePhraWaine. He found us again on the western continent but we lost him on the green seas. We knew he would find us again. But there may be hope for the moment. We believe the Geketz was killed, yet we found no body, so we are not really certain. The last time we saw it, it was fleeing in the direction of the Williamson Glen."

VelMud's eyes grew even wider. "You think you *killed* a Geketz?" he asked in astonishment. "This has rarely been done before. They're supposed to be very hard to kill. How did you do it?"

"Come," Migalik rose. "Perhaps Star Bright will tell you."

Star Bright was awake but still weak and in her bed. Aelrondenne and Fierrondenne were with her, and they were singing an old song of the ancient wars, a song of a victory that had never taken place. Some said it was written by a sage who could see the future. In times like these, Elves of all kinds sang it to those they loved, to inspire hope and comfort. VelMud and Migalik had heard it many times before, but now they listened respectfully.

> There is a Strath, a magic flowing flood
> Which washes stones somewhere and lays them down,
> To dry in warmth of day beneath the shining sun
> Then washes more with pleasure and with fun.
>
> In peace and freedom it adores the light
> And guarding what it loves it lays them right
> Within their beds for sleep when night abounds
> Not hiding days, concealing every sound.
>
> Once upon a day the folk of light
> Shall widely wander far enough and fight.
> The Magic waters of the Strath shall flow
> In glens of green and sun in day we'll know.
>
> The secret passion of the Strath conceals
> Mortal darkness in its loving will;
> Finding deep within its secret dream,
> That key to Elvish victory will be seen.
>
> The scarr-ed chest and hands, the darkest fight
> With dreadful pain and solitude and passions right
> The river dancing in the valley, 'neath the very air
> With darkness filled, we'll conquer all that's there.

"Have *you* solved the mystery of the song?" asked Migalik softly. It was a ritual question, the answer to which none knew except the Society of the Brith Gar-Nunsum. It was one of the recognition secrets of the order and all were obligated by dark vows to repeat the quotation after hearing the song.

"Have you solved the mystery of the song?" VelMud asked Migalik.

> When time is full and the waters of the Strath have flowed
> From the lofty hills through all the valleys down below,
> The time when Vile Darkness to the Faithful light will bow
> And Elvin Folk in freedom live where all can see and know.

The rhyme danced through Migalik's mind as it did for every member of the order when asked the question in the presence of others who have not been initiated, and he could not reply out loud. Instead, he gave the sign that he was obligated to give, in answer to a brother's challenge. That secret sign was the raising of the right hand in front of the face with the palm turned inward, as if to shield one's eyes from the sunlight. This was symbolic of the hope of the Elves that one day they would be able to live in broad daylight, instead of hiding their lives in darkness. This could only happen after their victory, when the Enemy could no longer hunt them. VelMud reciprocated with the sign but with his back turned so Migalik's daughters couldn't see.

Star Bright was also an initiate and made an effort to reply, but she was still weak. "It's good to see you, VelMud," she said softly. "It has been a long time."

"Too long," he replied with a sharp sideways glance in Migalik's direction reminiscent of their old rivalry for Star Bright's hand.

After the polite how-are-you's and the catching up, VelMud came to the point. "Am I to understand that it was you who killed the creature?"

Migalik answered for Star Bright so she could be spared the effort of speech. "It was in the days at YeePhraWaine, where we lived so many generations in peace and believed the Enemy to have forgotten us, that we gave up the ways of war and forgot many of our ancient secrets. The secret of the Wine Well is one that was nearly lost. It was passed on in fear from generation to generation, lest its need arise again some day. Other secrets have survived in such a way, and still others, only in legend."

"Yes," responded VelMud, "but the Order has also preserved many of them in secrecy against future need."

"Star Bright is the light bearer, a teacher, and it is her position in the Order to preserve the innermost secrets of the use of light," Migalik continued. "Do you recall the legend of Hrotgar and the Lake Monster?"

"Yes," answered VelMud crustily. "Are you about to tell me she used the Bolt against the creature? It's impossible, a thing of stories only. But could it be?" His tone changed to one of wonder. "Is the Bolt more than legend? Did it really survive the darkness?"

"Some legends are made to preserve the ancient truths, my friend. Not all, but some. You yourself hold knowledge from the craft that is yours to protect and share in time of need. Do you deny that this is true?"

"You're right, of course. I am the bearer of the Goad--and Star Bright is the bearer of the Bolt?"

"For this generation, yes. There are also two others, one in the Firthlands and one in the Southerlands. All who bear it have passed on the knowledge to their students. In this community there are seven who can cast the Bolt. Star Bright cast it twice two nights past."

"Twice?" VelMud eyed Star Bright in astonishment. "According to the legend, when Hrotgar cast it twice, he died. The monster was dead but the effort cost Hrotgar his life."

Star Bright stirred at this, and indicated she wished to speak. "Don't think because of this, that my life force is more mighty than that of Hrotgar. We have learned some refinements. I also believe I may not be able to do it again. This pain and illness is not eagerly given. It teaches one the art of selfishness. Be wary of the use of the Bolt."

"I have taught none the use of the Goad," muttered VelMud. "I have been so selfish in my exile. I should have stayed and borne my shame with head held high. I am too proud."

At that moment there was a disturbance in Migalik's outer rooms. The two Elves left the bed chamber and entered the front room where they found Silver Leaf, a willowy young Elf, the son of Migalik's friend and neighbors, Guldockel and his wife Kareem. He was one of the scouts Migalik had dispatched. Silver Leaf stood in the doorway, out of breath, twigs and leaves caught on his clothing.

"Welcome to my house, Silver Leaf," invited Migalik. "Do you have news?"

"Forgive my intrusion, Sir. There is a party of six Humans forging through the forest, coming in our direction. They are cursing and angry, swearing revenge and death for the deeds of the unnamed creature we know of. They will be upon us in another hour unless they stop to rest."

"Do you know who they are?" asked Migalik.

"I believe Sir, they are from the Glen and they are Williamsons, Kinsmen to the young Human who rests here."

"Have you spoken with them?"

"No Sir, I have not. I thought it best to tell you of their approach first. Do you wish me to speak to them?"

"You have done well, Silver Leaf. Also, there is no need to be so formal. I am your neighbor and friends with your parents. My name is Migalik. You may use it if you wish," Migalik said kindly.

"But you are King in this part of Alba, Sir. I owe you the deepest respect."

"And I also owe you mine, for you and those of your generation will in the future bear the burdens I and those of your parents' age now bear. Should I call you Sir or Silver Leaf, your name?" Migalik was now smiling broadly.

Silver Leaf blushed and shifted his weight from one foot to the next. "Come, Silver Leaf, and share a glass of wine with my friend VelMud and myself. Be comforted, my good friend."

❧ ❧

In the forest, the six had spread out into a fan formation. Slowly, with great care, so as not to miss any possible clues left by their enemy, they worked their way through the trees and underbrush. They began by following the Strath Naver south to where Tristan said he had left Angus. Then they continued south beyond the falls to where they found Angus's fishing rod. There they spent the first night, in the "fairy circle," as MacBain, the storyteller called it.

The grass didn't grow high here, and it was a fairly level area, with no bushes. It happened to be the very place where Lurenne had extinguished the fire two nights before. After much deliberation, the six chose what appeared to be the trace of a path going straight up the hillside. It was difficult to follow, since it kept disappearing every ten or twelve feet, and reappearing again a short distance ahead. Hender and William were sure they were on the right trail, since they noted broken twigs at various places along the path.

"Look there, will ya?'" Hender called back, huffing and puffing from the exertion of the climb. "There's foot prints!"

"I've not seen others. Has anyone else seen any?" asked William.

With little further conversation, they all agreed it must have been Angus who had left the prints and that he had doubled back north, heading for home. Near the top of the ridge the path narrowed making single file hiking more practical. Carefully the group examined both sides of the path and hill as they trudged forward. The hike to the valley beyond the falls had taken much of the rage out of them, and the climb up the mountainside had consumed the rest of it. Broad daylight and being away from the village and the scene of the horrors made the whole enterprise seem less real, even though each knew this was wishful thinking. What was real was real; sullen and determined to avenge their wicked aggressor, they plodded silently on.

The few who saw this creature offered little information about it. It was big. It was small. It was wearing a dark cloak of some sort. It was a naked man. Comments ranged from insanity to lunacy. *The truth,* William thought to himself, *is that no one saw it, and if they did see it, they didn't look at it very carefully.* His first item of business was to find his son. Possibly it would be Angus who could fill in the missing details.

The climb was difficult, causing Ingram to swear openly; Hender and MacBain grumbled under their breath. Scobie, a small wiry man with thin hair and a lean face that gave him the appearance of a rat, was the only one of them, William thought more than once, who seemed to take the climb in his stride. Scobie was also quick of speech, and often William had to ask him to repeat himself. His movements were almost like his speech, hurried and impatient.

MacBain, on the other hand, was slow of movement in spite of his long legs. His bald head and thin beard gave him the appearance of gentleness, but his eyes seemed anything but gentle. They seemed more cunning, as though he was always watching for an opportunity for gain at the expense of others. But William knew that none had ever accused MacBain of dishonesty or even of guile, and William often felt guilty for judging the man so unfairly.

The hike was becoming dull, since they weren't finding anything. Nevertheless, they remained as vigilant as ever. Although they were all still walking single file, they divided their duties; three watched the west side of the path while the other three watched the east. They felt if Angus had come this way, he would surely have been following the path.

It was William who spotted the disturbed leaves along the west side of the path. "Hold here," he called to the rest. "I'd like to take a look down here."

"What dya' see?" from Scobie.

"Looks like somethin' heavy slid down here recently." He stepped off the path, slowly examining the ground as he went.

"Be careful there, William," Ingram warned. "You don't know what you might find in those leaves."

"Do you think we'd have snakes up this high?" asked MacBain.

"Sure. We probably have them everywhere," answered Hender.

"Hello, look here," William called out softly. He was about twenty feet off the path. Bending over, he studied the ground closely.

"What have ya' got, Will?" The group gathered close. William was holding a long piece of cloth in his hands. "Feel this, will ya'!" he exclaimed. "What kind of cloth is this? It sure isn't wool, and it's not like any flax I've seen before!"

"It almost looks like it's made of spider webs." Scobie ran his thumb and forefinger over the material.

"Spider webs aren't sa' strong," MacBain pondered, "but you're right, Will. It's not wool or flax."

They passed Lurenne's scarf among them, examining it carefully. Each expressed amazement and awe at its softness and the richness of its color.

"Maybe it ain't Angus we're trackin' after all," Hender suggested. "Did Angus have a scarf like this that you know of, William?"

"No he surely didn't," William answered. "I think we should look through these leaves very carefully. Maybe there's somethin' else we'll find. Let's spread out just a few feet apart and feel through these leaves with our hands."

"Come on then. We should start back here where the leaves are first disturbed," suggested Ingram.

All six went down on their hands and knees closest to the path and began spreading the leaves and searching with their hands, watching carefully for signs of anything that didn't belong there.

They had worked their way through the center of the area and were nearly through it, when Hender pointed, "Look there... there's another spot where the leaves are all tumbled about!" He strode a short distance away. "And what's this?" He bent over to pick something up. "It's a Skyn Dhu! Look you here, William. Was this Angus's knife?"

Hender handed William the black-handled dagger. Silently William examined it, turning it over. "See here! This Skyn Dhu belonged to my grandfather, old Aaron. This is where he scratched his mark in the handle." He pointed to the letters 'A.W.', carved deeply in the dagger's hilt. "I gave it to Angus for his fifteenth birthday. It's his all right!"

They spent several more hours at the site of the Geketz's attack, combing through the leaves and searching for any additional clue they might find.

Finally William Robert rose to his feet, brushing loose leaves from his pants and dusting off his hands. "I don't think there's anything more here to find. I'm satisfied that Angus was here and that he had a struggle with something, probably a damned Elf. That scarf looks like the scarf of an Elf. What kind of cloth could it be other than some kind of magic weave?"

Nearly in unison the others began booing his words. "Where do you get this 'Elf' crap?" snorted Scobie. "There's nothing in these woods but trees and some very sick person who's a stranger to these parts. We'll know him as soon as we see him. And he'll know us as the life fades from his eyes."

"You're right, Scobie," Ingram agreed. "It's none more than a stranger to us, someone from some far away place where they have some way of making this kind of cloth. Maybe it *is* made from spider webs."

"Hell of a spider," muttered William.

"Yes," chimed in MacBain, "hell of a spider--maybe, but no damned Elves. There's no such thing."

William heard the annoyance in the voices around him and didn't wish to stir up trouble, but he knew if they spent enough time in the forest, sooner or later they'd be seeing Elves. He never had himself, but Laura had spoken about them enough that he believed her. "Have it your way, fellows. But what are you going to do when we bump into them in these woods somewhere? And we just might, you know!"

"I'll believe it when I see it," Ingram scoffed.

Tristan finally got up the nerve to try to say something. "A-a-a-angus -- h-h-h-he said th-th-th-that h-h-h-h-h-h-h-h- he s-seen 'em w-w-w-w-w- once."

"I often wondered why he wasn't chasin' the girls like the others," Hender joked.

"Looks like he was gettin' inta' some real wild stuff," chuckled Ingram.

"That'll be enough of such talk," William snapped.

They spread out and began following the path north. When the sun went down, none of them was feeling the need to rest. There was enough light from the moon for them to see where the path left the mountain's ridge and began weaving down through the forest to the west, the same side of the ridge where Glen Williamson was situated.

"Good Lord!" exclaimed MacBain who was in the lead.

"What is it?" asked Scobie, Hender and Ingram.

Ingram was next in line. "Good God Almighty," he muttered.

"Will you two stop swearing and tell the rest of us what's going on?" from William.

Before either man could answer, the others began to see a light up ahead that turned out to be a small fire burning in a cleared area.

They gathered close, still in the shadows and out of sight. "Be ready for a fight, me boys. Whatever it is we've been trackin' is right ahead of us," Ingram whispered.

"It could be Angus," William whispered back. "Let's not be so ready for bloodshed till we see who it is up there. It could even be more from the Glen, hunting for revenge."

"Let's sneak on up there and see," muttered Ingram through clenched teeth.

The six spread out farther, each picking his way stealthily through the twigs and leaves so as to not make a sound. Finally they were right outside the circle, half surrounding it. In the firelight they could see the figure of a small man clothed in deep forest green. He had a long gray beard, large pointed ears and a nose that seemed to fit too perfectly into his face. His boots, which came half way up his calves, were a light brown, and William caught his breath, a moment, when he realized those boots were made of woven grasses.

With a loud shout, Scobie and Ingram charged, followed a split second later by Hender and MacBain. Then they all watched as the Elf vanished right before their eyes.

William knew before they rushed in that there was no way they could capture it. As Ingram and Scobie thrashed the bushes around the fire with their antique weapons, William stood up from his position behind one of the many bushes and strolled into the light, trying to calm the other wild highlanders. Hender and MacBain stood quietly waiting.

"Now you've frightened him away," William scolded them. "He probably could have told us where Angus is."

"He probably has a bunch of others nearby and we'll be attacked shortly," growled Ingram, still clenching his teeth.

"If we had been just a little faster," Scobie added, his eyes flashing, "we'd a had 'em." This last was with a thrust of his fist.

"Wait," demanded William. "Do ya' see this fire? Do you feel any heat from it? Put your hand near it and see." Tristan was the first to step forward, then immediately drew back. Then Hender reached toward the fire. He kept his hand there for a moment.

"It's cool, William!" Ingram and Scobie watched in disbelief as MacBain approached the flames and confirmed Hender's statement.

"Dontcha' see?" declared William. "Elves are harmless! It was no Elf that attacked our families. Calm yourselves. Maybe he'll come back. He probably wants to talk to us anyway, or he'd never have let us see him."

"There's no 'lettin' about it," Ingram argued. "We snuck up on 'em pure and simple. He didn't see us comin'."

"Yeah," Scobie and Hender chimed in.

"Let's see if we can hear him moving through the trees," William suggested, hoping to quiet the men so the Elf would feel comfortable enough to return.

The conversation gradually softened and faded and the men began listening to the forest, each watching the darkness. It didn't take long for them to start noticing the night sounds. An animal was foraging in the leaves some hundred yards away, and a mouse darted across a short expanse between hiding places and making the leaves rustle.

Finally they began to grow accustomed to their surroundings and they relaxed their vigil. It was only then that they heard a voice addressing them from the darkness. "I am Migalik, King of the Naver Grays. Who approaches my sanctuary with swords drawn and battle cries on their lips?" Migalik felt that a strong stance would be more believable to the humans than a congenial one.

The men heard the voice but could not see anyone. They exchanged glances. Ingram, Scobie and Hender all tightened their grips on their swords, readying themselves for action.

"Loosen up there, boys," William said softly. "This is no enemy." Then he raised his voice: "We are from the Williamson family of Glen Williamson and Clan MacAodh. We are seeking the slayer who entered the Glen two nights past and killed kith and kin. What brings you to the forest, Migalik, King of the Forest Grays?"

At the more peaceful tone of William's voice, Migalik felt less danger and he approached the clearing. He was well within the light of the fire before any of them adjusted their focus enough to see him. Scobie was closest and saw him first. Again his hand reached for his sword.

"Stay your hand, Scobie. You too, Ingram. We'll shed no Elf blood tonight," William ordered. He was as shocked as the rest at the sight of Migalik standing before them. How had the Elf managed to do that, without being seen?

"So," Migalik began, "shall we sit and confer as brothers and the neighbors that we are, or shall we continue to play the game of distrust which those of the Glen so love? Don't you know that we are among you much of the time, even though unseen? If we wished you harm, it would have come swiftly, long ago. The creature that attacked your families also attacked mine. We have a common enemy. We, the Naver Gray Elves would have you as allies rather than enemies. What is your will?"

As Migalik spoke, William became aware that they were completely surrounded by Elves. Some held bows with arrows set in their strings. Some held ornately carved spears, poised and ready to defend Migalik. Others held large swords that gleamed in the firelight, each with a shield in the other hand for defense against the Humans' wood and iron swords. All were fiercely watching the scene playing out before them, waiting for William's answer.

Will began smiling at the humor of his situation. Their little group had rushed in so fiercely and so cocksure of themselves, when all the time they were vastly outnumbered and held inferior weapons. He knew Elves wouldn't harm any of them unprovoked, and if provoked they would cause the least amount of harm necessary to defend themselves. Of all the things Laura had told him of her kinsmen, their peacefulness was what she spoke most about.

William's smile froze as he saw Scobie's hand flash toward his old rusted sword. Before William could speak, Scobie was on his feet slashing at the Elves. By the time Ingram reached his feet, Hender and MacBain were rising. William shouted "Hold!"

It was too late for Scobie. He had learned his lesson. He was flat on the ground with three Elves holding him down. His wooden sword was in the hands of another who was studying it in amusement.

"If he promises to behave himself, will you release him?" William asked Migalik.

"Of course," answered Migalik with a laugh. "But I still await your answer."

"May I speak to him?" asked William.

"Go and do it," Migalik chuckled, "but if you don't mind, please leave this formidable weapon that you carry, here on the ground. As you can see, my companions may misunderstand."

Migalik's joke about his cracked and rusting iron sword did not go over William's head, but he knew the Elf meant no offense. He rose slowly and strode to the edge of the circle. "Scobie, they won't harm us. Do you believe that now?"

"Yes," grunted Scobie in annoyance, "if you could just make this one stop tickling me."

The entire party of Elves began laughing. The laughter was infectious and the Humans began laughing too, even Ingram Williamson, who was known to distrust strangers.

"Damn it, let me up! I won't try to fight you again," insisted Scobie.

Chapter Four: Premonition of War

Migalik not only gave them warm dry places to sleep; he also fed them. As the Humans ate the wonderful sauce covered seeds, berries and nuts gathered and prepared by their host's people, Migalik talked of the troubles facing them. He spoke of the Geketzim and the history of his people, the flight from YeePhraWaine across the green seas, and the further pursuit of safety that had led them to these hills, in the Valley of the Naver.

When he got to the part about the Geketz, William interrupted and told Migalik about the attack in the Glen, ending with "and I fear it's also taken my son Angus."

"No, William Williamson. The Geketz tried to take your son, Angus, and it nearly succeeded, but Angus was protected and he lies near us, sleeping. He has been gravely injured. I sent for help from our people who live in The City of The Vision. Someone from there should be arriving soon, perhaps even tonight. You may see Angus if you wish."

Standing beside his son's bed, William felt a mixture of relief and worry. Migalik had told him Angus had been in a deep sleep for two full days and nights. "He may wake on his own, and he may not," Migalik told him. "It depends on his constitution. The sting of the Geketz runs deep. It draws out of the creature that force that gives it life. If his life force is strong, he will survive. Some of us from The City of The Vision remember cures for such things. It has been many generations of Elf-kind since we have even seen a Geketz, but the knowledge has been preserved against the need for it. Someone will come."

William spent the night tightly wedged into a chair built for Elves at the side of his son's bed, remembering scenes from better times. He wondered if this Elf maiden Migalik told him of, this Lurenne, was the one who had turned his son's head away from Human girls. How had he met her and what she was like? *She must be one dazzling female if she's all Elf,* he thought to himself, sadly remembering his Laura. *Light and willowy, yet hot and strong, as a woman.* The tears finally began to flow. He cried for Angus' misery. Then he cried for Laura who he couldn't save. When he had finished crying for Laura, he cried more for Angus, and when he felt he'd cried enough for these two, he cried for himself, who had lost such a wonderful wife, and perhaps lost his youngest son as well.

After crying, his rage returned and he envisioned his slaying of the beast that had caused him so much harm. In his mind, over and over, he planned its capture and execution. Each time he would take great pleasure in his imagined success and then he would start to weep again.

Overwhelmed with his helplessness and impotence William he sat watching his youngest son moaning and tossing in his sleep. If only he could help him. He had never seen his son looking so drawn and gray, as though he would die at any moment. It frightened him.

After several hours, Fierrondenne entered the room with a strange-ly carved pitcher and filled a mug for him. As he sipped, it seemed hot, then later it seemed cold, then hot again. It had a fruity taste, like grapes he thought at first, then it seemed more like apples. Then he was asleep.

Toward the end of the night he was awakened by much activity in the room. When he opened his eyes, someone handed him another mug filled from the same pitcher as earlier. It was Aelrondenne. The en-chanting, mystical quality of her beauty astonished him. Fierrondenne was with her, and they laughed at his obvious discomfiture. Then for the first time, he noticed Fierrondenne, who was equally beautiful. "You are the daughters of Migalik?" he asked.

"Yes," replied Fierrondenne. "I am Fierrondenne, which means in your language, 'the bud of the flower of flowing water'. This is my sis-ter Aelrondenne. Her name means 'the life of growing plants, which is about to break forth'. What does your name mean, William?"

William only half heard her question. His mind was focusing on the whole experience of Fierrondenne. Her voice sounded strangely famil-iar, as familiar as his own. He had never seen eyes that contained such depth, except--when was it? Her skin had the appearance of a certain familiar texture. He couldn't quite determine how he knew about it.

"It means, uh. It means, well. It's a name that came down to us from an ancient ancestor who was famous among our people." Then it struck him. She reminded him of his wife, Laura. "It's a name that my people feel I am honored to have. It's the name of William MacAodh, the founder of the Williamson family. When a child is given such a name it is the hope of the parents that he will achieve the same greatness as our ancestor or that the child will somehow be like him."

"What a beautiful tradition," Aelrondenne smiled.

Fierrondenne's older sister was as tall as Migalik, by human standards, petite. Her deep blue eyes contrasted Fierrondenne's dark brown ones.

But wait, thought William, *Fierrondenne's eyes seemed blue only a moment ago.* Aelrondenne also had golden blonde hair and the fairest skin William had ever seen. *It's no wonder Angus has fallen for one of them. I did it myself. These beauties look like my Laura.* He had never before been so aware of the dominance of his wife's Elfish nature.

As William gawked at the girls, his thoughts were interrupted by the entrance of Migalik, followed by an ancient-looking man--no, an Elf—no, a man... William wasn't sure. The figure wore a robe instead of pants and shirt as the others wore. It was a deep blue, as blue as the sky, right before a thunderstorm. The trim at the robe's hem was a lighter blue, *like the blue of the bottoms of the clouds as the storm approaches,* he thought.

The man or Elf had a long flowing, snowy white beard that was actually a bit stringy and black toward the end. His bushy, black eyebrows formed an unbroken line across his forehead and his large, deep, nearly black eyes were frightening. William felt himself drawing a deep breath, pulling back into his chair and stiffening, as though to receive a blow. Then he was on his feet. The man was taller than Migalik and heavier through his chest and shoulders. He carried himself with arrogance and didn't smile when he saw William, but he did not frown, either. It seemed to William, it was enough for this stranger to be aware that William was there, and a greeting or other acknowledgment would be superfluous.

Migalik saw that William was on his feet and awake. "I hope you rested well, my friend. I am pleased to present to you my old friend and teacher, Feshka. He has come to us from The City of The Vision with news and healing power for your son. His name means in your tongue, 'Eye of The Wilderness'.

"Feshka," he turned to the stranger, "this is the father of the young man. His name is William Robert Williamson MacAodh. He seems to not mind that we call him William."

Feshka bowed, not too deeply and not too long. William bowed also, trying to be as polite as possible to the man who may hold the healing of his son in his hands.

"Feshka has the double distinction of being half human and half Elf," Migalik continued. "He thus has the physical strength that you have, also the passion of purpose that we so sadly lack. From our side he has the intuitive instincts, the ability to communicate with all things, and our connectedness with the world's Magic."

Migalik paused and cleared his throat. His tone gathered respect as he continued.

"As a chair officer of the Ancient Order of the Brith Gar-nunsum he has studied and been trained in all of our ancient mysteries. Feshka was chosen to come not only because of his healing knowledge but also to gather information about the activities of the Enemy."

"First," said Feshka, "let us attend to the boy."

William thought Feshka's voice sounded like the distant rumbling of thunder after a lightning strike. *How appropriate that his robe looks like the colors of a storm!*

Feshka approached the bed, brushing close to William, and as he did so William felt a tingling sensation. My God! thought William, stepping back. *What powers are at work here? The very air around him crackles.*

Feshka ignored him, although William had the distinct feeling that the half Elf heard his thoughts. William watched as the strange figure approached his son's side. Without a sound, Feshka raised both hands and held them over Angus's chest, palms down. For a few moments William thought he heard a sound much like thunder rumbling in the distance. He wasn't sure if the sound was coming from outside or inside the room or if it was just a feeling and not a sound at all. He made no move and waited for Feshka to finish.

Soon the half Elf turned and faced the others present. The change in his face startled William. His eyes had lightened in color from almost black to a light brown, auburn shade. His brow seemed less intense and he had such an aura of peace about him, William felt slightly embarrassed for his previous misgivings. For a moment, he even thought the man was glowing with a gentle bluish light. He closed his eyes and shook his head to clear the sensation. When he opened them again, Feshka was about to speak.

"He'll waken in a few hours. Be sure to have plenty of food around and water, when he does. He'll be very hungry. He's had quite a shock. He'll rest better now."

William walked the few steps to the edge of the bed and was relieved to see Angus in such a peaceful state, asleep just as the half Elf had said.

William accepted the bed Migalik offered. It was the most comfortable one William had ever slept in, although his feet stuck out at the end. His dreams were happy ones. He was not surprised by this. Migalik told him the bed would provide "sweet dreams." William didn't believe him, but then, *why not?* He asked himself. Understanding of the power of Migalik and the Elves was sinking in.

It was about an hour past first light that Aelrondenne came to wake him. She brought him food and sweetened water with the news that Angus was awake and eating. William could now hear the sound of many voices nearby. Quickly he splashed some of the water Aelrondenne had brought him on his face, brushed his hair slightly and emerged from his sleeping quarters.

He was surprised to find Migalik's front room filled with a host of all manner of the strangest looking beings William had ever seen: dozens of Elves of all shapes and sizes, old and young ones, children of all ages. William was astonished at the tiny size of a baby that one of the ladies was holding in her arms. It was certainly a happy group. Some sang together, but most were talking animatedly as though at some family reunion. Seated among them were Tristan, Hender, MacBain, Scobie and Ingram Williamson, merrily eating and drinking as though they had been friends with these strangers all their lives.

Then he saw Angus seated next to Migalik at the table. Angus appeared to be the only one in the room who was not smiling. He had a stern look about him that William had not seen in his son before. *It looks like my son has done some rapid maturing in these last few days*, thought William. *Thank God he looks well.*

Beside Angus and on the other side of Migalik were two unusual characters, even for an Elf community. They had a stocky build, with thick tangled long hair and salt-and-pepper beards. They wore bulky clothing that made them look even broader than they were. Both were wearing huge cloth hats that sagged down over their eyes and ears. William was so overwhelmed by the host of strangers, it didn't even occur to him to wonder how Migalik got them all into a single small room. It was crowded, but no one seemed to mind; they were having such a good time.

Migalik had just finished filling Angus in on the events of the last few days and the relevant history of the Elves that had brought them about. But he did not yet know about the calamity in the Glen and the deaths of his mother and many others. Angus was obviously angry enough dealing with the loss of his newfound Elf friend, Lurenne, who Migalik was now calling Lurelei. He was apparently beginning to feel her loss. All other thoughts were being crowded out of his mind by the anger growing visibly inside him.

Ingram saw William come into the room and he rose and came

to his side. "There's talk of a council this afternoon," he told William. "Elves are arriving from all over. That one over there," he pointed to a tall Elf wearing tan colors mixed with greens, "that one Migalik calls WarNock. He lives among the Islemen to the north. And that one," Ingram pointed again, "he's from across the sea to the east. These boys have done some fast traveling in such a short time. And did you see the Dwarves? They're some tough customers. When they came in last night, I saw the packs they were carrying. I tried to lift one and couldn't. They treat them like back packs for hiking."

By now, Hender and Scobie had made their way to William. They were both carrying a mug in one hand and bread and cheese in the other. "So there ya' are William! Isn't this something else? When I think, two days ago I didn't even believe in Elves—hell--never seen one before, an' today I'm breakin' bread with 'em!"

"Have they told you what's afoot, here?" Hender asked William.

"Just partly," William answered. "Have they told you?"

"Sure did."

"Looks like there's to be hell ta' pay," Scobie added.

By now, MacBain reached them, bumping his head on the ceiling. It was then that William noticed Hender also was holding his head at an angle to keep from hitting the ceiling. "Never thought I'd be glad I wasn't taller," muttered William.

"Hello William," MacBain greeted him. "Where have you been?"

"I spent most of the night with Angus, then I took a bed in one of the back rooms here. Some bed it was, too."

"We all had good beds," Ingram took a long drink from his mug. "These Elves know how to live, I'll tell ya'."

"William, these folks seem pretty light-hearted just now," said Hender, "but don't let that fool ya'. They have an attitude of determination that sort of sets my blood cold. There's talk of war, around here. Did you know that?"

"I sort of figured as much," replied William.

"Look at that one over there," Scobie motioned with his head, "the one with the funny eyes. Well hell, they all have funny eyes, I mean the one with the flaming red beard--the husky one. See 'em?"

"Yeah, I see which one you mean," answered William. "He does have unusual eyes, doesn't he?"

"That one's got a mean look about him. He just walks around the grounds here scowling like he's mad as hell all the time. Migalik calls him VelMud, or something like that."

"I wouldn't want to meet him alone in the woods at night. Look at the sword he's got hanging on his belt," Hender cast a sideways glance at him.

"All of these fellas are armed to the teeth," Scobie said. "The East-erners, over there with the short leather pants, all have bows and ar-rows and some of them have a mean looking kind of bow that they draw back and set with a hook before they place an arrow to the string. Then they release the arrow by pulling what they call a trigger. They call it a crossbow. It takes both hands to draw back the string. They all have a Skyn Dhu stuck in a sheath under their shirts too, just like we do."

Some of the men were having a lively conversation with Aelron-denne and Fierrondenne and three other young Elf girls. William kept hearing the word 'StrathNaver,' followed by giggling. After the first few repetitions, he approached Aelrondenne and asked, "What's this I keep hearing about the River Naver?"

The girls started giggling and seemed reluctant to answer. "Oh, it's Angus," Scobie laughed. "It seems that when he first saw them he was so surprised, he fell in the Strath Naver and nearly drowned. He was barely rescued in time. Ever since then they've been calling him 'ole Strath Naver'. He doesn't like it much, but they say he answers to it, if they call him a second time."

William drew Migalik aside. "A few months ago my father came to us very disturbed. He said there was danger in the south and he was going to find out what was going on. We haven't seen him since. Do you know anything about this? Have you seen him?"

Migalik smiled. Picking his beard out of a shirt button where it had become tangled, he gazed off into the forest. "Old Will Roy passed this way. A fierce old man, is he not?"

"Yes he's that," remarked William. "A bit too fierce for his own good, we think sometimes. I wonder what he's gotten himself into now."

"Did you know that he fought on our side in the last war with the Dwarves?"

"That must have been before my time. I knew there was more to that old buzzard than he ever let on. Where and when was this?"

"You'll no doubt be hearing more about the last Dwarf war at the gathering this afternoon. He distinguished himself in our behalf. He's a most interesting human for having no Elf ancestry himself. We think his influence was what led Feshka into his later studies. In a way, be-cause of that, you most likely have Old Will Roy to thank for Angus's life."

"Do you know if he's all right? Or where he is?" asked William.

"No I don't. When he passed through here he said he was going to The City of The Vision, and from there, who knows?" Migalik shook his head.

"What did he do during the war that could have influenced Feshka?

He has never so much as mentioned Elves to us, not in any serious way. We always thought he was making up stories when he spoke of your race."

"Be wary of ignoring legends," Migalik tossed over his shoulder as he turned toward the door. "Myths and legends generally begin as truthful stories that gain embellishment as they go. The grain of truth they contain can be easily missed by those too wise to listen!"

The council was held in the open air in a natural amphitheater under the trees. What surprised William most was the fact that it was in the broad light of day. Angus, still sullen and quiet, was at his side. William was shocked at the ugly scars at Angus's throat, hands and wrists, wide blackened areas where William could actually see the outlined marks where the Geketz's fingers had grasped his son.

When William asked his son if they still hurt, Angus answered quickly, "Yes. It seems that the pain is fading but I think I'm just getting used to it."

"What was it like, this creature we're chasing?"

"It was darkness and ice. Even its teeth were black. It was as though I could see through it a little bit at the edges, but it was solid enough, and strong."

William's party was seated together on the ground. It seemed that hundreds had gathered on the sloping hillside, and although one would think such a large group would have produced much chattering, all were silent. The groups were mostly intermingled, with a few Dwarves together here and there. Other Humans were present also, who had come with the Dwarves. William started when he spotted the MacDonald plaid not too far from him. Some Islemen had come along with the Sea Elves. The Wood Elves from the mainland also had a small group of Humans with them.

Several parties had just arrived. It seemed to William that the council had been delayed in order to wait for these late arrivals, both Elves and Dwarves from other parts of the great Island, and some from the southwestern Islands. Many looked uneasy and were scowling distrustfully at the other parties.

William heard a voice speaking softly and he turned his head to look down the hillside. It was Migalik, in the center focus of the amphitheater, addressing the throng. Behind him a low table was set up, and seated around it were six creatures, only one of whom appeared to William to be Human.

Migalik began his speech. "Welcome one and all to the largest gathering ever to take place in the Valley of the Naver. I am called Migalik and I am King of the Naver Gray Elves, by popular election. I compliment you on this peaceful gathering, since many times in our history, Humans, Elves and Dwarves have not lived in peace. Songs are sung of our ancient battles together, and histories have been written of the courage and heroism on all sides.

"Today we gather as allies to plan and discuss strategies against a common Enemy, most dreadful, who has killed and slaughtered loved ones belonging to all of us. Before we begin, let me mention that a most unusual event has taken place this morning. To explain it and its significance, we are fortunate to have among us one who is very learned in such matters. He will tell his tale. He is Feshka, of The City of The Vision."

All eyes focused on the blue-robed figure striding over to stand beside Migalik. They shook hands and Migalik took a seat nearby. Suddenly a low cry came up from the Dwarves. "Must we bear the presence of war criminal?!" one shouted.

"Let's take him now, while we can," another cried. Very shortly the forest was filled with the shouts of angry Dwarves.

As quickly as the disturbance arose, silence returned. Angus and the others were astonished to see a small army of Elves before them, with spears and arrows at the ready. They were so fast, none had seen them approach. They had appeared in the blink of an eye. Again Migalik walked to the front and spoke.

"Friends, a long time ago, half a century in fact, there was a dispute between us concerning mineral rights in the Great Glen. It was a concern that disturbed all of us greatly, Elves and Dwarves alike. The issue was blown up to great proportions and we fell to warring over it. Many were killed on both sides. These blood feuds lasted many years, but our wise leaders proposed and accepted an agreement we call The Treaty of the Great Glen. Feshka, then called by another name, was one of the greatest of our Rebecks or generals. You are angry because he was often victorious. He is now no longer a Rebeck. He has spent many years in study and research and now acts as a consultant to our leaders. He is here today for that purpose, to serve all of us."

VeratNonn, one of the Dwarves who was seated at the table, came to Migalik's side. "The anger you bear him is understandable," began VeratNonn, "but his crime that we find so infuriating was one of mercy, that saved many lives on both sides. Some of you who are with us today may well have been killed if it were not for what you call this person's evil. He trapped our forces in a valley and kept us penned in until peace was assured. We called him a coward. We called him gutless, but his bravery and stubbornness in refusing to battle with us without need, saved many lives. Yes, it was embarrassing. Yes, it was humiliating, but today he is on our side. Today, he will be part of our victory. Listen to him."

"We can all be glad and happy that we are on the same side and allies," added Migalik. "He is no longer your enemy. Can we proceed peacefully now, concerning our mutual interest?"

The Dwarves continued to grumble but finally agreed. Feshka rose again and began speaking.

"In the days when Elves lived in YeePhraWaine there was a wise leader whose name was called BaynYamen. He was known first for his discovery of the treachery of the GreYen Circle who were a human species living among us then. They had represented themselves as traders from the north and they brought cloth and special, soft woods that we used in our work. It was BaynYamen who discovered the GreYen Circle were selling information about our people to the Enemy, who, several generations before, had driven us from our first home among the stars. It was through the efforts of the GreYen Circle that the Enemy was able to find us again.

"BaynYamen found out too late for the Elves to flee without a fight, but most of our race escaped across the Green Seas to the Great Island where we now live.

"BaynYamen was known and distinguished by an amulet he wore which was presented to him by the Grand Sovereign of all Elves in that day, the Great King of the Kings, BarDoschel. The amulet is described in the scrolls that are maintained and protected by the Brith Gar-nun-sum whose headquarters are in The City of The Vision. It is said to be the figure of an eagle with two heads, one looking to the right and one looking to the left. Inscribed on the body of the Eagle is the name in our ancient tongue, BaynYamen.

"The amulet commemorated the occasion of BaynYamen's discovery of the traders' deceit. At that time, BaynYamen engaged in a deadly battle with the GreYen Circle and he was wounded in his right shoulder. This deep wound left a scar that is remembered in song and verse.

"When the Elves departed from YeePhraWaine, BaynYamen was unable to come. He had been attacked and taken by a creation of the Enemy like the one that was in this place a few nights ago. It is unnecessary and dangerous to name this creature, and I believe that all present are aware of that name, so I will not now give it utterance.

"Three nights ago one of these creatures attacked and took a young Elf named Lurenne. It tried to also take an Elfkin who we now name 'StrathNaver', after the river, for his bravery in defending our Lurenne. Lurenne, although perverted by the creature, still had enough of her nature to fight for the life of the Human, and even now, she is near us and does not attack. We name her 'Lurelei' to honor her life that once was among us.

"We have learned more in these past generations about such attacks. The creature apparently drains the victim's life essence. The victims then become the Enemy's creatures themselves. In this case, others were present who were able to subdue the creature. We thought it dead since we could find no sign of it. But this morning we found an old Elf wandering in the forest, filled with madness. We have brought him here before you.

"He was wearing this amulet." Feshka held a gold amulet above his head for all to see. "Behold. His right shoulder is scarred."

A low gasp went up among the crowd. "It's BaynYamen," many voices were saying softly.

◈◈

The crowd was beginning to annoy Angus. He was used to a quiet setting with a gathering of only six or seven people at most. He was filled with thoughts of the past few days, and those memories were displacing all others. Laura was dead. His mother was dead. Visions of that last morning he had seen her, the last day of her life, drove any other feeling out of his heart; but then there was Lurenne.

'Lurelei', the startling little man had called her. His heart and mind were struggling to contain all the images. Lurenne was taken by the creature. The last thing he could remember was trying to rise to his feet to show Aelrondenne where she was lying. The struggle flashed by. It was too brief, too fast. It was a blur in his mind. Laura was dead. Lurelei was dead. His whole world was crashing, and at the same time his heart was trying to explode.

Angus rose to his feet and left the circle, gazing over at his father sitting with cousins and neighbors. Their families had been attacked too and their family members killed. Glen Williamson was a place he would no longer recognize. His family had been his home, and now with his mother gone and his father going off to war, there *was* no family.

"What of Robert?" Angus had asked his father.

"He was missed by the creature, thank God," William told him. "He's home with his wife and baerns. Someone needs to be watchin' over the home front."

Blindly, filled with loss and despair, Angus walked away from the gathering into the forest, stumbling over fallen trees and branches, no longer caring where he was going. He knew Migalik thought another Geketz was in the forest, but he didn't care. *Let it finish me off,* he thought to himself angrily. His wounds throbbed with a hot then cold burning sensation. When the pain let up for a moment, he would forget about its intensity; then the burning icy sensation would return, causing him to wince and suck in his breath.

He climbed over rolling hills and small ravines. He had no direction in mind other than to escape the visions. At length he grew tired; it hadn't taken much, since he was not yet fully recovered from his attack by the Geketz. He plopped down on the ground, angry at his fatigue, angry at his father's failure to protect his mother, raging at himself for failing to protect Lurenne and failing to recognize the danger in time, for not being home when he was needed. He sat in the bottom of a gully between two low, tree-covered hills, glaring at the ground.

❧ ❧

When Angus left the amphitheater, William thought nothing of it. "Where's Angus goin'?" Tristan asked William, for once not stuttering.

"Probably to take a leak," he answered, expecting him to return in a few minutes.

Feshka completed his speech and now Migalik introduced Broenann's representative, VeratNonn. VeratNonn was short and stocky even for a Dwarf. His beard was nearly black with reddish highlights. It reached almost to his belt, which was wide and thick with garish carvings in its fine leather. His leather tunic was a distressed, darkened brown. It had obviously been oiled and it gleamed with reflected light every time a ray of the sun would peek through and touch it. VeratNonn had huge ears, made larger than life probably by the huge earrings he wore, that pulled heavily on his lobes.

VeratNonn's voice was tinged with anger and suspicion. His small eyes darted around the audience quickly, stopping more often on the Elves than anywhere else. "Yes," VeratNonn began, "we have seen the Flying Shadows. Had none of ours bred with Elves, we'd have nothing to fear since GaudarKahn never had any interest in Dwarfs." When he pronounced 'GaudarKahn', he drew out the 'U', casting it with an evil sound.

A rush of fear passed through the Elves. They believed it to be unlucky to enunciate the name of the Enemy and they never did. They referred to him only as 'The Enemy'.

"Please, name him not," Migalik whispered loudly to VeratNonn. "Bring not this evil name to life in the peacefulness of our homes."

VeratNonn sneered but replied, "It is not our wish to offend your sensitivities. I apologize."

The Elves applauded loudly. It was the first time any of them had ever experienced a Dwarf apologizing for anything, or expressing the least amount of humility to them. The Elves feared an alliance with the Dwarves as much as the Dwarves feared it.

"That was not a concession," smiled VeratNonn, but the Elves, who knew differently, returned the smile and remained silent. The other Dwarves did not respond like their leader, but they had no intention of acting foolishly. They too recognized their danger and the necessity of an alliance with the Elves against a common enemy, so they bore the indignity with silence.

"As I was saying," continued VeratNonn, "we have seen the Shadows passing over our homes at night. We know that Gau--I mean, the Enemy has found us, that he knows of our interbreeding. This spreads the Elf light among the other races. All our families have been against it from the beginning. If this continues, we all fear the races of Elves and Dwarves will one day vanish and we will all be some kind of bastard race, which is neither Elf nor Dwarf.

"And now I see the Elves are also breeding with Humans. May it be for the best. Some of ours have done the same.

"In any case, this interbreeding has endangered all of us, Humans and Dwarves alike. The Enemy seeks the light, however diffused. Our King, the Lord BroeNann, has sent you this message."

VeratNonn pulled a scroll from an inner pocket hidden beneath his shining leather tunic. He unrolled it and read:

> To the Naver Grays, the Sea and Wood Elves, my old Enemies, I say this to you. In the past we never saw this Enemy of yours to be our own. We have held lengthy meetings and conferences concerning the matter. We have studied the nature of this foe. We have sent spies to the west to seek him out and learn what we can about him.
>
> This knowledge we will share with you. We too, for the first time in our history, recognize [and he names him] to be our enemy as well as yours.
>
> I have sent word to our Kinsmen, KaarNonn, the King of the Mountain Dwarfs, to the west, BereeshNonn, King in the Iberian mountains, and to ValNonn, King in the Bird Islands. I believe they will be eager to participate in the coming battles, but for the present I await their replies.

VeratNonn rolled up the scroll and handed it to Migalik. Then he continued to address the audience. "Our King BroeNann has also instructed me to tell you this. In the south, several months ago, we found three of the creatures that caused you harm here."

A hush went up among the Elves, and the Humans listened with careful attention. This revelation had been a secret none had known.

"Since they cannot harm a Dwarf or any other who is not Elfkin, most of us did not fear them. In fact, we captured two of them. We did not take the third one because we wished the enemy to know what we had done. We want no more of their kind among us. Before we captured them and drove the other one away, they killed many Elfkin among us. We followed the evil creature until he had returned to the western islands. We followed him because we wished no others to come to harm."

VeratNonn returned to his seat at the table.

Migalik was surprised by the news from the Dwarf; everyone had wondered why the Dwarves were so eager to join on the Elves' behalf in a fight. Now they knew. Migalik proceeded to thank everyone present and invited them to feast again at his table after the meeting was over.

William was becoming uneasy. Angus had not returned and darkness was not far off.

Chapter Five: Lurelei

Angus held little fear for the forest at night, even with the threat of the Geketz at large. At least that's what he kept telling himself. Anger has a strange way of convincing a person that danger dare not raise its head. Fear becomes an abstraction. Only when confronted with reality does the resolution fade and terror return. Such was the way with Angus at that moment. He glared at the ground until the anger faded to exhaustion. Then he lay back in the leaves and drifted off into a pleasant dream.

The dream was the same one he'd had before this tragedy had begun. He was at a picnic with many others, some of whom were Elves. Immediately he began searching the group for Lurenne. Ahh, there she was, cutting a pie with two other lovely young Elves looking on.

Angus was transfixed by her beauty. Her hair seemed to cascade over her shoulders in waves of light, its reddish darkness casting an aura around her. Her translucent skin glowed with a beautiful aura in a cast of white. Her long fingers gracefully drew the knife through the pie. A strand of hair concealed her eyes from him as, head bowed, she worked on cutting the pie into even pieces.

She felt him watching her and looked up, meeting his gaze. He felt the intensity of her eyes and wondered why his heart had started to pound, why his breath was so short. Then she smiled at him and it seemed that all of her was smiling the same smile. Her eyes had brightened when she first recognized him, and now in their deep darkness he could see dreams yet to be dreamed and hopes he hadn't even thought of.

"Hello, StrathNaver." How musical her voice was! He heard it not so much with his ears as through another sense.

"Why do you call me this?" his dreaming self asked her.

"All things grow and change, StrathNaver. We know these things. Our names tell others of our growth and how we have become different."

Her voice floated over him much like the waters of the river had done, but it was warm and brought with it a gentleness unlike the cold and turbulent river. Its sweetness lulled his other senses. "Your new name is one of strength, for is not the Strath Naver a mighty river? It also speaks of joy and laughter. Do you not love laughter, StrathNaver?"

"Yes," Angus replied. "I love laughter," and as he said it he remembered that she had told him her name meant 'laughter'. "Yes," he repeated, "I do indeed love laughter!"

Something awakened him. When he realized where he was, rather, that he didn't know where he was, he sat up with a start. *What have I done now?* he muttered. *I'm lost in the forest and it must be midnight.* Then he began to worry about what might have awakened him. He heard it again. Something was walking through the dried leaves near him. He froze, listening.

The forest was filled with night sounds. He could hear a cricket in the distance, and not too far off, a mouse or some other creature rooting in the leaves for insects. Then he heard something that terrified him. It was laughter, but not the friendly sort. This rasping and chortling was deep and threatening.

"So. You're awake finally," a voice confronted him. It seemed somehow familiar, but this made it all the more threatening. Silently he drew his Skyn Dhu, his only available weapon. The voice cackled and shrilled louder.

"Make no mistake, Angus, I can see you very clearly, as though it were day. Do you think such a trifling toy can harm a Geketz?" More laughter. "Don't you remember how it burned your skin? I can see the scars. How is it that you survived the attack? I wonder if you will survive again. And what is this you were saying as you awoke? You love laughter? Ha. You were dreaming of me, no doubt, or I should say, what I used to be."

His heart was pounding. He strained to try to see the creature. His night vision was good; he could thank the Elves for that, he grimaced, squinting in the dark. But it wasn't good enough to see the creature.

"The forest is filled with Elves and men tonight, Angus. They're looking for you. From all the creatures I've slain and left near his house, I'm sure Migalik knows I'm around somewhere close, so I'm sure they're very concerned for you. How tempting it is for me, with all those Elves in the forest. Do you know how driven a Geketz can be to consume the lives of Elves? You yourself glow in the dark like a beacon to me, calling for me to dine. My body grows eager for you and my limbs begin trembling when I look at you. Do you know that, Angus?"

Angus was still searching the darkness for the image of Lurenne or what she may have become. He found a place about six feet to his right that seemed darker than the rest of the forest. He wondered if there was any point in attacking it.

"I think this is funny, Angus," the Geketz continued. "My body trembled for your touch before I became what I am now. But it trembles now for a different purpose. My tongue can taste your light even at this distance. Do you know what you have done to me, Angus? Do you have any idea of my situation?"

"You trembled for my touch?"

"Yes, Angus. I know you were dreaming of me just now and probably many times before. I dreamed of you too. I dreamed of you for so long, I gave up on ever meeting you. And these were dreams Migalik did not make. These dreams of yours and mine were from some other Dream Maker, a Master Dream Maker, the one who makes Migalik's dreams, perhaps."

Angus realized the voice was now coming from another direction. Angus turned toward it.

"Angus, don't try to attack me. You can't hurt me with that thing. Even if its sharpness could cut me, I'm far too fast for you. Now listen to what I have to say to you. I must finish and get away from you before my resolve to not harm you or the others is consumed by madness. Do you have any idea of the madness my body now contains?" The creature's laughter reached a hysterical pitch. "When you attacked the Geketz to protect me, it was almost too late. Had you been any later it would have drained me completely. Had you been any earlier I would have been no more injured than you were. It did not take all of my light and even now it wars within me against the darkness and against the Enemy. Sometimes the light is in control, but the evil of the Geketz that I am, soon takes over. Then the war within me begins again. So far I have not harmed any Elves or Humans, but I know not how long that may last. The Enemy is furious that he cannot control me all the time. I can hear his thoughts.

"It is well that I stay away from my people because the Enemy will know what I know. But there is an advantage in that, because I also know his thoughts, just as he knows mine. His fear at the present is that the Elves will learn how to help me and restore me. If that secret is captured by them, all his Geketzim could be lost."

"What can I do to help you?" asked Angus. "I wish I could have been there for you sooner... I may have been able to save you, if I had just been able to get to my feet faster. I had no idea the danger you were in!"

"Seek the Gate Keeper in the House of The Brith Gar-Nunsum." The Geketz now started to pace before him, rolling its head back and forth as though in the heat of a terrible struggle. "That is the thought of GaudarKahn. He fears you will find the Gate Keeper and the Key." Then it turned and raced through the forest, screaming. As its voice faded in the distance, Angus was carried to his feet by its urgency.

Angus had no idea how he found his way back. Migalik had left his door uncovered so Angus could see the light. People, Elves and even some Dwarves were searching the woods for him. He had walked right through them without realizing he was the object of their search.

When Angus entered the doorway, William was the first to see him. Migalik was not there. "He's off with the others. They're having a secret meeting talking about war," William told him. "There's plenty of food. Here, eat something." William then stepped outside the door and whispered to an Elf that Angus had returned and to call in the searchers.

Migalik and VelMud arrived back at Migalik's underground home at about the same time, with Feshka close behind. "That was a very unwise thing to do, Angus. You know there is another Geketz around us."

"Yes, I know," Angus replied. "I spoke with it." As he sipped a mug from the Wine Well he told them the whole story, except the part about the dreams and his former hopes concerning Lurenne. When he got to the words 'Gate Keeper', the three Elves exchanged knowing glances.

After Angus had finished, Feshka was the first to speak. "There's more to this story than you've told us. Why would the Geketz speak to you so kindly? Why would she choose to speak to you at all, instead of her uncle or cousins?"

Angus didn't answer.

Feshka rose and stood squarely in front of Angus, glaring at him for nearly a full minute. At least Angus interpreted it as a glare. Actually Feshka was examining the boy closely. Such intensity in any person can be easily misunderstood. Then he said, "Tell me the rest of the story, Elfkin. It may be much more important to us than you realize."

"But it's very personal sir." Angus wasn't sure whether he should tell him of his private friendship with Lurenne.

Migalik, VelMud, Feshka, and the older humans present, Angus' Father William, Ingram, and Scobie, without exception knew from their own memories of their youth just what it was that Angus was trying to conceal, but William and Ingram thought it had gone much further than it really had. Tristan was filled with curiosity. He had the feeling everyone knew something amusing except him. Migalik's eyes twinkled and he winked at VelMud, who was just getting it. Then the Elves glanced at the Humans to see if they understood. Their eyes met as the Humans glanced back for the same reason.

They tried to conceal from Angus that they knew he was in love with Lurelei just as they tried to conceal the "been-there-done-that" look in their own eyes. Feshka was the first to speak.

"Angus, Elves have only been among Humans for about six hundred years, in this place. We have known for a long time that major differences exist between the races. Elves tend to be delicate, intuitive and what Humans find to be delightfully happy. Humans on the other hand have much stronger passions and generally much greater physical strength. This combination has created an attraction between Human males and Elf females which doesn't seem to work the other way around. Most Human and Elf marriages have been with a Human male and a female Elf. Elf women for the most part, embody every positive trait that Human males seek in their women. Most Elf women prefer Elf men, but every so often we find one with a wild bent who seeks the higher passions and finds the greater physical strength desirable. I, myself, am the product of such a marriage."

The light dawned in Tristan's eyes and he turned his attention fully on Angus. *So that's why he couldn't decide which woman to take,* he thought. *That rascal, and he didn't even tell me!*

"But it's more than that," Angus began. "Both of us dreamed about each other for a long time before actually meeting."

"The rest you may keep private if you wish," Feshka said kindly. "We're trying to understand why she chose you as her contact with us. Now I understand. She said she could be restored. She said the Enemy fears we might learn the secret. If he fears that, then it must be possible. And it must be easily within our grasp. But why did she seek you for that message?"

"It may become clear later," Migalik offered. "For now, the first course of action we must follow is this. Angus, do you plan to seek the Gate Keeper, as the creature suggested?"

"I'd do anything to help her," Angus declared with great passion. "If this Gate Keeper can lead me in the right direction to accomplish that, yes I will seek the Gate Keeper. Do you know where I can find him?"

"Possibly," Feshka answered. "You may find him in The City of The Vision, in the house of the Brith Gar-Nunsum. Do you still desire to go there?"

"Yes," answered Angus without hesitation.

"It is a place where you can never be invited," Migalik said. "You must personally request that you be taken there. That is why you were asked a second time, so we can be certain this desire arises from your own free will and accord."

"Fine." Feshka placed a reassuring hand on Angus's shoulder. "We will leave for that place at sunset tomorrow. Spend the time till then resting. It seems to me that you have not fully recovered from the attack, Angus. You will need your rest. Also, my young friend, from this moment on, and until you return to your home in the Glen, your name shall be called 'StrathNaver'. It will be your Elf name, representing not the water of the river, but the passion of its drive to the sea--the power of its passion."

Migalik could tell from Angus's expression that he didn't much like the new name and Migalik knew why. "Don't let a little teasing bother you, StrathNaver. The girls named you well!"

"What's this talk of a cure?" Scobie asked.

"Yes," answered Feshka. "We must think about that. BaynYamen is again among us. His body is apparently recovered, but he's filled with madness."

"Perhaps living the life of the Geketz is what drove him mad," suggested Migalik. I'll try to speak with him again."

"And the Bolt from Star Bright drove out that part of the enemy that was in him, holding him?" Feshka asked.

"It appears so," replied Migalik.

"This talk of Bolts and monsters is a bit much for me." Ingram headed out the door.

"What is this Bolt you speak of so much?" asked Scobie.

"Elves have a very strong life force," Feshka began. "We have learned to use its power for healing, as I did with Ang-- I mean StrathNaver, last night." He smiled, watching Angus wince at the name. "We also use it for all the other things we do, things that you Humans think of as Magic. We can help a plant figure out which way it wants to grow and how big to get. We can help streams and rivers choose their course. The Bolt was accidentally rediscovered when we lived at YeePhraWaine. It is said that one of our ancient teachers of that day, in a fit of rage and in the presence of one of the creatures, sent it forth from his heart."

"And then he dropped dead," added Migalik.

"Yes he dropped dead. But it was through him that we learned to cast the Bolt in a more controlled manner. Now we know how to do it without sending out all of our life force. The first teacher to do it also did not focus it as well as Star Bright's Bolt. Its force was scattered and succeeded only in driving the thing away, causing it little harm. Star Bright's Bolt undid the creature."

"It would appear," suggested VelMud, "that the restoration of the creature we saw today was accomplished by the use of the Bolt. Maybe what we're missing is the idea that this was accomplished by the act of restoring the life force that was taken from it."

"But the Geketz spends its time drinking life forces," said Migalik. "How could this be the cure?"

Feshka rose from his seat at the table with the others. His brow was deeply furrowed, his hands clasped behind his back. William and Scobie watched him start to pace. *Perhaps there really is a cure after all,* thought Angus. These Elves had accomplished things he could never have believed without being a first-hand witness. He remembered the vine climbing back into the tree after his rescue, Lurenne, now Lurelei, walking a foot off the ground, and how his hand tingled at her touch. Was this her life force he was feeling? He thought now that he could believe anything.

William sat watching Feshka. He was thinking, *what strange names these people have. When we left the Glen we never thought this was a supernatural affair. We thought it was some rogue Islemen out playing at raiding our settlement. I never really believed in Elves. Laura said she was descended from Elves but I never really believed her.* He shuffled his feet under the table and cleared his throat. "What can we do to help, I mean, me and Scobie and the others?"

"Come with us to this place they call 'The City of The Vision'," suggested Angus, leaning forward earnestly. "It looks like there are battles to be fought. If there's vengeance to be had, it must be there. There are some ill creatures abroad that need slaying."

Feshka stopped pacing. Facing them, he instructed, "Speak not of vengeance and of slaying. There is a grave wrong in the world and we must correct it by guiding it, as we do plants and trees and streams that wander astray. The Enemy is a Being who is horribly deluded and corrupted. Try separating in your thoughts the Being from his deeds. All things believe their actions to be justified in some manner. We must find a way to correct this illness rather than slay its victim."

William stiffened in his chair. "This 'Being' as you call it, caused the death of my wife and the wives and some of the children of the other men here. He has also been the cause of much death and sorrow among your own people. How can you so calmly discuss sympathy for him when his evil delivers butchery to your very homes?"

Migalik turned toward Angus. "StrathNaver, do you still love Lurelei, even though she has become what she is?"

Angus's frowned. He looked at the floor and began shuffling his feet to find a more comfortable position while he thought about his answer. He cleared his throat, stalling for time. He didn't want to answer because he would have to direct his words toward his father. But William knew what Angus was going to say long before the answer was actually articulated. He understood love. So did Scobie, whose expression was softening as he reflected about those he loved.

"Of course I do," Angus answered at length. "I love what she was and what she could be again. But I have no love for this monster that did this to her. Loving what a destroyed piece of art once was, doesn't justify treasuring what good may be left in the vandal."

"Neither does destroying a piece of art justify destroying the vandal. The vandal may someday be the artist who restores it," answered Feshka.

"So what do you have in mind?" William asked angrily. "Are we going to fight our way to his door, break down the door and capture him, then provide him with a *teacher?* Are we going to give him a cure? This makes no sense to me! A creature's nature can't be changed. Destroy him, I say!"

"Agreed," shouted Angus and Scobie in unison.

"If this is the consensus of the others, it will be done," said Migalik. "It has always been our way to share in such decisions. But some may feel if he is imprisoned in some dark place and instructed and cared for, that he may someday come to learn about the good in us of which he is now ignorant."

"Let me see if I have this straight." Eyes flashing, Scobie confronted Migalik. "You believe the Enemy slaughters you because he fails to see the good in you? Hasn't he had enough time to see that? How long have your peoples been warring?"

"From time out of mind," responded Feshka, "He has always killed us on sight. There has often been no warning that he was near, as in the killing in your Glen. He has planted poisons where we would eat it. He has filled our air with poisons that made us sick. He has killed our children and our wives, as he did yours. For as long as our history can be remembered, he has pursued us."

"Is it finally time to stand and fight, do you think?" asked William sarcastically.

"Yes," Migalik answered, resolution ringing in his voice. "The time has finally come to face the Enemy. We now have tools that we lacked in the past. Our peoples are gathering. Even the Dwarves join us in this, and other peoples who do not acknowledge us. There are Humans, for example. Has anyone ever seen Humans and Elves fighting side by side? Not in the living memory of anyone I know!"

Tristan was loosely following the discussion. He didn't really understand what was going on, nor did Angus and the other Humans. Talk of Bolts and life forces were concepts beyond the understanding of any of the Humans present. They were shepherds and husbandmen, not metaphysicians and sorcerers. None of them had ever considered their life force to be a thing separate from the rest of their existence. Tristan understood they were going on a trip. He understood there was going to be a fight--one that may well last quite some time. He also understood what Feshka had said about how those lithesome willowy beauties of daughters felt about human males. Tristan's mind was wandering far and wide about the issues at hand.

"But how can we be of help?" asked Scobie. "Would our weapons be of any use against such foes?"

Migalik smiled and rose from his seat at the table. "Wait one moment, gentlemen." He left the room and returned with four sheathed swords tied in a bundle by a woven vine cord. Angus and the others watched in astonishment as the vines came untied, seemingly at Migalik's command. As he laid three of them on the stone shelf with his cooking pots and plates, he lifted one of the blades and handed it to Scobie. "Feel the heft of this one, Scobie, and tell me how you like it."

Then he handed one each to Angus, Tristan, and William. "We've been busy during these years in the Valley of the Naver. We traded with the Dwarves for the secret of these weapons. During the time they have been in our keeping, we have charged them with the power we use for the Bolt. They are charged with the life force that we generate within us. The Dwarves called them 'steel', but since we have contributed to their hardness, they are now ours and we call them 'Elf Steel'. Use them carefully, for they have the power to slice through stone. They are as yet untried against the Enemy but we believe they can hurt his creatures."

As Migalik spoke, William and the others unsheathed the swords Migalik had given them. "Be careful to not touch the blades," Migalik warned them.

"Look at this," Tristan declared without stuttering. "It shines brighter than Migalik's lamps!"

"That's true," Migalik smiled. "They shine with the life force of the Elves who charged them. The cutting edge is not the sharpness of the metal but the brilliance of that power. If you touch even the flat edge, it may draw blood. Keep them covered unless you must use them. Their light shines as a beacon to our Enemy. Treat them well. It takes time for the Elves to recover the power they placed within each of them."

"I hope you have more than four!" Scobie exclaimed.

"We have many," answered Migalik. "But the power of a sword, even these swords, is not much greater than the power of the swordsman. Have any of you ever handled a sword before, or been schooled in its use?"

"My father showed me some of the moves of a swordsman," said William. "This old iron blade was his and his father's before him. But neither of them nor any of us was ever trained in its use."

"There's a school in The City of The Vision where they've made quite a study of the use of the sword," said Migalik. "They are known to have mastered its techniques. Perhaps you would profit from some time with the teachers there."

Chapter Six: A Dangerous Journey

The path to The City of The Vision led over the mountains and through the most difficult terrain in all of Alba.

"We try to avoid Human settlements," Migalik explained later.

When the path crossed rivers such as the Strath Naver, it was at the most treacherous locations, over white water rapids in the bottoms of steep gullies. The Elves had developed a type of bridge consisting of two thin ropes made from woven grasses stretched across the stream, one a few feet above the other. The idea was to stand on one while hanging onto the other. "We'll be killed by traveling before we even get to see the Enemy!" grumbled Ingram.

Scobie was handling the hiking better, as he always did. He may have been smaller than the rest of the men, but that didn't mean he didn't have comparable strength. He had proved that many times, by almost trotting up the sides of cliffs while the other Humans struggled just to keep moving. Scobie, Tristan and Angus were the only ones who were able to keep up with the Elves, even though the Elves seemed to be walking slightly off the ground and without effort. "There has to be some advantage to being young," Scobie joked, "or short."

Feshka was only half Elf and his feet were on the ground. But even with this disability, he was able to keep up with the others, strolling along the paths effortlessly as though he did it every day; perhaps he did.

Migalik had decided to go with them. VelMud had also joined the party; he hiked silently, keeping his strange eyes ahead and alert. The group consisted of a little over three dozen that Tristan could count.

Counting was difficult because not all of the Elves stayed on the path but walked alongside, ahead and behind the group, watching for trouble. A few of the Dwarves had come along but the rest had gone back to the Southerlands, they said, to raise an army and encourage their distant kinsmen to do the same. VeratNonn was the only one whose name Tristan knew. There were Wood Elves and Sea Elves, Dwarves, the Gray Elves of the Naver, and some other Humans who had come up from the Southerlands with the Dwarves.

Tristan was excited about the chance to see this Elf city, yet fearful about the possibility of war. But he was very pleased about being among these strange and wonderful creatures that he didn't even know existed, only a few days before.

The Dwarves were sullen but trudging along at a surprising speed for their size and the shortness of their legs. Tristan was as awed by their strange bulky clothing as he was by their huge ears and elaborate jewelry. The Elves were mostly young, like Silver Leaf and his Elf friend GarMawk. GulDockel, Silver Leaf's father was as strange to behold as was VelMud. Tristan couldn't decide which one was stranger or fiercer. VelMud's broad shoulders gave him the appearance of great strength, and his sullenness was almost like that of the Dwarves. But the wildness of his flaming hair gave Tristan the idea that VelMud might be just a little mad. When Tristan learned of VelMud's years of seclusion and the reason for it, he became more certain that VelMud was not someone he would want to meet alone on a darkened hillside.

GulDockel, on the other hand, was not so broad shouldered or wild looking. He was neatly coifed and clothed, so neatly done, in fact, that it gave Tristan the impression that GulDockel just might be a little overly involved with himself. His long, very neatly pointed graying beard that perfectly matched his thin eyebrows turning up at their ends, made him look sinister. His face was long and the beard made it seem even longer. To complete the impression, GulDockel wore a long pointed cap. *What a great distance from the tip of his hat to the tip of his beard!* thought Tristan.

All of them were carrying the Elf Steel blades, carefully sheathed. Some of the younger Elves were carrying bows and sheathes of arrows. Tristan suspected something must be unusual about the arrows as well as the Elf blades, because they were carefully covered and out of sight.

He wished Angus would stay a little closer so they could talk about all this, but all Angus wanted to do was listen to Feshka's conversation. Angus was better at keeping up with the Elves than Tristan, so he was unable to stay close to the two to hear their conversation.

William and Ingram were near the end of the procession. Neither of them liked hiking. Added to their dislike was the weight of their heavy backpacks. Scobie kept getting ahead of them, then dropping back to join them again. Elves were all around, ahead, behind, and in the forest on both sides. "It looks like they're guarding us," William observed.

"Could be they're making sure we don't get away," replied Ingram.

"That's ridiculous," William retorted.

Scobie tuned in. He had just heard the last of the conversation. "Ingram, what are you so upset about? These creatures are like children. All they want from us and anyone else is to be left in peace!"

"It isn't peace they're seekin' now," Ingram grumbled. "We're off to war, or so they're sayin'. And if they're so peaceful, why don't we ever see them in the Glen? They live practically on top of us and we never see 'em."

"That's a good point, Ingram. What do you say, Scobie?" asked William.

"Well, think about it like this," Scobie began. "I'm much shorter than other men. I'm shorter than either of you. Do you remember when we were kids, how mean the others were to me? I was beaten more than once for being short. You were part of it once, Ingram. Do you remember?"

"We were just kids then. We meant no harm," retorted Ingram.

"Well, I remember too. I had a bloody nose from you just because I was a little bit different than the others. There are a lot of people like you, Ingram, who don't much like strangers, and these strangers are a lot more different from you than just being shorter. I think they fear us a lot more than you fear them."

"What are you sayin', Scobie?" Ingram asked defensively. "I'm not a bad person. We never did you any harm!"

"No harm done, Ingram, but don't you see what I'm talkin' about? If they ever showed up in the Glen they'd have been lucky to leave alive."

"You're right there, Scobie," Ingram condescended. "You're right there."

The first night ended without incident, and the second as well, but as they grew closer to the city, the party began traveling slower.

"Why are we slowing down?" Angus asked Feshka. "It's a welcome relief, and my legs are a bit weary of the pace, but what's the reason? Do you know?"

"Well, it's like this," Feshka explained. "For the last few months there has been some activity around the city that we don't like very much. Some of us would go into the forest and not return. After that happened a few times, no one has been willing to go out alone. Sometimes when a person is standing at the edge of the city, an arrow has found its way into that person's breast. We've lost several like that. The city is now guarded. We have scouts in the forests all around, in threes. That has helped some, but the troubles haven't stopped. We believe the Enemy is gathering information about us and when it is finished, he will come in force. Do you see? The Dwarves have moved to the head of the procession. They can handle a Geketz. There are Elf Warriors right behind them in case we find a different kind of evil. There have been some reports of others in the forest tonight. We believe we may be in some danger."

The group also traveled more quietly. On the previous two nights there had been the hum of soft conversation, but on this night, there was no sound at all other than the usual forest noises. The path they followed was clear of leaves and twigs and the shoes of the travelers were of soft woven grasses. Every so often one could hear the heavy breathing of some of the humans, and that was as controlled as possible. After several hours of what Angus thought of as tiptoeing through the forest, he commented to Feshka, "This seems unnecessary. I haven't heard a single sound that was out of place."

"It's not so much what you hear, StrathNaver, as what you don't hear. Look aloft!"

Angus stopped walking with Feshka for a moment, and looked up at the night sky. It was darkened by low clouds broken in places and revealing a brighter moonlit sky above. Then he saw it. At first it seemed like just another cloud, a small one, but darker than the rest. Then he realized it was moving in a different direction than the other clouds, and more quickly.

Someone threw a blanket over Angus' head and at the same time he realized that all Elves and Elfkin in the party were covering themselves, including Feshka. "The blankets will conceal our light," Feshka told him. "Maybe it didn't see us."

"Unlikely," responded Migalik who was walking just behind them.

Then Angus began feeling the same dark foreboding as on the night he had first slept at Migalik's home. It started in the pit of his stomach and began spreading throughout his body. He shivered to try to shake off the feeling of fear and began listening carefully to the sounds around him to take his mind off it. "Some of the Humans behind us who are not Elfkin, and the Dwarves are uncovered. They can tell us when it passes," whispered Feshka.

After a few minutes someone called the "all clear" and everyone began uncovering and looking around.

"What was it?" asked Angus.

"We call them Flying Shadows," said Migalik. "We have seen only one near the Naver, but they tell us there are many around The City of The Vision."

"The Enemy moves slowly," said Feshka, "until he's sure of where all of our settlements are. The Flying Shadows and the Geketzim are his eyes. He knows now of the Naver Grays, but he has not found the Wood Elves or the Sea Elves. His servants are all around The City of The Vision and they tease us with bloodshed. They leap out of the dark and take one or two of us. They shoot an arrow out of the night now and again to strike fear into us, but they are not ready to attack. We fear it will come soon and we are ill prepared. Our people are gathering and our tools of war are made. This will surprise him. In the past we only fled."

Angus noticed that the Elves who had scattered on either side of the path to guard the way had moved in closer. More Dwarves had moved to the lead. The pace was slower yet. They were now moving down a steep hillside, half sliding down the path. The forest rose to its full height on both sides. An occasional outcropping of rock blocked the path and the hikers carefully skirted them. Thorny bushes grew on the path's sides, catching at their clothing as they passed. The Dwarves had reached the bottom and were turning to the right to follow a narrow ravine. A thin stream of water trickled through its center, washing over rocks and the grass that lived in the flow of the current.

As Angus reached the bottom with Migalik and Feshka he began to watch the steep hillside rising above them on both sides of the stream. There was barely room to walk between the elevated ground and water in the center of the ravine. The band strung out now single file, and the Elves who had spread out on either side of the path as watchers, also had to move in to join the single line because the sides were even too steep for them to maneuver.

"The path will begin to climb again shortly," Feshka told them.

Just then Angus heard a disturbance from the Dwarves ahead of them... shouting and voices that sounded like cries of pain. Then he heard what sounded like squealing. Suddenly something nearly knocked him off his feet as it rushed past. It was a huge swine with shining tusks. Then he saw gleaming blades of light surrounding them. Feshka was on the ground on his back with Migalik beside him, both struggling to get up again. With one hand, Angus drew the Elf blade Migalik had given him, and with the other he grasped Migalik's outstretched hand and pulled him to his feet.

Another swine came racing down the valley. It went for Feshka, who was now on hands and knees and about to rise. Migalik slashed at it with his glowing blade and struck it. The swine screamed and turned on Migalik. Angus drew back his arm to strike the beast, but VelMud was faster. His blow nearly decapitated it. "Watch out, there's another!" He pulled Angus back by the arm.

At that moment two more came racing down the path. This one tried for VelMud, but he was too fast for the animal. He skewered it and as it fell, he kicked it into the creek. The second animal grabbed Angus just above the knee. VelMud and the swine went down with Angus, who was trying to push it off as he screamed with pain. Angus finally managed to sink his blade through the animal's throat just as VelMud's sword sank threw the back of its neck. The stinking beast fell on top of Angus, pinning him to the ground.

He could hear the shouts of men and Elves in the rear and knew there was also an attack from behind. More swine ran past him and something fell on top of the animal that was holding him down. Whatever it was kept going and the dead pig lying on Angus rolled off and hit the creek with a splash.

Angus scrambled to his feet, sword in one hand and Skyn Dhu in the other, eager for blood. In the light from the swords he could see another swine charging toward them through the group ahead. Many were down and struggling to get to their feet. The swine were doing their best to cause as much harm among the Elves as possible, biting and cutting with their short tusks.

Feshka was on his feet between Angus and the oncoming swine. Angus saw him raise both his hands as though to greet it. Then Angus saw a ball of light, almost the color of fire, form in front of Feshka's hands and dart toward the swine, hitting it. The pig's hair burst into flame and it turned, charging up the hillside, screaming in fear and pain.

Angus looked around for more and saw Migalik behind him, slashing at one of them. Angus raised his sword and in one sweeping motion sliced into the back of the pig's neck. It dropped like a brick, blood everywhere.

"Where's VelMud?" Migalik asked Angus.

"I haven't seen him since I got knocked down."

"Look there!" Migalik pointed upward. Another shadow moved across the sky, circling. "Like a general watching the battle and calling out directions," Migalik muttered.

He reached behind his back, unhooked a long bow, reached back again and drew an arrow from a woven grass sheath. The arrow glowed more brightly than the swords and with the same hue. Migalik fitted the arrow to the string and pointed it to the sky, drawing the string back to his shoulder. As he released the string, the arrow shot skyward.

Angus thought he saw it leaving a trail of light behind it as it darted toward the Shadow.

The image in the sky was apparently closer than it appeared to be. The arrow struck its mark in just a few seconds, and then the air was filled with an eerie wailing sound. Angus watched briefly as the Shadow flew quickly in a westerly direction, away from them. He turned his attention to the remaining swine that were still attacking the travelers and began working his way down the line, helping where he could, blood streaming down his leg.

He had been aware of the pain only when the beast had its teeth in him, and as he fought and slashed at the remaining animals, his thoughts were only of killing. The fight ended with the last of the pigs running off into the forested hillside, leaving many wounded and a few dead among the party. VelMud was found at the end of the line, defending the Humans. Angus's father and friends were uninjured but thoroughly frightened. Angus's leg had begun to throb. The scars on his neck and wrists also started to ache. He sank to the ground, feeling weak and sick. Placing his hand on the ground next to him for support, he was disgusted to find it had landed in a puddle of blood, oozing from a dead swine lying next to him. He wobbled to his feet and then fainted.

Tristan caught his arm as he went down. William grabbed the other one, keeping him off the ground. "Wake up, Angus!" William snapped angrily. "This is no time to faint!" William slapped him briskly across the face. Angus opened his eyes and looked around, groggy.

"Where are we?" he asked, and fainted again.

The remainder of the trip to The City of The Vision was less eventful, although several hours were lost as they gathered everyone together again, tended to those who were wounded and made litters to carry those who couldn't walk. Some of them had been separated, chasing the swine into the woods. Several of the Elves had gone farther ahead looking for more trouble; others stayed behind. They had been expecting Geketzim, not swine. The Dwarves in the lead had suffered the most injuries because they had been taken by surprise. By the time the swine had reached farther down the line, the alarm had been sounded and the group was already prepared.

Angus awoke on a litter bouncing between two Elves with his father walking behind, struggling to keep up with them. His leg was swathed in bandages woven from the grasses growing in the stream. They had climbed out of the valley and were following a path on a mountain ridge.

"Let me get off of this thing," Angus demanded

"Stay right there, son," ordered his father. "Those cuts are fairly deep and you might start bleeding again."

"I'm fine. Let me get up," Angus insisted.

"Rest for now, Angus." The Elf GarMawk who was carrying the back end of the litter spoke up. "You're not so heavy to us and William is right. Those weren't ordinary hogs. Wild hogs avoid us. Its bite may be worse than we expect. Feshka says they were from the Enemy. Stay on the litter."

"Migalik says he wounded the Flying Shadow," reported Silver Leaf, carrying the front end of the litter. "Did you see it, StrathNaver?"

Angus' throat and wrists felt like they were on fire, but the burning was more like an icy sensation, and the combination of the two extremes of temperature seemed to work against each other to intensify the pain. His whole body seemed to be plunged into this icy burning sensation. He had never before experienced such pain as in his chest and shoulder where the Geketz had touched him. His leg was numb from its wound. "Yes I saw it," replied Angus weakly. "Why are the scars from the Geketz hurting me more than the wound in my leg?"

"Hush and rest now, StrathNaver," GarMawk answered him. "You'll need all your strength for the rest of the journey."

"Wounds from the Enemy work together," said Silver Leaf. "Every time he wounds you, all the old wounds work together to cause you harm. We must get you to the City as quickly as possible. Try to sleep if you can."

Easier said than done Angus discovered, to try and sleep while bouncing up on down on the litter. Yet he was thankful it was not Humans who were carrying him. They would be stumbling over the rocks and limbs lying on the path. His wounds seemed to be digging deeper into his body, reaching for his heart and vital organs. As the pain increased, Angus was beginning to grow angry. His thoughts turned to his mother, now dead. The Enemy had slaughtered that sweet and beautiful woman, who was William's wife and Angus's mother. Her crime? The same as that of Lurelei: beauty and light. Then his thoughts turned to Lurelei, Lurenne. His lips remembered the touch of hers and his hand the feel of her tingling presence. His returning fury drove back the pain of the wounds, which were reaching for his life's force, drawing on it.

Angus heard shouts ahead. Was it another attack? What was it this time? Geketzim? Wolves? Who would ever have thought that swine could form an organized attack... the perversion of animals and murder of Humans and Elves? What else would the Enemy invent to offend nature itself? The litter had been set on the ground; Angus forced himself to rise to his feet. His Elf blade was still at his side, but for now he left it in its sheath, since he felt it might affect his night vision. He scanned the darkness, searching for the disturbance. Elves and men were fighting nearby but Angus couldn't see what they were fighting. He saw a flash of fire and knew Feshka was in the fray.

Suddenly Angus felt a shadow moving toward him. He drew his blade and in the flash of its light he saw a creature horrible beyond his belief: distorted yellow eyes streaked with red and legs and arms like a Human or an Elf. But it was neither. Its skin was darkened with scars as if it had been burned. Angus froze, overcome with horror. He could see the delight in the creature's eyes as it lunged toward him with a short but ugly-looking blade.

The blade and sudden movement broke Angus's trance. With one sweep of his arm he struck at the creature. The edge of his Elf blade glanced off the creature's shoulder causing little damage. It stepped back out of the way for a moment to assess the situation. Angus was tottering on his feet, barely able to stand. The creature began to approach again, its blade drawn back, ready to strike. Angus watched as if in a daze as it drew back the blade and made a long downward swing straight for his throat. Suddenly out of the darkness a figure Angus could barely see swept past him in a flying tackle and knocked the creature to the ground. Angus watched as the new menace struggled briefly with the creature, then rose to its feet. It was a Geketz.

Still in a daze, Angus remembered the Elf blade in his hand and drew it back to strike the Geketz. "If you wish to kill me with Elf Steel, Angus," rose a familiar voice, "I will stand here and die at your hand. But if you do, your friend Lurenne, who I was, will no longer be here to protect you."

With a howl, the Geketz dived back into the darkness. Angus could hear it crashing through the trees and fallen leaves. Exhausted and relieved, Angus fell back onto the litter.

In the distance and through the trees Angus saw another flash of fire-colored light and he knew Feshka was still fighting. The sounds of the shouting had lessened and he heard others approaching.

Silver Leaf and GarMawk appeared. "So," panted GarMawk, "one got past us. Well done, StrathNaver! Well done."

"I didn't kill it. A Geketz came out of the woods and killed it for me. It was Lurenne."

GarMawk stepped over Angus's litter to examine the creature. "It has a sword slash on its shoulder, but the gash at its throat is what killed it. It looks like a bite of some sort. You say a Geketz killed it. That makes no sense. The Geketzim are servants of the Enemy. Why would it defend you?"

"What is this thing that was killed?" asked Angus, cringing as his wounds again started to throb. "How can pigs be organized to attack Humans and Elves? What kind of an enemy is this that we go to fight?"

"He is an evil Enemy. He is one who fights us for no other cause than his own hatred. Now tell me of the Geketz. Why would it defend you? Are you a servant of the Enemy?"

Angus began to realize he had placed himself in potential danger. "No," he murmured. "It was Lurenne. When she was attacked, the Geketz was driven away before it finished. She's only partly changed. I didn't know she had come with us."

"She is the one Migalik calls Lurelei," Silver Leaf said. "She is not an enemy, but a Geketz nevertheless. Beware of her but do not kill her," he turned to GarMawk.

"Rest, StrathNaver," Silver Leaf placed a hand on Angus's forehead. "All will be explained when we get to the City. For now we must focus on getting there. Talking can wait."

With great relief, Angus closed his eyes. "If there's more trouble, please wake me. This creature would have had me if I hadn't been awakened by the shouting and fighting."

Although he fell asleep at once, the pain of his scars and wounds affected his dreams. His last thought before drifting off was, "I'll have to remember to ask Feshka about those fire balls."

After the attack by the wild pigs, William, Tristan, Ingram and Scobie had chosen to stick together with the Elves near the front of the line. William knew Angus was in good hands farther back. "These Elves are some warriors," Ingram declared grimly. "Did you see that one over there? He killed four of those things faster than I could see his knife moving."

"Yes, I saw it," William nodded.

"Did you see that one they call Feshka?" Scobie exclaimed. "He has some kind of trick of throwing balls of fire at them. Did you see how they ran off into the woods squealing when the fireballs hit them?"

Tristan was even more silent than usual. He was becoming aware that there was a lot more to be learned from the Elves than he had ever thought possible. They were far more than the soft-spoken forest dwellers that he'd first taken them to be. It had never occurred to him that they even existed; he'd assumed they were simply the creatures of childhood stories. Now he was discovering they had a culture all their own. They had a history, enemies, wives and children they loved and tried to educate. What intrigued Tristan even more was the Magic the Elf girls had over him.

Ingram was having thoughts about the Elf Culture too, but he wasn't as quiet about it. "I hope they never turn on us as enemies," he declared to William.

"I don't think they will, Ingram, unless we make ourselves their enemies. Why do you fear them so much?"

"They could take us in a war as quickly and easily as we'd take a bunch of rabbits."

"Yes they could," agreed William. "Aren't you glad they hate warring?"

"They were going pretty eagerly into it just now," Ingram observed. "What makes you think they wouldn't turn on us the same way?"

"Ingram," William sighed, "my wife was descended from Elf blood and so was yours. Can you see someone like your wife or mine deciding to hate an entire race and declare war on them for no other reason?"

"My wife didn't hate anything," said Ingram. "She'd no sooner hate another than hate her own children."

"Mine too. Did you hear what Feshka said of the enemy? They don't even want to kill him. Why do you do distrust them?"

"I don't know," admitted Ingram. "It just doesn't feel right."

If Scobie and Ingram had been impressed with the skill of the Elf swordsmen before, they were now in reverence. "Don't think so much of it," Migalik smiled at the Humans. "Before you've been in the City a month, you'll be just as good as they are."

Not likely, thought Scobie.

The next few hours were spent in quiet and determined hiking. Angus was near delirium while the Elves and Dwarves kept a silent moving vigil. His was not the only litter among them. There had been several injuries. Feshka was surprised at all the resistance they found. His trip to the valley of the Naver had been quiet. So much trouble on the way home concerned him. He urged the others to keep careful watch on the darkness. If there had been so many attacks there were sure to be more before they reached the City. "There it is!" Feshka pointed.

"There what is?" asked William.

"The City of The Vision."

"All I see is a large hill with a lot trees growing on it," grumbled William. "It's just a forest."

"But what a forest!" Migalik declared. "How many Elves would you say live in the same community as I do, in the Valley of the Naver?"

"Not many," answered William. "I only saw a few homes."

"We like to unobtrusive," chuckled Migalik. "There are over fifteen thousand Elves living in the Naver Valley."

William wasn't sure how many fifteen thousand was, but he knew it was far more than the number of Humans living in the same valley. "If there are so many of you, why don't we ever see you?" asked William.

"For the same reason you fail to see The City of The Vision. Give me your hand and look again."

William placed his hand in Migalik's and turned his eyes toward the hill. He was astonished to see a doorway under every tree and rise. Some led underground and others led into the trees. Still others led to stairways and ladders that led to homes above, in the limbs. A multitude of creatures was looking back at them and many were waving. They had arrived.

Chapter Seven: The Gate Keeper

Angus awoke in a dimly lighted room. He had no idea where he was, but the bed was comfortable and his dreams before waking were far better than those he'd been having. He noticed a low table to his left with a small lamp resting on it. Beside the table was a chair of carved sticks covered with woven grasses of a light brown color. The ceiling of the room was also covered with woven grasses. *These Elves certainly do like their weaves*, he thought. *If there were a spark from that lamp, this place would go up like a wheat field in fall!*

He could hear voices nearby and strained to hear what they were saying. He thought he recognized Migalik's voice, and perhaps VelMud's. Then he realized he was thirsty and hungry. As he listened, he continued to look around the room. It was sparsely furnished and the walls, like the ceiling, were covered with woven grass. The wall weaves formed interesting patterns and designs. To his right was an open doorway where he could see light shining from another room. Then he realized there was also a chair on his right, beside the door, and in the chair was an Elf maiden, fast asleep.

Her hair was the first thing he noticed about her. It was long enough that as she sat in the chair with her head resting on its back, it touched the floor. He gazed at it with amazement. Then he allowed his eyes to wander to her face. She had delicate features that seemed to almost be interrupted by a broad mouth. He began to study her lips, remembering Lurenne's lips as she had spoken to him that day by the river's edge. Possibly to dissipate his guilt about failing to save her that day, Angus pretended the girl in the chair was Lurelei. Indeed, he thought, she did resemble Lurelei very much.

He studied her hands, folded in her lap. She had long slender deli-cately formed fingers. As she breathed gently in her sleep, he watched the rise and fall of her breasts and wondered if they would feel like Lurenne if he held her close to him. As again he studied her face, the Elf girl's eyes fluttered opened and met his in surprise. The wideness of her eyes startled him, and then he remembered she was an Elf. Of course, all Elves had larger than human eyes. Their brilliant blueness seemed to see right through him. He wondered if he would be able to reply if this apparition of graceful beauty happened to speak to him.

Then the worst possible thing happened. She actually did speak to him. She said, "I've been waiting for you to wake up and I fell asleep myself. How silly of me. How are you feeling?"

Angus began to smile at himself. *Now she has spoken what should I do?* He started by clearing his throat to see if he had any voice available with which to reply. The action proved to him that he did have some voice. He wanted to cover up his head, but instead he said, "I'm just getting awake too. I think I'm OK. How are you?"

"I mean, uh, you were injured yesterday. How do your wounds feel? Are you in any pain?"

"Oh," said Angus. "I seem to feel much better. I feel like I could get up if I wanted to. Should I try?" He was having a mixture of confusion now. He was remembering his determination to save and recover Lure-lei and at the same time he was hoping that this lovely creature would come closer and help him get out of bed, and she did.

"I am called Marnel," she said. "It means in our tongue 'Healer.' I did my best with your leg. How does it feel?"

"I have no pain at all," he said, then remembered, "except in my throat and wrists. They still burn a little."

"We've done what we could for those wounds, but there is nothing in our lore which teaches us the cure. The others were easier. If you are feeling better, then you don't need more of my help. When you're ready, come to the outer room," and she pointed toward the doorway." They're waiting for you." With that she left. Angus felt as though the lights had gone out when she was gone. Then his angry determination began to return concerning Lurelei. This was the place. This was The City of The Vision, where he hoped to find the Gate Keeper.

VelMud was there, with Migalik and two other Elves whom he didn't know. Feshka was absent. The Elves seated Angus at a small table and placed food and drink before him. "Eat," invited an Elf, seating him-self beside Angus. "While you do that we will talk. I am called Rohen-drel and this," he gestured toward the other Elf Angus didn't know, "is

Be'erMagrel. We are to conduct you to a place representing the Adytum of YeePhraWaine where you will be instructed about your further journeys. You have yet before you a rough and rugged road to travel, upon which legend tells us one life has been lost, and you may lose yours. Feshka tells us you seek the Gate Keeper. Is this true?"

"It is," answered Angus.

"Is this an act of your own free will and accord?" asked Be'erMagrel.

"Well," Angus thought for a moment, "I'd rather that Lurenne had never been injured but seeing that she was, her cure is something I must seek. I suppose I seek it of my own free will and accord, but I'd really much rather she hadn't been injured at all."

"Let me repeat the question," Be'erMagrel said. "A simple 'yes' or 'no' will suffice. Is this an act of your own free will and accord?"

"Yes." As he heard his own direct response, Angus suddenly felt lighter as if a burden had been lifted from his heart.

Be'erMagrel went on, this time addressing Migalik. "Is he worthy of this?"

"He is," answered Migalik. "He risked his life to save an Elf. See for yourself the scars at his throat and wrists."

"What scars are these?" asked Rohendrel as he removed the scarf- like wrapping around Angus' neck. When he had finished, both Be'erMagrel and Rohendrel stared in astonishment. "We didn't expect to see these on a Human," declared Rohendrel.

"He's Elfkin by his mother," Migalik said.

"If he's Elfkin it's not by much," retorted Rohendrel.

"He's Elfkin enough to bear the scars," asserted Migalik. "He is the one you seek. I have watched over him since his birth, waiting for this moment."

"What do you mean by 'I'm the one?'" asked Angus, his eyes darting first to Migalik and then to the other two, returning to gaze with great bewilderment at Migalik. "'The one' for what?"

"You'll find out soon enough. Finish your food and we'll be off," was all Migalik would say.

"Where are my father and the others?" asked Angus.

"They're near us. There's no need for concern about them right now. There's work to be done." He turned to Be'erMagrel. "Is everything ready?"

"It is," answered Be'erMagrel.

"Then give him the wine," instructed Rohendrel.

With that they all stood except for Angus, who remained seated, eating. Migalik went over to a corner of the room to a covered tray. He picked it up with both hands and carried it to the table where he placed it in front of Angus. "Do you still seek the Gate Keeper?" he asked.

"Yes," said Angus. "Why do you keep asking me that?"

"Because," said Migalik, "this road once taken cannot be turned from. As Rohendrel has told you, you have yet before you a rugged journey. Under this cloth is a mug of wine. Our tradition teaches us that this wine must be drunk alone. We will now depart from this place, leaving you behind. When you have eaten enough, lift the cloth and drink the wine. When you have done this, approach that door." He indicated a low oaken door Angus had not yet seen. "Make an alarm at that door by making seven distinct knocks. Knock four times, pause, then knock three more times. Do you understand?"

"This is all very mysterious." Angus felt like he'd been left out of whatever it was that was going on, and yet apparently he was the one who was responsible for all of it. "Is the Gate Keeper behind that door?"

"Perhaps you will find him there," answered VelMud.

"Why all the mystery?"

"This is something you must learn yourself. Now repeat the instructions," directed Migalik.

Angus finished eating and lifted the cloth off of the mug of wine. The mug was carved from a hard wood and was so heavy, he needed both hands to lift it to his lips. After he drank most of it, he went to the door and knocked as instructed.

 familiar flourish

Angus found himself standing alone in an open field. The meadow grass was knee high and so thick, when the breezes crossed it, it rose and fell in waves, *like ground swells on the sea*, thought Angus. Mixed between the blades of grass were tiny magenta wildflowers that appeared to Angus as tiny bubbles of foam cresting each swell. He had seen the sea once when he was young, on a journey to a Clan Gathering near Wicke, and this was much like it.

Behind him he could imagine the path he was leaving as he waded through the tall grass, weaving on and on, out of sight over the low rolling hills, *to where*, wondered Angus. *Where have I been?*

"You knocked," came the voice. "Now continue."

Angus kept walking, fear of the voice overwhelming his ability to appreciate the serene beauty of the place. One foot. Next foot. Next foot. Sweat. *Why do I sweat when I hear it?*

"It is because of your self-doubt," answered the voice. "And because you fear change."

"Do you hear everything I think?" snapped Angus out loud.

"Only when I'm listening. Keep walking."

The voice was resonant. It sounded threatening to him, but not evil. His fear of the voice was fear of the unknown; the unknown vacant blackness of the area under a small boy's bed at night; the unknown entity that lives in the closet and only comes out when the lights are off. It was the fear of that which is hidden in a deep forest where hunters go and some don't return... and afterward the other hunters won't discuss it.

Angus felt like he had been walking forever, although he knew it was only a day, or was it two, or three? He couldn't seem to remember exactly when he'd started, or from where it was he'd started. This uncertainty added to the deep primal fear of the voice, fear of the superstitious, that Hell would rise and snatch him unexpectedly because of uttering some evil swear word.

The land sloped slightly uphill now, over another low rise in the ground. *Why is this happening to me?* wondered Angus.

"You chose the burden," answered the voice. "Soon you will experience the result of choosing, and feel the weight of your choice."

Angus felt a prod from behind. Startled, he nearly leaped forward. Until now he'd thought he was alone except for the voice that was answering his questions. He whirled around to see who or what was behind him: nothing.

"Keep moving," instructed the voice. "We have waited long enough for you. The twenty-four are gathered and the time of waiting is ended."

Angus felt the prod again and saw a long staff extend out of a space about six feet behind him. It looked like a shepherd's staff, with a crook at the end.

Instead of moving on, he stood staring at the space. The sun was bright and he could see the ocean of grass and flowers, but nothing else. The staff had vanished.

But what was that? Angus could see an area that seemed to be slightly out of focus, a shimmering in the air that distorted the background. Angus began to sweat again, even though both the sun and air were relatively cool.

The shimmering had vanished. *Where did it go?* He studied the spot and could see nothing. It was then that he felt the staff around his neck, pulling him forward.

"Where are we going?" Angus almost whimpered.

The staff pressed on the throat scars left by the Geketz. Its pressure seemed like the tips of many knives cutting into his flesh. His wrists throbbed as if in sympathy.

He thought he could see something in the air ahead of him, but when he tried to focus on it, it would disappear. He was walking forward stiffly. He could hear the swishing of the grass as his legs brushed through it, and the crunching under his feet as he broke the stems where he stepped.

His fear was approaching hysteria. His rational mind could not accept even his presence in the field, much less being dragged forward to some unknown destination by a shepherd's staff which seemed to act by its own volition, and talk to him in answer to his very thoughts. *This is some trick,* he thought, his fear changing to irritation, then anger. *If I can work up enough anger, maybe I can control the fear.* He leaned back against the staff around his neck, enduring the pain with determination and growing rage. Gradually he added more pressure, a little at a time.

"You will only make your neck sore by doing that," said the voice. "If you continue to resist, I will carry you with my staff. That will make your neck even more sore."

"Who are you?" Angus leaned backward into the staff with all his strength.

Angus felt himself hoisted into the air by the neck. His head swam with the pain. "Please!" he gasped. In the next instant he was dropped to the ground. He fell to his knees.

"You will be on your knees soon enough, profane one," said the voice. "Now rise and walk without my help, or I will certainly help you."

The implied threat was enough to convince him. Angus rose and began walking. *"Who are you?"* He asked again.

"I will give no name to the profane," answered the voice.

"Then just tell me where we're going," Angus demanded.

"We are going to the Adytum," was the answer.

Angus was overcome by fear. The entity saw what was happening to him and snapped, "Stop a moment. This fear you are experiencing is distasteful to me and disruptive of our intent. You must conquer it before we enter the place of the Adytum."

"Why are you forcing me?" Angus demanded now.

"I am your Goad," answered the voice. "We go where you have chosen. Now continue walking."

Angus felt the prod behind him again. He was nearly at the top of the hill when he saw something rising from the other side. The creature appeared to be a man, but he was carrying his head under one arm. Angus stopped.

"Why are you stopping?" asked the voice impatiently. "Continue walking," it directed without waiting for a reply.

"Do you see that thing?" asked Angus.

"Of course I see it," answered the voice. "Ignore it and keep going."

The figure walked toward Angus haltingly. The eyes in the head watched where it put its feet. Occasionally the figure would lift the head high over his shoulders and turn it, as though to look around. The eyes were yellow and its face was streaked with blood and dirt. When it saw Angus, the mouth began grinning and its eyes hardened.

Angus heard a sound like a distant clap of thunder and the mouth stopped grinning. The man carrying his head, stepped aside and watched them crest the hill. At the bottom of the slope, the ground leveled off for a few hundred yards and stopped at what appeared to be a high cliff rising above the plain. Many more figures were scattered over the short plain, all of them as disfigured and grotesque as the first one.

"Let the area be clear," instructed the voice.

Angus could see figures on horseback riding out of a cave at the bottom of the cliff. He had heard of horses but he had never before seen one. He watched in amazement as they trotted toward him. Some of the riders were carrying swords and others had other ancient weapons whose names Angus didn't know. With a shock, Angus realized he could see through the horsemen, as if they were transparent. They seemed to have been created from different colored lights.

The disfigured people and creatures scattered before the horsemen, running off in every direction. With another shock, Angus realized when they reached a certain distance from the bottom of the cliff; they vanished as if through a door. Those who resisted were attacked directly by the horsemen. When a sword or other weapon of the horsemen touched them they would vanish on the spot.

This is too weird to be true, thought Angus. *I must be dreaming!*

"Dreaming is what many among the profane believe when visiting this place," answered the voice. "But you may find it is much more real than what you think of as waking."

The horsemen now approached Angus; he started to run. He had already seen what had happened to the others when touched by those weapons! Again, the shepherd's staff stopped him. The horsemen surrounded him. One who seemed to be a leader and who appeared to consist of pure white light, dismounted and approached Angus.

"Who comes here?" he demanded.

"This one calls himself StrathNaver," answered the voice. "He seeks the enlightenment of The Brith Gar-Nunsum and fellowship with us."

Does he also wish to enter the Adytum? asked the Horseman.

"He does indeed," said the voice, "for he seeks the Gate Keeper."

Angus watched the horseman's expression change at the voice's answer, causing him to remember his immediate past. That's right, he thought. *This is where the Gate Keeper is. He's in this, uh...*

"Has he a token?" asked the horseman.

"I presume he does," answered the voice, "since he knew enough to sip the bitter wine, find the door and then to knock. Let us see if he has a token."

Angus began searching for pockets, thinking he needed a coin or some other such symbol, but found his clothes had none. His pants and shirt were made of soft white wool, and the pants were ragged just below the knees. "These aren't my clothes!" he muttered.

"This is the only manner in which the profane may approach these gates and survive," the voice announced to him.

Again, Angus stared down at his unfamiliar clothing. Then he noticed a symbol over his left breast, a rune of some sort. He didn't recognize it. It was blood red.

The horseman drew a large heavy sword from a scabbard at his side and slowly raised it until it pointed at Angus. He advanced until the tip of the sword touched the center of Angus's chest. Angus looked down at the tip of the sword, expecting to watch it sink into his flesh, expecting to feel the pain and then die. His knees were trembling and he struggled to breathe between frightened gasps.

The sword did not penetrate the flesh, but stopped on contact. Angus saw the flesh around the tip of the sword turn pale, then almost a silver color.

The horseman tensed his arm as though to plunge the sword through Angus's breast, shouting, "He doesn't yet have the token. What shall we do with him?"

"Kill him!" They all shouted together, lunging forward.

"Wait," commanded the one with the drawn sword. They all stopped, and even slightly withdrew.

"Look at his throat," instructed the Horseman. "The scarring is the final token."

"If you seek the Gate Keeper, before you proceed you must take a vow to keep all that you learn within our gates a secret, known only to you and to the initiated."

"I swear it," vowed Angus.

Angus now found himself in a room of stone with no doors or windows. The stone was cold on his bare feet, but he was still perspiring from his experience on the plain. Where was the plain now? He could see only stone walls around him. "Where am I?" he asked in a low voice.

"I will not answer again until you ask the right questions," said the voice. "Now you must calm yourself. This is a good place for calmness. There is no one here but you."

"But you're here too," Angus pointed out.

"That's a possibility. Do your eyes confirm it?" asked the voice.

"My eyes confirm nothing but this small room of stone. It's cold in here as well. How did I get in here? There is no door. The ceiling is close and there's no opening!"

"Think about it, StrathNaver," answered the voice, "and when you have finished thinking about it, then ask me something more interesting."

"I want out of here," said Angus quietly.

"Then leave."

"How can I?"

"When you have figured that out, you will have more to learn. So begin. Time is short."

Angus sat down on the cold stone floor, folded his legs together and tried to analyze the situation at hand. *Maybe I really did drown in the Strath Naver and this is some sort of Hell where people go when they die.* He reviewed all that had happened to him since his struggle in the river. It seemed he had spent most of the time either in a bed or on a litter. He had dined with Elves and talked of Geketzim and an Enemy that seemed irrational beyond belief. Only a few days ago life was normal. His mother was alive and his friend Tristan was in love with their cousin Agnes.

Lurenne was no more than a dream. Oh yes, Lurenne. He now remembered meeting her and why he was seeking the Gate Keeper.

"Now you're getting somewhere, StrathNaver," said the voice. "Have you figured out where you are yet?"

"I'm dreaming," guessed Angus.

"Think further. What is a dream?"

"It's like when I'm asleep and my mind is wandering. A dream is a vision that comes to me in my sleep."

"Is it true that you really don't know what a dream is?" asked the voice incredulously.

"That's all it is. Migalik is the Dream Maker where I live. He makes the dreams and visions I see there."

"That's very interesting," said the voice in a tone that told Angus it was bored and he was wrong.

"So if that's not what a dream is, suppose you tell me," suggested Angus.

"No. You tell *me*, StrathNaver. When you are dreaming, do you have to follow the directions of the Dream Maker, or do you make your own decisions in the dream?"

"I make my own decisions, of course. They're my dreams, after all,"

Angus retorted.

"I say that you create the dream," said the voice. "Prove me wrong."

"There's nothing to prove. It's obvious that we don't choose our dreams. Why would anyone choose to have bad dreams? Like this one, for example."

"The choice of the dream may not always be yours, but what happens in the dream is yours to choose. Is that not true?" continued the voice.

"Not always. I didn't choose over and over again to dream of being attacked by that creature you call the Geketz."

"It was on your mind. I say that you *did* choose to dream of it. You chose to relive the horror to understand it better."

Angus didn't answer for a few minutes. He needed to think about that. Then he offered, "Then you're saying that I chose to dream of Lurenne too?"

"Of course you did. You met Migalik's daughters and saw their beauty. You wanted an Elf wife. So while you slept you thought about it. Her name, by the way, is no longer Lurenne, but Lurelei. You controlled the dreams in every aspect. She too wanted a Human mate, so in your dreams you met. You were in the same mind set, the same place, so to speak, spiritually. She also controlled her end of the dreams. Don't you understand?"

"Are you saying that dreaming is a real place?"

"Of course it is. Are you not now in a dream? You said you were," the voice reminded him. "Is this not a real place?"

"It seems real," consented Angus, "I may not be dreaming. I don't remember falling asleep."

"Do you think you have to be asleep to be in the place of dreams?"

"Of course I do!" Angus exclaimed. "How can one dream the dreams of sleep unless one is asleep?"

"Could it be possible that you only know how to find your way there when you are asleep? If it's true that the place of dreams is a real place, then there must be a way to enter it without falling asleep. Does that make sense to you, StrathNaver?"

"Well, if it's a real place then certainly, but I'm not so sure that it is."

"Is this a real place?" asked the voice.

"It seems to be."

"Are you dreaming?"

Angus thought about it for a moment. "It feels like a dream to me, but I can't seem to make myself wake up."

"And you don't like the dream?" asked the voice.

"No. I don't like the dream."

"Then change it," suggested the voice.

"How can I change it?" asked Angus. "It is what it is!"

"Was Lurelei at the picnic before you thought of her and searched for her?"

"Certainly she was. How could I have found her otherwise? How do you know about that dream?"

"The Dream Maker told me," said the voice. "But that doesn't answer the question very well. How could she have entered your dream without your choosing it? Did you see her first or did she appear only after you sought her?"

"She appeared after I looked for her," mused Angus.

"You changed the dream. How did you do it?"

"I don't know."

"You changed it by wanting it and believing in it," prompted the voice. "You can change this dream in the same way. Let me see you do it."

"But I don't know how," protested Angus.

"What would you most like to see in this room of stone, StrathNaver?"

"I'd like to see a door."

"Which wall?"

"The one in front of me." Angus pointed to the wall opposite.

"What do you see there now?"

"Stone."

"Change the vision. Visualize a door. Want the door. Believe in the door. Do you see a door yet?"

Angus obeyed the instructions, but as he looked, he still saw only stone.

"What *is* cannot be changed to what it *ought to be* by wishing it so," declared Angus.

"Your instruction was not to wish it so, StrathNaver. What was your instruction? Repeat it to me."

"You said to visualize a door. Do you mean to try to see a door on the wall in my mind's eye?"

"Yes," said the voice. "Try that."

As Angus carefully focused his imagination, he watched a door begin to form in the rock. It was just a plain rectangle.

"Not much detail there," prompted the voice. "What kind of door are you making?"

Angus began to focus more carefully. He thought he'd like a wooden door so he tried imagining boards. A wooden door now appeared, of oak, it seemed. It had two cross beams holding upright boards together.

Angus could see two hinges on the right side of the door.

"That's very good," praised the voice. Many have said a Human could not do this. You have forgotten one important detail."

"What's that"?" asked Angus.

"A handle to use to pull it open. If you wish to open the door, since you've made it to open inward, you will need a door handle."

Angus continued in his creative visualization and added a handle by which he pulled the door open. On the other side of the door stood Feshka.

Angus was surprised to find himself at the top of the cliff he had approached before. He could see the path he had made though the tall grass. He was standing too close to the edge; he stepped back. Feshka turned to face him. Marnel was also with him.

"Have you discovered the Gate Keeper yet?" Feshka asked him.

Angus liked Feshka. He knew it was the half Elf who had retrieved his life force after the attack by the Geketz, and he was grateful to him. But Angus was getting frustrated with the strange surroundings and the stranger experiences. He tried to make his voice sound as respectful toward Feshka as he felt, but the annoyance was clear.

"I have not found the Gate Keeper," he sighed. I don't understand why I have been put through this. Can you please explain?"

Feshka shook his head. "As you were told before you entered the Adytum, so I must tell you again. This wine must be drunk alone. Some truths cannot be articulated. You yourself must do this learning, but we will help you as much as we can. You may leave the Adytum after you have discovered the Gate Keeper. Until then you must stay."

"Where is this Gate Keeper?" Angus insisted. "I must find him because he holds the secret of Lurelei's cure. While we're wasting time here, she continues to suffer. Why can't you just take me to him?"

"We hope you will be able to understand in time." Feshka's tone was kind but firm. "For now, your lessons continue."

Angus looked out over the fields below him, his eyes automatically searching again for the path he'd left in the tall grass. There it was; he could see it weaving across the swells of the ground, lying in rows before him. At the bottom of the cliff he could see the mutilated figures wandering aimlessly. "Who are the creatures below?" he asked. He turned his attention back to Feshka, but he was gone. Marnel was still visible but she was moving away from him.

"Marnel!" he called out to her, but she didn't turn to answer. Then she too was gone. He started to run after her. He didn't want to be left alone in this place.

As he ran, the ground seemed to be sloping at an angle; he found himself heading down a gentle grade with trees on either side of the path. "Marnel! Marnel!" he called out again, running faster than before. But he couldn't catch up to her. Soon she was lost from sight.

Now the forest on either side of the path was growing thick. Gradually it curved around to the right until he was running in the opposite direction. The ground was beginning to feel softer under his feet and he slowed down, afraid of slipping. He began to see large boulders beside the path and among the trees, but he kept going, determined to catch up with Marnel. Then the path stopped suddenly, at the face of a cliff. He looked up and saw only sheer rock. On either side of the path was forest, but the ground seemed to slope downward to the left, beside the cliff. Since he had already traveled upward, he decided to follow the downward slope.

As he approached the cliff's face he noticed a thin path leading in the direction he had chosen, so he followed it. The path became steeper, making it more difficult to proceed. He could hear running water nearby and soon discovered a stream at the bottom of the path. It seemed to run into a hole at the cliff's bottom. Here the path entered the cave beside it. Once inside, Angus allowed his eyes to adjust to the darkness.

He wondered what had happened to the voice, glad he wasn't hearing it anymore.

"Do you think you can learn without the Goad to instruct you? Angus jumped. The voice was speaking to him! "Do not think you are alone, StrathNaver. Many watch you today."

"No one's here but me," Angus spoke aloud.

"How would you know that?" asked the voice. "Your eyes are closed so you can get used to the darkness. Open your eyes and tell me what you see."

Angus opened his eyes. "I can see only darkness ahead and the cave walls all around me."

"I understand only that you still believe your eyes are messengers instead of servants. Tell me what I mean by that, StrathNaver."

"You're crazy!" exclaimed Angus. "My eyes tell me what's around me!"

"Your eyes confirm what you have told them to see," said the voice. "It is always so."

Angus sat down on the ground. "Are we going to have another conversation here in the cave?" he grumbled.

"Oh," said the voice, "so you have made this a cave. And it seems that now you will stop creating, hoping I will do the rest of your chore. I think not. Continue, StrathNaver. Where were you going?"

"I am going to sit right here until someone explains to me exactly what's going on."

"You need an explanation, do you? All right, here's one. You are learning. This is a puzzle you must solve, and in the solution you will learn lessons you need to learn. You may sit until I am rested. Then I will lead you as before, if you are still reluctant."

Angus was startled to see the staff that had prodded him through the tall grass earlier, standing before him, resting with one end on the ground. He scrambled to his feet. "All right, all right," he grumbled. "Which way?"

"You have chosen already. Follow your choice."

Angus proceeded into the darkness of the cave. As his eyes adjusted, he could see the ground ahead of him well enough to step over rocks, roots and other objects that might trip him. Gradually he became aware that there was some form of natural light in the cave and that he no longer needed the light from outside. He turned to look behind him and saw that the opening of the cave was no longer visible. Then suddenly he discovered he had reached the end of the dark interior. The stream, still running beside the path, entered yet a smaller hole and plunged straight down into the ground. Directly in front of him was another door.

Angus again sat down on the ground, this time in utter frustration. "Why have you led me into this hole in the ground only to stop me at another door?" he asked the voice.

"You sound angry. You are frustrated that you have come to yet another door blocking your path. But have you tried to open it? No. You simply sit on the ground with your head in your hands wallowing in self-pity. You who allowed an Elf to fall prey to a Geketz! Have Human males no more substance than that? Open the door, you poor pitiful excuse for a life form! Have you never opened a door before?"

Angus was on his feet in an instant, angrily searching the darkness for someone to punish for these insults. His face was a mask of rage, but through this passion was a flash of light. Of course he had opened a door before, only a few minutes ago. He had not only opened it; he had also created that door he had opened. He tried to calm himself so he could visualize the door opening.

"What are you doing now, Human? You built up this fine rage and now you try to defeat it by calming yourself. So, go ahead and calm yourself and the lesson will take longer. Don't you know we could do your chore as easily as waking in the morning, except that we lack your passion? It was beautiful while it lasted. You were lighting this place with the red glowing fires of your anger. Now look at you!"

"So you insulted me to anger me?"

"Of course!" responded the voice. "You are here to learn to focus and direct your passions--and some fine passions you possess! Try to open the door."

Angus faced the door. In his mind's eye he formed a vision and tried to bring into focus every detail of the door. In that image he created a door handle. Then he opened his eyes.

"There's no door handle," he said softly.

"Of course not, you poor fool! What did you expect?"

"You're trying to make me angry again," shouted Angus, "and you're succeeding!

"That's wonderful," encouraged the voice. "Focus the passion behind your anger, on that door, and see if you can push it open."

Angus stepped up to the door and kicked hard. He pushed against it with his hands, then with his shoulder. "It doesn't move," he sputtered.

"Do what I said," directed the voice. "Imagine that your anger is a huge and heavy battering ram. Put all of the anger you feel against the Geketz that destroyed your friend Lurelei, into that ram. Now try making the ram."

Angus again closed his eyes and began visualizing a heavy log ten feet long and two feet thick, suspended in front of him and pointed at the door. He summoned up his rage and frustration and imagined the door was the very Geketz he had grappled with. He allowed the pictures from his memory to replay themselves. As they did, he watched in horror as the Geketz tried to place its mouth over Lurelei's. He watched its hands burning Lurelei's skin, then his own skin. The wounds at his throat and wrist began to burn and the pain moved slowly down through his shoulder into his chest. With the growing agony in his chest and throat, his rage grew into a whirling turmoil of anger. In his mind's eye, he hurled the heavy anger, which was now the ram, at the door.

CRAAASH!

Angus opened his eyes.

He found himself inside a large room lighted by Elf fire. Inside the room with him were many Elves of all ages. He looked around the room in astonishment. Behind him he could see the remnants of a heavy wooden door lying shattered on the floor. He recognized Migalik and Feshka arguing with VelMud and several others whom he didn't know.

"It's dangerous to teach a Human these secrets," an old Elf was arguing. "He may well later turn these things against us."

"He is our own kind through his mother. He'll never turn on us," said Migalik.

"But he could teach others who are not so fond of us," the old one argued.

"He doesn't have the tools to teach others. He's barely learning the secrets himself," Feshka declared.

"Did you see how he shattered the door?" another interjected. "We were all holding it shut. His passions are uncontrollable! We must stop him here and now!"

"But it was because of his passions that we chose him to do this," argued Feshka. "We have waited for many years for a Human with the signs. He is the only one we've found!"

Angus glanced around the room. The Elves were seated in raised rows of seats similar to bleachers. Concern was on every face as they followed the conversation. In the far end of the room were about two dozen older Elves wearing white clothes that seemed to have a glow of their own. This group was conferring among themselves. Finally one of them rose to speak and the room fell silent, listening.

"We have considered these questions many times. We have reviewed our knowledge of the issues at hand many times. I remind you that we have learned after much struggling and over many generations that the Enemy is somehow affected by the use of our life force directed at it. We do not understand why this is so, but we know it to be a fact.

"In the prophecies given us, it has been foretold that a Human with the same markings as this one, would find the answer and rescue us once and for all from the hands of our Ancient Foe. We have been told that the life force must be driven by a passion stronger than that of Elves. It has been given to us that we must instruct him in the knowledge we possess, and teach him to use it so he may direct his passions. If the secret of his success lies in his passions, then so be it. The experiment shall continue."

"I summon The Goad, The Light, and the Ancient Knowledge. We, the Elders of this place, call upon you now to Obligate this Human. Then proceed with the ceremonies." VelMud stepped behind Angus and placed a cloth hood over his head. His hands were tied loosely behind his back. During these proceedings, Angus recognized the voice speaking in his ear. It was VelMud. Angus almost turned to face him in surprise when he realized it.

"Be still now, StrathNaver," VelMud's instructed him. "There is much to be done. Be silent unless ordered to speak. Fear no evil or disrespect and follow your conductors."

Someone took hold of each of his arms and guided him on a long walk through a series of turns, with stops along the way. Then he was ordered to kneel. Another voice now addressed him: "You were received into the Adytum upon the sharp point of a sharp sword placed against your breast. This was to teach you that as this is an instrument of death to your flesh, so should you ever remember it, should you ever presume to disclose our secrets to the uninitiated. If it is ever discovered that you have done this, you will immediately be put to death lest you betray us a second time. Do you understand this, StrathNaver?"

"Yes, I do," answered Angus, feeling the cold point of the sword again touching his breast.

"Let your flesh always remember this injunction, StrathNaver. Elf folk love not the shedding of blood, but we understand its necessity. Lead us not to shed yours."

"I won't tell anybody," promised Angus quickly.

"If you are still willing to proceed, repeat after me." The vow was long and detailed. Angus's knees began to ache before it was over. His back was beginning to get stiff as the ceremony droned on. Even his arms and shoulders started to hurt before the Elf stopped speaking. Such were the vows intended to frighten him severely and cause him to renew them instantly in his heart, for fear of the penalties of betrayal.

Finally the Elf said, "My Brother, I welcome you to the Fellowship of the Brith Gar-Nunsum. Brother Goad, release him from his bondage as he is now morally bound to us by the strong chord of a just and rightful obligation."

Angus then heard the voice of VelMud speaking to him again, softly: "There's a chair behind you. You're welcome to sit in it if you think it would be more comfortable." Angus rose, and as he did so, the cloth hood was removed from him, allowing him to see the room again.

Before him was a low table with a plant in a pot in the center of it. Angus's eyes were drawn to it, while the Elves moved to form a loose circle around him, to watch.

"What have you learned this day, StrathNaver?" asked VelMud.

Angus sat silently for a moment before speaking. "This has all happened so fast. I'm going to need some time to think about it."

"We normally do this over a period of several months," said Feshka. "This time we felt it was necessary to push you faster. Our need is pressing and time waits for no one. In that interest, I will tell you what you have learned. You have learned and are learning that the separation between waking and dreaming is not as great as you thought. This lesson will become more apparent as the ceremony continues.

"You have learned that you are able to direct your passions, your anger. You will continue this lesson in a moment. You have further learned that once directed, your passions can perform certain tasks for you. This lesson shall also continue. As I explain these things, do you see and understand that my words are true?"

"Of course," answered Angus.

"Do you see the plant before you?"

"Yes, I see it."

"This is a young Elm sapling. Can you see the blight on its bark from where you are sitting?"

Angus examined the plant. He could see a discoloration on its bark, a grayer area in one section. "Yes," said Angus. "I can see the color difference on one side. Is that what you're talking about?"

"Yes," answered Feshka. "Do you know that today you will heal this plant?"

"Healing is not something Humans can do, like the Elves do. We lack your powers," responded Angus.

"That's true," Feshka conceded, "but you are Elfkin. You are like us, a little bit. Today we have awakened those powers within you. Now we will teach you how to use them, and just so you know, I will tell you this. You may teach your children the power of healing, which you are about to learn. You may not teach them the powers of harming, which you have yet to learn. Do you understand?"

"Yes," replied Angus, "but I don't understand how I could learn to do those things."

"Just as we don't understand the power of your passions--how you could destroy a door which all of us supported. It's important that you learn to control those passions. Let us begin. Do you love this plant, StrathNaver?" Feshka pointed to the Elm sapling.

"Of course not," declared Angus. "How could one love a plant?"

"So tell us this, StrathNaver, is there anything you love?"

"Yes of course," said Angus. I love my father and my brother. I love Lurenne and my mother. I love my family." The sense of loss returned again suddenly. Laura, his mother, was dead. His last moments with her had seemed like many others before them, feeling her love and hearing her voice. How he wished he had stayed with her longer that day. If only he hadn't gone fishing but had remained to protect her. It wasn't the last time he would think of her in this way.

"Then you know the feel of loving something or someone. Is that so?" Feshka continued.

"Yes." Angus had never before thought of his father and his brother in terms of loving them. They just always were. They existed in his world and he was used to having them there. But yes, he did love them, just as he did his mother. That she was dead didn't change anything, only that now he would never see her again except in the pictures he carried in his mind and memories.

He had never thought much about love before, concerning anything. He knew as a man he was supposed to choose a woman and love her, but as he grew he did not meet any he felt he could love. Many girls and young women were available, but they were still like the playmates of his early years, grown older like himself.

Angus didn't know what love felt like until he began having the dreams about Lurelei. Even then he wasn't aware it was love he was feeling. As he considered the word now, Lurelei's face, as it once was, came to his mind's eye.

"Yes," Angus repeated, "I know what it's like to love someone."

"In the earlier exercises you learned to use the power of visualizing, did you not?"

"It was an interesting lesson."

"And in this most recent lesson you learned to focus your anger, did you not?"

"Yes," Angus responded, "but I'm not sure I could summon up that much emotion at any moment."

"This exercise," said Feshka, "is similar to the other two, but this time I want you to start by visualizing the love you feel for your family as a ball of light in the center of your heart. Can you do that?"

"I'll try."

"Then do it now," instructed Feshka.

"I'm trying."

"Now feel the power of that love inside you. Can you feel it?"

"Sort of," murmured Angus.

"Now imagine in your mind's eye, just as you did before. Visualize that place in your heart as being a spring, but instead of water coming from it, the power of your love for your family springs forth eternally from there. Can you visualize that?"

"Yes," said Angus. "That's easier than trying to imagine a door!"

"I suppose so," smiled Feshka. "Now I want you to visualize that power coming from your heart and running all through your body. You can focus that energy anywhere you want. Try imagining that it is coming to your hands and that anything you touch will receive that love energy."

"Okay, I'm doing it."

"Can you feel the heat of it in your fingers?"

"Yes," said Angus. "My hands are beginning to feel hot."

VelMud lifted the pot containing the Elm sapling off the low table and presented it within Angus' reach. "Now," instructed VelMud, "give that love to this plant and watch it glow."

"Place your hands on the stem of this plant," directed Feshka, "and imagine the love flowing from the spring of your heart, through your hands and driving away the sickness that affects this plant."

Angus leaned slightly forward and placed his hands around the Elm sapling's stem. After a moment he released it. The bark was clean.

"Have you yet found the Gate Keeper?" asked Feshka.

"Yes," answered Angus. "I am the Gate Keeper."

The crowd of Elves around him began cheering and gathering closer, slapping him on the back and congratulating him.

"We do not know how Lurelei was able to give you the secret request," said Feshka. "She is not an initiate of the Brith Gar-Nunsum. We had hoped she would wish it, but now we fear it is impossible. She did not know that this request to find the Gate Keeper was the ritual request for initiation."

VelMud took him by the hand and helped him out of the chair. Then the Elves led him through long passages back into the light of day. "But I thought this was all a dream," said Angus.

"Life's a dream while the spirit sleeps," laughed Migalik. "Don't you know that?"

Chapter Eight: Marnel

A stream flowed past The City of The Vision. It started back in the hills not far away and picked its path down through the rocky forest to lower levels nearer the sea. Then it meandered across a short piedmont through old areas of riprap and tidal flow and into the nearest firth, or finger of the sea. Where it passed The City of The Vision it slowed its course and formed small pools in which lived fish and frogs and all manner of other water creatures. On the bank of the stream by the City, Angus sat with the lovely Elf, Marnel.

He had overcome his shyness with her somewhat and they were talking. At no time, however was Angus unaware of the beauty of this Elf or of her physical charms. He had no idea why she had chosen to accompany him on this little outing, but he wasn't really complaining very loudly. He had spent much of the early morning with his father William and the other men from the Glen. Scobie, Ingram and Tristan were the only ones remaining from the group who had left in search of Angus. They were concerned and fearful. "While they had you in there," William had said, "there was another attack. It was pigs again. This time they said they thought they saw some creature with them, sort of directing the action. I wonder how they ever were able to train pigs to be like that."

"Pigs are evil animals," Ingram answered. "They'll do any vile thing."

"But they aren't so bad to eat," said Scobie.

"The Elves don't eat 'em," said Tristan. Angus noticed with a smile that Tristan had not stuttered since he joined them at the house of Migalik.

"Did anybody get hurt?" Angus asked.

"There were some injured but none seriously," William said. "Just some scratches and cuts. Maybe a few bruises. We killed a lot of swine though. I can tell you that for sure. What did they do to you in there," asked William.

"Oh, not much," said Angus. "It's sort of a school and I don't really understand what they're trying to teach me. I guess I'll need a few more lessons."

"The old Elf, what's 'is name, Migalik, said to not ask you about it that you'd be sworn to not talk. Is that true?"

"It was all sort of hazy to me," said Angus trying to find a way to politely not answer.

"Well, maybe next time, you'll remember more of it," William placed closure on the conversation perceiving that Angus was not eager continue discussing the experience.

Angus really wasn't sure about what underlying purpose the lessons had or why he had been taught them. He'd have to give it a lot more thought. That was why he was with Marnel now. He had wanted to go and sit in quiet and think but she had seen him leave the area and went with him, "for your own safety," she told him. "You already know of the swine attack. We don't know what manner of creature may be wandering the forest today. I will come with you to be sure you are safe."

"Yes. And what a lovely protector," he said with a smile. "Was any Geketz spotted?" He asked that question thinking of Lurenne, and then he caught himself and restated the thought using 'Lurelei,' instead.

"None were seen," she answered, ignoring his compliment. Then she said gently, "we try to not use any words here referring to the Enemy directly or to his servants. Some of the others would think it rude if you did it in company with them."

"What should I call them then?" asked Angus. "I do need to talk about this somehow."

"I don't know," said Marnel, "but the proper name for them shouldn't be expressed here. Try to find another way."

"Something else I'd like to talk about is the experience I just had. I wish Feshka or VelMud were available right now."

"We thought you might like to talk about it," she said. "That's one of the reasons why I'm here with you now. It was a lot more strenuous for them. That's why they're resting."

"Is it safe to be out here by the stream?"

"We think so," she answered. "The Enemy's servants usually avoid getting wet and to reach us here, they would have to cross the stream."

"Do you know if any plans have been made for a counter attack?" He asked her. He was doing his best to not notice how close she was to him.

She even brushed against him slightly as they walked along the stream's bank. It made him feel very self-conscious, but she seemed determined to not notice.

"There is talk of an adventure toward the Great Glen and the nearest firth to see if he has landed any large boats. The Council believes he has set up his base on one of the outer islands and that he strikes at us randomly from there. I usually find that what the Council says they believe to be true, is true. We have no cause for serious alarm yet. But the day isn't far off."

"He seems so powerful, almost mystical in his evil."

"Oh he's that," said Marnel, "but we know him and this time we're nearly ready for him. He'll be surprised to find us standing to face him, for the first time ever. That's not why I'm with you. It's not to discuss the Enemy but to answer your questions about your initiation, to help you understand."

"Then it's alright for me to talk with you about this?"

"Of course it is," she answered. "That's part of why I'm here."

"What's the other part?" asked Angus.

"It will become clear to you in time, I hope," she smiled.

"After the experience in the stone room all I wanted to do was run home and hide from all of this, but I'm determined to go on and do what ever it takes."

"Oh?" she said. "You created a stone room?" My test turned out to be a boat floating out of sight of land on the sea. I was so afraid that I'd never see land again."

"What does it all mean?" asked Angus, still having difficulty not staring at her. "Why a room for me and a boat for you?"

"It's always different. The dreamer creates his own dream. The first initiation is intended to teach him that."

You were in this dream, I created, the thought crossed his mind. "And what about this Gate Keeper business?" he asked. "I was supposed to find the Gate Keeper, who is supposed to have all the answers and all I found was myself."

"You don't understand? You probably soon will," she said smiling at him so sweetly that it was nearly impossible for him to not lean over just a little bit and touch her lips with his. The nagging thought of his fidelity to Lurelei was the only thing holding him back, and the guilt he was feeling for allowing himself to be so tempted.

Does she know how I want her?

"I understood that the Gate Keeper is me, but I don't really understand it. Do you think you could explain for me a little?" Angus asked wanting to hear the sound of her voice and an excuse to watch her as she talked.

"What do you suppose the Gate leads to which this Gate Keeper tends?" she asked.

"I have the idea that behind the gate is some sort of creative force powered by my passions," he answered. "I thought The Gate Keeper was a person who was a member of the Brith Gar-Nunsum. I was told that the Gate Keeper lives in this City."

"I think rather," said Marnel, "you were told that you might find him here, not that he was here or lives here."

"So. It was a puzzle I was to solve?"

It's a puzzle," she answered with a broad smile, looking up at him. She was facing him as she spoke, not more than a foot away. Angus thought at first that she was so close because they were speaking very softly, but now he realized that there was no one near and no reason to speak softly. His hands were trembling with the desire to touch her face, her hands. His knees were trembling with the desire to make her his own. Then he placed one hand on her cheek for a moment. She didn't object or withdraw. He was at one of those junctures in life that demand 'speak or die.'

He chose to speak, and not forgetting Lurelei. "I think I have never seen a creature more beautiful than you. When I think that, it nearly makes me forget my pledge to Lurelei, who I love."

She reached for his hand and held it up where they could both see it. "See how your hand is trembling, StrathNaver?" Without waiting for his reply she said, "You keep the gate well."

Angus looked at her in astonishment. "All this time and all the trouble to come to this place seeking this Gate Keeper only to learn that all the time I was the one I was seeking? That's an outrageous practical joke and a cruel one."

"Not a joke, StrathNaver," she said. "It's an important lesson. You acquired self-knowledge and a deeper understanding of how you control your passions and how you can greater use them. In this place, you < will > find yourself and in the new strength you find there in, you will be able to help not only Lurelei but all of us. It is written in the Weaves. Come with me and see." She set off at a rapid pace back up the hillside away from the stream.

"Do you not see within the gate you guard so well?" she asked as they walked.

"See within my passions?" he asked.

"Yes. Have you never looked within that well of power which you possess?"

"I'm afraid I've only ever looked to make sure that the gate was locked tightly," he began chuckling. "If that ever got loose and out of control I'd be lost."

"But you keep the gate well. You never let it escape. Do you?"

"Not very often," he answered.

"In this place you will recognize yourself, eventually. You are the Gate Keeper. This power - these passions are in your control. You can focus them either together or one at a time. You can aim and direct them. Did you not direct your passions at the beast when Lurelei was attacked?"

"Are you saying that I can cast the Bolt?" he asked.

"Not necessarily. We don't know, yet. But we believe that if you can be taught what we know, that you can learn to direct your passions in ways unknown to us. We lack such passions, StrathNaver. It is a Human trait, not an Elven one. We understand the use of our life's force and we can direct it. Your life's force has a different dimension than does ours. It's much more powerful but Humans have never learned to use this force because they are so consumed by it."

"Consumed?" Asked Angus.

"Yes," she answered. "You will never see an Elf's hand tremble with desire as yours did. Do you understand? When your passions rise again, instead of standing before them and feeling their pressure pushing you to act, look behind them and directly into them. See if you can detect their depth and breadth. Look at the many aspects of your passion. There is far more there than even most Elves imagine. I myself watched them rise and fall in you today. They take many forms. There is love and lust, anger, hatred, compassion, the drive to accomplish, acquire, to defeat, pain, and anguish. The first thing you need to do once you can see them is to be able to isolate them and direct them one at a time. You must learn to control them well enough to use their force. It is a powerful force."

"This sounds very difficult. I've never thought of my passions as separate things before."

"Well, maybe they're not separate but fueled from the same source and focused in different directions, scattered, even. We usually think of the different directions as different passions."

"Well there's a thought," said Angus as he hurried along behind her, trying to keep up.

Marnel paused in front of one of the dwellings at ground level and waited for him to catch up. "This is the place I wanted to show you," she said. "Come in."

They entered a short passage curving to one side, opening into a well-lighted room, nearly as big as the hall where he had been. It amazed him that such a large room could exist underground. The ceiling was fairly high above him. That he had no memory of the hill outside rising above this area confused him somewhat. As he was trying to puzzle it through, Marnel led him to one side of the room. He noticed that the room was very well lighted for being completely underground. There were torches here and there, burning brightly but giving off no smoke or smell.

Throughout the room were rows of stands supporting grass weavings like the ones in the house of Migalik. The walls were lined with them and the rows were arranged neatly through the center of the room. "These are the Weaves of Vision," said Marnel. "The originals, of course, have been sent off to distant places for safe keeping. These are copies, but they're good copies and they can be studied as well as the others."

At that moment, Angus became aware that there were three other Elves in the room gathered around one of the Weaves. They would look carefully at it for a moment then discuss something among themselves. One would point at the Weave as though using it to illustrate a point, then continue talking. It seemed that they were disagreeing over some aspect.

"These Weaves represent a complete history of our people from the time we left the western lands to the time we will return," Marnel said. "They were created over a long period of time by many Weavers of Vision. Star Bright, Migalik's wife, is one of the Weavers. She created the last part detailing the history of our Exile after YeePhraWaine, the time of our Sojourn in this land. Of course, Angeline was the first weaver of visions. The rest are an elaboration of those originals. Some think that you are pictured in that section. Come and see it."

At one corner of the room Marnel indicated a series of large grass mats, the same as the ones Angus saw in Migalik's home during his first visit. He was again amazed at how clearly the details of the images were depicted without paints or any method of coloring other than different colored grasses.

"The three Elves you see arguing over there are Adepts. They're discussing a point in these mats here," she said indicating the copies of Migalik's Weaves. "They have gone back in the time sequence to verify what they think these mean."

Angus examined the mats in front of him. They displayed a wide variety of scenes, from huge battles involving thousands, to domestic depictions of family life. The weave to which Marnel had directed his attention depicted a large sailing vessel crowded with Elves. In the bow of the ship was a red-haired figure whose face was obscured. All Angus could see clearly were the scars around the figure's throat and wrists, indicated by some fine strands of a darker grass.

"That's not me," objected Angus. "Is this what all the fuss is about? They think this figure in the boat is me?"

"For quite some time, it was generally thought this person was Ariel the Rebeck. It was Ariel who led us to begin developing weapons to fight the Enemy. He arranged for the first swords to be acquired from the Dwarves and for their fine- tuning to what they are now. This is the color of his hair, but he lacks the scars. You have the scars, and your hair is the same color as in this weave."

"But that can't be me!" declared Angus. "I'm not an Elf. He may get the scars later. It's nothing more than a stupid coincidence!"

"Maybe so," responded Marnel, "but there are some who believe differently."

⚜

William and the others were staying in a small treetop dwelling near the center of the city. Migalik, Feshka and VelMud were guests in various other homes, as were the Dwarves and the rest of the party from the Valley of the Naver.

Until this morning, William hadn't seen the Dwarves since arriving in The City of The Vision. VelMud had dropped by to invite them to a meeting to be held early that evening.

"This is all very confusing," Ingram shook his head, rubbing his eyes.

"Not as confusing as coming home and finding your wife dead," retorted William. "At least we seem to have some purpose here."

Tristan was standing by a window-like opening overlooking the City. It seemed strange, knowing so many Elves were living nearby, yet not being able to see a sign of them anywhere. Why did everything have to be so unpredictable? He was no longer so sure he wanted to go into battle knowing the kinds of enemies he'd be fighting. He'd seen the creatures that had attacked them on the trail, and the swine, which were either possessed or had been trained to kill.

When he had agreed to go with William to help find Angus, he had no idea what was going to happen. He had decided to go with them to The City of The Vision because it had seemed like such a grand adventure. It would be fun getting to know the Elves and Dwarves better, and he would also have an opportunity to meet Elf girls. It had all seemed too wonderful to believe. The trail hike had been difficult and challenging, but even that had been fun until the first attack. The swine were larger than normal pigs, and their tusks larger than any tusks he'd ever seen before on a pig.

But that was nothing compared to the second attack. He had no idea what the creatures were. They seemed almost human. On the other hand they seemed like overgrown Elves that had been darkened and perverted, like the swine. Some of the Elves had referred to the creatures as Ogladim, but Tristan had never heard that word before.

He asked GarMawk what an Ogladim was. He said they were servants of the Enemy. "Most of them used to be Human, some Elves, some Dwarves," said GarMawk. "Now they're just Ogladim. An Oglat feels no pain or fear. They have no memories of their lives before being captured. They can be very fierce warriors. We only know of them from legend. None have ever been seen in any of our lifetimes. This is what the Enemy does to those he captures. Fight well, young Human, or you could be the next Oglat I kill!"

GarMawk's intensity frightened Tristan. The Elves were usually so happy when they spoke. They seemed to radiate peace and the joy of living, but these words from GarMawk were frosty, almost hostile.

William was sitting at a low table with Ingram and Scobie, discussing the reality they were facing. They had thought they were pursuing a lone villain, a clansman perhaps, but now they were beginning to understand the full meaning of the dangers ahead. The City was full of Elves from every part of Alba and from the mainland to the east. There were Dwarves from four distinct colonies, from places William had never before heard of.

Another party of Elves had arrived from the south while Angus was secluded with the Brith Gar-Nunsum. These were the Wesheshicans as they called themselves, from the Westerlands. Their leader was a short stocky Elf called Mishishel. William had not yet heard Mishishel's story but he expected to learn more about this group at the coming meeting.

William had been trying to keep abreast of what was going on around him. Ingram and Scobie, like he, had been doing their best to hide their fears, but he knew how they all felt. He was most concerned about Tristan. He hadn't heard him stutter in days and that didn't seem right to him. Even now he was pacing the floor, contemplating their current situation. All of them, including Tristan had vowed to pursue this matter to its end and he was sure each would come through when needed.

He was disappointed that Hender and MacBain had elected to desert the party. They were right, of course, when they said the Glen needed protecting, but he doubted they would make much of a difference to what happened to the community if it were attacked as they had been, for example, by Ogladim or swine. Also, it was quite possible, although he didn't like to dwell on such a thought--that the two would never make it home by themselves. Things were much worse than Hender and MacBain could even imagine. A comment Migalik had made after the last attack while on the trail had concerned William: "These aren't so bad. He's got much worse." William hadn't shared that remark with the other men. He didn't want to frighten them even more.

Unlike the natural amphitheater in the Valley Naver, the meeting hall was indoors. Angus sat with his father, and Tristan, Scobie and Ingram Williamson gathered near the two. They were surprised at the large number of Humans present, since they hadn't seen them enter the city. They were from the southeast of Alba.

Also present were other clansmen. Clan Gunn was represented by nearly fifty men. Clans MacIntosh, MacMillan and MacFall were represented from the Northerlands and Clans Lewis and MacKinnon from nearer the Great Glen. Tristan estimated there were over one hundred Humans present. Even with that swell in the ranks, there were vastly more Elves and Dwarves than Humans. William wondered if they'd be able to hear what was said from such a distance as far back as they were sitting.

His concerns dissolved as soon as the first Elf opened his mouth to speak. He introduced himself as Ariel, the Rebeck of the Firthlands. He also introduced Mishishel as the Rebeck of the Westerlands and two other Rebecks, one from the Southerlands and one from the Easterlands, BarNockel and Shashiel.

Angus was startled at the Rebeck's flaming red hair. He was also about the same height as himself. *No wonder they could confuse me with him in a vague image like the one in the weave,* he thought.

"What's a Rebeck?" Tristan asked Angus.

"I don't know," answered Angus. "I think it's some sort of leader, like a Clan Chieftain."

Tristan was bored by the speeches. He was surprised to see so many females among the Elves. The Humans and Dwarves had brought no women with them.

William and his friends were overwhelmed by news these groups reported. Apparently Geketzim were randomly scattered throughout the territories. There were never many, but as Mishishel pointed out, the Geketzim were no more than scouts for the Enemy. It was true they did their share of harm, but their real purpose was to gather information.

Some reported encounters with Ogladim, but these were rare. The consensus among the Elves was that these, like the Geketz, were scouting parties. As yet, the attacks had not been serious and there had been no direct assaults except on Angus's party on the trail.

William was listening carefully for any further indication of other warrior types the Enemy might throw against them. He had a feeling the Elves were relieved that Geketzim and Ogladim were the only enemies they had encountered thus far.

Angus was in a world of his own, thinking about his experiences in the Adytum. He was still trying to separate dream and physical realities and caught himself wondering if he could affect physical things here as in the Adytum; but he was afraid to try. There was a door in the wall behind the speakers and he was toying with the idea of pushing it open just a little, to experiment. He could imagine the surprised expressions on the faces of the Elves, who were speaking so seriously!

Tristan nudged him and whispered, "What are you grinning about?"

Just then, the crowd began rising and Angus and his party rose with them. Angus could barely see over the heads of the others, and when he found a comfortable viewing spot, he was surprised to see at the front of the room a tall dignified looking gray-haired Elf wearing brightly colored clothing and a woven grass crown. The crowd started applauding, and after a few moments, the figure raised his hands for quiet. Gradually the applause subsided and the crowd began to re-settle themselves on their benches and chairs.

"Who is that?" Angus asked his father.

"Weren't you listening? It is the king of all the Elves, the King of the Kings. Listen!"

Even though Angus could not understand what the great leader was saying, he could hear his voice. It moved like a resonant wave of peacefulness over the frightened crowd, calming them. As hard as he tried, Angus could not hear the Elf's articulation; it appeared that none of the other Humans could, either. Angus soon realized he was speaking in a language that was foreign to Humans. The words rolled over them like a warm breeze.

He knew he was uttering Elf words of reassurance because he felt reassured. In a few moments the tone changed and Angus began feeling resolve. He glanced at his father to see if he was reacting the same way. William's lips tightened and his brows moved slightly together. Angus then looked at Tristan and noticed the same response. Angus and everyone else seemed to understand the meaning of the Elf King's words.

He spoke only for a few minutes. Then the crowd rose as one, cheering and loudly applauding.

Ariel the Rebeck spoke briefly afterwards. "It is not often that one is gifted with hearing the song of the High Elves," he began. "Sleep well, for there is much to do."

Before joining the others who were leaving, Angus and his group sat for a moment, still bathing in the peaceful sound of the Elfin leader's voice.

"What did he do to us?" Ingram spoke first.

"I think he's just a really good orator," Angus offered.

"But what did he say?" asked William.

Angus shook his head. "I have no idea. Do you?"

"No. I don't either," said Scobie, "but I now feel like I can conquer the world. Don't you?"

"Yes!" Tristan chimed in.

"That one fellow called it the song of the High Elves," mused Ingram. "I hope we can hear it again some time."

Two young Elves were watching them from farther up and they now approached. Angus saw them first and the others followed his gaze.

"I am called Arikin," said the first one, "son of the Rebeck Ariel, and this is my brother AriMa. Our father has directed us to bring you with us. Will you come?"

"Where are we going?" asked William for all of them.

"To a smaller meeting," said Arikin. "There is planning to do. It was thought best to not reveal our strategies in such a large group. One never knows whose ears might be listening. There are plans for you if you choose to continue with us. We will be under the Rebeck Ariel. Of course, he will not come with us. He will oversee and direct. That is what a Rebeck does. We are his soldiers."

The group gathered in a rear chamber of the meeting room consisted of Angus's father and neighbors, Tristan, Ingram and Scobie. Others included Mishishel and another of the Wesheshicans; Feshka, VeratNonn and another Dwarf; Marnel, Aelrondenne; and Arikin and AriMa, the sons of the Rebeck Ariel. When Angus saw Marnel he wondered if her purpose for being there was to arouse his passions again. He also wondered how Lurenne would react if she found out.

The first order of business was with Angus. "On the trail," began Feshka, "it was reported that one of the Enemy's creatures rescued you. Is that true?"

"It was Lurelei," answered Angus.

"Where we are going, she may not follow, StrathNaver. I will not tell you where that is until you have spoken with her. She may be able to feel your thoughts and then the Enemy will know them too. She is the eyes and ears of the Enemy. What she knows, he knows. Do you understand this?"

"Yes, she said as much," answered Angus.

"She is apparently following and watching you. You must find a way to send her back to the Naver and away from this place. She must not see what goes on here and she must not follow us. Can you stop her?"

Angus's head was spinning. "I'll try," he promised.

Chapter Nine: The Meeting

Angus stood within sight of the City's edge during the last hour of daylight watching the woods beyond. He saw nothing out of the ordinary, but he hoped Lurelei would see him and be near. He continued to wait until an hour after the sun had disappeared and the sky was completely dark. He was filled with fear but knew he was the only one who could do this, since he was the only one he was sure Lurelei would speak to. It didn't help to be aware of the existence of the Ogladim and other unknown dangers in the forest. How could he even be sure Lurelei hadn't already been fully absorbed by the Enemy by now? For all he knew she could be a full Geketz.

He stood in the darkness trembling but resolute. Slowly he began walking toward the forest.

Several Elves were on watch and they stopped him. "You can't go any farther alone. There's danger."

"I know the danger," Angus responded. "I'll be safe enough."

"You can't go out alone! You could be killed or worse."

"Do not fear for me. I have a protector."

Realizing they would be unable to hold him back, they allowed him to leave the city.

The forest was more silent than usual. Angus jumped when a drop of dew fell off a leaf and struck his forehead. The silence was eerie. He walked as quietly as he could, but he knew if Lurelei were around, she would find him.

The pain of his scars seemed to throb more intensely than usual. He rubbed his wrists, then his throat. The wound from the swine had completely healed under Marnel's ministrations. There was no lingering pain from it at all.

Ah yes, Marnel, his mind wandered. *She is beautiful and fair. How I had struggled to not touch her. Then it seemed that she wanted my touch. She waited for it. Those deep blue eyes seemed like they were waiting for me, wanting me. Why did I hold back? Lurelei is as good as dead. She is unattainable, out of reach. How could I have her now? I couldn't love a Geketz. Its touch would burn my skin and leave more scars like the ones on my throat and wrists.*

On the other hand Marnel was indeed present, well and possibly available. Her skin looked softer than any skin he had ever seen. Her hair seemed to be begging his fingers to touch it. Her eyes seemed to look right through him knowing his thoughts and fears. He wondered what mysteries those eyes had seen and what stories she could tell. Her form had almost made him gulp when he first saw it. She was slender to the point of being willowy. He wondered if she would bend when the wind blew. Her lips were like those of Lurelei. They were full with promise. And what of Lurelei, who he was even now going to see?

Just then he heard steps behind him. He continued onward, ignoring the sound. He could tell it was gaining on him. He had his Elf blade in its sheath and felt he could protect himself somewhat... at least he could protect himself better than the first time. He stopped and turned.

"You know, Angus, you could be killed out here," sneered Lurelei in a voice so unlike her lovely Elf one. "There are Ogladim everywhere. There is another Geketz besides me. It knows not that I am not complete. It would kill me or complete the job if it knew. It would have already killed you, had I not driven it away. I should kill you myself, you miserable weakling!"

Lurelei stepped closer. "I can smell your blood Angus. Give me a reason to not drink of it!"

"There is only one reason, Lurenne," Angus's forehead was burning. "And that reason is that I love you."

"How do I really know that?" Lurelei accosted him. "How can you prove that you do not think of anyone else but me? I feel lust for your blood differently than before. I am nearly mad with the closeness of all these Elves, and you yourself are here before me, helpless and Elfkin. Give me a better reason to not kill you!"

"You will not kill me because you love me, and I love you and there is still hope for a cure, more so than before," Angus exclaimed with great passion.

"You speak of a cure. What nonsense! GaudarKahn listens to your words with me and he is deeply amused. He thinks I will kill you tonight, but he is wrong. Why are you outside the City's protection?"

"Feshka sent me to speak to you."

"That fool!!" Lurelei scoffed. "Doesn't he know the danger you are in? Doesn't he realize we could take you easily right now? It's with great effort that I don't kill you right this minute! Doesn't he know I am a Geketz?"

"You are not a Geketz. You are injured only. You are Lurelei, the Elf who I love," insisted Angus.

"Lurelei?" She echoed the sound of his longing, but her tone was icy and hostile. "So they're calling me Lurelei! Is that so?!!"

"Yes, but I don't know the meaning. Would you tell me?"

"They honor me as Lurel but they call me Lurelei, 'the spirit of laughter lost'. They think I am lost!"

"You will not always be lost," Angus reassured her. "You did say once that there was a cure, you really did say that. And if there is, I will find it and bring it to you. I swear it by my life!"

"Enough with oaths and vows, Angus! Did you find the Gate Keeper in this City?"

"Yes, I have found the Gate Keeper."

"And what does the Gate Keeper say of a cure? GaudarKahn fears the Gate Keeper. He thinks that such a one will be his downfall."

"The Gate Keeper is working on it."

"'The Gate Keeper is working on it!!'" mimicked Lurelei. "How comforting... those blind fools! If no cure has been found in all these generations of Elves and men, how could a cure be found so luckily in time for me? What kind of silly message is that?"

"It is a true message," Angus declared, feeling the heat rise to his face. "Lurelei! Listen to me! No cure has ever before been sought. It was believed there was no cure, but you have said from your knowledge of the Enemy's own mind, that there is a cure."

He could feel her breath, she was so close. "Seek the lone tower in the Great Glen," Lurelei's voice trembled. She seemed to be struggling to speak from her Elfen and not her Geketz self. "That's all I know. He keeps thinking, 'Keep him away from the lone tower of the Great Glen.' Now what is it that Feshka would have you say to me?"

"He wants to know first, if your heart is still that of an Elf."

"Tell him that I have been corrupted, but my heart is still that of an Elf. What else?"

"He says we will leave the City soon. If you want to help us, see that none follows us whose thoughts are heard by the Enemy."

"I understand, and so does GaudarKahn." Her voice grew harsh and cold again. "You are coming to spy on him, are you not? Of course you are! And what if you need my help? If I don't come with you, how will I know when you are in need?"

"Do you still dream?" pleaded Angus.

She remained quiet for a moment. Again Angus felt her struggling: "I can still see into the place of dreams. In the dreamtime, I am still as I was, but the creature that I am, sleeps rarely, and in the light of day. Light is painful to me now. For sleep, I sink into the ground. I know not how."

"I don't understand. Why does GaudarKahn not tell the other Geketz about you?"

"It amuses him to do this. He thinks if I live, maybe he will be able to get useful information out of me about you, and he's right. He just did. He's already sending out scouts to locate you and steal you. This way he'll get more than just your life. Be forewarned, Angus. I will go now and do as you asked. I will leave this area so the Enemy will not learn any more from me. Good luck in your search."

This time Angus did not hear the loud crashing as she left him. Or maybe she didn't leave after all. She could have remained nearby, to make sure he returned to the City safely.

It started to rain. The drops fell gently at first, then gathered momentum. Soon Angus was drenched. When he left the City he had followed a path, but now this path was obscured. He set out in a direction that he thought was the right one.

To make matters worse, a mist started to rise from the ground, further obscuring his path. It wasn't long before Angus realized he was lost. He felt his feet begin to climb a hill and he thought he had found the city, but it was the wrong hill. He tried to listen for the sound of the stream, but all he could hear was the heavy rainfall.

No need to ask why he had come out without a cover. He'd wanted Lurelei to be able to see him. A cover would have hidden his light from her, so he'd left it behind.

All his life he had never been far from home and he was never much of a camper except for short fishing trips. Once he'd spent the night in the forest while searching for a lost lamb. Now *he* was the lost lamb, searching for his shepherd.

Angus decided it would be best to find a sheltered spot out of sight, and wait for the rain to stop. Maybe Lurelei was still near and she would help him. Picking a large tree with thick bushes around its base, he crawled beneath the trunk and waited.

Angus had no means for measuring the hours, but it seemed his wait was too long for the rain to stop and for the darkness to give way to daylight. He kept his ears tuned, carefully listening for any night sounds that might be loud enough to be heard over the falling rain. He heard nothing. He felt it wouldn't be long before they sent out a group to find him--at least he hoped they would try to find him. *Where is Lurelei?*

He was a fool. Everything he had tried to do had failed. He had failed Lurenne miserably. If he had acted faster he might have been able to save her.

But wait... he thought he had been over all that too many times before, and had accepted that he'd done what he could. But then... he could have attacked the Geketz more quickly if he had only known her danger. *If he had only known her danger.* And on the trail he had fouled up again. He let that pig get a hold of his leg and ended up making two Elves carry him like a baby for the rest of the trip.

He had tried to get up and walk, but his legs wouldn't carry him. Then there was the Oglat. He couldn't pull himself together enough to even defend himself. If it hadn't been for Lurenne—Lurelei--he would have been killed again. She had saved him twice and what had he done for her? He'd allowed her to be attacked by a Geketz. What betrayal! What unfaithfulness! How could he live with himself?

And now, to compound stupidity with stupidity, he had got himself lost in the woods, like a child. Any child would have been more careful. How stupid to allow himself to get lost and become prey to any of the monsters prowling the forest tonight. Would Lurelei have to save him again? How could he ever face her? Even if he did find a cure for her, he had sent her away. How would he ever find her again?

The night wore on, the rain causing little rivulets to run around his legs where they touched the ground. The rain had chilled the air and soaked through his clothing. He was cold and miserable..."I don't know why you're sitting there in the rain, Angus, but there are four Ogladim coming this way," said a voice almost next to him. "Don't make a sound!"

Lurelei! She had stayed close and was still watching over him! How embarrassing. Now she had saved him yet again by warning him of the approaching Ogladim. If he could only stop his teeth from chattering, they were making so much noise!

It wasn't long before Angus heard the Ogladim's voices, but he couldn't make out what they were saying. They were speaking in a language he didn't understand.

They seemed to have stopped within a few feet of him. They looked around carefully, almost as though they could smell him. Were they following his scent? That couldn't be. It had been raining. The scent would have been washed away even if they could smell it, but they lingered still, talking excitedly.

Angus was tempted to cut and run, but he didn't know which way to go. Cold and tired as he was, they could easily catch up with him and kill him. His legs tensed just in case they came closer. If they did, he would leap up, kill the closest one with his Elf blade then run as fast as he could until he'd lost the other three.

Maybe he could run just so far, then stop to catch his breath behind a tree. When they got near enough he could kill another one. Maybe he'd be able to kill all four of them. They were inching closer, examining the ground as they moved. He could smell them; it was an odor of filth and sweat. He was revolted. His stomach started to heave, but it was stopped by his fear. His teeth had stopped chattering and he tried to keep himself as still and quiet as possible. He was even holding his breath.

Finally the four gave up whatever it was they were looking for and moved on. The rain was beginning to ease a bit. It was still coming down hard but in almost solid sheets that obscured Angus's vision. The Ogladim seemed to be following a path. Maybe it led to the village. When they were gone and out of hearing, Angus rose to take a look.

"Maybe you are smarter than GaudarKahn thinks, Angus," Lurelei's voice again, from the shadows. "Do you understand the language of the Ogladim?"

"No. What were they saying?"

"They were grumbling about being recalled," answered Lurelei. "GaudarKahn is expecting trouble in the west. He has enough scouts in the countryside and he doesn't need so many around a village where he expects the Elves to flee. You should try to learn the tongue if you can. It's a variety of YeePhraese. The older Elves know it."

"While you're here, Lurelei, do you know which way on this path leads to the city?"

"Ha! I thought you were lost. I was right. It's to your left, Angus. To your left. I will go ahead of you part of the way. Try to walk quietly."

He could finally see her a little. She had been close before but the darkness was too thick. She had felt like she was nearly close enough to touch but he was afraid to try. "I can see you," he said.

"Then I am too close." She moved away.

"No, wait!"

"*Don't touch me Angus!* My touch brings death and pain."

"Not for long. I swear it, if it is within my power!" Angus cried, his voice filled with anguish. "Where should I look for you?"

"I will wait for you in the Valley of the Naver, at the place where we first met."

"When I come to you it will be with the knowledge of your cure."

"I will expect it to be a long wait," she said, and ambled off into the shadows ahead of him.

Then she was gone and he was alone again on the trail. It was still raining but not as hard as before, so it was easier to make his way. He was beginning to feel cold again. His terror of the near-encounter with the Ogladim was subsiding. He set off in the same direction as Lurelei.

When he reached the gate to the City, the two Elves acting as guards refused to let him in. Feshka came to the rescue.

"Ho, StrathNaver," he called in greeting. "What's this? Come," he exclaimed to the two Elves. He's with us, now, not to be feared. Come along, Angus!"

MarNosh and his wife, Lee-Eesh were standing in the doorway waiting for him. The strain of Lurelei's capture was beginning to show on the parents' faces. Lee-Eesh's cheeks had tear trails and MarNosh looked as though he hadn't slept in days. His thick black hair was uncombed and his clothing was wrinkled.

"We're leaving in the morning," said Feshka. "Most of the Enemy's servants cannot follow in the light of day. Get some sleep Angus."

Angus's dreams were wild and confused. He kept returning to the experience of the initiation. He would find himself in the plain again, fighting off the creatures he had seen there. Then he would be on top of the cliff looking down on the plain with Marnel beside him.

"Why was VelMud so unkind in the beginning?" he had asked Marnel. "It's very much unlike him."

"He was trying to make you angry," Marnel told him. "We've never tried to raise a Human's passions before. We didn't know how to do it."

"He was trying to make me angry? I was only afraid!"

"He knew that," said Marnel. "It was very confusing for him. He only succeeded in raising your passions when he suggested you call to mind some pictures of those times when you've been angry, or pictures of things you love."

"Why did he want me to do that--'raise my passions'--as you said?"

"Some think that since you are part Elf that you will be able to do some of the things we do, like casting the Bolt, and so forth. But you are also part Human and Humans have strong passions. We have little of that in our natures."

"That still doesn't explain it," insisted Angus.

Angus again found himself in the cave where he had broken the door, but this time he was watching. He could see himself pushing against the heavy door as hard as he could, yet unable to open it. In his sleep he was grunting and straining so hard, he woke himself up.

He poured a drink for himself from a pitcher beside the bed. As he drank, Marnel entered the room. "They sent me to wake you. It's time to be off."

Angus pulled on his clothes, wondering why it was Marnel who had come into his bedchamber. Then the confusion began again. Why did he have to have this temptation in front of his face when he was trying to help Lurelei? It was going to be hard enough completing the task he had set for himself without the constant temptation of this beauty so close at hand.

"Did you know Lurelei," he asked her.

"She is my sister," she answered. "And it is you who will save her."

Angus watched her eyes as she said it, trying to understand the emotions they evoked in him. He saw longing, fear, hope, all rolling across her face, one replacing the other, then returning, combining. She turned quickly, hiding her face from him. Angus now had a completely different slant on things. He finished pulling on his boots as he thought about it. Marnel left the room so she didn't see Angus's cheeks burning.

Chapter Ten: Evil Dreams

"Why are we traveling in the light of day?" Angus asked.

"In the daytime we have less to fear," answered VelMud. "There will be no Geketzim around, since they only live in darkness. The Flying Shadows can't see Elf Light as well, in the brightness of sunlight. We have only Ogladim and Humans to fear and the Humans won't be looking for us."

"Why do you fear Humans?" asked Angus.

"Because the Human communities fear us. We are strangers to them. Most people are like your friend Ingram. He fears and distrusts us. Look at the suspicious way he eyes us!"

Ingram was walking behind Arikin, and Angus had to admit VelMud was right. Every so often Ingram would glance at Arikin distrustfully, then glance behind him again at the other Elves. "You would think that with the amount of time we've spent with you by now, he'd relax a little," commented Angus.

"One would think," muttered VelMud. "We need to keep a watch on that one. He could turn on us at any time."

"I don't think he'll turn on the Elves," Angus reassured him. "My father and the others have come to be more trusting. Look at them."

William was walking with Feshka in front and Mishishel of the Westerlands behind him. They had a lively conversation going about sheep and women, which needs no repeating. At a remark from Mishishel, William burst out laughing. Feshka's contributions were sardonic.

"They seem to be getting along all right, wouldn't you say?" grinned Angus.

"For the time being," VelMud chuckled. "We'll see how it goes when it comes to fighting. I'll still keep an eye on Ingram."

Angus was so busy looking at everyone and watching the Elves, he had little time to worry about his neighbor Ingram Williamson. Ingram could keep watch on himself. Many of the Elves and Dwarves in the party were new to him. Studying them was taking his full attention.

Mishishel was the most interesting of the Elves. He was shorter and rounder than any of the other Elves Angus had seen so far. The Wood Elves and Sea Elves were long and lean, as were the Naver Grays. The only apparent difference between them was the way they dressed. But the Wesheshicans were distinctly different. When Angus remarked about this to VelMud, he was told, "The Wesheshicans eat too many potatoes. They can raise them there easier than we can in the north."

Angus didn't know what a potato was. He thought about it for a moment and when he asked, VelMud laughed and exclaimed, "It's a dirty little tuber that grows under the ground. It's shaped like a Wesheshican. No one knows which is the cause of the other!"

Mishishel was clothed in browns instead of the forest greens that seemed common among Firthlanders and the Grays. His long jacket hung low over his waist, almost giving the impression that his head was mounted on his hips. His companion, PoleeShimel was dressed the same way, but his hair was lighter than Mishishel's sandy-color.

Angus tried to watch them without being noticed, but the Elves were too observant. "The Human thinks your nose is bigger than mine," laughed Mishishel to his servant, PoleeShimel.

VeratNonn the Dwarf also had a servant. Angus was surprised to learn he was in high company. Not only was Mishishel the Rebeck of the Wesheshicans, but VeratNonn held a similar but lesser post with the Dwarves. Mishishel was in command of the small army that had been raised in the Westerlands, and he was on his way home. VeratNonn was more like a sub-commander. Angus knew VeratNonn was used to being in charge of things not only by his manner, but the fact that BarNeesh was carrying both his own pack and VeratNonn's as well.

BarNeesh seemed to carry them without much effort and without any apparent resentment. Mishishel had enough of a job carrying all the jewelry he was wearing, Angus thought with a smile.

The trip had begun just after first light. They seemed to be less cautious than on the previous journey. No Elves were ahead or on the sides of the path as lookouts. They were walking at a more relaxed pace, and talking as they went along. The path they had taken was more or less level and well cleared of any debris they could trip over. The rain of the night before had stopped, and the sky was clearer, with scattered clouds. Angus was glad to see the sun peeping here and there through the trees, but he was concerned about the apparent lack of caution.

"VelMud, there are no Elves or Dwarves ahead and behind to watch for danger. Is there no cause for alarm on this journey?"

"Perhaps there is," answered VelMud, "but there aren't enough of us to spread out like that. We're a small enough party that if the Enemy knows about us, we hope we won't be worth bothering with, but as you can see, everyone is well armed."

"So, you're saying if we're attacked by the swine again, we'll have no warning? And what about the Ogladim?"

"Those who drive them don't like the daylight," answered VelMud. "The only real danger for us is that we might stumble onto one of their camps. That's why Marnel and her cousin Aelrondenne walk ahead of us. They have the keenest eyes of all of us and they watch for our protection."

It was only then that Angus noticed Arikin did not keep his place in the procession. He dropped back for awhile and disappeared from sight. Then he'd catch up again and pass them all to join Marnel and Aelrondenne. He would walk with them for a short time, then disappear ahead of them again.

"Arikin also keeps watch, doesn't he?" asked Angus.

"Arikin leads this party. He has plenty of advice though, with Feshka, VeratNonn and Mishishel in his company," answered VeratNonn. "Our safety is his responsibility. Since there are so few of us, we must not be discovered. Our only real defense is secrecy. He watches even the trees and rocks. He thinks some of them might see us pass."

Arikin was the tallest Elf among them. His clothing seemed to Angus to be only what was necessary to cover him instead of for adornment, like that of VeratNonn. The other Elves, including Feshka, wore some additional garments. "We need our pockets," laughed VelMud when Angus asked the reason. "Arikin says he likes to travel light."

Angus watched as Arikin disappeared again ahead of them. As they walked, he wondered if any of the trees and stones did have ears and eyes. At the beginning of the journey he had been tense, but with the conversation and good weather, he'd become much more relaxed. Now, however, with VelMud's comments and Arikin's vigilance, he became more wary and watchful.

They were on their way to the Great Glen first, to search its shores for ships. This had been decided in secret councils. It was feared that GaudarKahn had sent more than scouts. It was the task of this party to learn if their fears were true. They had been instructed not to engage in any fighting that was avoidable, but to gather information only.

As the day wore on, the clouds overhead thickened. VelMud was interested in Angus's impressions of his initiation and encouraged him to talk about it, but Angus was having trouble thinking of anything but Marnel and Lurelei.

His scars were not hurting him as much as before. He had been concerned about that, and also concerned that he might have caught a cold in the rain the night before. He hadn't told anyone about getting lost and having to be helped to find his way back. Some warrior he was! If Ogladim attacked them on the trail, how would he ever defend himself? The one time he had a chance to cut one down, he'd missed and nearly lost his life. If it hadn't been for Lurelei he would be dead. To be saved by a Geketz was beyond shame. It was beyond embarrassment.

His first thought at all times had to be finding the cure. How could he even know how to search for it? Finally he decided to ask VelMud. "The Geketz told me the Gate Keeper could provide a cure for Lurelei. I found the Gate Keeper, but I'm no closer to finding her cure than I was before!"

VelMud listened but did not respond.

"How can I search?" persisted Angus. "Where should I look? Who should I ask?"

"No Geketz has ever been cured," VelMud said at length. "It's a ruse on the part of the Enemy. It's part of the torture he puts her to, to give her false hope and tease you with it."

"What about the one in the Valley of the Naver? That one was cured!"

"But he was lost in madness. Even now he is kept like a captive. He is imprisoned to protect him from himself."

"I can't give up hope for a cure," declared Angus. "It's the only reason I'm here with you."

"Ask Feshka," VelMud suggested.

Angus was growing angry. Was this just a game? Was the hope for a cure nothing other than more cruelty? He had already been badly used--and now this! He dropped back in the line and matched paces with the half Elf.

They walked next to each other for a short time without talking. Finally, Feshka said to him, "Let's drop back if you want to talk."

"I think I'm still searching for the Gate Keeper," said Angus as soon as they were by themselves, at the back of the line.

"What don't you understand, StrathNaver?"

Angus' anger had abated. Now he was with Feshka whom he respected and admired. The half Elf was more like a wizard or sorcerer to him. He had an aura of mystery about him, and in the blue robe he wore over his gray tunic and matching pants, he did indeed have air of mystery and magic about him. Angus had seen him throw fireballs at the Ogladim and was even a little fearful of him because of his power.

"Lurelei told me to seek the Gate Keeper because through him I might be able to find a cure for her. I have found the Gate Keeper, but I'm not closer to a cure than I was before. I don't know what to think of it," Angus began.

"No one knows of a cure for a Geketz, but after recovering BaynYamen we now think it may be possible. We know no more about it than you do," Feshka answered.

"But how does the Gate Keeper fit in?"

"First let me ask you a few questions. Do you know what lies behind the Gate?"

"Well," Angus shrugged, "my passions, I guess. What do you think lies behind the Gate?"

"One more question, StrathNaver. Where is the Adytum and what is it? I guess that's two questions."

"The Adytum lies behind a door in the House of MarNosh," Angus answered quickly. Then he reconsidered. "No. The Adytum is in that large hall where so many were gathered."

"Think again. And tell me," chuckled Feshka.

"The Adytum is a stone room with no door. Well, where is the Adytum then?"

Feshka continued walking in silence for a moment. Then finally he spoke. "You don't know where the Adytum is although you entered it. You probably don't know *what* it is either then... do you?"

Angus didn't answer. He waited for the half Elf to say more. When Feshka didn't continue, Angus retorted, "No, I guess not."

"Do you know the story of the Phoenix?" asked Feshka. "The Phoenix is a bird that lives forever. When it grows weary with age, it builds an Adytum."

Feshka looked at Angus and saw that he had missed the joke. "He builds a huge fire in which he burns his old body. Then he emerges from the flames with a new young body of Gold. His Adytum is a Pyre. It is a place where his spirit evolves into a newer and higher level of existence. Is this not what happened to you?"

"I was not burned," Angus shook his head, bewildered.

"You were not burned? Did you not fear for your life? Did you not find yourself in desperate circumstances and through your own efforts you rose from the ashes of what you once were, with a new and higher understanding of your existence?"

"I guess you could say that," Angus mused. "I do have a different understanding, but I really don't know what to do with it. How does this tie in to a cure for Lurelei? She says, if I touch her I'll be injured. I can't cure her like I did the plant!"

"No. But you're one step closer. We all are. You have not yet answered my question. What lies behind the Gate you keep?"

"Is it not my passions?"

"That and more," smiled Feshka.

"Is it the dream world you're talking about?"

"Yes. We thought you would understand that. We think the Geketz lives half in the physical world and half in the other. In the dream world, as you call it, you can approach it without the same fears. The way it causes injury is to pull its victim out of its normal reality. Is that a step toward the cure you seek?"

"Do you mean if I approach it in the dream world it can't hurt me?" asked Angus excitedly. "It looks like I should practice going behind the Gate!"

"We aren't sure. It's a theory. Be careful. I'll go with you if you want me to. Just ask."

The path they were following was now winding up the side of a large mountain. To accommodate the Humans, the pace slowed slightly. Angus could now see BarNeesh struggling with the double load. Verat-Nonn told him to stop, and then he took his own pack and carried it up the hill himself.

The trees thinned out and the Elves were more on the alert, fearful of being seen from some distant point. Arikin led them off the path and under a line of trees for cover. As they climbed higher, the trees grew smaller and finally disappeared altogether. The group then stayed among the bushes and bracken as they proceeded on their upward climb.

"This is the most dangerous part of the journey," VelMud told Angus. At a signal from Arikin, they all pulled out their thin grass covers and put them over their heads.

"These will conceal us from anyone who is watching the mountain from a distance. None will see us who are close either," VelMud said.

Late afternoon was upon them. As the sun began creeping closer to the western horizon they came upon a small cave. Angus was surprised to see it, but understood that this had been the planned refuge for the first night. The sun was still above the horizon when they entered, and the contrasting darkness reminded Angus of the other cave he had been in, or thought he had been in. What was it anyway? Had he created the cave just as, according to Marnel, he'd created the stone room?

How could he have created any of those things? He hadn't been thinking of a stone room or a cave! They were "just there," like this one was. After he entered the interior, he wandered back into its depth, looking for a door. He came upon a narrow area and as he entered it, the light grew dimmer. Finally the light was so dim, he couldn't see ahead of him. *No use continuing*, he decided. When he returned to the area where the group had spread out their bedrolls, he found Feshka watching him.

"Find anything back there?" he asked Angus.

"Just darkness," answered Angus.

"Let's look again, shall we?" suggested Feshka.

Together they walked deeper into the cave. As it grew narrower, Angus took the lead. The light disappeared faster this time, since the sun was sinking below the horizon outside, and less daylight penetrated the cave.

"I can't go any farther," said Angus. "The light is gone."

"If you can't see," said Feshka, "you may as well close your eyes. They're of no use to you without light are they?"

"Close my eyes? I won't see anything for sure, if I do that!"

"Try it," urged Feshka. "Stand where you are and close your eyes. I'm right behind you."

"All right." *What a stupid exercise!* thought Angus. "My eyes are closed. Now what?"

"What did you do in the other cave when things weren't going your way?"

"But that was a dream of some kind."

"Was it? Really? What did you do in the dream?"

"I imagined whatever I wanted, and there it was. That can't work unless I'm dreaming again."

"Are you dreaming again?"

"I don't think so," answered Angus.

"It can't hurt to try, can it?"

"All right. I'll do it your way! What should I imagine?"

"Well, if you can't see and you'd like to be able to see, imagine that you can. Try that."

After a moment of silence Angus called out, "It's not working. I can't see a thing. This seems ridiculous to me."

"Try this, StrathNaver. Sit down on the ground. Lean your back against the side of the cave." Angus followed Feshka's instructions.

"Now find a comfortable position that your body can relax into, so you don't have to exert any effort to hold yourself up."

"I'm in position. What next?"

"Now let go of your body. Relax every muscle you have control over. Start at your feet. When your body is so relaxed, you can no longer feel it, tell me."

Angus tried to obey Feshka's suggestions. It took him a while to be able to approach the condition described. His foot itched in protest. He tried to ignore it but the itch became too insistent. He broke his concentration and scratched his foot. Then he tried again. The same thing happened but this time it was his eye that started to itch.

"Don't be discouraged," Feshka assured him. "It can take some time to master this. Keep trying."

Finally, he signaled he was ready for the next step.

"Now try this. Imagine your body is asleep and your conscious self is not. Your mind is still active. Imagine you have a body made of light living inside your flesh body. Visualize this body made of light, standing up, outside of its flesh body. This body has its own eyes and ears, legs and arms, just as your flesh body does, but this light body is your real self. Can you do that?"

"I think so."

"Try it now."

Angus opened his imaginary eyes and discovered the world of astral travel. He was standing in the cave that was lighted somehow with a dim white light. He could see his body resting on the cave floor and Feshka seated beside him. But Feshka was also standing next to him.

Angus became alarmed at the realization of the contradiction and found himself back in his own flesh body on the floor of the cave.

"That's enough for now," said Feshka. "You can practice when you have time. The sun is down and we must leave very early. Get some rest."

"What was that? What happened?" asked Angus.

"You became frightened and lost your focus. But now you know how to walk behind the Gate, don't you?"

"I see," exclaimed Angus. Was what I saw real?"

"As real as you believe it is. Sometimes you might accidentally create what you're seeing. It takes time to learn to distinguish between what you're imagining and what's really there. You'll learn in time, with practice."

Sleeping in the cave was strange to Angus. The mattress was uneven hard rock. Several times during the night he imagined something had crawled across his face and he awoke with a start.

The Dwarves were taking turns at watching for danger. Mishishel took the first watch and traded with BarNeesh every three or four hours. Tristan was sleeping next to Angus; he wanted to talk.

"What do you think of Marnel?" whispered Tristan. "And Aelrondenne? They have such strange names. Have you ever seen such beautiful females?"

"Just one, who was more beautiful than both. It was Lurenne. They call her Lurelei now. I met her above the falls after you left that day."

"She's the one who was made a Geketz?"

"For now. Yes."

Tristan grew silent, realizing he had touched on a subject that was causing Angus much pain.

Angus's sleep was not restful. His dreams kept him half awake and tossing under his blanket. First he was in the Glen back home with his mother. She was doing household chores and at the same time cooking something in a large pot. For the moment he forgot she had been killed. He was glad to see her.

"What's in the pot?"

"Stew," she answered as she went back to untangling wool for spinning.

"Is it mutton or rabbit?" he asked with a grin.

She smiled at him. Brushing her rich auburn hair out of her eyes, she stopped her work for a moment. The look in her eyes was one he had never seen before, one of longing yet fearful. It was the look that any mother has when a son is going into danger. "What's in your pot, Angus?" she asked, and went back to her wool.

He found himself back in the Naver. It was a dream he had not had in several days and thought he had finished. This time, he was on the bottom of the river with a rock on his chest. He couldn't budge the rock. He tried rolling so it would fall off his body, but he was stuck between two other rocks that were holding him back. Again he struggled to turn onto his stomach. Then he tried to push the rock up and off with his hands and knees. It was too heavy and he was running out of breath. As he started to choke on the water, he woke up, or thought he did.

Now he found himself on the mountain trail with the rest of the party. They were half sliding, half walking down a steep path toward a river. Suddenly out of the forest on either side of the path, a band of Ogladim rushed out at them. There were many more Ogladim than people in his party.

Behind the Ogladim was a small herd of swine, squealing and making a strange growling sound Angus hadn't heard before. The swine rushed in behind the Ogladim to finish the work of killing. Angus was down. He had been struck by one of the filthy blades and was leaning against a rock, waiting to die. In the forest just out of the sun's light he could see a dark figure riding one of the pigs. Its eyes were red and large. It was foaming at the mouth. Its thin black hair hung in loose strands in front its face and around its oversized ears. It called out to

Angus as soon as Angus spotted it.

"Soon you can join your Lady, Human. The one to help you is near." Angus saw the dark form of a Geketz approaching him from behind the figure. Angus awoke screaming.

When he fell back asleep he dreamed again of his home before his mother's death. This time she was preparing an evening meal. It was a peaceful domestic scene. His father was outside tending the sheep. His brother Robert was at home with his wife and babies. The room smelled delicious. Laura was roasting mutton over the fire. The smell of the succulent meat had reached as far as the sheep pen. "Smell's great," William called out to her.

Angus was learning to make cloth out of the spun wool. He worked at fitting the strands together in a tight weave. Some thought of this as women's work but he had no woman yet, and thought it would be best to know how to do it if the need should ever arise. Laura turned the meat on the spit. "Would you throw some more wood on the fire, Angus, please?"

Laura thought it was Angus behind her but it was a Geketz. Angus rushed to push it off her but his hands went right through it. He was again tossing in his sleep, the dream filling him with fear and anger. This time he awoke shouting in rage and impotent frustration.

He could no longer sleep. Instead, he spent the rest of the night at the cave's entrance under his Elf cover, so that he could not be seen. At first light VelMud began waking those who were not already stirring. Angus looked back into the cave, absent-mindedly counting the group. One was missing. There were only thirteen. Concerned, he counted the group again, this time running through the list of names in his mind. Arikin was missing.

Chapter Eleven: Flight

The day was hotter and the path uphill, with rock cliffs ahead of them for what looked like several hours of hiking. William and the Humans watched with envy as the Elves stepped over rocks as though they weren't even there. William had to stop and carefully crawl over them. Ingram was having the hardest time of all. His age and bulk were working against him. Ingram was tired before mid-morning. The party slowed in deference to him.

Scobie was as energetic as usual, now keeping up with the Elves. Tristan and Angus were following behind the lead Elves, Marnel and Aelrondenne. Tristan had been trying to engage them in a conversation. "What do your names mean?" he asked them.

As Aelrondenne was explaining the inflections, Tristan listened in rapture. Angus could see on her face that she wasn't pleased that so many of her peers had reached the mark of distinction with the 'el' ending while she had not. Angus didn't think Tristan noticed, but he felt sorry for her frustration.

"Sometimes it's just a matter of coincidence," he reassured her. "You can't defeat an enemy if none is present to defeat."

"My field is guiding the lives of plants," Aelrondenne sighed. "There isn't much of a chance for glory there. But my mother has taught me the Bolt."

Angus hadn't thought about Star Bright since they'd left the Naver. Now he wished she had come along. He had never seen such a beautiful older woman before. She seemed to be surrounded by an aura of peace. *Her influence would have been good for us on this trip*, he thought.

"She taught my sister too. Together we could cast the Bolt in Trine without it hurting any of us. Now the Trine is broken and the Gift is lost."

"Gee," exclaimed Angus. "They should have kept the three of you together."

"That's what we told the old King, MarGaynsiel, but he said we should each teach others."

"MarGaynsiel? Is that the name of the one they said is the King of the Kings?" asked Tristan. "We missed his name at the introductions."

"Yes," answered Aelrondenne. "MarGaynsiel is the High King. It was his order that we form new Trines and perfect the Bolt with as many as possible. He thinks it may be the only truly effective weapon we have. Star Bright is with MarGalas-Siel, his wife. Together they will teach many."

"Where is your sister?" asked Angus. "She knows it too, doesn't she?"

"Fierrondenne has gone with the Sea Elves. They will send others to the Wood Elves. We are trying to spread the knowledge as quickly as possible. Marnel has learned it, but we are only two. We need a third. Arikin and Mishishel are also learning in case the Trine is broken again. We'll be able to keep the weapon in use."

"What about Feshka?" asked Tristan. "He could probably do it."

"Possibly," grinned Angus, "But he has his own weapons. I saw them in use."

At that moment they saw Arikin approaching quickly from ahead. He seemed to be agitated. When he reached them, the group gathered around to hear.

"I climbed to the top of the mountain while you slept. For a better view around us, I went to that outcropping, there," he pointed to a jagged cliff to the east of them. "From there I watched until I saw a fire spring to life far below. I saw no one around it at first, but I watched as the sun rose. Its light showed me seven Ogladim around it, some of them cooking over the fire."

A murmur rose among the group but died quickly as Arikin continued. "They travel in the night and rest while the sun is high because they work with the Geketzim who live only in darkness. If there are Ogladim, there must also be at least one Geketz."

"What do you suggest we do?" asked Mishishel. "Is there a hiding place near here?"

"I haven't been in this place before," answered Arikin, "but I've heard the songs. One tells of a Haven, but it's on the other side of the mountain. If we hurry we may be able to make it there before nightfall. The Ogladim are nearly a day's journey from here. It could be that they won't catch up to us. I thought we'd have plenty of time, since I thought they would sleep for the day, but they're not doing that. I watched while they ate, and instead of sleeping they set out along the trail toward us. They're faster than we are. We must hurry."

"If there are only seven, we outnumber them. We could face them on the mountain, right here," suggested Ingram.

"That's true," William agreed.

"But there may be more that I didn't see," Arikin reminded them, "and when night falls they may have one or more Geketzim with them. We must flee."

"I was close to four of them on the trail two nights ago," said Angus. "They said they were going west to join the Enemy, that the Enemy was expecting trouble."

"You can understand the tongue of the Oglat?" asked VeratNonn menacingly.

"How do you know the tongue of YeePhraWaine?" asked Marnel, frightened.

Angus stepped back from them, frightened himself. "Lurelei was with me. She told me what they said."

"You were with a Geketz?" BarNeesh face grew red with anger. "What kind of traveling companion is this?" he demanded of Feshka.

"Calm down," Feshka laid a hand on Angus's shoulder. "Angus was in the forest at my bidding."

"We can discuss this later," Arikin interrupted impatiently. "We must move on, right now. Come." With that, he led the way back up the path, calling over his shoulder, "Keep up, Humans!"

"With that," said Ingram, "I'm a dead man. I may as well sit here and wait for them."

"Come on, Ingram," William urged. "We'll help carry your pack. You have to keep up with us!"

Tristan was the first to take Ingram's pack and add it to his own. The group tried to hurry, but the climb was steeper than yesterday's. "Take heart," called Arikin back to them. "The top is nearer than you think!"

"The top is beyond tomorrow," muttered Ingram as he struggled to carry himself up the steep slope.

"When ya' get tired of that Tristan, I'll take it for a while," Scobie offered.

"I can take a turn too," said William. "We'll get him up there."

"Then when we get to the top, I can just roll down the other side," grunted Ingram, half to himself. "Why did I ever decide to do this?"

"Because you loved your wife, I thought," snapped William, "just as I loved mine and Scobie his. Tristan's the only one without a grudge here and he's doin' half your work right now. Quit griping!'"

If Ingram was unhappy about the increased pace, the Dwarves were downright ugly. Angus had never before heard such language from anyone. They were cursing the mountain, cursing the Ogladim, the Enemy, and most of all they were cursing the fact that they had to sweat.

The day didn't seem any different from before: sunshine and blue sky and birds here and there. The urgency of their passage didn't press itself into Angus' mind. Maybe it was because he was still groggy from lack of sleep, and shaken by his dreams. The image of the red-eyed creature riding the swine was still fresh in his mind and he feared it was a vision instead of a dream. The danger of the Ogladim below held little fear for him compared to what he felt from the image in the dream.

The Elf cloaks they wore made him feel hotter than he thought was necessary. He was tempted to throw it off so he could enjoy by the mountain air, just for a minute. He envied the Humans as well as the Dwarves, who had no Elf blood. They didn't wear the covers unless they were in plain view from below. Most of the time the path wound around through ravines and kept them out of sight. But the Elves feared they might be seen from above. They said the Enemy would pay no attention to humans, but Elf glow could be seen by the Flying Shadows, or perhaps other creatures the Enemy had perverted.

"Did you see any swine below?" Angus asked Arikin.

"No, but that doesn't mean they're not there. Pigs don't like to be in the sun. They don't have enough hair to protect their skin and they get sun burned. They try to stay under some sort of cover. They like trees. There could have been swine under the trees."

Angus dropped back again and asked no more questions. His fear, he felt, was confirmed. Probably there were swine with the evil creatures below, and they were coming this way. The Swine could smell them out, no matter where they were hiding. There would be no escape for them. *Pain would pass. Death is like sleeping. There was nothing wrong with dying.* He felt sorry for himself for awhile and let a few tears slip down his cheeks. Quickly he wiped them away, fearful the others might see him crying and think him less than a man.

As he climbed the mountain his thoughts turned to home and his mother. His anger returned. He had to help find and kill this Enemy that had caused him so much harm. His mother was dead. Lurelei the Elf of his dreams was a Geketz. It was a fate that would deprive her of even the sweet peace of death. He was her only hope. And what hope was that? He had learned much in his days with the Elves, but not enough to find the cure.

To add insult to injury, the exertion of the climb was causing his scars to begin to ache again. His wrists and throat were burning. He was afraid if this continued he wouldn't be able to keep up with the rest. He'd have to drop back and wait for the Ogladim to come and kill him, or the swine would do it.

He looked for Ingram among those in the rear. There he was red-faced and puffing. But he was keeping up. Tristan still had his pack; he seemed to be tireless. Angus looked more closely. He could see how hard Tristan was breathing. His shirt was wet from sweat under the Elf wrap. Angus was ashamed of himself again. Here he was, moaning and feeling sorry for himself. There was Tristan donating sweat and energy to help cranky old Ingram. "Give me that a while," he said to Tristan.

With a grin, Tristan handed him Ingram's pack. "Take it to the top, Angus!"

Angus glanced back at Ingram, feeling he was finally doing something worthwhile, then headed on up the hill. The path was no longer as steep as it had been, but the sun was rising and he was hotter than ever under his wrap. "I wonder if there's a spring ahead. I think I'd like to dive into it, if it's deep enough."

"There should be a bit of a breeze when we get to the top," Marnel told him, "and that should be pretty soon."

As they rounded the next turn in the path, Angus noticed she was right. The path leveled off. Ahead he could see that instead of an ascent, it became more of a rolling terrain. He turned and looked behind him. In the distance, he could see more mountains shrouded in the clouds. "Where is the Valley Naver in all of that?" he asked no one.

Feshka was close behind him. "It's over there," he pointed. "The second ridge from the right. See it?"

"A bird could be there in a few hours," said Angus.

"More than a few hours," smiled Feshka. "Maybe a day. You can see farther than you think from up here. Remember how long it took you to get this far away? The sea is beyond the last peak there."

Angus strained his eyes to see through the haze that hung over the last peaks.

They continued walking along the rolling path. Angus gave the pack back to Ingram who grumbled a "thank you."

"No problem," Angus responded. "It was my pleasure."

Arikin had lingered at the top. He studied the paths below, brow furrowed distrustfully. "Keep them moving," he instructed Feshka and VelMud. "I'm going to go and see where they are. I'll catch back up before you reach the Haven."

Arikin disappeared back down the path. Angus watched him go. Deftly Arikin made his way over the rough terrain below just as easily as he had on the way up. Angus had watched him in amazement and envy. His long legs carried him smoothly and quickly out of sight. Angus continued along the path, trying to keep up with the new pace set by the girls.

I wonder what she ever sees in me, Angus thinking again about Lurelei, comparing himself to Arikin, *when she could have a mate who looks like that.* His hand moved up to feel his sweaty red beard. His mother had kept it trimmed with a knife. She said it looked good on him; he hadn't washed or trimmed it in more than a week. He wondered what he looked like now. He glanced back at his father. William's dirt-streaked face seemed tired and worn, his hair mussed by the wind. *He looks as dirty as me.*

Marnel dropped back, urging the Humans to hurry. Ingram was resistant but her smile and cheer brightened even his sour demeanor. Catching up to her position in the lead with Aelrondenne, she smiled at Angus in passing. Even Marnel was suffering from the heat and work of climbing.

It didn't take long for them to reach the other side of the mountain. There the path turned downward abruptly. Ingram stopped at the top. "Now it's time to roll or slide."

"There'll be none of either," declared William. "You can make it just fine. Let's go."

Aelrondenne had gone on ahead looking for danger. She was already out of sight. Angus was becoming frightened again. Why had he come on this adventure? What good could he do them here? This was a job for one person who could slip in and out of the trees easily, for someone like Arikin, not for old Humans like his father and Ingram. He was beginning to run through the emotional gamut again when Aelrondenne returned.

"There's a camp below," she was gasping for breath, "it's more Ogladim. There are many, I couldn't count them. When I tried, they would walk under the trees and then more would appear. It's almost an army. There must be a hundred of them, but they aren't coming toward us. They seem to be waiting for something. They may be waiting for the party behind us."

"What shall we do now?" asked Mishishel. "We can't go forward. We can't go back. Those behind us will smell our trail and be hurrying toward us soon. If we try to slip away through the tress, they'll simply follow our scent."

"There are too many to fight," VelMud frowned. "We must do something clever to get around them. Is the Haven that Arikin spoke of, on this or the other side of the Ogladim camp?"

"I don't know where it is," Aelrondenne answered.

"I too have heard of this place," said Feshka, "but I don't know where it is. I'll go ahead and search for it. The rest of you continue as before. I see no other choice."

"We could stand and fight," from Ingram.

"Certain death is not as good a choice as possible survival," retorted VelMud. "The idea is foolish and the action a waste of blood. Let's do as Feshka says. Come," he continued, turning to Feshka, "I'll go with you."

Feshka and VelMud vanished on the trail ahead. "Our party grows smaller," VeratNonn reminded them. "Let us not run into any trouble."

The party began moving ahead as quickly as they could. Angus was frightened. Tristan's face had turned ashen gray. Angus glanced back at his father. William wore a grim look of determination. Scobie's expression was passive but he pressed on with the others. Angus noticed Scobie was now carrying Ingram's pack.

"This is hopeless," Angus called out to Marnel, who was just ahead of him. "Wouldn't it make more sense to stand and face the four behind us, than to rush headlong into the hundred ahead of us?"

"If there were only the four, yes," answered Marnel. "But we don't know what all is behind us. Arikin may be able to tell us when he returns."

"Arikin could be captured."

"No lone Elf could be captured by Ogladim," Marnel replied. "They harm us by attacking in force or by sneaking in the dark and attacking our camps and cities, like vermin. Arikin will be like a ghost to them. They won't even see him, and he's smart enough to avoid leaving his scent where they'll find it."

"But there was a concern that there may be other creatures with the Ogladim," Angus reminded her.

Marnel glanced back at him again. "He will be safe," she reassured him, but Angus could see the fear in her eyes. Aelrondenne did not join the conversation. Angus could see her back stiffen as Marnel answered him. He had never seen an Elf express fear. If they were afraid, then the group must be in serious danger. Angus checked to make sure his sword would easily come free of its sheath. He felt for his Skyn Dhu, the knife his father had retrieved for him from the place of the Geketz's attack. He knew it would not harm a Geketz, but the Ogladim were not so supernatural.

The other side of the mountain had trees, as though it had warmer winds or perhaps more rainfall. Angus eyed the trees suspiciously. Anything could be concealed behind them. As they descended, the forest grew thicker. Underbrush concealed the lower tree trunks. Small animals began to appear and there were tracks in some places, from squirrels or some other rodent. Angus wasn't sure.

The party was tense. There was no conversation as before. All were intent on scanning the forest, watching for some fierce enemy to leap at them from the trees. Angus was developing a new respect for the girls. Aelrondenne and Marnel led the group as swiftly as before, never faltering or expressing any hesitation. Aelrondenne had gone farther ahead, watching for any sign of danger. But she stayed within sight of the rest of the group.

"The main fear now," said Marnel, "is beasts. Aelrondenne saw none to be feared when she came this way before, but an Oglat scout may have picked up her scent. If so there may be dangers here that she didn't see."

Angus did not pass this information back to the others. He kept a watch behind him as they traveled. He was concerned about his father. None of them had ever traveled like this through the mountain trails, and at such a hurried pace. He was fearful and jumpy about the unknown dangers. A rabbit had been hiding beside the trail and when Angus spooked it, he had his Skyn Dhu in his hand before he knew it.

He heard laughter behind him. It was VeratNonn and BarNeesh. Then Mishishel and PoleeShimel began chuckling. William and Ingram were between them and had not seen the rabbit, but they heard the noise. "What was that?" William called ahead.

Marnel turned quickly, indicating silence with a motion of her hand and a stern expression. "We must be as silent as possible," she cautioned Angus. "There is no way of knowing what may be in the forest around us. Let us not announce our presence with foolishness. Pass it on to the others."

Mishishel and PoleeShimel indicated they'd heard her. William already knew what she was talking about. Mishishel turned to William and said in hushed tones, "It was a rabbit."

Aelrondenne who was still ahead of them, stopped to wait for them to catch up. "The camp is getting too close for comfort." Let's wait here for Arikin."

"Maybe we should get off the path and wait in the forest where we won't be so easily seen," suggested Mishishel.

They left the path for the forest. The thickness of it surprised Angus. After hiking so many miles with no trees at all, the plush leaves were refreshing. Aelrondenne and Marnel both insisted that the group move well away from the path so they wouldn't be seen or smelled. Aelrondenne stayed closer, to watch for any passersby, welcome or unwelcome.

"What do you think happened to VelMud and Feshka?" Angus asked Marnel.

"There's no way we can know that yet. Aelrondenne thinks they left the path. She said she hasn't seen a sign of them, including footprints in the last hour."

"That's just great," retorted Angus. "Now we've lost them. Arikin is somewhere behind, Feshka and VelMud are either ahead or behind, and here we are close enough to the path to be found by our scent. I feel like we should be doing something other than sitting here waiting."

Just then Aelrondenne came running back to them from the path. She looked frightened and was breathing hard. "Be extra quiet. Someone is coming." She disappeared again in the direction of the path.

The group settled to the ground exchanging glances. Everyone was frightened. VeratNonn had his hand on the hilt of his sword and was glowering in the direction of the path. BarNeesh was beside him, dagger drawn. Almost absentmindedly, he was testing the blade with his finger. He too was watching. Mishishel and PoleeShimel each were clutching a bow they had pulled from their packs. Their arrows were still sheathed but the quiver covers were removed so they could easily extract their arrows.

William was standing beside a tree that he could step behind. His Skyn Dhu was in his hand in readiness. Tristan couldn't seem to make up his mind how best to be ready. He had his hand on the hilt of his Elf blade and was pulling it partway out, then pushing it back in. Ingram and Scobie were squatting on the ground, not sure of what to expect, their faces tense.

Not a sound could be heard from them, not even breathing. It was as silent as though they weren't there. Angus listened to the forest sounds, trying to detect anything unnatural. He could find nothing. This made him even more nervous. There should be some sound indicating the presence of the intruder, something louder or different than the background sounds. A twig snapped to the right of the direction they were all watching. All eyes turned. It was Aelrondenne and with her was Arikin. The two looked at them and chuckled. Angus looked around to see the cause of their amusement. He saw that every one of them was ready for a battle, including himself. Swords were drawn, arrows cued and ready to fire. Ingram was in a crouched position, ready to spring forward. Scobie was on his feet with his Elf blade held high. The tension of the group was obvious.

"It's only us," whispered Aelrondenne. "Let's hear what Arikin has to tell us."

"Where are Feshka and VelMud?" asked Arikin.

"They went ahead to search for the Haven," answered Marnel. There are more Ogladim ahead and not far away."

Arikin lowered his head as though to consider what he had been told. He brought his palms to his forehead and held his head for a moment. "There's little time to lose. The Ogladim have found our trail and they're coming faster than before. They're not far behind me. If VelMud and Feshka aren't here, we can't wait for them. I hope they're safe. The song says that from this path where the land slopes to the south and the east, there is a narrow river. When we find the river we must follow it upstream to a falls. Let us be on our way, quickly."

Arikin set out, beckoning the others to follow, forward and to the left. "Come now," he called back to them over his shoulder. "The Ogladim will be in this place very soon!"

The Dwarves were the last to follow. The sun was on its way to the horizon and darkness would be upon them soon. Angus wondered which would find them first, the Ogladim or the darkness. Arikin followed no path this time, but he kept up just as quick a pace as before. Ingram was having a problem again. The forest floor was strewn with fallen limbs and rocks. Ingram was tripping and stumbling, trying to half-run to keep up with Arikin.

"Slow down a little, Arikin," Marnel called to him. "The Humans are having a hard time keeping up!"

"If they don't keep up they will die. The Ogladim behind us have a Geketz and swine. If they catch us after dark we will have little chance of escape and the darkness is as close as the Ogladim. *Hurry!!*"

Tristan was by Ingram's side in an instant. "Give me your pack again, Ingram. You must keep up. Even the Dwarves are ahead of you."

Ingram answered with a curse and handed his pack to Tristan. Angus dropped back to join them. When William saw this, he also joined them, followed by Scobie. "We've got to stick together and help Ingram if he needs it. Come now, we must hurry to not lose the Elf."

With the heavy pack off his back Ingram was better on his feet and soon they began to gain on the Elf. "Let's not get too close," puffed Ingram, "he'll speed up more."

"Not so," Aelrondenne exclaimed. She had come back with the Humans to help watch over them. "He won't leave us behind."

"I don't think he wants to," Angus added.

"He's as frightened as you are," declared Aelrondenne. "A Geketz is very dangerous to us. It can come close without our seeing it, yet it can see us easily because of our light. Even with our covers it can see us in the dark, but we hope not as well. Come, we must hurry!"

As the ground fell away, the underbrush seemed to thin slightly for a while and there was less debris. Angus could hear running water ahead of them. Arikin was nearly out of sight but Marnel had lagged behind him to keep in touch with the others in the party. Angus could see her not too far ahead, looking back at them as she hurried to keep Arikin in sight.

"Why this damnable hurrying?" insisted William. "I don't hear a sound behind us and I see no reason to fear."

"Arikin said they were near us and they had picked up our scent. That means they're hurrying to catch up to take us. He also said they have swine. The swine can run faster than we can, and they have keener scent than the Ogladim. If we don't hurry they'll be upon us," answered Aelrondenne. "It's also possible they sent word ahead, for help in finding us. Instead of four or five Ogladim we may well have a hundred and four or five."

He knew the situation. He only wanted to grumble a little, like Ingram was doing. With the scolding from Aelrondenne, even Ingram stopped mumbling to himself and concentrated on keeping up with the others. Soon the Humans had Arikin in sight again.

The ground finally stopped dropping and leveled off. Angus soon saw why. The river at the bottom of the ravine had washed a wide flood plain.

"The songs say to go upstream from here, but I can't see why," Arikin shook his head, bewildered. "I choose to follow the song." He turned left and hurried off into the gathering darkness, following the stream.

"I wish he could travel a little slower," complained William. "My legs feel like they're about to drop off."

"Tell me about it," Ingram chimed in. "Mine already have."

The party turned to the left to follow Arikin. Mishishel and the others had surprised the Humans with their ability to travel through the brush and forest so quickly. VeratNonn's jewelry had started tinkling with each step he took. Without breaking his stride, he took it all off, wrapped each piece in a cloth from his pocket and without a word, continued pumping his legs and carrying himself along behind Arikin.

Angus could now hear voices behind them. There was a shout and a loud sound that he couldn't identify. Then he heard many voices talking loudly. The distance was still great and he felt they had not been seen, but they knew the Ogladim were nearby. The others had grown silent and were walking as quickly as they could to keep up with the seemingly tireless Arikin.

Ahead, Angus could hear the sound of the water more loudly than before. A rapids. "Can you hear it, Tristan?"

"Yes," he answered. "It sounds like a falls."

"I think you're right," replied Angus. "It does sound like a falls. Do you hear the voices behind us?"

"How could I not? I don't know where we're going but we'd better be getting there fast!"

Ahead Angus could see that Arikin had stopped. As they all caught up to him, he indicated the high waterfall in front of them. "This is the place," he announced. "The Haven is under the falls. Follow me." Stepping across a few rocks over the water, he disappeared behind the falls. One by one they followed him into a cave hidden by the water.

When they were all inside Arikin said, "I thought I heard the voice of VelMud behind us, struggling with the Ogladim. Mishishel, PoleeShimel, BarNeesh and VeratNonn, Aelrondenne and Marnel, now that we've found this place, come with me to help VelMud and Feshka, that they may also reach safety."

Angus and Tristan jumped to their feet. "We'll come too," Tristan offered.

"You Humans can't see in the night. You are not accustomed to racing through the mountains and forests. I can see that you're tired. You may not make it back if you come. Stay here," Arikin ordered.

The Elves and Dwarves vanished into the night. Angus looked around to see where he was. The darkness was nearly complete; no light penetrated behind the wall of roaring water. It was surprisingly dry in the cave. The only moist areas were closest to the falls. The area behind them seemed like another cave. Angus wondered how deep it was, and after catching his breath, began feeling his way back.

"Angus," William called after him, "stay with us now and don't go wondering off. We're alone in this place. Anything could happen. You don't know what might be back in there. If there's fighting you should be here with us."

His father was right. He too was tired and ready to rest with the others. "This place seems safe enough."

"The rocks we stepped on to get in here were wet," said Scobie. "It seemed that the water was splashing over them. No scent will stay on them after being washed."

"That's for sure," Ingram agreed, relieved to be able to sit down with the prospect of sleeping for a while.

"What if Arikin and the others are overcome by the Ogladim"?" asked Tristan.

"That's something I'd rather not think about right now." William stretched out, making himself as comfortable as possible. "They seemed to know what they were doing. Let them."

Angus listened to the sound of the waterfall, upset... and troubled... angry and frustrated. How could he have gotten himself into such a situation? His life and the lives of the others depended on the success of the Elves and Dwarves who had gone off to fight for them. But no. They had gone to help Feshka and VelMud. He should have gone also. He and Tristan could have helped them, and here they were, sitting in the darkness and hiding, like women. At least it was consistent with the rest of his failures. He began running through the litany he had developed for himself, to support him in his self-pity.

By the time Arikin and the others returned, he was so lost in his fears and misgivings, at first he didn't hear them enter. Then there was so much noise and confusion, it took him a few seconds to figure out what was going on. He saw only the flashing of Elf Steel. Then he heard the squealing of at least one pig followed by another. In the light he saw the last of the group entering behind the waterfall. A swine had followed VeratNonn. Letting loose with a string of invectives, Verat-Nonn decapitated it, and as it fell he kicked it into the water. Another one followed VelMud into the cave and was immediately dispatched by VeratNonn, who was apparently taking great pleasure in the slaughter.

Finally they were all inside. Scobie started to speak but was cut off by Arikin. "We can talk later. The area is filled with swine and Ogladim. The Geketz was right behind me when I entered the cave."

"I got the Geketz," grinned VeratNonn. "It will trouble us no more."

"You killed it? How?" asked Marnel."

"These blades you call Elf Steel bit into its flesh as though it was another swine. Didn't you hear it squeal?"

"So the Elf Steel does what we had hoped!" exclaimed Arikin gleefully. We must get word to The City of The Vision about this as quickly as we can!"

They stopped talking. A light had appeared beyond the veil of water. They couldn't see what was carrying it or what sort of light it was, because the falling water distorted their vision.

The light danced closer to the waterfall and paused. In their imaginations they could all see different perspectives of the crowd of Ogladim that had gathered beyond. Some saw them as heavily armed and others saw only dark shadows. The Elves knew if the Ogladim found the entrance to the cave, it would be impossible to resist them. The Humans thought the entrance to the cave was magically concealed.

The pool under the falls was wider than the river itself, and wider than the falls. The river's water spilled from a cliff high above, straight down in an almost unbroken fall. In daylight if any of them had moved, they would have been detected from the outside. Anyone hiding inside would have to remain perfectly still to remain concealed. But at night, the waterfall served as a shield because it reflected the light back on the group. Also, the stepping stones were far apart and not obviously placed. *Good thing pigs can't talk,* Angus thought.

The Ogladim were puzzled. Where had the Elves gone? The Ogladim leader had ridden in behind them on one of the hogs. He was now pacing in front of the waterfall beside the stream. His torch reflected off the water, making the river and waterfall look totally black. Maybe the party had somehow scaled the cliff and was laughing at them from above. Maybe they had somehow crossed the stream and were even now climbing away from them on the opposite hillside. Clearly, he had lost them. GaudarKahn would be angry.

No one took GaudarKahn's anger lightly. "Pitch camp," he ordered the others. "We'll find them in the morning."

Chapter Twelve: The Castle

Angus and the others watched the light beyond the waterfall. It moved around like a firefly, but they all knew this flickering was hardly innocent. No sound could be heard over the roaring water and nothing was visible inside the cave but the flickering light on the screen of water before them. They knew the Ogladim were still out there. Then there was a second light; this one stayed in the same place. Apparently the Ogladim had built a fire and were setting up a camp.

Angus's eyes were becoming accustomed to the darkness. The light shining through the falls was providing just enough illumination for him to begin to see shadows. The first shadow he saw was Arikin's. He was standing by the narrow entrance to the cavity behind the falls, his sword carefully sheathed to conceal its light. He was covered with the wrap of the Elves to conceal his own light. Angus too was covered up. They all were, except for the Humans and the Dwarves.

VeratNonn was standing behind Arikin with a long dagger in his hand. The dagger was of iron and cast by the Dwarves in the Southerlands. It gave off no light. VelMud was resting, farther inside the cave. Feshka was beside him and seemed to be tending to a wound on VelMud's arm.

No sound could be heard over the water. What were the Ogladim doing out there? Had they figured out where the Elves and men were hiding? They had no interest in the Dwarves except for their interference in protecting the Elves, since Dwarves had no value to their Master, GaudarKahn. They were simply regarded as a nuisance. But they made good slaves. They were strong and hard workers, taking pleasure in their handiwork of weapons of hardened iron and their homes in the caves of the Southerlands. They could dig caves for GaudarKahn someday, but for now the leader of the Ogladim was interested only in the Elves and the value of their light. Light is power and power is control.

⤙❧

Agri-ifone paced angrily. As the leader of this Kaduetza of the Ogladim, he was expected to bring information to GaudarKahn. His orders were to harass and tease the Elves only. He was permitted to kill as he pleased but he was not to attack directly. His force was too small. He was not to lose his warriors to the Elves until it "was time" and that time was not yet but would be soon.

Booreetza, the watch, had said that he saw the Naver with this group, but no one else had seen him. GaudarKahn also had his methods of scrying. None among the Ogladim or even the OeberKaduetzim knew how he did it, but he was usually right in his projections. If the Naver was at large, then he had to be captured. GaudarKahn wanted him badly.

The description was sketchy. Booreetza wasn't sure, but he said the human had the right markings, the bright red hair and the scars. Agri-ifone was outraged and frustrated at his failure to capture the party. His rage was driven by fear; if he came this close and failed, not only would he not win the award offered by GaudarKahn; he would probably also be punished. Those who failed GaudarKahn usually were severely punished.

He had won the status of OeberKaduetza only half a year ago by demonstrating cunning. All the Ogladim by nature had valor, so no reward was given for duty performed. But if an Oglat proved intelligent, he received recognition. If he didn't follow orders, however, he was killed, sometimes cruelly. Agri-ifone did not fear death. None of them did. What they feared was continuing to live while GaudarKahn killed them.

All that was not an issue right now. They were now focused on finding and capturing the party they had found that night. They had word that some had left The City of The Vision and their orders were to capture and kill all of them except the Naver; he was to be brought to GaudarKahn alive.

Agri-ifone sat down on the riverbank to think. They had found two traveling alone. The Naver was not with them. They pursued the two for an hour and then suddenly there were five of them. Booreetza had reported eleven travelers, some Elves, some Humans, and two Dwarves.

So there were eleven, then there were two, then there were five. How many parties of Elves and Dwarves were roaming the woods tonight? Where had they all gone? There could be as many as eighteen that he knew of, or as few as eleven.

The five had fled to this riverbank, then turned north. They had the swine pursue them, but the swine could run faster than the Ogladim, so none saw where they went. He himself had ridden a swine and was in the thick of it, but he'd also lost sight of the five. They'd just disappeared. How could five Elves disappear? It was impossible. If they had climbed the cliff by the falls they would have been seen. Even if they'd climbed a rope, they would have been visible for awhile. He would have seen them.

If they had crossed the water they would have left a boat that would have been seen by now. Maybe they sank the boat on the other side and fled into the forest. Maybe they had some kind of watercraft that folded up, and they carried it with them for the next time. They could have done that. They were so skilled in weaving the grasses. They could make a floating weave that could carry five. None had ever heard of Elves doing that before, but he remembered the stories of the escape from YeePhraWaine. The Elves had sailing ships that used the wind to push them. The wind pushed them wherever they wanted to go. Amazing, these Elves.

And where did they get the ships they used, to flee GaudarKahn at YeePhraWaine? They made them of woven grasses, of course. The grasses seemed to obey the will of the Elves. How could they command grass, Agri-ifone wondered, tossing his torch into the stream?

The night passed slowly. Agri-ifone sat in the darkness listening to the same sound that filled Angus's ears. The Ogladim were scattered and sleeping on the ground. The swine were sleeping too, mixed in with the others. The area smelled foul, but it was a smell that Agri-ifone was used to, one to which he himself contributed. He was tired, but his anger kept him from joining the others in sleep. He felt they were nearby. He could feel them. They had to be holed up somewhere close. He scanned the treetops thinking, maybe they had climbed into the trees to hide. That would be a good hiding place because the swine never look up. Neither did the Ogladim, unless they were climbing a tree like Booreetza did when he was watching the path today.

Carefully he inspected every tree near him, watching for places where the night sky didn't show through the leaves and branches. He saw nothing. Then he began to wonder if perhaps one of the trees was hollow. He'd heard of Elves hiding in hollow trees, but he'd never seen it done. That was an easy question to settle. None of the trees near him were thick enough to contain five Elves, much less eleven. He guessed there were eighteen of them altogether. They had seen eleven, then two, then five. Elves were tricky that way. But was the Naver an Elf? Booreetza had said it was a Human, but Elfkin.

❦

Angus had questions too, as had everyone in his party. One of the biggest questions troubling everyone present, except Feshka and Arikin, was when the Ogladim would figure out where they were. Angus felt no one could be so stupid as to not realize there was a cave behind the falls. Where else could they have gone?

Another question troubling Angus, Arikin and Feshka concerned the Geketz. If there is a second Geketz where was it? They knew a Geketz would be unwilling to come too close to the water, but it had to be out there when the fighting was going on. Why didn't it tell the Ogladim where they had gone? Then a thought came to Angus that frightened him much worse than the other one. Maybe it already had told them and they were waiting for morning before coming after them. Were they trapped in the cave? Where could they go if the Ogladim rushed them en masse?

Arikin left his post at the entrance and slipped slowly back through the group until he was completely past them. He continued back into the darkness of the cave. Angus could barely see in the dimness and soon lost sight of him. He noticed VeratNonn had also begun moving in that direction. Then he too was out of sight. *Well*, thought Angus grimly, *if there's a bear back there, we'll all soon find out.*

After what seemed like a long time, Arikin came back out of the darkness. He whispered something into the ear of the person farthest from the entrance and closest to the back of the cave. It was Mishishel. Then Mishishel passed the message on to the next person and that one to the next and down through the group until it got to Angus: "Very slowly, one at a time, as quietly as possible, start working your way back into the darkness. Make sure that you are well covered so no light may be seen from you. Keep your sword covered, and come."

Shortly the entire party was far back into the darkness of the cave. They felt their way as best as they could. The Elves seemed to walk as though they could see where they were going. Angus could see only vague outlines of those ahead of him. He could hear nothing but the roaring of the waterfall and soon that too dimmed. "Where are we going?" he whispered to whoever was in front of him.

"I have no idea," came Scobie's voice softly. "It looks like the Elves have something up their sleeves we don't know about."

Soon the path through the cave started climbing. It grew steeper until it was nearly straight up, like the path they had followed up the mountain. The progress slowed and Angus had to wait every few minutes for Scobie to make his way after the others. Then he would follow. Suddenly Angus realized he was standing under the night sky. Verat-Nonn and BarNeesh were beside him urging him to keep going. When everyone was out of the cave, Arikin counted them. After he was satisfied, he nodded to VeratNonn. As Angus watched, it seemed that the mouth of the cave closed and what had been a dark opening was now just solid ground. Angus blinked his eyes and looked again. William stepped onto the place and stamped his foot. "Well I'll be damned," he declared.

Marnel was standing next to Angus. "The Dwarves' reputation for working with Earth and Rock is well earned," she smiled.

Arikin was nearby and motioned to them, whispering, "Let's go. We have yet a long way to the next Haven." He set off through woods at a rapid pace, but not as fast as when he'd fled from the Ogladim earlier.

"Oh no," moaned Ingram. "I thought we'd get a chance for a little rest in there."

"Some rest," retorted Scobie, "with death at the door."

"It's a soldier's life for now," added William. "There may be time for rest later."

"Arikin says to keep it quiet for a while. There's no way to know what's ahead of us or near us," Aelrondenne cautioned. They stopped talking and walked... and walked... and walked. The terrain wasn't as rough as what they had already crossed before, but the problem now was fatigue. Even the Elves seemed subdued. The bounce was out of Marnel's walk. Aelrondenne lagged behind, but Angus thought it may well be to watch their rear rather than out of fatigue. Arikin's pace was gradually slowing. They were tired but afraid to stop for rest in the open forest.

When they had emerged from the ground, Angus could hear the falls again. It seemed they had crossed the river and were well on the other side, away from the Ogladim and upstream. Maybe the Geketz was still over there too. Had they escaped completely? No sounds emerged from the forest other than those made by the little animals. They could see no lights anywhere and the noise from the river had faded in the distance.

They had climbed back up into the hills. Arikin led them south, as before. After several hours of sneaking along as quietly as possible, Marnel dropped back to join him. "Since we're following no path, it's less likely we'll be seen. Arikin thinks we were seen on the path before.

He says it's unlikely that the camp I found would not post someone to watch to see who might be approaching. Now he thinks we're safe for awhile."

"Where are we going?" asked Angus. "How far is the Firth?"

"Half a day from here," guessed Marnel. "Arikin had thought to go first to the head of the Great Glen. We are working our way west to watch for boats or ships that the Enemy may have sent."

"Why am I along on this journey?" Angus asked. "What good can I do here? I'm only in danger as you are. For that matter, why did you come? If all they wanted was information, Arikin could have done it alone much more easily. This way all of us are in greater danger."

"You are the one in the Vision," Marnel reminded him. "How could it be otherwise? You are the one who will lead us home."

"That's crazy," exploded Angus. "I'm just a shepherd! I'm in more danger from this sword I carry than those I might try to attack. I told you it wasn't me!"

"None can say what the fates may decree for you, StrathNaver, not even you. The winds will blow where they will, but the course a man follows is decreed by a Greater Power. He doesn't even tell us, the Elves, what is in his mind. Sometimes he gives us a Vision like the ones in the Tapestry. You have seen it."

"But I'm telling you, it's not me," Angus insisted. "The picture in the Weave is the Rebeck Ariel, just as the others think. It's not me!"

"What is to be is up to thee," Marnel smiled. "I believe in you Strath-Naver, just as Lurelei does!"

Mention of her sister's name set Angus off again. *Where is Lurelei now? Probably wondering through the woods this very minute, killing squirrels and rabbits. How can I save her?*

Marnel sensed his mood change and said nothing for a few minutes. First light was near; they had been up all night. Angus was going into his second day with hardly any sleep. His eyes felt dry and his stomach tight. He wondered how long he could go without sleep. Maybe tonight they'd have a chance for a few hours.

The land started to drop again. Apparently they'd picked up a path leading down through a narrow glen. Arikin had gone on ahead again to watch for danger. Another encampment of Ogladim could be below. There was no way to know without going to look. Aelrondenne took the lead again as before.

"This is how it started yesterday," Angus remarked to Marnel. "He went ahead, then behind. Aelrondenne then went ahead and soon all hell broke loose. I hope he finds nothing ahead of us."

"He looks for the next Haven. There is one on the north side of the

Great Glen," Marnel told him. "We think it should be clear of any danger."

The sun had risen and the path was now descending more steeply. The forest was thick with pine trees and pine needles on the ground cushioned their footsteps so they were able to walk more quietly, even though occasionally someone would slip and then slide a few feet.

Angus was now getting glimpses of a large body of water ahead of them, below. Its deep blue reflected the sky above. Angus thought he could even see some clouds reflected on its surface.

For a short time, the glen they were following took a turn away from the water. Its depth between the rising ridges allowed less light to penetrate through the trees. The sudden shadows made Angus shiver slightly. He wondered what had happened to Arikin. Would he make it back to rejoin them this time? No sooner had the thought occurred than Arikin appeared from below. His walk was slow and casual. This was a relief to Angus. Yesterday when Arikin came back to them he had been out of breath and hot from running. But the news he brought today wasn't much better than yesterday's.

"There's a black ship," Arikin told them. "It's not as big as we feared, but it's a ship nevertheless. It seems that few are on board. It's anchored by the old castle. I think there are more Ogladim there."

"It makes sense," mused Mishishel. "If they're close to land they would probably rather sleep on solid ground than on a rolling boat."

"This boat you speak of--was it big enough to carry a hundred?"

"I think so," answered Arikin, "and over the sea as well."

"Are you sure there was only one boat?" asked Feshka.

"I saw only one, but there could be another around the point.

"Let's go and get it," declared Mishishel. "With a boat we don't have to walk the length of the Great Glen."

"Go and get it?" Angus turned to Mishishel in astonishment.

"What do you mean by 'go and get it?'" retorted Ingram. "Are we just going to go and ask them for it?"

"That's a hell of a note," fumed William. "How many Ogladim do you think are down there?"

"There aren't many in the boat," Arikin reassured them. "It shouldn't be too hard to do. We'll have to slip up on them from the west side. The east has a lot of cover and they'd probably be watching it, but the west side is more open. They'll be less careful there."

"What if there are more than you think on the boat?" asked Ingram. "What if we can't take it and they take us instead? I don't think I like this plan."

"If there are too many, we'll have to create a diversion to draw them off of it," said Arikin. "My father would enjoy a game like this one. Let's move on."

Angus had forgotten that Arikin was indeed the son of the Rebeck of the Firthlands and these were the Firthlands. Even though he was tired, he started off in the direction of the Lake after the others, eager to see what Arikin had in mind.

Even in its ruined state, one could tell that at one time the old castle must have been beautiful. Its walls had mostly fallen and the main hall was exposed to the elements. Its only remaining tower on the east side overlooked the lake; its roof had collapsed. Old King Brude's bedchamber was no longer capable of sheltering even the wrens that summered there. The servants' quarters were below the main level and the path was obstructed by fallen building blocks and other rubble. The rooms below would be inaccessible to the Ogladim without extensive physical labor.

The earthwork done under the instruction of old King Brude's Masons still stood but it was overrun with bushes and trees that had not been permitted to grow there in the days of the Castle's splendor. To the west the earth dropped away, leaving only the rocky beach of the lake. To the east the land sloped out toward the lake and was overgrown like the rest of the castle grounds. Trees had been growing there for more than a hundred years, since the castle had fallen to some unknown lord of a now forgotten city lying at the eastern mouth of the lake.

The castle was no longer remembered by any except the Elves and water creatures that lived in its shadow. Vines crept up the sides of its thick high foundation. A second tower on the west side was in ruins. Only its original base could be seen, and there an OeberKaduetzim had set up a small cot. Most of the rest of his crew were scattered in the mountain seeking a small band of Elves. Earlier he had received a message that the group consisted of Elves, Dwarves and Humans... strange indeed to hear that those species were in each other's company.

He waited in peace, guarding the small ship in which they had arrived. He expected the hundred to be back by the end of the day with the Humans who would be given to GaudarKahn for slave labor. The Elves would be dead and the Dwarves probably dead too, since they were such fierce fighters. But he hoped some would have been captured with the Humans. Dwarves made excellent slaves. BooGraTom liked Dwarves. They were tough, hard to kill. Because of their hardiness he could torture and tease them all he liked without being concerned for their lives. They swore well too. BooGraTom loved nothing better than forcing a Dwarf to tunnel, while driving them with a spiked whip.

The day had been like the others he had spent in this old stone fort. The remaining crew he had kept to watch over the boat lay scattered around the castle grounds. There were six of them counting two on the boat itself. They caught a rat here or a rabbit there to lunch on. They weren't much at fishing although the lake seemed to be teaming with fish. He wondered idly what kind of fish they were when he heard splashes now and then, when fish would jump out of the water, rising too fast for a floating bug.

BooGraTom thought himself a good leader of the Oglats or Ogladim. He only killed his soldiers when they failed to obey quickly enough. He knew of others who killed for pleasure, but he feared the anger of GaudarKahn. If he came back with too few of those he took with him, he could be punished. GaudarKahn knew OeberKaduetzim sometimes killed their own for pleasure but he thought it humorous unless it interfered with his own plans. GaudarKahn had plenty of Ogladim and there were plenty more to be had.

The Humans he expected to be captured would probably be future Ogladim. The conversion process was cheap and fast; it had been done to him a long time ago. It was similar to converting an Elf to a Geketz. They hated the process but it was fun to watch and they were more useful afterwards.

He glanced to the west again. The area was mostly open and he didn't want the stupid soldiers he commanded to be near him, so he ordered them to watch the east and north walls. The east side was heavily wooded with plenty of cover. It would be easy for a foe to slip up on them from that side. The west approach to the castle had only scrub bushes along the banks. No one could approach unseen, which is why he chose this spot for himself.

BooGraTom was enjoying the leisure. The sun felt good although it was now slipping into the sea to the west of them. He'd had a good sleep that day while he was watching the west wall, and would sleep well again that night.

He was unconcerned. The hundred had scoured the countryside around the castle before heading into the mountains to pick up the scouts. The Geketz was to remain. No one was found living near the castle and there was no sign of any Elves. It was pointless to watch for an attack, since no one was near.

BooGraTom enjoyed watching the moon rising off the lake. A night bird sang in the distance and he could hear one lone cricket on the rocky beach below where the water would sometimes lap up as far as the castle's foundation. He glanced out over the water and saw that the black ship was riding peacefully. The two Ogladim who were watching the boat had traded with two from the castle. Even duty on the boat was easy, since they knew no enemies were near.

The two on the boat had eaten well and were sleeping soundly. BooGraTom felt that was all right. One more peaceful night would be just fine. They would have plenty of hard days ahead and going into them well rested would be to their advantage. BooGraTom thought maybe he should make the two on the boat stay awake and keep an actual watch, but he was too comfortable to bother getting up.

The remaining four Ogladim were distanced from him, thankfully. Two were on the high tower watching to the east and the other two were at the old entrance to the castle. It was useless now as an entrance, of course. One needed only to step over the wall to enter the former interior. BooGraTom could see one of them standing just beyond the castle's gate.

The cricket from down below chirped one more time. The sound annoyed him now because he wanted to go to sleep.

That was BooGraTom's last conscious thought. VeratNonn had slipped up on him in the darkness and with his long dagger had half cut off BooGraTom's head. The motion was silent and swift. The OeberKaduetzim didn't even gurgle as he died. At the same instant Arikin slipped in behind the Ogladim standing guard by the castle's gate. Arikin had a garrote. It wasn't a weapon he preferred. Actually he preferred to not kill at all, as did most Elves, but when necessary, he killed without hesitation. The garrote was fast and silent. He hated having to get so close to the Oglat, but later he could wash in the lake.

The two remaining in the tower had not seen the silent actions of VeratNonn and Arikin. They were fighting over who got to eat the last dead rat they had caught. VeratNonn waited at the foot of the tower with BarNeesh. They had argued that one of them could easily handle the two guards above, but the Elves insisted it would be better to use two to do the job. Others would go after the two in the boat.

Angus and the rest of the troop were waiting just north of the fort on the hillside, with Feshka. They had been there since before sunset. Tristan was whittling a stick he had picked up. The others were sleeping. It was Tristan's job to make sure none of them started snoring loudly. That would be enough to give them all away. They were close enough for Tristan to hear the same cricket in the distance that BooGraTom had been listening to.

It was Arikin's opinion that the Ogladim they had encountered the night before probably spent the day searching for them, but that wasn't certain. No sign had been seen or heard of them all day. Now, near the fort, they were particularly cautious. They thought the band might show up at any time. They had seen smoke in the distance before the sun went down and Arikin thought it might be them.

"Could be anybody," VeratNonn shrugged.

"Not in these times," VelMud frowned. "It's probably them. We should thank them for telling us where they are. They'll probably be here in late morning."

"I wonder why there were so many of them," Marnel mused. "If they were coming to pick up a small scouting party, why would they need so many?"

"Maybe they know we still have the ships we used, to leave Yee-PhraWaine," said Feshka. "They could be expecting trouble from us at sea."

"The Enemy should know by now that we're not using any ships. He probably won't send so many again for such a reason," countered Arikin.

"Do you really think that's why he sent so many?" Aelrondenne glanced from one to the other.

"How could any of us know his mind?" exclaimed Arikin. "There are as many as there are. We have at least a hundred to deal with."

Tristan was reviewing this conversation as he whittled his stick. Ingram had started snoring twice so far. It was easy to make him stop. He just gave him a push and Ingram rolled over onto his side and stopped. "I hope they're having as easy a time below," Tristan said to himself.

The cricket Tristan had been hearing in the distance stopped its song. In a few minutes he heard the signal to come down to the castle. It was the call of a sea bird. It cried twice, then silence, then three times. Tristan woke the others.

The castle had a terrible smell about it. "That's the blood of the Ogladim. Their blood is filthy," Feshka grimaced. "The others are below," he pointed over the castle wall at the beach below. "Come this way," he motioned, heading toward the low wall of the west side.

Angus and the others followed. Angus started when he saw the headless dead body of BooGraTom, but he held his breath to avoid the odor and stepped over the wall after Feshka and the others. The beach below was strewn with pebbles and course sand. "This is the Haven I mentioned," said Arikin when they had all gathered. "Watch this."

Carefully he began feeling the rocks of the castle's foundation. After a few minutes he cried out, "Here it is!" He pressed hard on one of them. The rock gave way to reveal a low door. "Inside, now, all of you!"

Once inside, Arikin pushed on the other side of the stone and it rolled back into place. As an extra measure, Arikin placed a rock wedge against the underside of the large stone to keep it from being opened from the outside. "The Elves of the Valley Ness, which this is, built this

Haven after Brude was driven out," he told them. "No one ever comes here."

"Are you sure this is a safe place?" asked Angus.

"Yes," Arikin reassured him. "It's very safe. The Ogladim will be here soon. I want to see that they get a safe departure," he added with a grim smile.

Angus was surprised to see there was enough moonlight coming in through the cracks in the foundation to make out the details of the room they were in. Beds were set up like bunks, in rows against the walls. In the center was a table with chairs and a lamp. On the floor beside the table was a clay bottle. "With oil?" he asked Arikin as he picked it up.

"Yes, but don't light it."

"What are we going to do in here?" Scobie asked. "This is going to be a long night."

"The bunks are there," Arikin pointed. "Sleep. And when the Ogladim arrive, I'll wake you. This will be fun to watch!"

"Why didn't you sink the boat?" asked Ingram. "I saw it out there on the lake. It looked like it was tied to a line of some sort."

"Yes. The line comes in to the shore so they can pull it in when they want it."

"So why didn't you sink it?"

"And what would we do with a hundred Ogladim terrorizing the countryside?" Arikin retorted.

"Well, they'll be here shortly, and what if they stay?" asked William.

"Watch and see," grinned Arikin. "Now, if you don't mind, I'd like to have a little rest, myself."

"Anybody know what this place is called?" asked Tristan.

"This is Castle Urquhart," answered Feshka.

The group settled down to sleep on the bunks. For the first time in days Angus felt safe. If the Ogladim stayed or left it meant nothing to him at this moment. He'd had no sleep since before they'd crested the last mountain, except for that brief nap on the hillside. He was out before his head hit the mat.

His first few hours of sleep were dreamless. But then he found himself walking on the pebbly beach of the lake, kicking stones into the water. The castle was nowhere to be seen and he didn't miss it. The water had a light chop whipped up by a strong westerly wind. He thought he heard birds in the distance but it could have been something else.

Not far ahead was a large rock resting in the sand. He decided to continue until he reached it, then sit there and watch the water lap the shore. As he walked toward it, he studied the sand for what might have washed up. When he was closer to the rock he looked up at it again then did a double take. It appeared there was an Elf sitting on that rock.

"Hello there, friend," Angus's dreaming self called out.

"Speak not, but listen, for time is short," answered the Elf. "And there is much to tell."

Angus had never before seen such an Elf as this one. Its clothing was one shade of gray. He was wearing a peaked hat that was also gray, perfectly matching the shade of his long pointed beard. His boots appeared to be made of leather, something that Elves never wore. To wear leather, something had to be killed. As Angus studied this creature, it began speaking. Angus usually couldn't remember much of what people said to him in his dreams so he paid little attention at first. But then he began listening carefully as soon as he caught a few words from the Elf's song:

Oh I'm the one of wisdom high
You seek to cure your Elf.
Yes I can tell as you draw nigh,
You've a burden for youself'.

Three woundes foul she has been given,
As many as woundes three,
And only one, by the god in Heaven,
Can be healed by such as thee.

For deep they are and festered well
So festered well are they
That magic not of any man
Shall make them go away.

But I am not a man, says me,
And I laugh at my own joke.
I'm an Elf and Forest Old.
I'll help remove the yoke.

Three magic gifts there are for thee,
With threefold Magic power,
For Lurelei the Elven Maid
That lovely Naver's Flower.

But heed this warning, mortal man,
As only once it's given.
Touch not these magics with thy hand
Or you'll be burned by heaven.

The Elf began to fade into the mist of the night. Angus could see through him as though he was a ghost, but Angus needed more information. He was confused as it was, and not sure what to ask. But he thought quickly enough in his dream to ask at least this:

How then, Old Sire, can I these gifts
Deliver to my lady,
If I must not lay hand on them
Or touch them to my body?

The Elf replied without hesitation:

Thou must advance yet more, my son,
Than I can now impart.
Your dreaming self must carry them
And lay them in her heart.

The Elf was gone. Angus was again alone on the pebbly beach. Then he drifted back into dreamless sleep. Some time later, a hand on his shoulder drew him gently from sleep. He jumped in fear, then caught himself from calling out. It was Marnel who had awakened him. "Come and see this!" she urged.

It was full daylight. The sun's rays were streaming into the small room under the castle and Angus could see clearly. "When they got here, it must have been an hour ago," Marnel said. "They raised a lot of noise. I was afraid they would wake you. They found the dead we had left for them. We didn't want them to waste any of our time while they hunted for them so we left them in plain sight. You should have heard them yelling!"

Angus had gone to one of the cracks to peek outside. The boat was full of Ogladim. They had raised a sail and were slowly making their way out into the lake. "The lake is very deep, StrathNaver," she said. "No one knows how deep."

Angus watched as the boat drifted before the east wind. As it went farther out over the lake, it also began making its way west toward the sea. When it was well off and into the deepest part of the lake, Arikin pushed the stone door open.

"Wait," warned Ingram. "They'll see you."

"I hope they do," declared Arikin. "So they know who sent them to their deaths."

He strolled out into the daylight. Then he pulled a flute out of his jerkin and started to play a melody. The Ogladim saw him and began shouting. Slowly the boat turned toward shore, but it was too late. As Arikin played, the boat began to sink. Angus saw an Oglat pick up a piece of wadded grass and throw it into the water with disgust. Arikin continued to play. Within moments, the boat had sunk beneath the lake's choppy surface. The Ogladim disappeared from sight.

"After the guards were killed," VelMud explained, "Arikin cut wide holes in the bottom of the boat. As he did that, Aelrondel filled the holes with woven grass. She instructed the grass to hold back the water. Then they covered the woven grass with whatever they found available, so the holes wouldn't be seen. The sound of Arikin's flute released the grass from its charm and the water filled the boat."

Angus did not miss the change in Aelrondenne's name. She was now Aelrondel. *She will be pleased*, he thought as he walked outside into the open sunlight, smiling.

Chapter Thirteen: Havens

The party did not remain at Castle Urquhart because of the stench left by the dying Ogladim. They gathered their things and headed west along the lake's shore. "Our task is to see what's here," said Arikin. "It's doubtful that we would be as lucky as we were this last time, if we find another ship, but we must know if there are more."

"How did the boat come to sink?" asked William.

"Yes," Ingram chimed in. "That was quite lucky if you ask me."

"It was lucky that we didn't have to wait longer for them to leave," exclaimed Aelrondel. "We thought they'd spend another day searching for us before they left."

"What was that trick with the flute?" asked Scobie.

"I used to have a flute," said Tristan, "but it wouldn't do anything like that."

"It wasn't the flute, but the tune," Arikin told him as they walked along the pebbly beach. Then he explained how it was done.

A path led along the lake, then wandered off the beach and out of sight. "Where to now?" asked Angus.

"We're going to walk the length of the lake, then come back on the other side. We're to see what's what in the Great Glen," Marnel told him.

"How much longer do you think this will take?" asked Tristan. "We've been walking for days."

"And days more it will be," responded William. "We're in a war. That's what soldiers do. They walk till their legs are shorter. Then they die in battle or starve to death on the way."

"There'll be no starving on this trip," declared VelMud. "We have plenty of food!"

"While it lasts," retorted Ingram.

"Mine'll last about a week," sighed Scobie.

"Then we'll have to stop and gather some more," Marnel stated matter-of-factly. "There's plenty in the forest all around us for those who know what to eat, and I do."

"Berries and nuts," grumbled Ingram. "A man can't live on berries and nuts."

"A man can live and live well on them," Marnel smiled. "What do you think is in the biscuits you've been eating these many days on the road?"

"She's right," agreed William. "They're not bad eating, either."

"We'll be tired of them soon enough," Ingram grumbled. "What I'd like right now is a good mutton chop."

"We'll have mutton enough when we get home," from Scobie.

"If we get home, you mean," Ingram added dourly.

And so it went for the day and a half it took to get to the end of the lake. Ingram and Scobie grumbled while William tried to look on the brighter side that was not visible to the other two.

Tristan was still eager to engage the Elf girls in conversation. He wanted to know everything about them, and asked again about their names, what they dreamed of, and on and on. Aelrondel and Marnel were patient with him, and even a little amused.

Angus stayed with Feshka, listening to the stories he had to tell and trying to learn a little of the Elf tongue. Feshka then suggested that Angus learn the Old Elf language instead of the current version they were speaking, since that was the language the Ogladim knew. None of them understood why the Enemy spoke Old Elf, and although most Elves could understand it, they couldn't speak it. Only Feshka and Mishishel also knew how to speak it.

At the word 'old' Angus remembered his dream and told it to Feshka. "Forest Old," Feshka told him, "is a legend among Elves today. It's his name but in all the stories he never tells it as though it is. He says it as though it's his age instead. It's a play on words that our myths say he loved."

"Myths?" repeated Angus.

"Oh yes. Forest Old is remembered in myth only. Some say he never existed and others say that stories of him are remembered to teach lessons. They are an allegory made up to teach and amuse children. Others say when an event becomes so old no one can remember it and no history records it, then it's remembered in stories which later come to be thought of as myths and therefore untrue."

"But I saw him," remonstrated Angus.

"Many have seen him over the centuries, but always in dreams," Feshka explained. "When this has happened it has always been said that the dreamer invented him from the stories, but you have never heard the stories, have you?"

"No," replied Angus. "Maybe the Dream Maker invented him for me!"

"The Great Glen has no Dream Maker, StrathNaver," Feshka shook his head. "There has been no Dream Maker in the Great Glen since the days of the Dwarf wars."

"We call them the Elf wars," VeratNonn chimed in sarcastically. "And you played a part, old fool."

"I will accept the name 'Old Fool' if we can begin to call it 'The War Between Friends,' and remember it in sorrow. How's that, VeratNonn?"

"Well said, Old Fool," agreed VeratNonn, thinking he had won some small victory and liking Feshka in spite of himself.

"The Dream Maker in the Great Glen was killed in the War between Friends," Feshka tried to conceal a smile. "The dream that came to you last night was not of that kind. Can you repeat what he said?"

Angus furrowed his brow trying to remember, then slowly he began:

Oh I'm the one of wisdom high
You seek to cure your Elf.
Yes I can tell as you draw nigh,
You've a burden for yourself.

Three woundes foul she has been given,
As many as woundes three,
And only one, by the God in Heaven,
Can be healed by such as thee.

For deep they are and festered well
So festered well are they
That magic not of any man
Shall make them go away.

But I am not a man, says me,
And I laugh at my own joke.
I'm an Elf and Forest Old.
I'll help remove the yoke.

Three magic gifts there are for thee,
With threefold magic power.
For Lurelei the Elven Maid
That lovely Naver's Flower.

But heed this warning, mortal man,
As only once it's given.
Touch not these magics with thy hand
Or you'll be burned, by heaven.

Thou must advance yet more, my son,
Than I can now impart.
Your dreaming self must carry them
And lay them in her heart.

"I think that was all of it," said Angus.

"The instructions are clear," Feshka eyed him solemnly. "What do you intend to do about this?"

"It was only a dream," protested Angus. "What does one do about a dream?"

"But it was not just a dream. It was a dream of Forest Old. This is what he's known for in myth. He comes to those in need and helps them."

"Who was Forest Old?" asked Angus.

"He was a King among the Elves," answered Feshka, "while Elves still lived among the stars. Of course, it's also a myth that Elves came from the stars. Angus, what do you intend to do about the dream?"

"What can I do?"

"You can do what Forest Old suggested. Advance further."

"How can I do that?"

"I will help you, Gate Keeper," Feshka smiled fondly at Angus.

They continued on, finding no further sign of Ogladim along the lake. When they reached the narrows, they crossed it using one of the bridges that seemed so easy for Elves to make. Then they turned the other way and hiked back many miles along the other side of the lake.

Arikin stayed far ahead of them. Sometimes Aelrondel or Marnel would take a turn with him or go ahead alone to give him a break.

After three more days of hiking they were about to reach the narrows again at the northeast end of the lake where it formed the source of the River Ness when Arikin came running back to them.

"There are Ogladim ahead and the nearest Haven is more than a day's march to the southeast!"

"Did you see how many there are and if they have any other pets with them?" VeratNonn asked.

"I saw their fire and heard their voices. I also heard the voices of swine. But they're camped. At least this group isn't about to stumble on our trail."

"Do they have scouts watching the path?" asked Feshka. "That last bunch that was following us had one in a tree. VelMud took a shot at it with his bow but it was too fast for us."

With that last comment, the Elves strung their bows that had been at rest and hanging on their quivers. The Dwarves were already scanning the trees within sight of the path.

"There's one," muttered Arikin as he released his bowstring. An arrow darted upward. Within seconds they heard a cry and then a thud as the Oglat hit the ground. "Keep looking," he instructed the rest. "There may be more."

They heard a scrambling noise just ahead of them and turned to see what it was just in time to see another Oglat slide the last few feet down the trunk of a nearby tree. Three arrows flew toward him at the same time. All three hit him and he dropped like a rock.

Arikin, Aelrondel and Mishishel congratulated each other for their marksmanship. They were interrupted by the sound of feet in the forest above the path. All turned again. The Humans and Dwarves had drawn their swords. The Elves had arrows in their bows ready to shoot, but no target could be seen. The sound of the footsteps stopped. The group froze, listening in silence. An arrow struck a tree within inches of Arikin's head. They all started at the sound, then ducked and ran for cover in the direction from which they came.

After a brief pause, the Elves and Dwarves charged in the direction from which they thought the arrow had been shot. There was a sound of struggling. Then Arikin emerged from the forest. Behind him were the others. The Humans had taken refuge behind some trees about fifty feet down the path.

The Dwarves were angry that the Humans had hidden. "Some allies you are," BarNeesh snarled. "We could have been killed while you skulk behind the trees."

"There could have been more arrows," Scobie said defensively.

"If there could have been, there would have been," retorted Verat-Nonn.

"We charged before he had time to re-string an arrow," snapped BarNeesh. "Try to be a little braver, weak Humans!"

William spoke up. "He who fights and runs away, lives to fight another…"

Feshka interrupted William. "Let there be no more of this. We must act and not argue. What do you suggest we do now, Arikin?"

"If we got all the guards," said Arikin, "*if*... then we need to back-track a little so we can confuse our trail. If we didn't kill all the guards, they'll be coming after us shortly. I suggest we assume the worst."

"Agreed," chorused the Dwarves.

"Agreed," chimed in Feshka and the rest of the Elves.

"Have we got into another scrape?" grumbled Ingram.

Setting off at a brisk pace, west bound, Arikin rolled his eyes, muttering "Let's get moving. Follow me."

They were backtracking. The Humans were getting used to life on the trail, and even Ingram was able to keep up, pack and all. Angus watched the trees and bushes rush past him as he nearly ran down the path after Arikin. He thought he would see these trees only once, when he'd passed them the first time. He'd never wanted to come this way again.

The group trotted about half a mile before they came to a stream running down the southern hillside. Arikin stepped into the water and began wading against the current. The others fell in behind him.

"If they don't discover us too soon," called Arikin over his shoulder, "by the time they get here, the mud we stir up from the creek bottom will have either settled or made it into the lake. If they get here too fast they'll see the mud from our tracks and follow us up the stream. If they don't see the mud, they'll follow the path and our scent until they realize we've tricked them. And they *will* eventually realize that. Then if they want us badly enough they'll start wading in creeks trying to pick up a new trail. If all goes well, they won't find our trail until sometime tomorrow, unless it rains. Keep your fingers crossed."

"So this won't get us free of them at all then," muttered Ingram.

"We'll just have to keep moving till we either lose them or have to face them," William reasoned out loud.

"I wonder how many there are," Scobie paused to wipe his forehead with the back of his hand.

"It could be another hundred," exclaimed Tristan.

"If it's a hundred we won't have a chance if we have to face them," said William.

"*Let's hope we don't have to face them,*" Ingram muttered.

"They had three watchers," Feshka reminded them. "If that's any indication of the size of the group, then it must be large."

"On the other hand," said Mishishel, "if it was another situation where a party of four was joining another party of a hundred like last week, then we failed to find the fourth one. He's gone and told the hundred and they're on our trail already."

They had made surprising headway up the stream. Walking in a stream is not easy. The rocks are often slippery, making it treacherous. Those ahead often kick loose some of the rocks the water then carries downstream into the path of the ones behind. Angus was the first to stumble. Now completely soaked, he struggled to carry not only his pack, but all the cold mountain water that traveled with him in his clothing. The next to fall was Ingram. He didn't handle it as well. His face flushed with anger, water dripped from his beard as he stumbled a second time. William grabbed one arm and kept him from falling yet again. Scobie moved up on Ingram's other side and together the three of them supported each other whenever they started to falter.

Angus lost track of how many hours they had been trekking through the water. Surely the Ogladim wouldn't climb this high to check the stream's banks for scent or tracks. If he was getting tired of the water, he knew what the others would be thinking. He looked at the stream where his feet were pushing against the current. Each time he lifted his foot it stirred up mud from the bottom. He looked ahead and behind and saw that it was the same for the Elves and the Dwarves. It was good that the stream was wide and deep in enough places for the sheer volume of the water to consume the color of the mud they were stirring up, and thus erase their tracks.

The stream itself made a lot of noise as it flowed over the rocks. It wasn't as loud as a waterfall, but it was enough to drown out all other sounds around them. He wished Arikin would slow down but understood the need for hurrying. The stream was narrowing quickly.

Ahead, Arikin was slowing a little because he was having a problem keeping his footing in the water. Angus was thinking, maybe they should have followed a different stream. Maybe one of the tributaries would have held its size longer. His feet were cold, his clothes were wet and he was tired. Looking back, he could see that his father and the others felt exactly the same way. For all the walking they had done over the last week, very little of it was actual climbing like they were now doing, and none of it was in creeks.

He was proud of Ingram, who was keeping up with the others without much comment and also keeping his footing in the stream along with the rest.

Finally the stream narrowed to a point where they could no longer follow it. Arikin stopped and waited for the rest of them to catch up. "We must now leave the safety of the water. As we do, everyone should follow the steps of the one in front of him as closely as possible, to keep from spreading our scent. It would be best, and I know we can't do that, but try to put your feet in the exact place where the person in front of you stepped. If they do find the tracks they will think there is only one of us, and that we split up. That will keep some of them away from us as they search for the rest. Can we do this?"

"How can we follow your tracks like that, when you walk a foot above the ground?" VeratNonn balked. "Also, some of us have longer legs than others!" He eyed Angus and Tristan.

The Elves tried not so smile and the girls looked away. "Do your best," urged Arikin, and set off to the east.

Angus could see that ahead and farther up the mountainside were sheer cliffs. He knew they could not be climbed easily. They didn't want to go any farther south anyway. Home was to the north. They had to get around the lake, but first they had to get around the Ogladim. Could they do it this time? He doubted it. They had been lucky until now. With Arikin's cleverness they had evaded the Ogladim on the other mountain, then killed them easily in the boat. He wondered if this group also had a boat.

So far there had been no sign that the new group of Ogladim below had found their trail. Still they traveled at a fast pace. Arikin had said there was another Haven, but it was more than a day's march. Were they headed there? He knew they were near the end of the lake. They were descending toward the eastern sea. But as the land began to drop away, Arikin turned southward, keeping toward the high ground. The sun was going down; Angus hadn't noticed how late it was. Were they going to have to travel all night again? It appeared that was what was in store for them.

Again they began to climb. There was no path to follow. They were going straight through the open forest with the cliffs above them, but more to the right now. It looked like they were going to go over the top, and just as that thought occurred, the ground began dropping away again. They had crested the eastern end of the mountain. Arikin had led them around the top rather than over it. But then they turned west again. "To find another stream," Marnel whispered to him.

When they did find another one, Arikin waded right in. "Now wait a minute," protested Ingram. "I was just starting to get dry!"

"We won't be in here as long. You can dry off in a few hours," Arikin reassured him. "Now we'll continue upstream as before. If they find our trail at all and come to this stream, they'll think we went down, not up. That will lead them away from us for maybe another day. By then we can make it to the next Haven."

After two more hours of wading and slipping over the mossy rocks they came to a shallow pool below a low falls. "Wait here. Stay in the water," instructed Arikin. Leaving the stream, he climbed above the falls, walking just off the ground.

"How do they do that?" wondered Tristan enviously.

Aelrondel, Marnel, Mishishel, VelMud and PoleeShimel all went with him, careful not to touch the ground. Only the Humans and Dwarves waited in the water with Feshka.

Soon Arikin and the other Elves appeared at the top of the falls and dropped a rope. Some climbed and some were pulled, but none of those left below touched dry ground on the passage up the falls. "Just a little farther," Arikin told them. "There's an island ahead. I'll have to remember to sing of this at the next gathering. It's a Haven as safe as the others."

"Why is this so safe?" grumbled Ingram as he stripped off his wet pants and boots.

"If they do come up the stream looking for our scent and footprints, they'll think we couldn't have passed the falls. If they think to look beyond the falls they won't cross the water to check an island unless they have a fresh trail at the water's edge. It's as safe a place as there is," Feshka patiently explained.

"How do we know they even found our trail?" asked Ingram. "We could well have gone to all that trouble for nothing. For all we know they never found out about the dead scouts and there were probably only three of 'em to begin with."

"Then it's certain that we're safe. Would you like to build a fire to warm yourself, Ingram?" suggested Feshka.

"I don't feel that safe," argued Ingram.

Angus looked around at the trees. The island they had found in the middle of the stream was just like the rest of the forest, with thick bushes circling it. The sides of the stream were the same. The only way they could be seen even in the light of day would be if one of them stood up and waved. Angus noticed everyone was on the ground either preparing for sleep or eating some of the trail bread from their sacks.

It was as good a place to camp as any Angus had seen. The ground was relatively clear of roots and rocks, covered with what appeared to be the soft silt that a stream deposits when it's high. Of course that's what it was, since the island was composed of soft silt that had piled up among rocks that used to be in the stream bed. He leaned back on the ground, using his pack for a pillow. Then they heard voices. It was unmistakable. Someone was calling out from one side of the stream. Then someone answered from the other side. Angus couldn't make out what they were saying. There it was again. He almost stood up to see but caught himself first. He was now thankful that Arikin had insisted they keep themselves covered to conceal their light.

What was that? He thought he heard splashing in the stream. The voice seemed closer now. One of them must have stepped into the stream to investigate the island. He started to sweat.

"No one move. No one speak," Arikin whispered unnecessarily.

The splashing grew closer. Angus felt himself tensing; his heart was pounding. He didn't know how many there were, or even *what* they were. The language they had used to call across the stream to each other was the same one he had heard on the trail the night he went looking for Lurelei. It was the old tongue of the High Elves that Feshka was teaching him. But he hadn't learned enough yet to be able to make out what they were saying.

The sound of someone splashing as they walked through the water was getting louder. He knew that meant the "whatever" was getting closer. He turned over so he could get his knees under him in case he wanted to get to his feet fast. The splashing was now on the downstream side of the island. A voice called out again in the ancient tongue. It was almost on top of them, answered by a voice that apparently was from the opposite bank.

The entire group was getting ready to charge, all but Arikin. He was motioning with his hand to keep quiet and stay still. He was smiling. Then Angus noticed that Feshka and Mishishel were also looking very relaxed. Suddenly he realized they could understand what was being said. He began to calm down.

The Oglat splashed on by and crawled out of the stream on the other side. "What were they saying?" Angus whispered to Feshka.

"I'll tell you when it's safe," he whispered back.

The Ogladim had found their trail and had followed it to the logical end. Then they split up and followed the stream down to the sea without finding where the party left the water. But for that night a large number of them were camped at the base of the falls, where the others had camped a few nights ago.

The voices faded into the night, but they all remained quiet, close to the ground. "Someone should go and see what's going on," murmured Arikin. "I'll do it." Pulling his cover over his head, he slipped into the water and vanished from their sight.

Angus was amazed by his fear. One gets used to most unpleasant things in time. Unpleasant odors, even pain eventually diminished. But his heart was pounding and he was sweating just as hard as that night when he was lost and alone on the trail. This feeling of panic seemed to afflict him whenever danger was near. He wondered if he would ever get used to it. Probably not.

Some of the others were stirring, rolling to one side or the other to find better comfort for the night. *How could anyone sleep under such conditions?* He certainly wouldn't shut his eyes much that night, with Ogladim at the foot of the falls and who knew what else, wandering in the forest. If there were Ogladim there could very well be swine or even a Geketz. He listened to the silence around him, broken only by the sound of the rippling stream.

Finally his thoughts turned back to Lurelei. *Where is she now?* What kind of a life could she be having as a Geketz alone in the mountains? He wondered if she had made it back to the Naver yet or if she had followed him against his wishes. If she had, it would be dangerous for both of them, especially if it was true that the Enemy knew her thoughts.

Arikin crawled into the bushes with them, soaking wet. He started pulling off his clothes and wringing them out. "I saw only four," he whispered. "They have no swine with them, but there's a large white dog, almost like a Wolf. It seems that it can smell us but it can't figure out where we are. All the time I was in the stream, it was running up and down the bank as though it wanted to go into the water but was afraid. It's gone now, but I don't know where it went."

"Do these Ogladim have Wolves?" asked Marnel. "We feared that the Enemy might bring Wolves. He did that before, didn't he?"

"Yes," said Mishishel. "In the flight from YeePhraWaine our people were pursued by Wolves. This is the first we've heard of it this time."

"The stories say they were vicious," said Aelrondel. "They could outrun us."

"It could just be a wild dog." Arikin settled himself on the ground. "Maybe it was hungry and thought there might be food on the island with us. What do you think, Feshka?"

Feshka was silent and thoughtful. Until he was asked, he didn't say any more. But at Arikin's request he replied, "There is a very ancient story about a race of dogs. None have reported seeing them for many generations of Elves and men, but that doesn't mean they're all dead. An immense black male led them. As the story goes, his name in the Old High Elf tongue was Barreal. His family was large and they were friendly to us."

"What happened to them?" asked Angus.

"They met our people on the beach when we first landed on this large island. They said it belonged to them but we were welcome to share it. We offered them food but they said they prefer meat. We offered to make sleeping mats for them but they said they preferred the hard cold ground. They said they too had come here as refugees. Since we fled an enemy as they once did, they said we were a brother race. Then they vanished into the forest never to be seen again."

"Do you think this dog that Arikin saw was one of them?" asked Marnel.

"No," said Arikin. It's just a dog and it probably belongs to the Oglad-im who are sleeping below the falls."

"The story of Barreal is just another legend," said BarNeesh. "It's just a myth."

"That's what my people always said about Elves," said William.

Chapter Fourteen: Island in the Sky

They managed to sleep quietly. Sometimes, when the body is in grave danger, it can do that. The person knows even in sleep that any sound he makes could be his last. Angus slept without dreaming. Ingram didn't snore. None of them did. At one point William started talking softly in his sleep, but as soft as his words were, they woke Angus who nudged him. William woke, rolled over and went back to sleep.

They were taking turns at watch, as they'd been doing ever since they'd left The City of The Vision. Arikin watched first, then Aelrondel took a turn. William had insisted on taking a turn and at his example, Ingram and Scobie joined in. It seemed that Angus had been sleeping only a short time when he was awakened by voices. It was Ingram.

"He says there are only four of them below us. We could take them easily."

"But if we do that," Arikin argued, "the larger party will know."

"How can they know? We don't even know where they are," countered Ingram.

"That's right," agreed Aelrondel. "But they could as well be close as they could be far."

"And we don't know for sure how many there are," added Marnel.

"What's all this about?" whispered Angus, rubbing his eyes.

"Ingram wants to attack the four while they're sleeping," William informed him. "He thinks we should kill as many as possible while we can."

"They killed my wife," Ingram's voice was harsh and bitter. "I'm in these woods for bloodshed, not for skulking in the bushes when a few of the enemy are near. Kill them, I say."

"They killed mine too," said Scobie, "but I can see the wisdom of waiting. We may be able to kill the four without much trouble, but Arikin's right. There could be another hundred within earshot."

"We couldn't kill a hundred," Tristan shook his head dubiously.

"We couldn't handle even fifty," agreed William.

"But four's a manageable number," Ingram argued.

"Wait," Arikin scrambled to his feet. "If we kill the four we alert the others to the fact that we're here and we could be in great danger. Do you intend to risk all of our lives?"

"I'm here to fight and die," snarled Ingram. "If that's not why you're here, then go home. With my Maggie dead I care not for living."

"You're here to gather information," Arikin reminded him, "not to wage your own war and risk the lives of others."

"I'm goin'." And without a backward glance, Ingram waded into the creek, one hand on the hilt of his sword and the other gripping his Skyn Dhu.

"I can't let him do this alone," William declared, following him.

"Me either," added Scobie.

The party began wading across the creek with the Humans in the lead followed by the Dwarves. The Elves came last. Angus was full of turmoil. He agreed with Arikin but he couldn't stand by quietly while his father went to his death. Mishishel and Arikin were arguing quietly and the Dwarves were angrily interjecting and calling softly to the Humans to come back.

"If they're going to do this we have to make sure they do a clean job of it and none of them get away," whispered VeratNonn hoarsely to BarNeesh.

"We *have* to stop them!" PoleeShimel demanded.

Arikin was rushing ahead to get to Ingram before he reached the side of the stream and placed his scent on the dry land, but he wasn't fast enough.

One by one the party left the stream and started creeping down around the falls as quietly as possible, toward the Ogladim. By now, Arikin was beside Ingram with the other humans crowded just behind. The scene they found was almost domestic in nature. A fire was burning in the center of a ring of sleeping forms. There were some cooking utensils near the fire. One of the Ogladim was snoring.

"Go on," Arikin challenged Ingram sarcastically. "You can probably kill all four of them yourself if they don't wake up fast enough."

Ingram rushed into the group, his sword held high over his head, shouting at the top of his lungs. Angus, Tristan, Scobie and William followed closely, wondering why Ingram chose to shout and wake the sleepers. All four rose at the same time. With a wide swing, Ingram brought his blade down over the neck of the closest one. Without waiting for it to die he turned and with another swing of his blade and nearly hit Angus.

The five of them had each killed one Oglat except for Tristan who had held back. "There weren't enough for me to get one," he said later. "There were only four."

Angus stared at the creature he had just killed. It was lying on the ground partly on its side as though in sleep. He had never killed anything before except for chickens and maybe a few sheep, but these were intelligent creatures.

"Come on, Angus." William understood what Angus was feeling. "Let's get moving or they'll leave us behind."

Angus noticed that the party had set off at a brisk pace toward the south. The hill descended with the stream to the east so they were still walking crosswise to the hill. The night wasn't over yet. Angus hadn't had enough sleep, but Arikin had said the Ogladim below would now be alerted to where they were, so they had to lose them again.

"Stupid Humans," VeratNonn grumbled. "Always wanting to kill something. Why couldn't you allow us to sleep, then get away easily?"

"We shouldn't have brought them," muttered PoleeShimel.

"But we did bring them," Marnel reminded them. "They have a part to play in this just as we do."

"The hell with all of you," snarled Ingram. "You should have let me kill all of them."

"Maybe we should have let you kill the hundred too, oh mighty warrior," retorted VeratNonn. "Then we wouldn't still have to listen to you. You'd be dead."

Arikin stopped the group and came down to the end of the procession. "Enough of this," he ordered firmly. "The Human did something stupid. Let's not add to it by making so much noise that the rest of them find us."

VeratNonn closed his mouth in a thin line of anger and snorted through his nose. BarNeesh did the same. The others folded their arms and waited, standing with their legs apart. Ingram also drew his lips into a thin line and glaring at Arikin, snapped, "We're here to fight and kill. Why do we spend our days hiding and our nights fleeing? It's time to stand and fight."

Arikin stood squarely in front of the group and addressed them. "My father, the Rebeck Ariel, ordered me to come here and gather information. I agreed to do it alone, but he wanted me to also conduct

Mishishel to the southern side of the Great Glen where he would meet others to conduct him safely home to Wesheshica. My father Ariel commanded me to do this. I agreed to do it alone, but my father said I must also take StrathNaver to expand his knowledge and that it would be unfair to take him without the rest of his party. Since StrathNaver was to come, it was necessary to have additional guards. My father said he also wanted VeratNonn to come with us to observe for his people.

"You, Ingram, are here because StrathNaver is here and for no other reason. This is not a war party. It is a scouting party. We are here to gather information. I am in charge of this expedition. This is not a time for kindness and forgiveness. It's a time to be efficient and to work as a team. What you did tonight was not efficient. It has exposed us to danger. Now we must compensate for you, again. Can you keep up quietly, or would you prefer to find your own way home?"

Ingram drew back his arm to strike Arikin but William caught him. "Calm down, Ingram. Calm yourself!"

Scobie was on his other arm by now, with Angus and Tristan close by to offer help if needed. "We can't survive alone out here, Ingram," said Scobie. "Not with all that's about."

"He's right, Ingram." William tightened his grip on Ingram's arm. "We have to work as a team to survive."

Ingram stopped struggling, overwhelmed and outnumbered. "Release him," said Arikin, simply.

"He'll tear you limb from limb," William warned.

"I hope he tries," Arikin answered calmly.

William and Scobie released him and Ingram began to warily approach Arikin. But in the distance they could hear voices.

"See what you've done to us, Human?" snapped VeratNonn.

"Let's go. Come on," urged Arikin, setting off again.

Angus knew more Ogladim had found their trail. He also knew Ingram wouldn't be able to keep up the pace with the others, and kept watching to see how he was doing. He wouldn't be able to abandon his neighbor no matter how foolish he'd been. As he hiked along over brush and bracken he glanced from time to time at his father, trying to read his thoughts. William was grim-faced and puffing with the exertion.

They were all in better condition than when they had started out, more than a week ago. Ingram wasn't lagging behind. Tristan was trotting along as though it was part of his daily routine, which by now it had become. Arikin and Marnel were nearly out of sight. Aelrondel had dropped back and disappeared behind them. "I guess she's going to see how they're doing," Angus commented to Tristan.

Mishishel who was near to Angus, poked him in the arm and made a motion with his finger to his lips to keep quiet. Angus was terrified. Here they were again with the Ogladim closing from behind and no help anywhere. Arikin's pace was faster than he had set before, except maybe the second night out. He could hear the voices sometimes far behind them. The Ogladim had to be on their scent by now. He hoped there were no swine this time.

Tristan's face was pale. Ingram's anger had apparently faded in the face of the fight to come. Surely there would be a fight this time. Angus wished he had taken the time to learn more about the use of the sword he was carrying. His only knowledge of swords was that they cut. He could swing it and cut from the side as he had seen Ingram do earlier. He could jab with it and cut with its point, but he knew nothing of thrust and parry. His only consolation was that he knew the Ogladim were not renowned for their skill either.

The ground was uneven. He was having a problem keeping his feet if he went too fast. He glanced back at Ingram. He was having the same problem. Angus admired the Dwarves for their sure-footedness. Their legs were shorter than his but they were keeping up just fine and they never tripped. Their grim faces told him they knew there would be a fight this time.

Aelrondel came up from behind so quickly, Angus didn't notice her until she passed him. Catching up with Arikin they conferred briefly. The only result was that Arikin picked up a little more speed. Angus could see on the faces of those around him that this was not a welcome change. Doing his best, he tried to go a little faster to keep up with Arikin. The voices seemed closer now, but that could have been Angus's imagination.

Angus watched as Aelrondel disappeared again, this time ahead of them. The direction they were taking was still south and now they seemed to be descending. It would be easier walking than it had been, on the side of the mountain. Angus wondered what was at the bottom and where the fight would take place. Maybe they were heading right into a trap. There could be more Ogladim below, or worse.

Feshka and VelMud kept together just ahead of Angus. Verat-Nonn and BarNeesh brought up the rear, following Mishishel and Pol-eeShimel. Aelrondel had run ahead again to watch for danger.

The forest was nearly silent. The birds had taken warning and were either gone or in hiding. The wind was silent. It was already past the first hour of daylight. On they went. "We have two means of escape this time," Marnel told Angus. "We can outrun them or we can lose them."

"Arikin said there is another Haven," said Angus. "Do you know how close it is?"

"No," she answered. "The land has many Havens. Most of them are a day's walk apart but some are closer to each other. Arikin said this is another water Haven, but unlike the others we've seen."

"Who built these Havens?"

"Some were built by our people when we first came to this land. Some are natural and were discovered when necessity arose. Some were here before we came. It seems there was an ancient race that lived here before us and they built many of them."

"I wonder what they were like. I wonder what happened to them."

"Peoples come and go," said Marnel. "Everywhere our race has traveled there have been signs of others who came before us. In some future period, others will find signs of us after we've left this place. It may be, as some have said, that our races will blend. Someday maybe there will be no Elves and Dwarves and Humans, but a wonderful new race that combines all of our qualities."

"I hope no day comes when Elves don't live in the forest near my home," declared Angus.

"If it does," Marnel smiled, "something else will be there in our stead. Life springs forth where there is none. Its need to express itself is urgent. There is life under rocks, beneath Earth and above. Some creatures have learned to live even in the air and upon the star we call the Sun."

Angus speculated how his life would change if the Ogladim caught up with them, or how it would end. The thought saddened him that the species he called Human and Elf and Dwarf may someday no longer exist, as though a species was no more than an experiment performed by this force called life. Then there is the constant struggle, the constant competition between life forms, between rabbits and foxes, mice and hawks. He chuckled to himself at the thought that competition is the acid test by which all things live or die. Even now he watched as Tristan tried to compete with Arikin for Aelrondel's attention. The group of which he was a part was in competition with the Ogladim for speed and cunning. He wondered if maybe there was a way, somewhere, somehow, in which he could drop out of the contest and live as a spectator, watching it. He was tired of running through the woods in pursuit or flight.

Angus was also weary of the anger he felt over his mother's death and the attack on Lurelei. It still gripped him and his heart still hurt, but his mind was weary of hating. How could he step aside from the current of events? Could he somehow distance himself and let all these circumstances and events pass by, without touching him?

His legs ached. His clothing was sticking to his skin because of his sweat, and also getting stiff from repeated sweating day after day with no chance to wash or bathe. The Ogladim were still behind them. Occasionally he could hear a shout. Aelrondel now passed him again from behind and disappeared ahead of them. Angus was grateful for her and the Elves. They knew the forest better than any except, maybe the squirrels, but he doubted that. There was Aelrondel again, racing ahead to watch for danger. Marnel had taken her turn at the watching and running, as had Arikin. Angus wondered how they could move so quickly without apparent effort. He wondered how in the world they could keep up this pace and still take turns at going even faster.

His thoughts returned to the fantasy, the escape. How could he step aside from the mainstream of the competition? How could he make himself uninteresting to the Enemy? If he could do that, he would be able to live in peace, except for the occasional spats with other clans. There were always troubles that needed attending, but that was part of the fray he was trying to figure out how to avoid.

His leg had blistered where the Elf Steel blade chaffed him. Its sheath protected him from any real danger, but even with the sheath, its weight and rubbing were enough to irritate his skin. Pain from the wounds he had received from the Geketz had almost subsided. Only occasionally now would he wake in the night with the burning and throbbing sensation.

Aelrondel appeared again at the front of the procession. This time she stopped to speak with Arikin, who also stopped. A pause was a welcome relief. Angus's legs hurt from the constant push through the forest. But what was wrong now? Nothing had changed. Why had they stopped? Without a word, Arikin waved to them to follow him and he started off across the hill. He had changed directions again too, and at a faster pace even than before.

Word was passed back through Angus to the end of the line. Another hundred Ogladim were also ahead of them. *This is hopeless*, thought Angus. Arikin was leading them out from between the two groups, but as soon as they found their scent, the Ogladim would surely follow.

As they marched west, the ground once again began to rise. The group had become toughened by the regular exercise and they were keeping up pretty well, but Angus knew he couldn't sustain this new pace much longer. He was nearly running, jumping over fallen trees and rocks that lay in his path. He had youth on his side but he feared for his father and Ingram. Ahead he could see Tristan sprinting through the woods like a deer. Every so often he caught a glimpse of Arikin and Marnel. Aelrondel was out of sight again. Ingram and his father were a short distance behind him. Scobie was handling the new pace with ease.

Now the ground rose sharply and they had to slow a little. Angus thought he was climbing a new hill that seemed almost unrelated to the mountain they were on. It turned out to be a separate ridge that broke to the left in a low cliff. It seemed to him that Arikin had turned again slightly to the left as though to approach the ridge and as they proceeded, the direction continued to turn to the left.

The group ahead had stopped and was waiting near the edge of the cliff Angus had seen a few minutes earlier. Then he noticed that the approach along the ridge was narrow, widening toward the cliff's face. They had found another island, but this one was in plain sight and easily approached by following the same path Angus had just climbed.

"There's no point in running farther," Arikin told them. "The Haven we sought is beyond the Ogladim camp ahead of us. To get to it we have to pass them or go around them. The Ogladim behind us are gaining on us. We wouldn't be able to slip past the ones ahead before being overtaken. We're trapped."

"What do we do now?" asked William. "Just wait to die?"

"We're not without defenses," answered Arikin. "Come and view the Ogladim with me." He stepped to the edge of the cliff and pointed to the north. "Do you see them there?"

All eyes turned to the direction indicated. "I don't see anything," declared Angus.

"Look between the trees," directed Arikin. "They're coming quickly. Look to the south. Can you see the smoke from their fire? They seem unaware of us as yet, but they'll know soon. Everyone step back. We must form a Trine."

Aelrondel and Marnel approached him as the others backed away. Angus watched as they gathered closer. Aelrondel and Marnel stood on either side of Arikin with their hands on his back. Angus glanced back to the north, trying to see the approaching Ogladim again. This time he spotted the group coming quickly in a line of pairs. It was a long line. Some had spears, others were carrying jagged swords. What amazed Angus the most was their pace. They would have overtaken the group shortly, so it was just as well that they had stopped.

Angus was weary. He didn't want to fight any more, he didn't want to run any farther and he didn't want to die yet. He had to find a cure for Lurelei and he also had to find a way to protect his home from the invasion, now growing immanent. The woods were full of Ogladim. He had never seen one near his home, but these southern mountains had too many.

Suddenly a Bolt of lightning flashed across the sky. The sky was clear of clouds and rain, but now a clap of thunder followed the lightning He looked at Arikin in amazement just in time to see it again. His face raised to the sky, Arikin raised his arms over his head. He then lowered both arms bringing his hands together. At the same time he brought his gaze from the sky back to the Ogladim approaching them from the north. As his eyes and hands pointed in the same direction, he saw Arikin light up. Aelrondel and Marnel also lit up beside him, with visible power coming from them into Arikin. Then the Bolt struck again.

He felt a hand on his shoulder and turned sharply. "Sorry to startle you," Feshka had come up next to him, with VelMud. "This is a trick of visualization and balling your energy. You could do this. We think you could do it without the exhaustion the Elves feel afterwards. Your passion would be the power behind it, instead of your life force."

Angus continued to watch. The Ogladim had stopped their approach. Several bodies, maybe six at the head of the pack, lay on the ground, inert. Arikin was watching to see what they would do next.

"Do you think the Bolt will alert the Ogladim to the south?" asked Angus.

"They may not know about the Bolt," said VelMud. "If they do know, they'll come now."

As they watched, a cry arose among the enemy in the north. Arms and fingers pointed to the cliff and the Ogladim began running toward their attackers.

Arikin and Marnel traded places. Now they stood with Marnel in the center and Arikin and Aelrondel on either side of her with their hands on her back as they had done before. In a few seconds there was another loud crash as another Bolt descended from the blue sky. Feshka stepped up beside them, placing one hand on the back of Arikin and one on Aelrondel. VelMud joined also. As Angus watched, Mishishel and PoleeShimel also joined the former Trine. Another Bolt flashed across the sky.

Angus watched in astonishment as the Elves worked together to make an even larger and stronger Bolt than the first ones. Below, the Ogladim were scattering. More lay dead on the ground, but most of them were still approaching as fast as they could. The two Dwarves were at the edge of the hill beside the cliff with bows and arrows ready for the Ogladim when they came within range. The Elves set off Bolt after Bolt. Each time more Ogladim fell, but as they scattered, they were too far apart from each other to get more than one at a time with each blast.

The Elves broke up their group. "This takes too much energy for killing so few at a time." Arikin removed his bow from over his shoulder.

The Elves now rimmed the hill's edge, kneeling. They were poised to release arrows as soon as the Ogladim came close enough. Angus took up a position at the entrance to the new island they had found in the sky. His father and Ingram were on his right with Scobie and Tristan on his left. Together they would stop any that tried to gain entrance to their Haven. Although they were cornered, it was a corner of the world that could easily be defended.

"Don't let any of them get to the top," instructed Arikin.

"They'll stay below till we run out of arrows," said Mishishel.

"Which do we have more of?" asked PoleeShimel, "arrows or Ogladim?"

"Just hope that they don't have any swine. I haven't seen any," added Feshka. "Has anyone else?"

"I've seen no swine," reported Marnel.

"I've not seen any either," from Arikin, "but they could be under the trees on either side of the path. They could be anywhere."

Just then the first Ogladim to come within arrow's range was announced by the twang of Aelrondel's bowstring. A second was close behind, announced by Mishishel's bow.

"Brace yourself," called William. "They'll be past the Elves shortly, and then it's our turn."

The Elves were firing away as fast as they could pluck arrows from their quivers. The air was growing foul from the blood of the creatures below, but the Ogladim kept coming. Feshka approached Angus and stepped between Tristan and himself. The approach to the promontory was only wide enough for two men to walk abreast. The six should be able to hold it for a while unless the Ogladim had arrows of their own, but then the first of the swine arrived.

It was a large bore hog with bristling black hair, tiny black eyes and four-inch tusks rising from its lower jaw. Its pointed hooves left tiny holes in the dirt as it charged, squealing with rage. Shortly behind it were two more. William stopped the first one with a hard slicing blow of his Elf Blade, but the swine's momentum carried it beyond the defensive line before it fell. The second was a fat old sow. This one charged toward Ingram and met its death with a sword directly plunging down its throat.

This was not a good move on Ingram's part because he had difficulty extracting his blade before the third swine got to him. Scobie stopped it just in time. More came hurtling across the threshold but it was not wide enough for a rush. Since only one or two could come at the same time, the men were able to kill them as they approached.

Angus heard barking. At first when the sound registered, he was too busy striking at the oncoming swine. The Elves were still firing arrows as fast they could draw their bows. Angus saw Ogladim beyond the entrance to their promontory; some had made it past the Elves. Sooner or later the swine would accomplish their job and the Ogladim could lazily stand by, watching. Then Angus saw one of them take a bow from his shoulder. With a grin the Oglat reached over his shoulder. A second later its hand appeared again with an arrow in it.

In the back of his mind he heard barking again, the deep-throated voices of many large dogs. Finally the sound forced its way to his consciousness and he remembered what Arikin had just said to VelMud. *Oh no. They have Wolves!*

The Oglat fitted its arrow to its bowstring and stood there grinning, as though he wanted to gain the full amount of fear from his victims. It wanted to draw out the torture of wondering who would receive the arrow. They all saw it, but nothing could be done. The hogs were still coming. William was busy stabbing and slicing. The ground was littered with the stinking bodies of pigs. The new ones entering the scene had to pick their way over the bodies to get at the Humans, only to be struck themselves.

"Kill more," shouted the Oglat in his own tongue. "We'll have a barbecue later!" He drew his bow and aimed it at Ingram. At that moment Angus remembered Feshka's fireballs as one flew in the direction of the Oglat. The arrow passed through the fireball and fizzled in mid-air. Then the ball struck the Oglat, who burst into flames and fell silently on the ground.

Two more Ogladim stepped in to replace their fallen comrade. Both had bows ready to be fired. One aimed at Angus and the other at Feshka. Another fireball flew forth followed by a second, but more Ogladim appeared, and the barking grew louder. It seemed they were finally at the end of the hogs. No more rushed into the area. Now there were only Ogladim—and Wolves. Angus, now watching for them, hadn't seen any yet.

The Ogladim didn't look as confident as before. They exchanged fearful looks, replacing yet more fallen comrades as they continued to approach. Angus was wondering how long Feshka would be able to stand there and throw fire balls, when he was startled by another Bolt which struck the two Ogladim now facing the men. Angus turned and saw Arikin, VelMud and Mishishel Trined. Aelrondel, Marnel and PoleeShimel formed a second Trine.

The first of the Wolves arrived. As yet they had only a few paces to go before they would be upon them. The first one Angus saw was coal black with fierce-looking blue eyes that seemed cold and remorseless.

Its back was as high off the ground as Angus's waist. Its head was bigger than a man's and as high off the ground as Angus's throat. "So this is how I'm going to die," thought Angus. "It could have me by the throat without even reaching up!"

"My God," gasped William. "What a big dog!"

"What a beautiful dog," added Tristan.

"It's a Wolf," shouted Scobie. "It must be a Wolf. Dogs don't get that big!"

Angus watched as the dog stopped just beyond the fray, watching. Several more approached behind it and stopped, also watching. Then a pack of dogs numbering around fifty descended on the scene. When the rest of the pack arrived, they all leaped into the fight. There was horrendous barking and snarling. Angus had never before seen dogs fighting. He was completely overwhelmed with amazement and fear at their viciousness.

But the Wolves, if Wolves they were, attacked the Ogladim, not the Humans, Elves or Dwarves.

The Elves broke their Trines and the Humans sheathed their swords. Feshka tumbled to the ground in exhaustion. All watched in astonishment as the Wolves drove the Ogladim back down the hillside. They were everywhere, racing through the forest like wood sprites, above the island and below it, along the trails where the party had fled earlier. As they ran, they slaughtered the remaining Ogladim.

Arikin rose and headed toward the entrance to their impromptu fort, waiting. Finally the barking and fighting stopped and the huge black dog Angus had first seen, approached silently. Arikin knelt on the ground with his hands behind his back and his face to the sky, baring his throat to the dog. The huge black dog trotted up to him and with a bark took his throat in its teeth. It did not bite but stepped back and with a voice that seemed almost human it said, "Greetings, newcomers. I see that your lore remembers the signs of friendship among Wolves."

"Our lore remembers your friendship of long ago, and our stories for many generations will remember your help today. Thank you, son of Barreal."

"Any who would help us rid our home of these creatures who defile it are welcome to our help," said the dog. "I am Banneall. Barreal was an ancestor of my line. I welcome you in his name, but our task is not completed. There are more of these vile creatures to the south and they approach in large numbers. We have blocked your scent with our own. Let us watch to see what they do."

So it was to become another waiting game. Angus gazed at the perimeters of their island in the sky. The narrow ridge that formed it ended in the cliff facing south. Just before the cliff was a broad level area. Its approach was restricted by sharp drop-offs on both sides, like another island, surrounded by air and sky.

We must lie low then," said Arikin, "so that they don't see us."

"But they know you are here," agreed Banneall. "The other party sent them a messenger before they ascended to fight you."

"Then they'll stay and search," said Feshka. "They're determined."

"We must find a way to get word to The City of The Vision and to my father," determined Arikin. "We knew there were Ogladim in the area but we had no idea how many there were."

"What is this with the talking dog?" Ingram muttered to William. "Dogs don't talk."

"It looks like this one does," grinned William.

"Banneall is the descendent of a very special race," Feshka informed them. "Is that not so, Banneall?"

As Angus gazed at the dog, he thought he must have been getting sleepy because suddenly it went out of focus and then Angus couldn't see it anymore. When the dog faded back into focus, it wasn't a dog any more, but a man. Then it faded again, and when Angus looked again, it had become an Elf. Angus felt lightheaded. He closed his eyes and rubbed them. When he opened them again, Banneall was once more a dog. Angus shook his head to clear it and looked at his father, wondering if he had seen the same thing.

William was also rubbing his eyes. "As you can see," explained Banneall, "there is more under heaven than you know of. We were made at the same time as the Elves, from light. This land is our sacred home over which we are designated as watchers, protecting the light. When the Elves came we welcomed them. When Humans came, we ignored them because they had no light and they were not an enemy. Now a new enemy has arrived. This one we must fight."

Chapter Fifteen: The Cudgel of Boer

The battle had taken longer than Angus had thought. The sun was no longer high in the sky. It was already touching the western horizon. He had never felt so tired; he was trembling with fatigue. He hadn't had a good night's sleep since they were in the bowels of Castle Urquhart.

That night, for the first time since he had left his father's house in Glen Williamson, he felt safe. Even with the Ogladim pitching camp at the foot of their cliff, he still felt safe. The Wolves were prowling the forest tonight. Their scent had covered what little their own group had left in their rapid passage through the woods. They believed the Ogladim below would think the wolves had killed them along with the rest of the Ogladim.

The Wolves in the forest kept the Ogladim from doing much searching on their own, especially after dark. The Ogladim spent the first hour after they'd arrived, counting bodies. Then as darkness fell, they cowered around fires they had built. Angus could occasionally smell smoke from below, but it wasn't strong.

All he could think about now was closing his eyes and not opening them for at least eight or nine hours. He hoped he could have some undisturbed sleep. The Elves were trading watches and the Dwarves were keeping a close watch on Ingram. Angus felt Ingram had had enough of fighting for one day. Maybe he would be satisfied to get some sleep.

For several hours Angus slept peacefully, but then his dreaming self awoke. He found himself standing at the top of the cliff he had so staunchly defended that day. Around him were sleeping Humans. One Dwarf slept while the other sat awake watching and listening. Marnel was awake, her light carefully covered, like the rest of the Elves. Angus looked down, and at his feet he saw his sleeping self curled up under his cover. He marveled at the experience of seeing himself asleep while he was standing, awake and alert.

"StrathNaver," a voice addressed him. He turned to look. It was Feshka. "We wondered if you would ever leave your body without assistance. I see that you did."

"I haven't left my body," protested Angus. "It's right here!"

Feshka smiled. "That's not what I mean. See, your sleeping body is there, and your consciousness is elsewhere. You awoke in your dream. Do you understand?"

"Are you saying that I'm dreaming?" asked Angus.

"Not exactly. Look around you. Do you see my body sleeping nearby?"

"Yes. It's there," Angus pointed.

"But I am here, not there," Feshka reminded him. "Your spirit can travel without your body if you want it to. Do you understand?"

"But that's me lying there," insisted Angus. "How could I be here and there at the same time?"

"Where do your eyes tell you that you are?"

"Am I my spirit or am I my body?" asked Angus.

"Some believe they have no spirit, that they are only a body. What do your senses tell you?"

"My senses tell me there's more than there appears to be most of the time. Is this a dream?"

"No, StrathNaver. You awoke in your dream. Do you remember Forest Old?"

"Of course I do," replied Angus. "He told me of the gifts for Lurelei."

"Where did he say to look for them?" asked Feshka.

"He said my dreaming self must carry them."

"Then your dreaming self must seek for them. I have been waiting for you to try. Do you want some help with this?"

"If I'm to help Lurelei, then I will need help myself. I have no idea what to do or where to look."

"Follow me," instructed Feshka.

Angus watched as Feshka stepped off the cliff, but he didn't fall. Angus stepped toward the edge, but didn't have the courage to follow those footsteps. Feshka stood in mid-air, a smile on his face. "Look down, StrathNaver. Look down!"

Angus discovered he was standing about a foot above the ground. In his dreaming self he was weightless. He had drifted upward without even knowing it! "How do I get back down again?"

"Visualize yourself gently falling until you touch the ground." Angus did as he was told and shortly he was standing on the ground again. Then, to experiment, he visualized himself again a foot off the ground, and instantly found himself there.

"Now that you see how easy this is, how would you like to take a little trip with me?" asked Feshka.

"A trip? Where?"

"Take my hand." Angus reached out and took Feshka's right hand. Suddenly he was in another forest, floating about thirty feet off the ground. It was colder and drizzling, but he couldn't feel it. Below him he saw a dim light moving through the trees. "Do you know what that is?"

"No. What is it?" asked Angus, thinking it was an Elf's light that he saw.

"That is a Geketz named Lurelei. See how it seems fuzzy and out of focus?"

"Yes. That's how it was when I saw it close up and in person."

"This is because the Geketz exists partly in the place of dreams, partly in spirit. If it touches you even now it can hurt you. Stay away from it."

"Can it fly?"

"No one knows for sure if they can fly or not, but I don't think so."

"I think I'd like to speak with her."

"Stay away now. She'll see you and think you're dead. Let's not take away her hope."

"Where shall we look for the gifts?" asked Angus.

"First we must teach you to navigate in this form. Do you know how to get back to your body? I don't want you to be out here running around by yourself if you don't know how to get back. I may not be able to find you if you get lost."

"I guess what I have to do is visualize my body and I'll just be there. Is that right?"

"Try it," suggested Feshka.

Suddenly they were back on the low cliff with the rest of the sleepers and watchers. Angus noticed now that the forest was full of lights, most of them traveling at different speeds. "Are the lights I see from the Wolves?" he asked Feshka.

"Yes. Now would you like to set out to try to find the first gift... or do you wish to rest and try that another time?"

"I'll try now," Angus exclaimed without hesitation. "Where should I begin, do you think?"

"The items you are to find are probably not hidden if indeed you are intended to find them. I will summon a friend." Feshka made a whistling sound.

For a few moments there was no change in the forest's night sounds. Angus's hearing was different in this state. He could hear things that his ears would not normally detect, and he could also depict undertones that he couldn't identify. Then suddenly he heard an odd thundering, loud and growing louder. *Where is it coming from?* Angus wondered.

Feshka smiled at his concern. "He's coming!"

In the sky to the south, Angus noticed a shadow appearing; the thunder grew louder. Angus began to draw back in fear, but Feshka calmed him. "It's only Geemayel, young Elfkin. Fear not, for this is a friend."

Finally the huge apparition stopped before them. It walked on four long legs and its back was above Angus's eye level. Its eyes bulged from a head that was overlong and as it stared down at him, Angus had the feeling this large beast was amused by him. Angus finally realized this was a kind of horse. Its color was ash and it wore no saddle. "Climb on his back, Angus. Geemayel has come for you!"

"Fear him not, StrathNaver," another voice said. Angus realized VelMud had joined them. "I'm here to see you off. This is a journey you won't soon forget!"

The animal didn't seem to be able to stand still. As it waited for Angus to climb up on its back, nostrils flared and breathing hard, it danced around him. "Come now, Angus," urged Feshka softly. "Geemayel knows where you need to go. He can take you there."

"What is this--a dream horse?" asked Angus. "What beast is this that rides into dreams?"

"He is more than a horse," explained VelMud. "He is Geemayel. The Aeser god Odnir gave him his name when he was created. His task in the old days was to carry Odnir and his wife across the dismal abyss that lies between the islands of the living and the place of their home that they called Asgard. The Aeser gods have left this place but Geemayel and others of their creation remain."

"All who travel in the place of dreams one day meet Geemayel," said Feshka. "He is a friend to dream travelers. He won't wait much longer. Go now, StrathNaver. He will bring you back safely. Trust him! Leap upon his back and hold on tight. And Angus," instructed Feshka, "drink no wine tonight."

Angus leaped, one hand holding onto the horse's mane and the other held high for balance. As soon as he was on Geemayel's back, the horse galloped away. Angus looked down at the Earth as it disappeared beneath him. In the distance he could see a fire that the Ogladim had built at the base of the cliff. The light from the Wolves faded in the distance and soon all that Angus could see was the blackness of the night. He now knew that the thundering he had heard earlier was the pounding of Geemayel's hooves on the night sky.

Angus marveled at the animal's strength and appearance. The Aesers were gods of the Norse peoples in an age beyond his ability to imagine. They had been gone for a long time. As a child his mother had told him stories about them, but she had never told him about Geemayel. The animal's dusty hide and short mane were barely enough to hang onto. His surging strength pulled hard as Angus struggled to keep his seat.

Angus began to again experience fear. If he fell, what then? Was there Earth still beneath him? The beast forged on through the night sky as though on a mission of its own. Its thundering hooves echoed against the clouds and seemed to rattle the stars.

Would Lurelei believe all he had to tell her about his quest for the gifts? He hadn't even had a chance to tell her of Forest Old and his message. She was alone, somewhere in a vast forest, without hope. He feared for her and as he did, his love rose within him, giving him strength to hang on while Geemayel leaped through the sky.

Geemayel seemed to be racing at full gallop on a path only he could see clearly. His feet seemed to hit a solid surface as each in turn touched down. Then Angus thought he could see a path with ghostly trees on either side, towering over him. His speed was so great, the trees passed quickly, but he could see branches hanging down sometimes as they approached and whizzing over his head.

Now Geemayel turned and took a side path that seemed to be less traveled, Angus thought. He could see tall grass ahead and sometimes the path would vanish before his eyes. But Geemayel knew the way. He charged through this phantom forest as though it was the way he traveled daily to find his food. Angus could see a light pass by now and then that could have been from some weary camper sleeping beside the trail, their cooking fire burning low.

What of his own camp, Angus wondered. Would the travelers he was with, be safe and still be there when he returned? Could he return? Where was this beast carrying him so fast and far? This was unfamiliar terrain. The rises and falls of the Earth this path followed were strange to him.

In the distance Angus could see a castle with banners waving on high turrets. This was no deserted fortress like Urquhart. The windows were lit up and so was the courtyard. The lights shone into the night sky, reflecting off the bottoms of the clouds overhead.

As they approached, Angus saw a deep moat with a draw span pulled up tight against the castle wall. Someone had seen them coming.

He heard the creaking of ropes and pulleys as the span began to drop.

Geemayel waited at the foot for the bridge to touch the ground and when it did, he began prancing as he had done before. A small figure came out across the span. It was shaped like a man or Elf but was smaller than either, with Earth-colored skin and prominent veins across its face.

"Who comes here?" asked the creature.

"I am Angus of the Valley Naver," answered Angus. "Some call me by its river's name, StrathNaver. What place is this?"

"You have reached the home of Boer, but the Master is not in just now."

Another voice from inside the walls called out, "And he's not likely to be in. He's gone now a thousand years."

"But we watch over it for him," said the first. "I am Caleel, the servant of Boer. How can I help you?"

"I have been sent by Forest Old to claim Three Gifts for Lurelei. This is the place where Geemayel has carried me. Has he carried me astray?"

"Dismount, Elfkin, for Geemayel it would seem has other business this night. See how he prances in his eagerness to leave!"

Angus was afraid to dismount, but he still had his Elf Steel Blade and his Skyn Dhu. He doubted that Feshka would send him into danger, and after all, his sleeping body was far away and safe. This was only a dream. He dismounted.

"What are these gifts and where can I find them?" he asked Caleel.

"Your Humanness is showing," the creature laughed. "You are in such a hurry, too much of a hurry to even drink a drought of wine with me."

"No wine for me tonight," Angus declared, remembering Feshka's words. "This is a night of serious business in which I must find the Gifts for Lurelei."

"You Mortal Men can be so single-minded! Is there no time to enjoy the night? Share with us some food and wine and then if you still want to, we'll help you find one of the Gifts."

"One? There is one only in this place? Where are the other two?"

"Such a hurry. Such a hurry. And don't you know these Gifts of the Aesers are hard to find and make? Do you think it so trivial a matter that all one needs do is drop by a shop and pick some up for a price? "

As he spoke, Caleel grew in size and shape. He now towered over Angus. His shoulders had spread and looked very powerful. His arms hung to his knees and in one hand he held a mace, a spiked ball on a long chain. Angus had never seen a mace before and he drew back as though to remount Geemayel, but the horse was gone.

"And who is this who comes from Forest Old to claim such treasures? Do you not know that the Cudgel of Boer is not to be carried by a man?"

"What is the Cudgel of Boer?" asked Angus, trying to steer the conversation away from whatever was annoying Caleel. The creature raised its voice so much that, when it spoke, Angus trembled. Angus did not want to go against this huge servant of the Aesers with its mace, using only his sword.

"Ah, the Cudgel of Boer," exclaimed Caleel, his voice softening somewhat. "Its essence only remains. Boer took it with him, but that is not what you have come for. You are here to remake the Cudgel. The original was lost when Boer fell off of Geemayel on the way back to Earth."

"A god fell off of Geemayel?" asked Angus in astonishment and fear. "If the horse's own Master couldn't stay astride of him, how could I do so--I, a mere mortal, Elfkin or no?"

"Boer beat Geemayel because he refused to steal the wife of another for him. Boer created Geemayel to have integrity and this order offended him. Boer beat him with the Cudgel. Be kind to Geemayel, Human. He is a beast but not mindless."

"How is the Cudgel to be remade and why are the other Gifts not here?"

"Don't be a fool, Mortal. The Cudgel of Boer is the weapon by which the Holiest of the Holies is protected and guarded from the approach of Barbaric Force such as the one that caused the malady of Lurelei. Forest Old had told us of it. That is why you are here. It must be forged to keep the afflicted one whole. Without this protection there is no point in such healing, for once healed, the victim will again be afflicted. Without the Cudgel of Boer, the most Sacred of the Healing Gifts will be useless, for it will be stolen and consumed by the Wraiths which dwell upon the plain you must cross in order to return home."

"Forgive my ignorance," exclaimed Angus, "but how can one such as I cause this Gift to spring into being? I have never seen it, nor do I understand it!"

"No living Mortal has ever seen it. Knowledge of its existence has passed from the minds of Men. Forgetfulness reigns below, young Mortal. Only here is it remembered, where time does not rule. We told Forest Old of its power and how to use it."

"What next?" asked Angus.

"Remember this, young Mortal. No power on Earth or above it or below it is greater than love. Love is the root of all passion and all power. Perverted love is the root of all evil. Love is a creative healing power and forms all things anew. It makes an old man young and it can make a young man old. It was a perverted love of youth that caused old Boer to lust after another's wife. It was love of self that caused Geemayel to drop the god into the Abyss. Love creates the Cudgel of Boer, but its passion must be directed. Can you direct your passions, StrathNaver? As the power of the river, your name's sake, channels its energy down one path into the sea, so you must channel your full power to manifest one idea. Can you do this?"

"I don't know," responded Angus meekly.

"That is not good enough! The three forces within you must be in concert. Those forces are your will, your faith and your passions. If your faith is weak the feat cannot be accomplished. Your passion is the power. Your will directs the force. Your faith is the horse that pulls the cart. No faith, no cart. *I ask again, StrathNaver: can you direct your passions?"*

Angus remembered the door he had burst. He remembered the battering ram he had created in his imagination. He remembered the power of the anger he'd felt at that time that he had directed to form the ram and burst the door. "I can do it," he answered confidently.

After he spoke, there was silence. Angus listened for a sound but heard nothing. Even the sound of the night air, moving through the castle windows had stopped. The banners still waved in a mysterious breeze that he couldn't feel or hear. Faces watched him from above and within the castle walls. As he listened he felt stronger and more courageous. He dismissed all his self-doubt. He was here for a purpose. He would have one chance. Lurelei's life depended on his ability to focus. "I can do it," he resolved.

"Before you on the ground is a staff. Lift it," instructed Caleel.

Angus bent over and picked up a wooden stick on the ground in front of him. It was about an inch-and-a-half in diameter and about six feet long. At one end was a short slightly tilted cross piece. He inspected the stick of wood for markings or any sign that it was other than a stick of wood. "Is this the Cudgel?" he asked softly.

"No," answered Caleel. "It is the form only. Now you will create the Cudgel, using this form. Hold out the staff before you."

Angus held the stick at arm's length in front. "Now focus your energies on the staff itself. Call forth that part of you that wishes to defend the one you love. Call forth your protective love for her. Fire it with your passion for her and drive that passion with the anger you feel for the injustice done to her."

Angus focused on the staff. In his mind's eye he imagined it was near Lurelei, defending her against the Geketz. Suddenly the area around his hand supporting the staff began to glow with a blue, then a violet light.

"That's good," Caleel was pleased. "Whatever you're doing is the right idea. Keep going."

Angus called up all the love he could find in himself. His love for Lurelei was not enough, so he called up his love for his lost mother as well, and his father and the joy of his childhood and that of knowing the Elves. He called on all of it. Behind the passions he was raising, he felt the smoldering anger of being deprived of those he loved. All of this, he focused on the staff. As he did so, the staff's glow changed from the violet hue to a nearly white brilliance. The light spread throughout the length of the staff. The crosspiece at the end seemed to be a focal point for the power. It glowed so brightly that Angus could barely look at it. Then the staff burst into flames, but he felt no pain from the fire. He continued to build his passions and focus on the task at hand. Soon the staff completely disintegrated, leaving only the burning image of brilliant white light.

Angus removed his hand. The staff floated in the air before him without any means of visible support. "You have recreated the Cudgel of Boer," Caleel informed him. "Now you must take it and go."

"Forest Old said to not touch it with my hand," Angus shook his head, bewildered. "How can I take it?"

"Your conscious hand is sleeping far away from this place, Strath-Naver. You couldn't reach it if you tried. Take it now with your dreaming hand and hold it to your breast."

Angus reached out again and took the staff. Obediently he held it to his chest and watched as it vanished inside him. "You now carry the Cudgel of Boer within your heart. Find the other gifts and the healing of Lurelei will be within your power."

"Where can I look for them?" asked Angus. "Where are they?"

"You will find them, StrathNaver. You have found a cause to lead you that the Aeser gods favor. They will help you."

Turning his back on Angus, Caleel strode back inside the castle. As he approached the end of the draw span, the noise of ropes and pulleys again filled the night. Angus turned to discover that Geemayel was dancing with impatience as he waited for him. The drawbridge was back in place against the castle's wall and the castle itself had begun to look fuzzy and out of focus as though it was fading into the night.

Angus leaped upon the horse's back and again rode through the night. When they arrived at the cliff's top, the island in the sky, Angus leaped off Geemayel's back and turned to thank the horse; but Geemayel was already gone. Feshka and VelMud were not where he had left him but were now sleeping with the others, surrounded by the Wolves.

Chapter Sixteen: The Haven of Barteel

When Angus awoke he still felt groggy, as though he hadn't slept at all. Then he remembered. What a strange journey! What a weird dream! Was it a dream or a journey? He decided that it must have been a dream. Then reflecting on it, he decided he must have been on a journey. Feshka was in it. If it were real, he would probably mention it. VelMud was there too, briefly. Angus looked around.

At first he was startled because he saw no one. *My God! Am I here alone?* He lay back in his bedroll and tried to figure out where he was. This didn't bother him too much. He had awakened more than once since this journey began, not knowing where he was.

He was alone on the small plateau. The forest rose around him in silence and the smell of rotting flesh nearby assailed his nostrils. Then he remembered the Elf covers that were meant to conceal. Everyone was under covers and they were transparent at the same time blending into the surroundings. The covers were better than the camouflage that the Grouse wears. Although the party was nearly invisible, he had learned to see them even with the covers. He looked again and there they were, all around him.

It was first light. Had he even slept at all, or had he spent the entire night galloping across the skies on that phantom horse? His face felt wind-burned and his hair was blown straight back. How had that happened? It had to have been a dream. He was right here with the others. He had just awakened. There was his father, William. Tristan was sleeping not far away. There was Scobie with Ingram right next to him. They were still all together. Over here were Feshka and VelMud. Mishishel and PoleeShimel were just beyond them with Aelrondel and Marnel. VeratNonn was snoring loudly with BarNeesh beside him. Arikin was standing near the cliff's edge, watching them.

As consciousness filtered its way into Angus's mind he also became aware that the sky was slightly cloudy and the air cooler than it had been. Maybe this run of sunny days was nearly over and the typical rainy foggy days of northern Alba were about to begin. Angus didn't look forward to that. Constant hiking and sleeping out of doors was shock enough to his system. Foul weather added another undesirable factor to all of this.

As he recalled some of the details of his dream, his skin started to prickle and he felt a chill move down his spine. What a dream! What a horse and flight! How could he have conceived of such dream-adventure? What was that creature? 'Caleel' it had called itself. He sat up, aware that VeratNonn's snoring was a danger to them. He scrambled to his feet to try to wake him or somehow make him stop. The Ogladim were still near.

Arikin moved to stop him. "They've fled. Barreal returned an hour ago and said they've taken the low road that returns to The Great Glen and the Lake. We'll have to take a wide path around them to return to The City of The Vision."

"Then we're safe?" asked Angus.

"For the time being, yes," Arikin smiled. "VeratNonn may snore if he wishes."

When everyone was awake, they left the island in the sky for cleaner air, away from the stench of dead Ogladim and hogs. The path Arikin chose this morning was north by east, finally in the general direction of home. Aelrondel and Marnel took turns running ahead and behind as before, but their reports were of empty forests and paths. No Ogladim had been sighted, and no hogs.

They felt free to talk again. For the last few days they had been afraid to make any unnecessary sounds. The Elves chided the Humans and Dwarves for making so much noise as they walked, but Angus knew they were joking because they also talked, and sang as they hiked along. Arikin had said, if they encountered no more problems they should be home in two, maybe three days. Their hearts were lighter. Fear was gone.

Their pace was more relaxed and the path they followed was more level. No need to flee through mountain passes and steep slopes. No more hard climbs or descents because they didn't have to hide in the mountain. There was nothing to hide from, or so it seemed. The Ogladim had moved away quickly.

As before, Angus chose to walk with Feshka. VelMud followed closely behind. The dream was the main topic of conversation. Had Feshka ever heard of the Cudgel of Boer? No, but he had heard of Boer. Had he ever heard of Caleel? No, but wait... wasn't he a servant of Boer? And on it went, as the sun climbed into the sky and their feet again began to grow weary; but not as weary as before.

Suddenly Marnel burst upon them from ahead, calling softly but urgently, "They're coming again! They're coming again! We must flee!"

"How many this time?" asked Arikin.

"There must be eighty or more and they're running as fast as they can, and shouting. We'll hear them any moment. We must flee immediately!"

With a mixed look of fear and apology, Arikin instructed, "Quickly, follow me! The Haven we sought before is near. Come quickly!"

He took off at a run toward the southeast and soon was out of sight. Angus hitched up his pants and took off after him, with the others close at his heels. The Dwarves took a rear position with Mishishel and PoleeShimel. Arikin continued to lead and Marnel and Aelrondel stayed with the Humans, urging them on. Angus could hear the shouting behind him. This encouragement seemed to add speed to his legs. Looking back, he was glad to see Ingram keeping up. He could see the fear in Tristan's eyes but there was no time to think about it. On they ran, stumbling over the bushes and fallen limbs.

The next time Angus looked back, Ingram had disappeared. William called to him to keep going. "Better lose one than all!" Angus was torn between going back to defend his neighbor and fleeing for his own life. Good sense overwhelmed honor and he continued after Arikin. The shouting was getting louder. A glowing arrow whizzed past Angus's head and stuck in a tree in front of him.

"Keep your head down, Angus," called Scobie. "That one was close."

Angus glanced backward again, trying to see the marksman who had missed him. He saw no one. It had to have been fired from a good distance. His lungs were burning. He wouldn't be able to keep running like this much longer. How could this have happened? He had found the first Gift of the three and was about to be overrun with Ogladim. What would happen now to Lurelei? His life would soon be over.

His legs pounded over the uneven terrain. A branch snapped back across his face, stinging and tearing his flesh. Blood was now dripping into his right eye, mixed with sweat. William was close behind him, keeping up. Scobie was in the lead, with Arikin, Marnel and Aelrondel ahead of him. The ground they were following had begun to slope down. Angus guessed it went toward the sea. *And what then?* When they reached the sea they would be cornered. They would have to stop. There was no escape.

With the effort he was putting forth to keep up with his fleeing friends, his wounds were beginning to ache again. His throat was burning and freezing at the same time and the pain had begun to move down across his shoulder and into his chest. With the effort of the past days, he thought the wounds had abated, but now they reached further into his body than ever before.

They came to a stream; Arikin, running at top speed, was following its flow. Angus got a glimpse of him leaping over rocks and bushes just as he turned a corner and was then hidden by trees. The Humans in the party were beginning to wear out. The Dwarves were closer behind than before and grumbling at them to hurry along. Angus could now hear the shouts and voices even over the sound of the stream. Glancing back, he thought he could see movement in the forest behind him.

As he rounded the bend in the stream, he was amazed to see that it had come to an end. The stream had not been very wide. It was hardly more than a brook. Still, it would have required three or four steps in the water in order to make the crossing. This would have been impossible, since the water was too deep and the current too swift.

Yet now the water had just stopped. So had Arikin. Marnel and Aelrondel had also stopped and they were waiting for the others to catch up. When Angus reached them Arikin called, "Jump in!"

Angus eyed the pool at the stream's end. It wasn't wide but appeared to be deep. It was dark blue, almost black and very turbulent. The water seemed to dance a rhythm of its own, and the surface had tiny chops and waves from the stream, transported to a low cliff face on the other side. The center of the stream had a small hole or whirlpool that danced around in small circles as though the water was draining into an invisible source. Angus could hear an intermittent sucking sound, as the water sucked air down into the hole with the water.

"Jump in!" repeated Arikin urgently. "This is the Haven. Do it now, and then get out of the way. The rest will follow. Show him," he turned to Marnel.

Obediently Marnel jumped into the center of the pool and vanished. Aelrondel followed. Mishishel had caught up to them with the others and he now followed the two into the pool.

"Do it," directed Arikin. "There's no time to explain. Trust me!"

Tristan closed his eyes, and holding his nose, leaped after Aelrondel and vanished into the water. Angus was trembling. His only experience in deep water had been in the River Naver. It seemed like it was so long ago, he could barely remember the day, but he remembered Lurenne.

He remembered the bubbles floating away from his mouth and nostrils, joining with that big bubble way up above him where he could not go to breathe.

William leaped into the pool and vanished. Scobie leaped in behind him. Arikin picked up Angus and threw him into the water.

In horror and fear, Angus felt the cold mountain stream close over his head. He didn't know which he feared more, the water or the Oglad-im. Without Arikin's help he would have been willing to stand and fight any number of them single-handed rather than brave deep water. Better to die in battle than drown in a brook.

He could feel the clamminess of his wet clothes clinging to his skin. *Now to die by drowning.* He had never really feared death. His father had often talked of it with the others in their small community. Stories of distant battles were favorite topics among the men. They saved souvenirs from battles their fathers and grandfathers had fought. The stories were of war with Norsemen and other clans. The biggest war with the most stories about it was the one with the invading Italians. That had been a long time ago, yet they still talked of it.

Angus had always thought he would die like that, hand to hand with some invader. His brother, friends and family would talk about him for hundreds of years afterward, sharing stories with their children and friends at community gatherings. *"Remember Old Angus Williamson,"* they would say. But now all that was dashed from his thoughts. Drowning was the way it would be for him. *"Old Angus drownded in a brook,"* they would say. *"Was he fighting?"* some would ask. *"No,"* would be the answer. *"He was running for his life. Abandoned Old Ingram, so they say."*

Angus plucked up his courage and looked up. The surface was as he remembered it, but something was different. This time he wasn't attached to any bottom. No vine was wrapped around him. He wasn't stuck to anything. The water was sucking him down like wine out of an upturned bottle. Down it gurgled and down went his last remaining hopes for a rescue. How could Arikin have done this to him? What cruel streak ran through the Elf that he had kept hidden all this time? What betrayal! Trying to lead them to safety was his plea, but here he was leading them to death in what was hardly more than a puddle.

The surface was disappearing rapidly. It was now just a tiny glimmer of light at the top of what looked to Angus like a long tunnel. His ears felt a strange pressure in them and he longed for air. Would he ever smell a fresh spring breeze again? Would he...

SPLASH!!! He hit bottom. This time he really was in over his head. A hand gripped his. It was William's. Shortly he felt the earth under his feet again and air around his face. He inhaled, then coughed. Suddenly there was another splash. It was Feshka. A third splash turned out to be VeratNonn.

"Sorry I never taught you to swim, boy," William helped Angus out of the water, "but I see that you're all right. When we get home, I'll teach you if you want to learn. It's not hard."

Angus looked around him. They were in another type of cavern and a strange light was emerging from the rocks around him, causing them to glow. The rocks themselves were strange. He had never before seen stalagmites and stalactites and these were coated with phosphorescence.

Angus was still out of breath. He stretched out on a short beach beside the now underground stream and puffed and huffed till his heart slowed. The group was all together in the cave, with the exception of Ingram.

Angus now had time to reflect about the loss of Ingram. Here was another death he could lay at his own door. There were three now. If he had been home he might have been able to protect his mother. Maybe not, but if he had been home at least he could have tried. Hell, his father was at home at the time. Why didn't he protect her? Angrily he glared at his father, then caught himself. His father loved Laura as much as he did; his loss was probably greater. How must William feel? How should Angus feel?

But what about Lurelei? Angus realized with a shock that Arikin was lying on the beach near him, sound asleep. Then he realized that Aelrondel and Marnel also appeared to be asleep. Of course. They had been deprived of sleep for days, trying to watch out for everyone else. They had been watching out for him. Arikin even had to physically pick him up and throw him in the water for his own protection. Angus now felt embarrassed about all these thoughts.

William patted him on the back. "Don't worry Angus. Ingram probably had a quick death. Those creatures don't fool around. You saw how vicious they were. They had us trapped on that little ridge. They just stood back there with their bows and arrows behind their pigs and shot at us like it was target practice. Ingram had a quick death. There was nothing we could do for him without being killed ourselves."

"It still seems there must have been something we could have done to help him." Angus bowed his head, feeling a hard knot in the pit of this stomach. *So that's what loss feels like.* How did one make that knot dissolve or go away?

"We can live to fight another day," added Scobie. "We can live to fight another day. That's what my Dad always said. There's no shame in running from an overwhelming force."

"If we live to fight and we keep fighting, someday we'll prevail," VeratNonn chimed in as he rolled over to go back to sleep.

"We should follow his example." William laid a hand on Angus's shoulder. "Sleep if you can. We'll probably have a lot of long days ahead."

"I don't think I'll be able to sleep much. I'm pretty hungry and I'm out of food. We all are, I think." Part of his inner turmoil, he realized, was caused by lack of food. None of them had eaten much of anything in days, and they had carefully rationed whatever they had, making it last as long as possible.

"I have none," said William. "We ate the last of it this morning. We were going to do some foraging today but all this happened and prevented it. Try to rest. The Elves will have something in mind. They always do. Look at this place, for example. I believe the first person to jump in that hole was made of some stern stuff."

"I wouldn't have done it," declared Angus.

"I'll say," exclaimed Scobie. "What could he have been thinking? I sure wouldn't have done it either!"

"It was fun, kinda,'" Tristan piped up.

"Fun?! You can have it," Angus snorted. "I thought I was going to die!"

"Worse things can befall a man than death," declared Feshka. "What of the Ogladim? Many of them were once men."

Angus was looking at the waterfall where he had just fallen. "Do you think they would try to follow us? Do you think they saw where we went?"

"They might have," answered Feshka, "but they don't much like the water."

Arikin stretched out on his back, his hands behind his head, listening to them talking. "I know who the first person was to jump through the pool."

"Who was it?" asked Tristan.

"It was during one of the wars between the Dwarves and Elves. VeratNonn and BarNeesh, do you mind if I tell the story?"

"I was there," said VeratNonn. "I know who it was. But you may tell it if you wish."

"His name was Barteel," said Arikin. "He was young then. He'd gone away from the camp, not far from here, to scout the area. He hadn't gone far before he found a troop of Dwarves on the trail. He knew if they continued in the direction that they were traveling that soon they could come upon the Elf encampment. It was his intention to distract them, but these Dwarves were faster and more cunning than Barteel thought. He was, after all, not of full Elf blood and couldn't run as fast. He wasn't as nimble as we are, even when he was young."

"Did they catch him?" asked Tristan.

"Nearly. They chased him through the forest for quite a distance. He ran blindly downhill trying to find a stream where he could lose his tracks. The Dwarves were using dogs. Finally he came to this stream, and since he was hot and sweaty, he decided to swim across rather than wade. You can imagine his surprise!"

"How did he get out again?" asked Angus.

"He is now called Feshka. Ask him," Arikin grinned.

"Well, how did you find your way out?" asked Tristan. William and the others were trying to hide their chuckles.

"There's a way," Feshka smiled wryly. "There's a way."

As they watched, it seemed to Angus that a rope was hanging in the water. He thought at first, it was his imagination, a trick played by the eerie light coming from the tall strangely pointed rocks. As they talked, the rope seemed to grow longer, with something hanging on the end of it.

"Look there," Angus pointed at the waterfall. "Do you see something odd there?"

They all looked. "It's odd," exclaimed Feshka. "It's an Elf grass rope with a sign at the end. I'll look closer."

Feshka rose from his sandy bed and waded back into the water. As he waded deeper, Arikin turned to watch. Finally the water was too deep to wade and Feshka began swimming against the current toward to waterfall and the grass rope.

"Do you think the Ogladim are trying to trick us?" asked Angus. "That couldn't be from Elves unless they were captured."

Arikin now sat up to watch more closely. His clothing was soaking wet and his hair hung in strands over his face. Mishishel also sat up to watch. The rope was now all the way into the water and the current began to carry it downstream toward the place where the water disappeared into darkness on its way to the deep. Feshka caught the end of it and began to make his way back toward them. The rope seemed to grow longer as it came down through the waterfall.

"Give me the end," instructed Arikin as Feshka waded out of the water. He handed the rope end to Arikin. On it was a wood carving of an Elf. Arikin gathered some of the rope into his hand. Grinning, he tugged hard on it. A moment later there was another loud splash. All of them were on their feet in seconds, with Elf Blades glowing brighter than the phosphorescent stalactites and their brightly glowing mates below. In a moment a head appeared above the water's surface.

"Ha!" shouted Arikin.

"A mean trick that was," the head called back to him.

"A good one, I thought," Arikin shouted back, laughing.

Then Marnel and Aelrondel recognized him at about the same time and began laughing. "It's AriMa, Arikin's brother," Feshka informed them. "Something has gone right today!"

Suddenly the water stopped falling, leaving a gaping hole in the cavern ceiling. "It's safe to come out now," called AriMa.

"Come above and break bread with us," a voice called through the hole.

One by one they were pulled or climbed up the rope and soon they were all gathered on the stream's bank above. Angus was surprised to see Fierrondel standing by the stream. She seemed to be having a regular conversation with the water. When the group had all been removed from the cavern, she walked toward them and the water began to flow once again. Angus was further surprised to see the stream surrounded by a huge mass of people and Elves.

Migalik was among them, with his wife Star Bright. What most surprised Angus was the fact that MacBain and Hender were there among a large number of heavily armed men wearing the MacAodh plaid. Not only did he see MacAodhs; there was also a hoard of men from Clans Gunn, MacDonald, MacDonell, and others. Included in the gathering were also Wood Elves in their browns, and Sea Elves. Angus had never seen such a large gathering before.

Finally he began to understand. And wonder upon wonders, there in their midst stood Ingram with a strange glowering grin on his face.

"What happened?" Angus asked him.

"The bloody creatures weren't chasing us at all," he told them. "They were fleeing from this army you see before you. They ran right over me as though I wasn't even there. The only injury I got was when one stepped on me as he ran. I'll probably have a bruise."

Hender came up to Ingram with MacBain. "We found them on the way north. I guess we owe you some explanation. We did not head home, back, to the Glen, as we told you. We were on another mission. The Elves sent us back to raise the clans. They sent others north to fetch the rest of the Elves from the forest and the Islands. Ariel is around somewhere. He's the Rebeck of the Firthlands and he's in charge of this small army."

"Small?" Angus shook his head in wonderment. "There must be thousands here."

"There are many, but not thousands. We hoped we would run into you somewhere," continued Hender. "We killed lots of these creatures on the march south. We were afraid they had got you."

"Ariel said his son was with you and you'd be safe. How was he as a leader?" asked MacBain.

"Amazing," William approached them. "Did you see where he took us to hide from them?"

"Looks like a hole in the ground to me," declared MacBain. Then he turned to look. The stream was running again and appeared to them as it had before, when Angus first saw it. MacBain simply stared.

"Was it like that when you went in there?" asked Hender.

"Just as you see it," answered William.

"How did they stop the water to get you out?" asked MacBain.

Angus smiled and nodded his head toward Fierrondel. "She has a way with water. It's her specialty."

Arikin had been speaking with some of the other Elves and he now approached the humans. "There is a massing of power from everywhere. The Enemy has never in our history been confronted with such a force. It's win or die for us. The word is that the Dwarves are marching from the south in huge numbers. All the Elves of the north are represented here. All the northern clans are here with us. We'll drive the Enemy into the sea."

Angus felt chills run over his skin at Arikin's words. He might live to fight real battles yet. Maybe his death would be as he hoped, one his family would tell stories about for generations to come. Maybe they would even start a new clan with his name, like they did for old William MacAodh. 'MacAngus,' or something like that, it would be called.

Everywhere he looked he saw strange faces. Then he had another shock: there was an Elf who looked just like Lurelei! In the next instant he realized it was Lee-Eesh, Lurelei's mother. Beside her was MarNosh, Lurelei's father. Marnel was standing with them, and so was Feshka. They were talking earnestly.

Migalik and Star Bright approached the group. "We're glad to see that you're safe," Migalik embraced them warmly.

"And we're glad to hear that StrathNaver is progressing in the way of the Brith Gar-Nunsum," added Star Bright.

"Progressing?" repeated Angus.

"Have you not been to Asgard, the home of Boer?" she asked. "Have you not begun the journeys which will lead to the healing of the daughter of MarNosh and Lee-Eesh?"

"I guess I've made a start," admitted Angus reluctantly. "But--"It is our hope that your quest to heal Lurelei will result in knowledge that we can use in our effort against the Enemy. Lurelei is harmed by his power. If you can find a way to break his power, you may be able to find a way we can use to break him."

"I hadn't thought of that." Angus shook his head, holding out his hands in a helpless gesture. "But what I've got so far doesn't seem like much."

"Feshka has told us what you have done," exclaimed Star Bright, smiling at him. "You now wield the Cudgel of Boer. Do you know what that means, StrathNaver?"

"Not really," Angus shook his head.

"Perhaps one day you will find out," she declared. "In the weave, the figure that represents you is holding such an instrument."

"But it's not me," Angus protested. "It's the Rebeck Ariel who is in the weave. It's not me!"

Chapter Seventeen: The March South

Angus slept fitfully. The crowd around him was never completely silent; there were always voices. Someone would rise to walk briefly into the forest to relieve himself and Angus would hear rustling leaves and awaken. Many were snoring; others were as restless as he and were strolling around the encampment, lost in thought.

This was the first time Angus had been close to the MacDonalds since he was a boy. He was almost instinctively afraid of them because of that first experience. He would never forget the fear he felt when he was racing away from them through the forest. He had been afraid of its darkness and the legendary creatures that lived there. It was the first time he had met Migalik and his family, and the first time he had ever seen Elves. What an experience that had been! It was also the first time he had ever seen—or felt the Flying Shadows. He now knew that was what had brought on the feeling of terror he remembered from that night.

Now, he was surrounded by Elves, and not only Elves, but Dwarves. And he had met new creatures he had never heard of before, not even in legends and stories. The people of Barreal were a total surprise to him. The giant dogs or Wolves were fearful to encounter, and a terrible foe. He was glad they were on his side. The dream experiences he had been having were unbelievable. He wasn't sure yet that he believed them. The Castle of Boer was a thing of myth and legend. Boer was not even one of the gods his people remembered. Ever since the visitation of Columba, and that was a long time ago, they had honored only the One God. It was a time when Castle Urquhart was still occupied. In fact Columba had stayed there for a while as a guest.

The Norseman or Vikings, who had raided this land long before he was born but who were still feared in the land, worshipped the Aeser gods. And what of the Cudgel? None he knew had ever heard of it in lore or legend. Feshka had said it was logical to expect that Boer had carried some sort of weapon. In legend, it was a sword, but it could also have been a club or both. No one knew.

What was he to do with this weapon? To him it had just been an interesting dream. He had no Cudgel with him. He did not see it around him when he awoke that morning. Feshka had said it was a metaphysical tool, whatever that meant. It was something he could only see or use when he was dreaming. What good was such a thing? If he could only use it when he was dreaming, what use could it possibly have? None that he could think of. Feshka had said it may become clear to him in time.

Angus had told his father about the dream he'd had about the Elf who called himself Forest Old. "Quite a dream," William had said. "I wouldn't think it was more than that, though. Don't believe all this claptrap from the old half Elf. Feshka may be well respected among the Elves but he's just an old fool with crazy ideas." Angus had given his father's comments a lot of thought. That in itself was an important step for Angus. He had never before questioned his father's opinions and ideas, and he wasn't sure if he agreed with him about Feshka.

The experiences he'd had with dreams since he'd met the Elves had certainly been vivid. If Elves and Dwarves and all these things of story really existed--and he'd seen for himself that they did--then maybe these other things were also true. He had to hope so, for they were the only hope he held for Lurelei.

There was a disturbance in the camp. Some were shouting. Many were on their feet with weapons in their hands, running into the forest. Angus had no idea what was going on, but he rose as did his father and the others and drew their weapons to defend themselves if needed. Ingram was the only one who did not arm himself. "What for?" he grumbled. "The fight's up there."

In a few minutes a large group returned from the forest. There was still shouting but they were now more orderly and most swords had been sheathed. The returning group was led by four large Dwarves. Three of them held long poles with loops on the end which were around the neck of a Geketz. They held it away from themselves by the poles. When Angus saw what they had, he took a few steps back in fear. The Elves all gave it a wide berth. It struggled as the Dwarves dragged it toward the camp. Its shrieks could probably be heard for miles.

Arikin strode toward them with a raised hand. "Don't bring it any closer." He instructed the Elves to build a wooden cage where they would keep it in for a while.

"They captured another one up near the Naver," Migalik informed him. "Don't worry, StrathNaver. It was not Lurelei, but she has returned to us. She lives in the forest near our home and waits for your return."

"Have you seen her?" asked Angus anxiously.

"No. She stays away from us, but the number of squirrels and rabbits in our area is not what it used to be. She feeds on our animal friends and neighbors. She must be stopped soon. If you cannot find a way to save her, she must destroyed. We have not done so yet because we have hope for her cure."

"What about the one you captured? How can you keep it? Why not just kill it?"

"We don't know who it is," said Migalik. "The Geketz that was stopped by Star Bright turned out to be one of our ancient heroes who we thought had been captured. No one knows how these creatures are made and what they were before. If you find a cure for Lurelei, maybe we can cure more of them."

"Then you think you may be able to cure this one too?"

"Not we, StrathNaver, you."

"I have a long way to go before I've completed the journeys I have before me," Angus protested, "and when they're finished, how can I be sure there will be any success?"

"If you fail, then we will kill the Geketzim we have captured, and Lurelei as well. It is cruel of us to allow her to suffer in this way if it is within our power to end it for her. If you have more work to do, then you should begin, without delay."

"We have been busy fleeing and fighting." Angus was annoyed with this expressed dependency on him. What could he do, after all? And what if he failed?

"I meant no reproach, StrathNaver, only encouragement. Your project is urgent."

Angus's annoyance melted into guilt. It was his fear and worry that prevented him from pursuing his task with more eagerness. His self-doubt had bound him in moral chains. These creatures, these Elves believed in him. Lurelei believed in him. How could he waste any more time? Now there was a Geketz among them, but subdued. Perhaps he could learn something from it.

He approached the Geketz for a closer look. It glowered at him, its red-streaked yellow eyes so dark, at first he didn't notice any color. Its darkness was so complete he had difficulty focusing on it. It seemed to fade at its edges, and as it moved, parts of it seemed to disappear into the night's darkness. Nearby fires provided some light so he could continue to examine it. Angus had never seen a Geketz close up with the time to study it. It looked like an Elf but it was larger than the Elves he had seen so far. It was somehow taller yet not filled in. It almost seemed that it was stretched to fit another dimension that was too large for it.

"Do you like to look upon death?" it addressed Angus. Its voice had a rough quality, almost as though it was ill, yet the strength in its voice was obvious. Angus was glad it was tightly tied to a tree. Three Dwarves still held the loops over its neck on the ends of poles, to be certain it couldn't escape.

"Don't come any closer, StrathNaver," one of the Dwarves warned him. "This thing's a lot stronger than it looks and it's very fast."

Almost as though to prove the Dwarf's words, the Geketz lunged at Angus but was restrained by the grass ropes holding it to the tree. In frustration and anger it then lunged at the Dwarves restraining him. The Geketz shrieked again, a piercing wail that caused Angus to cover his ears and retreat.

"They know they can't hold me for long. These strings they tied me with have Elf Light. I'm absorbing it as we speak," it sneered. "They don't know which ones will break first, but I do. Come closer, Naver. You are the one I seek."

It lunged again, trying to break the ropes that held it. Angus stepped back, frightened. As the creature struggled, it seemed that parts of it overlapped and flowed through the ropes. Angus had the feeling it could probably plunge through its restraints as though they weren't there, like air moving through a spider's web, dark air with little substance. Angus stared at it in anger and hate. This was the kind of creature that had attacked him on the mountain. It was the same kind of creature who had attacked Lurelei and made her what she is today. He hated it. He hated what it stood for. He hated its hatred. He wondered if there was a way that he himself could kill it. Such a monstrosity did not deserve to live.

Then he remembered what Caleel had said to him and repeated it for the monster's benefit, also to see it try vainly again to break free:

Remember this... No power on Earth or above it or below it is greater than love. Love is the root of all passion and all power. Perverted love is the root of all evil. Love is a creative power, healing and forming all things anew.

"Tell your Master that he can't prevail against so many and against the powers that these creatures bear in them. We are coming to get him even now. Your days are nearing their end," Angus added, wondering where all these words had come from.

The Geketz surprised Angus. It did not lunge again. Instead it began laughing. Its voice rose and fell, but all the while it did not take its eyes off Angus. It stared at him coolly and held its head level as if waiting for a chance to get to him, watching for any opening. "GaudarKahn is amused at such puny weapons and such puny armies. He has a hundred times as many eagerly waiting to punish your insolence." It paused and looked around and behind Angus. Then it added, "And theirs. You think you can change a Geketz? Ha. The thought spends your energies and wastes your sleep. GaudarKahn is Master. He is your Master, Naver. You will see."

Angus broke free of the creature's gaze and sought out Feshka who was sitting by the stream. The Geketz's arrogant self-confidence and determination shook Angus. Why did the Enemy hate them so much? What had happened in that ancient past that had aroused so much enmity?

"Feshka," Angus said softly. He didn't want to startle the half Elf, who was lost in thought as he stared at the moving water.

Feshka looked up at Angus. "Come and sit with me, StrathNaver. Quite a catch tonight, wasn't it? See there?" Feshka pointed. "Star Bright and two others are ready to form a Trine if it breaks loose."

"Can it?" asked Angus.

"We don't know. It could break the ropes as it says, but it hasn't so far. What do you think?"

Angus realized that Feshka had no experience with the Geketzim except through stories about them. It made him uncomfortable that Feshka didn't know everything. For the first time he looked old to Angus. The lines in his face seemed deeper and his skin dryer and more pale with age than before. *But he can still run like a deer*, Angus thought. He had seen Feshka keeping up with Arikin even though Arikin was a foot off the ground almost flying through the trees.

"He says he can break the ropes," said Angus.

"He says many things. He says that Ogladim are better fighters than Elves. We know that's not true. The only thing the Ogladim have that is better than the Elves is numbers. They are many, or so it says. We may be few by comparison. And they have the Geketzim. We are only now learning to fight them."

"They are very strange. He seems to be almost like a character from a dream. He seems to be not there completely, like he's partly here and partly somewhere else. Did you see how his skin fades in and out?"

"He exists partly in the place of dreams--bad dreams. Sometimes we think the Enemy hates us so much because we can enter and leave that place at will and it cannot. We do not even know what he is. He is to us only a fierce and fearful name that has represented death and destruction to us. In the past we have only fled from him. We fight now because there is nowhere else to go."

"You can enter and leave the place of dreams whenever you want to?" Angus asked, surprised.

"Yes, of course. So can you. Did you not know that?"

"How is it done?" asked Angus.

"This is something you already know, StrathNaver, but I will remind you. You must first relax your body. Make your body go to sleep but keep your mind awake. You exist partly in the place of dreams just as the Geketz does, but your body, unlike the Geketz, does not. It exists only in the place of awakening. You simply let that part of you go to sleep. It then releases your dreaming self - your spirit."

"Of course," exclaimed Angus. "That's how I did it the other night! My body was tired so it went right to sleep, but my mind was restless and stayed awake."

"That's right."

"If it's so easy, then I must complete the other two journeys and find the gifts for Lurelei."

"There may be other things you would want to do also. Let your dreaming self look at the Geketz and then later, tell me what you have seen."

"I looked at it," said Angus. "There is nothing there but darkness and hatred."

"There may be more than that. There may be something buried under all that savage anger and illness. The Geketz that Star Bright struck before, turned out to be BaynYamen, a hero of our past. I wonder who this Geketz may turn out to be, and if we can save him without driving him insane as we did to BaynYamen with the Bolt."

"Maybe it was being a Geketz that drove him mad. Lurelei fears madness. I hope I can help her before this happens to her. Are all of the Geketzim Elves who have been attacked?"

"We don't know for certain, but we think that may be true," answered Feshka.

"I will look at him when my dreaming self is again awake," said Angus.

"When do you think that will be, now that you know how to do it whenever you want to?"

Angus smiled. "In a few minutes, Feshka. Will you show me how to call Geemayel?"

Once again Angus was riding the wildly powerful horse through the night sky, westbound it seemed it him. Clouds whizzed past and for a few minutes he felt rain in his face. The ground dropped far away and soon there was no Earth, no clouds, only Geemayel's pounding hooves. Angus hung on tightly. He had no idea if he would fall or how far it was to the ground or even if there was ground below. He was less frightened this time, and in a different way. Why had he waited so long to do this? Feshka was right. He did know how to do it, how to enter the place of dreams! He had simply not thought of it. It had been easy.

Geemayel thundered on. Angus was alone with his thoughts, waiting for the horse to arrive at wherever he was going. He couldn't help wondering what the horse's hooves were pounding on, since they were certainly not touching the ground. He was tempted to lean over and look down but he was afraid of falling. Caleel had said Geemayel had dropped Boer in the Abyss. *Was Boer still alive perhaps, and angry that another was riding his horse, that another now had his Cudgel, or a copy of it? Where was Boer now,* Angus wondered. Then he wondered if he should be frightened of meeting up with him somewhere.

As they raced through the forest, Angus could see the misty paths ahead once again, as when he had first come this way. Here and there were campfires that made him wonder what sort of creatures lived in this place. How far would they go this time? Angus saw the path they took before as it rushed past him. There was the way to Asgard. Were they not going there this time? Then the ground disappeared again and Angus saw light in the distance. Was it another brightly lighted courtyard as before? He was eager to find out.

As they approached the light, it grew brighter. Before long Angus realized they were catching up with the sun on its journey west.

In the distance to the right, Angus could see another castle, a strange-looking edifice, half in night's darkness and half in the full light of day. The side that faced the sun had banners flying from its turrets and towers and Angus could make out people or creatures; but he could hardly see the dark side. It was hidden in its own shadows and lying in the night behind the moving line.

Geemayel landed carefully on the speeding draw span that had been lowered, and leaped off the moving platform as soon as Angus dismounted. Angus turned to look at the place where he now found himself. At the castle's wall was an ancient door made of heavy dark wood, thickly grained and oiled. At the top was a jagged edge as though a gate was hung above inside the wall, that could be lowered to prevent entrance or departure.

Angus approached the door and pounded on it with his fist. Then, without waiting for a response, he pounded again. The door vanished as though it had not been there. Before him now was pitch darkness, a deep dense cavern of nothing, the stone floor vanishing into the darkness. A malevolent male voice addressed him: "Who comes here?"

"Tis I," Angus called out. "Angus Williamson of Glen Williamson of the Clan MacAodh."

"What do you want, Angus Williamson?"

"I came seeking the Second Gift for the Lady Lurelei of the Gray Elves of the Valley Naver that she might find relief from the touch of the Geketz."

"The names Angus and Williamson I have not heard and that person may not enter here without the Pass. Have you the Pass?"

"I am also called StrathNaver by the Gray Elves and I have no Pass."

"If you have no Pass," boomed the Voice, "then you must be cast from this Great Monument to Evening, and the gods pity you."

As he spoke there came from the darkness a great host of Human forms but without faces. All of them had body armor and were wielding halberds, maces and staves. They started to advance on Angus. Unwilling to leave without achieving his purpose and of course completely unaware of how he would survive a fall from the flying castle, he drew his Elf Blade and stepped forward to engage them or die trying. *After all, this is only a dream*, he thought. *What can they do to me?* At the same time, thoughts of Boer's fall into the Abyss troubled him. He had no choice but to fight.

Angus steeled himself, ready to start swinging his blade, to take whatever blows he must. The closest one drew back with his mace to strike Angus, but Angus caught the chain on his blade and pulled it from the creature's hand. Several more approached him with swords drawn. Angus struck at them but each one he struck vanished only to appear again a few feet away.

Suddenly there was a blinding flash of light and it was as though a hundred clansmen were at his side. A blade of light flashed and something flew forward driving the horde back into the darkness. In shock Angus realized the hundred clansmen were not there with him after all. It was the Cudgel that had come forth in his defense.

The voice spoke again, this time in anger. "You said you have not the Pass yet it springs forth to defend you. What poor and foolish mortal are you, so steeped in ignorance that you know not the Cudgel of Boer when you carry it on your person, or that only one so well armed may enter this place?"

"I have come not to war," said Angus, "but to serve the Gray Elf Lurelei. Is this the place I seek where I can forge the Second Gift for Lurelei?"

"Perhaps it is," answered the voice. "Advance and receive darkness."

Angus stepped boldly forward, not wanting to reveal his fear after so brave a show as the Cudgel had performed for him. Stepping into the darkness from the light, he had to pause for his eyes to adjust. When they did he saw a candle far ahead of him. As he approached it he discovered more candles, a circle of them, mounted on short staves which seemed to be planted in the stone floor. Behind each stave stood a white-robed figure, faces mostly concealed by the hoods of their robes. Long white beards flowed from their faces. On each robe was a large rune apparently stitched into the cloth; each one was different. In the right hand of each of the robed figures was an ornately carved staff and on the head of each staff was the same rune as on the bearer's robe.

The scene was strange and threatening. Angus counted twenty-two robed figures standing in a circular pattern; twenty-two candles, staves and runes.

"Stand forth and wait," one ordered.

For several moments, Angus stood there and listened to the silence around him. Finally one of them began to circle the candles in a clockwise fashion. When he had completed his first circle, another stepped in beside him to continue circling. When the two had completed one full circle, a third joined them, and so on, continuing until eleven pairs were walking around the circle of candles. Then they beckoned to Angus that he should walk behind them.

Angus could see no purpose to all of this but he also saw no harm, so he did as requested. Now twenty-three circled the floor, and it seemed to Angus that the room was growing brighter with each completed circle. Angus soon realized the additional light was coming from a globe in the center of the circle. With each turn, the globe of light grew brighter until the entire room was as bright as the daylight on the other side of the door where he had entered.

Inside the globe appeared to be a fire whose tongues of flame were licking its sides and chasing each other up and around, up and around. Angus was so mesmerized by the circling movement around the circle of candles and now the vision of the flaming globe, he didn't realize the figures and he had stopped moving. Now they were standing side by side in a circle, eyes focused on the globe's brilliant light.

"Behold, mortal," began a soft gentle voice, unlike the former speaker. It was the aged voice of a grandfather as though speaking to his son's child. "Before you is the Globe of Sheeawn. It is made of the pure white light of truth and wisdom. It is the Second Gift for Lurelei the Gray Elf of the Naver.

"I have many questions, Wise Ones," faltered Angus.

"We're sure you do," said the kindly voice. "What is its purpose?

What is its use? How can it help the Gray Elf? We know your questions, young mortal. But ask."

"Forest Old said she has three wounds, yet I know only of one. I have no knowledge of how the Cudgel of Boer or the Globe of Sheeawn can help her. I trust your wisdom and that of the Elves. Thank you for your wonderful help in its construction."

"All will become clear to you, my son," responded the voice. "In the making of the last Gift, the Holiest of the Holies, it will become clear to you. For that Gift is the greatest Gift a human can give another. Rest well before you try to make the Third Gift because it will require not only bravery and strength. It will require all that you are."

Another spoke: "Sheeawn, my son, is the secret fifth element contained within the fourth, which is Fire. It is the Creative Force. Sheeawn is the Creative Force and the Globe enshrines it. You will carry it in the same manner in which you carry the Cudgel of Boer, until such time as you can deliver all three to the Gray Elf."

Some of them began urging Angus toward the globe. He approached with great caution. When he stood directly in front of the glowing object, he stopped to study it. Then he stretched his hand toward it. As he did so, it seemed to sink into him as the Cudgel had done. It was as though he were somehow absorbing it.

"With the Cudgel and the Globe," one of them said, "you are well armed for your journey into the light. But remember to rest well before the next sojourn, for it will be the most difficult. The Third Gift has the most power of the three; even the knowledge of it is well protected."

Angus was nearly consumed with curiosity. It had been his idea to go straight on his way to the next journey, but with the caution he had received from the white-robed brotherhood, he decided to wait and rest.

When he returned, Feshka was still seated by the stream, as though waiting for him. He roused himself and went to sit with the half Elf. "What do you have this time, young Human?" asked Feshka.

"They called it the Globe of Sheeawn," Angus eyed Feshka hopefully. "Does that make any sense to you?"

"None whatsoever," answered Feshka. "Do you have any idea yet, how these things can be used to help Lurelei?"

"None whatsoever," Angus echoed his words, "but everyone keeps telling me that it will become clear in time."

Chapter Eighteen: Another Geketz

Angus then related his most recent dream experience to Feshka, who listened without comment. The noise of the camp was greater than before. The voices of many blending into one dull rumble rose into the night air. Some feared there were more Geketzim near them but others said that they always travel alone or with Ogladim.

Some had seen Wolves in the area, but reassurances from Arikin and the others calmed their fears. The shrieking of the Geketz interrupted Angus' conversation with Feshka. It sounded as though it was in dire agony. Angus and Feshka went to see what was happening.

They found a group of Elves watching the Geketz. "They're trying to find a way to overcome it, to bring back the creature that it once was," Migalik told them. "We don't know yet how to do it. If we don't find a way before the sun rises again, we'll have to kill it. We can't keep it in the daylight."

"Could it be covered somehow?" asked Angus.

"They seem to disappear when the sun rises, if they're not kept underground. They just sort of sink into the earth when the light of day arrives. No one knows what becomes of them. But we can't keep him in this cage they've built, after daylight. He'll get away only to cause more harm. Four Elves were injured before we caught him."

"Four?" echoed Feshka. "Who were they?"

"Wood Elves from the central mountains. I didn't know them," answered Migalik.

The Geketz began shrieking again, making it difficult to continue their conversation. In the interval between shrieks, Angus asked, "What are they trying to do? I mean, how are they trying to cure it?"

"We have ways of healing sick and injured animals," replied Migalik. "They're giving it healing energy as we would to a rabbit that has been attacked by a dog; but it only seems to cause more pain. That could mean our efforts are successful, at least partially. It's the same type of healing energy that Feshka gave to you after your attack. And now you're here, Feshka, would you try?"

"In a few minutes," said Feshka. "I need to gather my energy." Angus watched him return to the rock where he had been sitting by the stream.

"Where is this large army going?" asked Angus.

"We received word from Wesheshica a few days after you left The City of The Vision," said Migalik. "We are told that the Enemy has landed and taken a large fortress by the sea. Since then it has enslaved the human population, a very large number of people. There was a major city on the seacoast there. The Enemy has been gathering its power, making Ogladim and Geketzim for its troops. Many Ogladim have been spotted in the forest around the city, but it seemed that all at once they were gone. The ones you found were returning south and west, were they not?"

"The ship that was sunk was headed west toward the sea. The Ogladim we found on the trail were moving south, generally," said Angus.

"It seems that he's calling in his troops for one massive maneuver, one hard march through the country. Our hope is to reach him before he has gathered his full power. If we can get there while his forces are still divided we may have a better chance of success."

Angus turned to see what Feshka was doing. Still seated on his rock, he was now surrounded by a large glowing egg-shaped ball of brilliant blue light. Angus observed that the light was the same color as Feshka's clothing.

William also noticed the light, as had many others. They were watching the half Elf gather his energy and inadvertently illuminate the area around him. "How does he do that?" asked Angus. "What is he doing?"

"It's a trick of visualization. It's very effective."

"It looks as though he's gathering light right out of the stars," exclaimed Angus. "Out of the Earth itself! Where does he get it?"

"I don't think it's a matter of finding the energy," said Migalik. "I think he generates it himself. It's from him."

Feshka now rose from his sitting position and began walking toward them. "See if he speaks while he's in that condition," commented William, who had just walked up to join them. "His voice will sound really strange."

As Feshka approached, those in his path stepped aside, more out of awe than fear. Angus watched as he moved toward them, leaving a residue of blue light in his trail. As he approached, it seemed that his glowing grew brighter. "All stand back now," he ordered.

William is right, thought Angus. His voice sounded like distant thunder. It was as though they were listening not to the source of the voice but to an echo from faraway cliffs, that was reflecting Feshka's words back to them. The half Elf's eyes now glowed with a bluish-white light; Angus took a cautionary extra step back and away from him.

Feshka approached the Geketz, stopping several feet out of its reach. He raised both his hands, extending them in front of himself, his palms facing the creature.

"You make me want to laugh," the creature cackled. "If I wasn't so hungry I would laugh even more. Your light looks so good I could just about bust through this weak little cage you built and suck it right out of you. In fact, maybe I will." The Geketz began struggling violently to free itself. To break loose, first it would have to sever the ropes by which it was tied, and there were plenty of ropes. Then it would have to break the neck loops that were still around its throat. If it managed to do that, it had to avoid the Dwarves who were standing near the cage with Elf Steel Blades drawn in readiness. Finally, it would have to break through the heavy wooden bars the Elves had built around it.

Feshka ignored its taunts; Angus wondered if he even heard them. Feshka raised his hands and stretched his arms toward the Geketz, his spread fingers pointed up, palms facing the Geketz.

Angus wasn't sure, but it seemed to him there were little streaks inside the ball of light surrounding Feshka. They looked like tiny bolts of lightning only a few inches long, and blue instead of white like real lightning. Angus wasn't sure he believed what he thought he was seeing; he looked again more closely. There they were, little streaks of concentrated blue light shooting from Feshka's eyes and fingers. They were like little spurts of electricity that continued to build up a series of charges. When the charges became too strong, they popped into the air.

Angus noticed a change in Feshka's light. The ball of light surrounding him seemed to be extending in the direction of the Geketz. The creature started shrieking again... *was it out of fear or was it trying to break Feshka's concentration?* The light continued to extend toward the creature and now touched its skin. As it did so, the Geketz shrieked louder than before, causing everyone to clap their hands over their ears.

As the light touched the creature's skin it seemed that what had been translucent and transparent before now had solid edges, like real skin, yet pale and thin. As the light further penetrated the creature's space, it writhed as though in great pain, shrieking even louder and more urgently. The ball of light surrounding the Geketz was now elongated, like an egg that had been stretched. The small end of the bubble was still surrounding Feshka, but the larger end was now completely surrounding the Geketz. Its cries finally peaked and its struggles grew less frantic, as though it was losing some of its strength. Finally the cries stopped altogether and the Geketz fell limp.

Feshka did not back off. His light intensified, becoming almost white. Angus noticed a bead of sweat running over Feshka's brow and down his cheek. His lips were drawn tightly together and his frown of concentration grew more intense. As Angus watched, the light grew even brighter until it was a pure and brilliant white; but Feshka's hands were now trembling. Then the light began to fade until there was only night. Still, Feshka stood, his arms extended, palms facing the creature. Finally it appeared to dawn on him that the light had faded and the creature's cries had stopped. At that point, Feshka collapsed.

Angus and others rushed to his side. He was still breathing and conscious, but exhausted. Angus helped carry him to a small tent that one of the Dwarves had constructed. Angus was amazed at how weightless he seemed. He didn't know if it was because of Feshka's age or the fact that he was half Elf. The Elves were also light in weight.

Everyone except the Geketz's guards had forgotten about the creature. But as Feshka was stretched out on a bedroll to rest, Angus suddenly remembered and rushed out to take a look at it. It was lying in the pine cage, no longer a Geketz. Angus wasn't sure what it was, but it was definitely not what it had been. Star Bright also stood nearby. "That's no Elf," she declared. "I don't know what it is. It appears to be sleeping."

It was too dark for Angus to get a good look at the creature, and he was tired. It had been a full night for him and dawn was not far away. "We'll take a better look when the sun comes up." Migalik joined them. "It must be from the peoples of YeePhraWaine."

The rain woke Angus; he was soaked again, and as so often before, cold and shivering.

He had been dreaming again, a confusion of ideas and places where he'd been. During part of the night he was hiking through the mountains with the small group that had been his companions in recent days. He fell into the water again and again, down through the hole in the bottom, continuing to relive the terror of drowning. Sometimes it was in the Naver and other times it was in the pool, still nearby. He watched the surface far over his head, and the bubbles rising from his mouth as he tried to call for help.

Then he was fleeing from or fighting Ogladim. Angus's first thought on waking was a wish for the day when he could sleep peacefully again as he had done in his father's house. How he longed for home, even though it would never be the same with his mother gone.

There was plenty of activity the next morning. The army was packing up their tents and bedrolls and getting ready to move out. Angus sat up and rubbed his eyes. His father was sitting with Scobie and Ingram, talking at length with Hender and MacBain. One thing that got his immediate attention was the fact that they were eating. He hurried to join them, all thoughts of Geketzim, turbulent water and flying castles suddenly fleeing.

"The thing's dead," William said to him as soon as he was close enough.

"I'm not surprised." Angus picked up a piece of bread and crammed it into his mouth. "Where's Tristan?"

"Over yonder," Mouth full, Scobie pointed.

Tristan was seated before the cage where the Geketz had been imprisoned. "He doesn't want to leave it," said William. "He's been sitting there for almost an hour."

Angus took a chunk of the trail bread and strode over to where Tristan was sitting on the wet ground. The rain had passed but the air was misty and damp. "Did you eat anything?" he asked Tristan.

"Yeah." Tristan glanced away briefly from the cage to acknowledge Angus.

Angus looked into the cage. The creature was still there but obviously dead. Angus wondered why he was surprised to see that it was naked. "What is it?" he asked Tristan.

"Nobody knows," Tristan shrugged. "They think it's one of those who peopled the place they call YeePhraWaine, but no one is sure. No one living has ever seen one."

"The creature must have been tall. Look at how long its legs are."

"It was tall all right," Tristan agreed. "Taller than any of us, at least. I was near them when they caught it. It was the ropes around its neck that kept it from standing straight up."

"I'm glad it's dead," said Angus, "but at the same time I'm sorry because it means we haven't yet found the cure for Lurelei."

"But Feshka says you've made good progress. How's it going?"

"Strange dreams is all it is," Angus sighed. "Feshka places more importance on them than I can. I don't understand them at all, but they'll make a good story some day, if I survive this little war we're headed into. What are they going to do with this thing?"

"Some said they were going to bury it in the forest. They should be coming for it soon."

"Why do you sit here staring at it? Come and join the others."

"Before it died, they said it woke for a moment. It looked around in fear, very quiet. Then it laid its head on the ground muttering some strange words that no one knew. Migalik was here and he said the words were Old Elf and they meant, "Where are you, my Beloved? They think when it awoke it was sane."

"Maybe they've stumbled on something important," Angus mused. "But it's dead now. It doesn't matter."

"I can't help but think," said Tristan, "that it had some wife and children somewhere. It must have once had a home. It probably wasn't always evil. It had a normal life somewhere among others of its kind. I know it doesn't make much sense to think of such things, but I can't help it. I feel sorry for it."

Angus' mind was alive with the possibilities. Tristan said when the thing woke it appeared to be sane. Maybe there was hope for Lurelei after all. What had killed it, he wondered? If Feshka's energy had been a little less intense, would that have saved it? If the energy had been a little different, would that have done the job? He had to speak with Feshka.

The army was finished packing and most of them were standing around now waiting for the order to move out. The march to Wesheshi-ca would be a long one for this large mass of people. They would have to take time to forage for food every day and to make the trail bread. Sometimes they could find enough to last for several days, but the forest had been foraged before. Usually they found barely enough. They would have to take a different path home because the forest needed time to replenish itself. Food could turn out to be a bigger problem than they'd thought.

Ariel was seated near the edge of the encampment under a large oak worrying about this. His specialty was strategies and organization of force. He did not like to have to think about such mundane and rudimentary subjects as food. That was the responsibility of others. But they had brought it to him. He had never commanded such a large force in the past and had never before been faced with supplying a large army. This wasn't even a question of maintaining supply lines because there was no main source of food. They couldn't herd sheep like the Humans were accustomed to doing. The Elves do not eat sheep. He was glad that at least that part of his problem was answerable. Some of the clansmen had actually brought sheep of their own to feed themselves.

How disgusting it was for him to listen to the cries of the animals when they were being slaughtered. But what was worse, he had to smell the cooking flesh and watch these Humans consume it. He was revolted at the very thought, but glad he didn't have to feed them as well as the Elves and Dwarves.

Ariel had not thought that the Council of The Kings would make the decision to fight. His preparations had been for flight, not war. His thought had been to flee to the north and the east. The rough seas and cold climate might deter the Enemy's pursuit, but now with the use of the Bolt being rediscovered and the manipulation of the Bolt's energy, the Council of The Kings had decided it was time to face the Enemy once and for all.

News of the Enemy's approach had first come to them many years ago. They had thought for many generations of Elves that they were finally free and could live as they chose, without fear. Then came the sightings of the Flying Shadows. The Elves knew if they had been seen by the Flying Shadows it would only be a matter of time before the Enemy followed up with a larger force.

Then there were the first attacks by Geketzim in Wesheshica. News had been sent to The City of The Vision when they first began. The attacks had spread. And then there were sightings and minor incidents with Ogladim. Still the Council of The Kings was not alarmed enough to take action. Ariel thought they were frozen in fear and couldn't act. He was afraid the Rebecks would have to take charge if nothing was done. Finally, the Geketzim had penetrated as far north as the Naver, and when they did, The City of The Vision began to have more incidents. They were minor to begin with, but still troubling.

It was only when Mishishel, the Rebeck of the Wesheshicans, sent pleas for help that the Council of The Kings was called. Members of the Council arrived reluctantly. Only those who had first had troubles came willingly and with forces. Ariel was glad Migalik was among them. But this rumor about the boy they called StrathNaver troubled him. Ariel wasn't a glory hound. He had no dreams of his descendants and friends telling stories of his bravery and leadership. He wanted only the safety and the well-being of his people. Reluctantly he accepted the medallion of the Rebeck. He understood he was needed, and at the urging of his wife, the mother of Arikin and AriMa, he'd agreed to take on the responsibility.

He doubted that Angus had any special abilities or gifts. He had no idea who the figure in the Weaves of Vision might be, but he doubted it was StrathNaver. He was hardly more than boy. He looked strong enough and he showed promise that someday he might become a powerful person, but for the present he was just a young man. He hadn't filled out yet.

Ah, Glowamel. The mother of his children was the centerpiece of his life. She was the light that brightened his day and the warmth into which he drifted when he slept. She was the dream of his childhood, his heart's desire and the love of his life. He had asked her to stay in The City of The Vision to watch over the people there, to make sure the food supply to the city was protected and that all was well in that beautiful place. But the real reason he had asked her to stay was a selfish one. He feared for her safety. He wanted her as far away from the fighting as possible. He had tried to find a way to protect his sons as well, but could find no excuse to keep them home.

He feared what was to come. Reports from Wesheshica were not good. Mishishel's people said the Enemy grew stronger day by day. The Enemy had no problem with food and feeding the masses it was perverting. It simply killed the old and weak and the children and used their flesh to feed them. If it ran out of people to kill, it could fall back on the wounded among its forces; and there were plenty of them.

It had not been an easy battle. Wesheshica was not falling willingly. They were a stalwart people, proud of their homes near the sea. They loved their families and defended them with fierceness unrivaled among the Elves. Stories of their forays into battle made Ariel feel proud to be an Elf. They gave him chills and filled him with determination to back their effort with everything he had. Even now, the troops he had mustered were pacing and waiting for his order to march south and overwhelm this hideous evil that was invading their homeland.

Some of them even now were standing near him, waiting respectfully but with obvious impatience. Ariel rose reluctantly. The old oak under whose shadow he sat seemed almost like a friend. Leaves still clung to its branches and filtered the light that fell on him. Leaves that would soon be on the ground, he thought, grateful that they had fended off some of the rain that had fallen earlier.

This had not been a peaceful night. The Geketz had destroyed any chance of sleep for him. He'd stayed near it during most of the night, wondering what it was and where it came from. But now it was dead and buried, and it was time to march south.

Angus was glad the original party was back together, and glad MacBain and Hender were with them again. With this vast host of warriors—Elves, Men and Dwarves, he felt nearly invincible. There would be no more problems with Ogladim for a while, and little fear of Geketzim with the Dwarves to help them. Feshka had rested well and was on his feet again. He looked a bit drawn but seemed to be ready to move out with the rest. Angus fell in naturally with the men from Glen Williamson, friends and kinsmen all.

The clouds still hid the sun's light, but they were higher clouds than before and no rain fell from them. The ground was slightly muddy and became even more so toward the end of the procession after so many footsteps had passed over it. Angus was in good spirits. He was fed and rested and had obtained the Second Gift for Lurelei. He felt he was well on his way to the end of his journey.

This war was an interference, however. He had little real interest in it except as to how it pertained to his rescue of Lurelei. She was his only concern. But of course there was the matter of avenging his mother's death.

They had killed a Geketz. In fact, two Geketzim had been undone so far, the one near the Naver and the one that was killed last night. And a third Geketz had been captured and was being held underground near Migalik's home, so there were three out of commission. But the head of this snake remained. GaudarKahn was still alive, and they all knew that until he was killed, the battle would not be over.

GaudarKahn must pay. If the task of killing GaudarKahn was to be left to him, Angus thought, he would do it. Although he had no idea how, it was enough to know it had to be done in order to bring peace to the land. When Angus thought about it, he was overcome with anger. GaudarKahn was the source of all the evil in his world. He had caused Angus to lose his mother and Lurelei, the Elf of his dream. Of course, GaudarKahn had not done it personally, but he was the snake's head. It had to be cut off before the snake could die.

Angus was glad it was rainy. Had there been sunshine and dry air, the army would have raised so much dust it would have been difficult to breathe. Angus also noticed that as they marched south the land grew more level and was easier to tread. The mountains were still visible behind them but Angus understood for the first time that they were headed for the low lands of which his people had always spoken with such disdain. Wesheshica was in the low lands.

The Army stretched out far ahead, and when he looked back he couldn't see the end of the line. It looked like a great migration from the north, traveling with grim determination, and anger. He still tried to stay away from the MacDonalds, but as he grew used to their presence, his fear of them began to ease. So many strange people were around him, a few MacDonalds didn't seem to matter much.

They kept going without stopping to eat. Angus had bread in his pack again and William passed him a skin with water that he then passed on to Tristan.

Rumors circulated that GaudarKahn had a greater force than theirs and they were waiting for them, but none believed it. How could there be more warriors than those gathered here? It seemed to Angus that most of the peoples of Northern Alba must be there with them.

Chapter Nineteen: The March to BungFeddor

Angus had lost track of how many days or weeks he had been away from home. Some of his adventures had been so intense that each seemed to have involved a number of weeks. He knew the year was moving on. The weather felt more like early fall now than the late summer in which he had gone fishing with Tristan. What a peaceful day that had been, with Tristan catching the fish and Angus daydreaming! He sometimes wondered what would have happened had he stayed below the falls that day. Would he ever have met Lurelei? Would his mother be alive today? That thought annoyed him.

Had he not suffered enough guilt by now? Had he been home when his mother was attacked by the Geketz, he would probably have been killed as well. And he may even have drawn his father into the battle; William could have been killed. *What if what if what if,* worried Angus. But he did venture above the falls. He did meet Lurelei. Maybe his curiosity had annoyed some god who had made all this happen to pay him back for his trespass. *Some payback.* Lurelei was now a Geketz. His mother was dead. *What capital crimes did they commit against this god? Would a god be so small as to kill an innocent woman like Laura or the Elf Lurelei, to pay him back for such a foolish error?*

He'd heard stories when he was a child about the falls above them on the Naver, but no one believed such things. He was trying to remember what the stories had been about, but he couldn't. He only remembered it was said that no one had ever gone beyond those falls. Maybe it was because the hills rose so sharply on either side of the river at that point. It was hard to walk there and was even dangerous. He had almost fallen

in several times. Hell--he did fall in. He felt a mixture of fear and embarrassment when he thought of it.

How could he have been so awkward in front of the Elves? Thankfully the Elves had been there to rescue him, but if it weren't for them,
he never would have fallen in. Maybe when he fell into the river he fell
through a hole in the world and when he came out again he had come
out the other side just as when Arikin had thrown him into the pool.
There was another side to that hole. Maybe when the Elves fished him
out of the water he had come out the other side into a different world
than he was in when he fell.

He had been walking for most of the day without a break, and was
beginning to feel the physical strain. When he went hiking with the
Elves the first time, they stopped periodically to rest, but he guessed
that was because of Ingram, who had needed to rest now and then. But
now Ingram was getting used to the constant push and maybe he didn't
need to rest as much. He looked behind him. There he was, his pack on
his back, hiking along with the rest; and he wasn't even sweating.

There was a disturbance ahead. Angus couldn't see what was going on but a ripple effect was coming back to him from the others. Too
many were ahead of him on the path for him to move to the front of the
line to find out, so he waited. Word would reach him soon.

The disturbance turned out to be a group of refugees fleeing from
BungFeddor, a small city on the coast of Wesheshica; about fifteen
Elves, by Tristan's count. Mishishel knew some of them and was talk-
ing with them. Three were on litters that were carried by six others.
The remaining six were injured and some of them could barely walk.
Mishishel was giving them bread and Elf wine that Migalik was pour-
ing from an ornately carved pitcher that was vaguely familiar to Angus.

Angus could see Ariel approaching, and he moved as close as he
could so he would be able to hear what was being said. He didn't want
to seem too obvious and he didn't want to be regarded as an eavesdrop-
per, so in passing he slowed his pace and lingered. All that he learned
was that Ariel was frightened; and this frightened Angus. If the imper-
turbable Ariel was openly showing fear, it was not a good sign. Angus
glanced back again to see if his father and the others of their party were
near enough to see. Maybe by the time they caught up, Ariel would have
a better handle on things; he hoped so.

Information from the refugees was the first Ariel had received from
Wesheshica in weeks. GaudarKahn had taken the island of Anglesheel
as his main base. They said a great number of black ships had arrived
there about a month ago. GaudarKahn was said to be aboard one of
them and surrounded by a horde of Geketzim and other strange crea-

tures that no one recognized. The Wesheshicans had begun calling these creatures Groessmunden. It was not one of their words; the name came from one of the visiting traders from the mainland to the east, who said they had mouths that were bigger than his mother-in-law's. Everyone thought that was humorous back then. But the Wesheshicans began to realize these creatures had more use for their huge maws than talking.

They were a furry beast that could walk on their hind legs like Humans and Elves, but they had only three fingers or claws on each paw. They also had ears like Humans, but they were covered with short coarse hair similar to a rat's. They did indeed have wide mouths, but their jaws were short and well muscled. Two of the fleeing Wesheshicans had bites from these creatures. As they discovered later, the Groessmunden had venom like a snake.

Ariel feared there would be more to fight than Ogladim and Geketzim but he was glad to learn that at least these creatures existed in the material world instead of half in and half out like the Geketz. That meant they could be killed and injured conventionally, by arrows and swords. They needed no new magic, yet.

The bites inflicted by these creatures were wide and jagged. The venom did not spread through the victim's blood like that of a snake, but it stayed around the wound, creating infection and festering. The wounds would eventually kill a person if left untreated, but the healing arts were not unknown to the Elves. Feshka was called to examine them but Marnel did the actual healing work.

The march to the southwest seemed endless. They spent their days from dawn till after dusk walking... and walking. Angus was bored and tired. When he slept at night, it was soundly, with few dreams or none. He had tried to leave for his last dream journey several times, but fell asleep as soon as he relaxed. The march was basically uneventful except for the rain and occasional groups of refugees they encountered.

They all told stories about the capture of the island of Anglesheel and enslavement of the population. GaudarKahn was building a fortress for himself on the island's coast facing east. The distance between the two lands was not far. On a clear day one could see the coast of Anglesheel and those who dared to look saw a frightening scene.

The stone walls of GaudarKahn's stronghold were going up at an alarming rate. Their slaves were the free peoples of Anglesheel and BungFeddor, a city that faced it on the opposite coast. These slaves could be seen working on the walls, moving like droves of ants, pulling and lifting large stone building blocks that continued to pile higher with each passing day.

⧄⧅

GaudarKahn remained on his boat during the building activities. He had found a secure anchorage, directing the labor through selected Geketzim who acted as his generals. He felt fortunate to have found Geketzim who could think a bit on their own. He had tried many before he'd settled on the few he trusted with such work. They were mostly Elves whom he had converted, but the conversion usually stole their abilities.

GaudarKahn mostly used his Geketzim for reconnaissance and harvesting. It amused him that the Elves were planning to put up a fight. It would be easy to overcome them. Usually they just fled as soon as they learned of his approach. This time they were marching to the slaughter.

It was the first time he'd ever lost any Geketz to the Elves. It angered him that the impertinent little creatures thought they could toy with him this way. And the Dwarves! He had never encountered Dwarves before who were troublesome. Now he was going to have to waste time killing some of them. The Dwarves had taken some of his Geketzim; they had actually taken and imprisoned servants of GaudarKahn! This was unforgivable and would be punished.

He liked this place. The climate was cool and there was plenty of water. The fortress, now nearing completion, would serve him if he had to return. Maybe the fortress was rising too quickly. There was really no hurry. The Elf and Dwarf army would arrive soon but there was no need to defend against them. When they arrived he would send out the army of Geketzim. He could also use the ZarFusim. What a party it was going to be! What a harvest.

The only other aggravation GaudarKahn was dealing with right now was his problem Geketz; he had failed to completely subjugate it. The original attack had been interrupted and the initiating Geketz had been undone. That one of his pets had been recovered by the Elves was aggravation enough for GaudarKahn, but that he had a rogue Geketz running around the forest was worse. His telepathic communication with these creatures was imperfect, so he didn't know exactly where it was. He had withheld the information about this Geketz on the loose from his other pets because he feared the knowledge would harm them. If they knew there was hope, they might not be as eager to please him.

Yes, Lurelei, as the Geketz thought of itself, was a problem. He was confident he would conquer its resistance, but it was taking longer than he'd thought. A Geketz needs a little Light now and then. Most of them took what they needed from the energy they collected before passing it on to him. This Geketz was a waste of his time. It consumed the Light that lived in the plants of the forest, and it also took small animals that had Light. He was becoming increasingly annoyed with it. He could sense its anxiety and frustration and that annoyed him even more. He did not like to have to deal with these emotions in his servants.

Winter was coming. He was told that in the winter season all green things go to sleep and remain underground until spring returns. If that were true, then Lurelei would have to capture Elves or Elfkin to stay alive during that season. The hunger for Light would drive the creature to it. It would have no choice. He hated the wait, but he knew there was no point in taking action. This was a problem that would solve itself.

Lurelei spoke to him sometimes of a cure. This foolish Geketz thought some Human or Elfkin could save her; maybe he could... but surely not before winter. After the final perversion of her Elf nature there was no hope for it to ever again be anything but a Geketz. He needed to wait for winter. It would be only another four weeks or so before the snows began... not long to wait.

❧ ❧

The army trudged on. All were weary of walking and of the rain and drizzle. Soon they knew they would have to deal with sleet, then snow. Angus had no winter clothing with him. The thought now occurred to him that he may have to spend some of the cold season in Wesheshica. The thought of the blistering cold and blowing winds was enough to send chills through him. Winter was no time to be outside, and poorly clothed.

He watched as William and the others turned distrustful eyes skyward to survey the clouds and winds, and he knew they all shared his thoughts. As they walked, the Elves sang away their fears with marching songs, battle songs, love songs... and one song that puzzled him:

There is a Strath, a magic flowing flood
Which washes stones somewhere and lays them down,
To dry in warmth of day beneath the shining sun
Then washes more with passion and with fun.

In peace and freedom it does love the light
And guards all it so loves and lays them right
Within their beds for sleep at night abound
Not hiding days, concealing every living sound.

Once upon a day the folk of light
Shall widely wander far enough and fight
The Magic waters of the Strath to found
In glens of green and the sun at night gone down.

The secret passion of the Strath conceals
Mortal darkness in its loving will;
Finding deep within his secret dream,
That key to Elvish victory soon be seen.

With scarr-ed chest and hands, the darkest fight
With dreadful pain and solitude and passions right
The river dances in the valley, 'neath the very air
With darkness filled, and conquers all for Light.

Once after they sang it he heard Feshka say to VelMud, "Have you yet solved the mystery of the song?"

"Have *you* solved the mystery of the song?" was VelMud's response. Feshka answered with:

When time is full and the waters of the Strath have run
From the lofty hills through valleys of its own
The time when Vile Darkness to the Faithful light will bow
And Elf Folk in freedom live beneath the shining sun.

"Not yet," he added with a smile, "but it may happen any day now."

Star Bright was near them when they spoke and Angus watched her shield her eyes, wondering why, since the sun wasn't bright. "What does the song mean?" asked Angus.

"It refers to the weaves," she answered. "It refers to the story of hope for all Elves, for the day when the Enemy will come no more."

Angus was sorry he had asked. She had brought up the idea again that he was to somehow be their rescuer. He knew it was to be Ariel. Just because he had the red hair did not mean he was the hero of the weave. Lots of people have red hair. Ariel for one had hair the same color as his. What could possibly make them think it was Angus pictured in the Weaves of Vision? Maybe the markings around the figure's throat represented a scarf or some item of clothing. Why did they think it was scarring--and why his?

He ran his fingers over the scars at his throat. The skin felt raised and it had a different texture. Angus knew he was no rescuer or hero among Humans or Elves. He would perform no heroic deed that would win the victory. He was barely a soldier, much less a hero. Clearly, the Vision was flawed.

The party continued southwest, and after a few days turned in a more westerly direction. Angus was glad these Elves knew where they were going because he certainly didn't. They continued to amaze him. The trek didn't seem to stop them from their daily tasks, but the tasks had changed. As they walked along they snatched a branch here and there from trees hanging over the path. They made arrows from the shorter branches and spears from the longer ones. Some of them picked up stones of a certain color that they favored. From the stones they shaped arrowheads. When an arrowhead was formed, they would pass it on to another who would hold it tightly in his hand for a moment, then pass it on to another, who would fix it to the end of an arrow.

The most interesting person in this loosely organized assembly line was the one who held the arrowhead for a moment. As he did so, his hand would glow brightly enough for Angus to notice it over the light of day. These Elves were charging the arrows with their life force, adding the element that made the arrows dangerous to the Geketzim and Flying Shadows. It seemed that an Elf could not make more than a few arrowheads before becoming exhausted of whatever energy they were using. Then another Elf would take over for a while, during which time the resting Elf would strip bark off of more sticks, to prepare still more of them for the bow.

Other Elves would disappear for a time into the forest to return an hour or two hours later with sacks filled with nuts and berries. Some brought back wild rice and wild wheat. These would be passed on to others, who would toil over the material to prepare it for baking later, when they camped.

Angus's mother had been like that. She could have three or four projects going on at the same time and never miss a beat. He had seen her many times spinning, cooking and watching over the shearing of the sheep all at the same time. It had seemed to him that she was never idle, except for those moments in the morning when she watched the sun make its way out of the hills where she thought it slept at night.

Angus noticed during the last day that the march had slowed its pace. He asked Migalik if he knew why this was so. "We're drawing closer to BungFeddor, closer to the western sea. Ariel expects to find trouble--more and more--as we approach its gates."

"So the walking is nearly done and the fighting about to begin?"

"Yes, StrathNaver. The fighting is about to begin."

Angus forgot about being tired. He forgot about his aching feet and throbbing scars. As the refugees passed them on the trail and he heard stories of GaudarKahn's disdain for anything living, of his power and ruthlessness, Angus had grown increasingly more fearful. Now they were nearly upon him! Arikin said BungFeddor was only a day's march or less. He expected to get glimpses of the sea at any time. Angus was lost in a wave of panic.

His feet felt heavier than ever before. Now they were no longer fleeing. They were rushing directly and deliberately into harm's way. They knew where the Enemy was and they were going directly to him. How powerful was this GaudarKahn? Did he outnumber them as overwhelmingly as the Geketz had said, or was that just another lie? Would any of them survive? Angus did not expect to survive the first battle. He hoped others from the Glen would be left after all the battles were over, to tell the stories.

And these Elves thought he was a hero! What a laugh that was! Angus began to wonder if there was some way that he could avoid this conflict. He couldn't just turn and run away. His father had walked miles and miles with him. His neighbors and kinsmen were among them. The MacDonalds were there, and the Gunns. If he turned and ran, what stories would they tell of him then? "The Elves thought he was some kind of hero," they would say, "but you should have seen that coward turn his yellow back to us and run away!" Clan MacAodh would be the shame of the Highlands. There must be some legitimate reason he could find to flee. What could it be? What reason would be understandable that everyone would agree with?

Angus's feet slowed and gradually he dropped back. His father passed him by and then Scobie and MacBain. Tristan dropped in step with him for a while and was full of talk about Aelrondel. This brought Angus back to his own sorrow concerning Lurelei. Since the march was slowing, maybe they would stop earlier to be certain everyone was well rested. If they were going into battle the next day, it would be important that everyone be as well rested as possible. They would need time to make extra trail bread for the days to come. It was common knowledge that there was no food to be had in BungFeddor. Anything they got to eat there would be what they brought with them. They would have to bake extra bread.

If they stopped long enough, maybe Angus would have time and be rested enough to go on the journey to find the Third Gift. That would be good enough excuse to leave the party. He would have to return to the Valley of The Naver to give the Three Gifts to Lurelei. That was it. That would be an excellent excuse. He would be able to go home. That's all he really wanted to do. Yes. Go home.

The last few days, their path had taken them through low hills that bore no resemblance to the mountains of the Highlands. They could cross them in a day or less, and climb half the next hill as well. These low hills also had a different kind of beauty than the ones around the Valley of the Naver. Many of the trees were of a different species than the ones he knew. Some of the Wesheshicans in the party pointed to them as they passed and explained what they knew of them. Angus found this interesting, but his thoughts were on other matters.

Ariel had chosen their campsite for this last night on the trail. It was as Angus had hoped. The sun had not yet disappeared behind the trees ahead of them; it was early. On this night he would rest well and perhaps he would make the final journey into the place of dreams.

Even though he had made his way nearly to the end of the procession, Feshka and VelMud stayed near him, watching over him. As the army settled and each found his special place for sleeping, Feshka nodded to him. Angus understood that Feshka thought this would be a good place and good time to do what Angus had in mind. The place Ariel had chosen was on top of a small hill. If Ogladim or any other of the Enemy's creatures attacked with the forces they expected, this would be an easier place to defend. No matter where the attackers came from, they would have to attack - up hill. The defenders' arrows would carry farther and their weight would be behind any blows delivered to the lower footing.

"I don't like this place," VelMud inhaled deeply. "It smells of Ogladim."

"Do you think they would attack such a large force?" asked Angus.

"If there are enough of them, yes," answered VelMud, "and we're very close to BungFeddor, only a few hours' march."

"It's very possible," said Feshka. "Many of us won't sleep tonight. We've been traveling in the daytime as an insult to the Enemy and for the benefit of the humans in the group, but his Geketzim fight at night. We must be ready to change our routine."

Angus watched as many Elves took up stations behind trees around the perimeter of the hill. Marching in the daytime was an open signal to GaudarKahn that they were coming. They put away their Elf covers and when darkness fell, the sleeping band looked like lights from a city. Not even Tristan had to squint to aid his night vision. The campground was bright. Only the guards surrounding them covered themselves.

As an extra precaution, Ariel ordered that torches be planted in the ground around the perimeter below the campers. When darkness finally came, Angus saw that the approach to the hilltop was completely lighted. It would be impossible for anyone or anything to approach them unseen. It would also be impossible for anyone or anything to pass them without seeing all the lights. To Angus's way of thinking this was an act of overt arrogance on the part of Ariel.

Because of the size of their force, Ariel was so confident, he stopped taking precautions, almost as though inviting an attack from a Geketz. Many of the others agreed with Angus, although no one voiced anything publicly about it; Ariel was in fact the commander of this legion of Elves, Dwarves and Humans. They were waiting to see what would happen.

The loudest complainers were the Dwarves, but surprisingly the object of their unhappiness had little to do with their physical safety or the dangers ahead. They were more interested in maintaining segregation of the three races of Elves, Dwarves and Humans.

"Look at us even now," a fat hairy one declared. "A good third of us are mixed with other races. If this continues the races will fade away and become some hybrid mixture of half-breeds and quarter-breeds. Those of us who have Elf or Human blood can't tunnel. They lack the strength. The Elves who have human blood can't do many of the things Elves do. They can't communicate with streams, rocks, water and lower animals. The natural skills of all our peoples are being bred out of us. I for one don't want to live in a world that has no true Dwarves. There may even come a day when the races of Dwarves and Elves are forgotten."

Stretched out on his bedroll, Angus listened for a while to the argument, and nearby, Feshka was also listening. "Do you think what that Dwarf is saying is true?" Angus asked Feshka.

"Without a doubt," replied Feshka. "There are a great many among the Elves who are like me and many among the Humans who are like you, and you have chosen Lurelei for a mate. Your children will have more Elf than you, but less Human. They won't be as strong and they won't be able to manipulate light as well as an Elf. He's right."

"Maybe I should select a Human for a mate," said Angus, "if this is going to cause so much trouble. I don't think I like the idea that there may come a time where there are no Elves and no Dwarves. I don't like it very much either that there will come a time where there are no Human Beings, only this race of halflings that the Dwarf speaks of."

"There's nothing you can do to stop it," smiled Feshka. "The die is cast. It has been happening for generations. It's inevitable."

"Then it's pointless to worry about it," sighed Angus. "But I still don't like the idea."

"Change is difficult for Humans, but you are still going to take Lurelei for a mate, if you can, when all this is over. Aren't you?"

Angus grew silent. As he lay back in his bedroll, a smile formed on his lips. He forgot how wet and cold, chilled to the bone he was. At least he was no longer hungry.

Chapter Twenty: Trapped in BungFeddor

The campsite was peaceful and well chosen. Angus stretched out in his bedroll and tried to get comfortable. He wished he could take a swim somewhere to wash all the accumulated sweat off of his body. He hadn't bathed since the dunking in the pool, way back when they thought they were being chased by Ogladim. It had been a cold dunking but at least he'd gotten himself rinsed off a little bit. Now he had been on the trail for at least a week, and water for washing had not touched his skin.

At home Angus or William would carry water from the Naver which Laura would heat over their fire and then pour into the big bucket. When Angus had been young he was small enough to actually get into the bucket, but as he grew larger he could only use it like a sink. He'd thought when he had his own home he would like to have a larger bucket, more like a low barrel that was big enough for a full-grown Human to climb into for bathing.

That was odd. Before he'd started this long trek for war, he would have thought that he'd wanted a bucket big enough for a "man" to get into. Now with his association with so many species and races, he even specified in his private thoughts, what race the wash basin would be built for. He chuckled quietly at his own joke.

There had been little enough time in the last weeks for joking. He missed his brother Robert; Robert liked to joke. Even in the coldest winters when they were out of firewood or low on food, Robert always found a way to somehow lighten the atmosphere and make everyone feel a little bit better. Although he missed Robert, he was glad his brother hadn't come along. *It would be good if some of our family survived*, thought Angus. He fully expected if he and William continued on this mission, they would both be killed. Then his thoughts returned again to Lurelei.

How lonely she must be. She had a sister and parents and many friends in The City of The Vision and in the community of the House of Migalik. She had joked and laughed with Aelrondel and Star Bright. She'd been fun to watch... He closed his eyes and tried to remember how her kiss felt on his lips. He tried to remember the pressure against his lips, if there had been any warmth in her lips, if they felt warm to him. Yes, that was it. What had she said? Oh yes, it was: "Now is not the time for promises, Elskin. Now is the time for traveling." Then she'd leaned into him, put her arms loosely around his neck, and lightly kissed his lips. "But a time for promises may someday come. Now we must go."

A time for promises may someday come, she had said. And she had called him 'Elskin', or 'beloved'. She had called him beloved! He listened in the relative silence of the camp, trying to hear her words in his ear again. Her voice had been soft, low-pitched and rich in his ears as she'd spoken to him. She had made no promise to him, but the kiss was like a promise. He didn't see the Elves going around kissing each other very much. They weren't really into kissing, it seemed, unless something was going on between them. He had seen Migalik and Star Bright kiss once. He had even seen Lee-Eesh and MarNosh kissing when they thought he didn't see. Elves did kiss. So maybe the kiss was like a promise. Whatever it was, he couldn't wait to find out.

Her cure was nearly at hand. He was almost ready to go to her--but wait a second. He was going in the wrong direction. She was north and he was headed south and west. How far away she must be at this moment! The River Naver entered the sea to the north of his home and now he was nearly as far west as one could go without a boat. He was in Wesheshica and almost at BungFeddor, its capital. And oh yes, the war was about to happen. As his mind wondered, he accidentally fell asleep. He had intended to go traveling, to find the Third Gift or make the Gift for Lurelei. But now he was dreaming out of control.

In the dream he was walking, over hill and dale. He was with a large group of Elves and Dwarves and Humans. His father was there and also Robert, his brother. As they walked they sang marching songs and told stories. It was a happy dream, but all of sudden hundreds of Ogladim carrying long knives and clubs rushed out of the forest. Some of them had weapons that Angus had never seen before. The party he was traveling withdrew their swords and Skyn Dhus and readied themselves for a fight. And then it began. His father was down, then Robert was surrounded and overwhelmed.

Now Angus could see the source of the fear that was rising in his throat. It was a herd of swine rushing at them from the forest, but in the forest's darkness he could see a hog that was standing still as though watching. On its back was an Oglat bigger than the others. In the shadows Angus couldn't get a good look at it, but he could see the reddish glow in its eyes. It was watching him closely. As Angus looked at it, the creature raised its hand and pointed at Angus. He could hear its voice as it called out to him: *"You."*

Angus couldn't make out what it was saying, but it kept looking at him and pointing. Then he was surrounded with swine emerging from the forest. As he stumbled over the first one that hit him, he lost sight of the creature with the red eyes, but his fear and panic were rising so quickly and violently, he woke up gasping.

He wasn't sure if he was awakened by his dream or by the reality in the camp. Everyone was shouting and rushing around. Some of the Elves had their bows at ready, with arrows to the strings. The arrowheads glowed dully in the darkness with the energies placed in them by the Elves. Suddenly one flew past Angus. It seemed to leave a trail of light behind it as it flew quickly across the camp. Angus' eyes automatically followed its path. When it stopped there was a soft thud and Angus could no longer see the glowing arrow's head. It had plunged into something soft, and vanished. Then Angus realized it had struck a Geketz; its shrieks were unmistakable. In rage it was racing toward the Elf who had fired the shot. A second arrow was loosed at the Geketz, then twenty arrows flew at it.

The air was lit with the glow of arrow trails. All of the arrows struck the Geketz, but they hardly seemed to stop him. Another barrage of arrows was loosed at its legs. That brought it down. It was quickly dispatched by one of the Dwarves who had drawn an Elf Steel Sword. But that was not the end of it. There was an outcry all over the hill where they were camped; more Geketzim were on the small plateau where they slept. Angus was on his feet in the first second that he realized a Geketz was present. His sword was drawn in one hand and his Skyn Dhu was in the other. Angus was ready to start fighting for his life.

Out of the corner of his eye he could see his father swinging his sword at a dark shape before him. Swords drawn, MacBain and Scobie were running to help him. Hender was dealing with yet another. Two Dwarves were helping him with their own heavy blades. All around Angus was heavy fighting. The Elves' arrows seemed to fill the air for a while, but the Geketzim kept coming. *There must be dozens of them,* thought Angus, *maybe more.* The Ogladim had joined the fray and four of them had now formed a circle around Angus.

Suddenly Marnel was at his side with three other Elves, including VelMud. As more came to Angus's aid, more Ogladim swarmed out of the forest. *What happened to the torches they set out?* Angus wondered suddenly. The forest around them was in darkness and the torches were gone. So that's how they had sneaked up on them! But how had they extinguished the torches?

As Angus fought, swinging his Elf blade with both hands, he noticed the Elves that had been hiding out of sight and watching in the torch-light were lying on the ground, very still.

The fight continued. Angus felt he was the center of the attack. As more came to his aid, more Ogladim appeared from the forest. Then more hogs arrived. Fortunately they were not smart enough to differentiate between the Elves and Ogladim. Maybe they were so worked up with all the excitement, they forgot which was which--but whatever the reason, in their rush to get into the action, they knocked over the Ogladim as well as those fighting them. For a few minutes the warriors took time from their own fighting to kill the hogs. Then they went back to their bloody task of trying to exterminate each other.

Angus wondered what had happened to all the Geketzim that had attacked them. He no longer saw any of them; only the Ogladim remained... *but wait...* there was one coming now! Arrows again flew through the air as the Geketz raced up the hill to join the fighting. Angus could see from the path of the arrows' light that many had already struck it. As it approached, a number of Dwarves stepped in to deal with it. After a short time, probably less than a minute, the Geketz joined its brothers on the ground. Gradually the fighting tapered off. Some of the remaining Ogladim fled while others remained and fought till they were killed.

Angus couldn't believe he was still standing. He hadn't even received a wound, but many others were on the ground. Some were quiet while others moaned for help. Angus glanced anxiously around, looking for his father and the others. There was William, all right and Tristan. But those were all he could see of his neighbors and kinsmen. William was hurrying toward him with the same concern for his youngest son. "You all right?"

"Yes I'm fine. What about the others? Is everyone else okay?"

"I'm not sure about MacBain." William pointed, "he's down back there. One of the Ogladim snuck in on 'em. Scobie and Hender are down that way," he swept his arm in another direction. "We did some killin', didn't we?"

"I killed five, I think," Angus was feeling slightly weak in the knees.

He tried to steady himself. "How many did you get?"

"I don't know," William wiped the sweat from his forehead with the back of his hand. "I was too busy swinging this heavy blade to count bodies. I'm sure Ariel will be telling us shortly."

Angus turned to Marnel, who was still standing near him, guarding the shadows. "Thanks for saving my butt," he grinned ruefully.

She replied by practically jumping on him and holding him in a tight embrace for a second. Then she let go of him and darted into the crowd. "I wonder what that was all about," said Angus to his father.

"Don't think too hard," said William laughing at his innocence.

Angus noticed that there was one long blond hair clinging to his shirt. He smiled as he took it off with his fingers. Then he placed it in his pocket. His cheeks were still flushed from the sudden hug.

As thoughts of what had just happened came filtering back to him he began anxiously looking at those around him and those on the ground. He tried to brush away his fears by focusing on searching for the rest. Where was Feshka? VelMud? Was Migalik all right? What about Aelrondel? What about Star Bright? Where were they? Then Angus saw Feshka speaking with Ariel and Aelrondel was with him. AriMa was nearby speaking with Mishishel and with a Dwarf that Angus didn't know. VeratNonn was listening to the conversation.

"What happened to all the Geketzim?" Angus asked, coming upon them.

"We killed twenty-two of them," Feshka responded proudly. "We also killed somewhere around three hundred Ogladim. The Enemy will now know we are not here to sacrifice ourselves to him, but it cost us one hundred twenty-five Elves and at least fourteen Humans. The Dwarves came through it unscathed. They are very fierce fighters and stronger even than Humans."

"How many new Geketzim does the Enemy have?" asked Angus fearfully.

"Since you've asked, I'll tell you, but you must keep this to yourself. It won't help anything if the others learn this. Also, keep in mind that none of the attacks by the Geketz went uninterrupted. If you save Lurelei, these others can also be saved. If they have the strength of purpose that Lurelei has, they will stay away until the time is right and not join in the fight against us. They may even become allies."

"I won't tell anyone," promised Angus. *"How many?"*

"Ariel estimates about fifty," Feshka said grimly.

For a moment Angus wondered if he had heard correctly. *Fifty!* "We can handle the Ogladim, but the Geketzim are winning by better than two to one," he said finally.

"We did not use the Bolt," Feshka reminded him. "We'd hoped we wouldn't have to, since we have these new weapons. The new weapons helped, but now we know we must use the Bolt against Geketzim."

Angus was shocked at the number of bodies lying on the ground. If there had been more Geketzim they would not have been able to drive away the attackers. It now seemed a shallow victory. The Ogladim were slaughtered, but it took more effort to kill a Geketz. He wondered when the next attack would come and if GaudarKahn realized the same things he did about this exercise.

Angus helped gather the bodies. It was the custom of the Elves to cremate their dead. Some of them were gathering firewood and building a huge pyre and some were dragging the bodies toward it. Others were observing exactly who had been killed so they could report to their families, and still others were tending to the wounded.

The dead Ogladim were cast down the hillside and left to rot. The dead Geketzim were pushed over the hill by the Dwarves. Even dead, the Elves were afraid to touch them. Their darkness was fearful, their bodies disgusting.

The cleanup took the rest of the night. As soon as it was finished, Ariel ordered that they move on toward the city of BungFeddor. The other Rebecks of the Sea Elves, the Wood Elves, and Mishishel the Rebeck of Wesheshica argued it would be better to wait for the Dwarves of the Southerlands to arrive; but they had agreed to follow Ariel and ultimately did as he wanted. It was Ariel's opinion that they should press on and attack the city before they had a chance to recover from last night's defeat. "We need to keep in mind, that the army from the south is hoped for only. We do not know for sure that they are coming." The army marched west toward the sea.

As they started out, Angus allowed his mind to wonder as before. But now his thoughts were more on the subject of fear. The few Geketzim that had attacked had done incredible damage. Every Elf that fell to them was a new Geketz adding to GaudarKahn's forces. The Ogladim were little more than a distraction used to free the Geketzim to do their work. His father had nearly fallen to them. He had nearly fallen. For the first time he was glad his mother was dead. It would have been far worse for her and her family if she had become a Geketz. How horrible to think of the gentle Laura as a Geketz, hunting Elves and leaving death and devastation behind her. It was no wonder that being a Geketz drove Elves insane. And what of Lurelei?

Angus wiped his eyes with the back of his hand. Why was life so difficult? Why couldn't Lurelei be with him right now, at his side? But then, he reminded himself, that was one of the most foolish thoughts he'd had. If she were here with him, they wouldn't be here at all, fighting this battle!

They had almost arrived at the City of BungFeddor. The terrain was hilly but not mountainous. Angus was surprised that BungFeddor was primarily a Human settlement, with many houses. Some of them were larger than any Angus had ever seen. One house would appear as two houses piled on top of each other, and some even had three piled together; well, not piled, but built that way. They were two and three stories above the street level. Angus had no idea that houses could be built that way. He was filled with awe and his neck was getting stiff from gazing up at them.

It didn't occur to Angus at first that there were no people around. The entire city seemed deserted. Then he realized they hadn't seen an Oglat all day. They'd had no resistance as they approached the city. It had been a quiet march, as though everyone had been expecting trouble, but nothing had happened. As they walked farther into the city, Angus became aware that some of the houses and other buildings were made of stone. Angus had seen only a few stone houses before, and these amazed him more than the others, especially the ones that were four and five stories high. Then he saw the top of the fortress across the water.

The march had slowed as they waited for those in the rear to catch up. Then they could approach the waterfront in one mass. Angus kept his eyes on the black walls in the distance. It seemed he could see figures moving over its surface, many figures. He squinted to try to see better, but that didn't help.

For many days they had encountered no new refugees from the city. No one was left. Angus wondered what they had fled from, but as he approached closer to the sea he began to realize that those who had not fled were working on the fortress. At the bay front was a wide clear area that had been paved with stone blocks. At the water's edge were long piers, but no boats or ships were docked there. Farther out on the water he could see several large boats just sitting there. Then he noticed each had a rope coming off the front or bow leading down into the water.

At the eastern end of the cleared area Angus could see large buildings that seemed to be for storage. They had large openings in the front, as though for keeping goods that were either coming or going from boats that could dock at the piers. Angus didn't like this place. There were no trees to hide behind or disappear into. Before them and on both sides as far as he could see, was only ocean. There was no escape. This could be a trap.

He was in the center of a large mass of Humans and Elves. There were also some Dwarves but not as many as the others. They all had crowded onto the huge loading and staging platform to see the sea and fortress in the distance across the water. There was barely enough room between them to move quickly, much less swing a sword, but it was still daytime. The Geketzim could not come out to fight until the sun went down. Apparently Ariel believed GaudarKahn would not order an attack until it got dark. He moved through the mass of his army giving orders as to how many should take cover here and there, pointing at the various buildings around them. Mishishel was with him giving advice.

He stationed the Elves at the higher places in the buildings that overlooked the site. They had collected a great many arrows; during the entire trip they'd been making them, and the Humans and Dwarves had helped carry them. Before long all the windows were filled with of Elf eyes watching the streets and waterfront. The Humans and Dwarves were stationed on lower levels, since most of them would do their fighting hand to hand.

Ariel was wise enough to separate the Humans by their clans. Clan MacAodh took up a position in a large warehouse facing south. It was located on the north side of the harbor and afforded them a clear view to the south. Clan Gunn was stationed on the south side of the harbor in another warehouse facility, giving them a clear view facing north. Clans MacDonald, MacDonell, Sinclair, Munroe, MacCleod and MacNicols took the facilities that faced the water. The area was well secured, and the sun was touching the horizon in the west. More Elves were at the corners of the yard, nearest the sea, readying themselves in Trines and in larger groups for the casting of the Bolt, if necessary.

Angus could see Marnel with Aelrondel and Star Bright at the far end of the yard near Clan Gunn. They were on a raised platform that was just large enough for the three. As the sun sank into the sea, Angus was overcome with the greatest fear he had known thus far. He couldn't sit down. He couldn't stand still. He paced. Some of the men were playing a gambling game in one corner. Others were honing their swords. Few of them were Elf Steel. Some of the men were eating trail bread they had carried in their packs. Most were simply sitting at the edge of the building's shadow, waiting.

Angus could see the colors of the other clans fading in the darkness. No one had built a fire and the night air was growing chilly. Some food helped that situation. Angus finally took a seat among the others and pulled some trail bread out of his pack. He didn't know what the Elves put in this bread but he never got tired of eating it and it never failed to lift his energies and his spirit.

He was thinking he shouldn't have joined this group. He should have stayed below the falls. If he had gone back with Tristan that night, none of this would ever have happened. His mother might even still be alive.

As the darkness deepened, Angus pulled on his Elf cover to conceal his light. The Elves had not been wearing their covers on their approach to the city, but now Angus felt the need for that extra protection.

Angus's fear had a draining effect on his energy and spirit. It was a hopeless feeling that started in the base of his stomach and moved through his groin and into his legs. Then it began climbing into his chest and arms. His throat felt tight and his scars began to throb with pain, burning and freezing.

Angus tried to disappear beneath his cover at the same he tried to peek out from under it to try to figure out what had happened that was making him feel this way. He could see nothing that he hadn't seen before. He was glad to notice that Marnel and her companions had also put on their covers and thus were totally invisible to him.

He allowed his eyes to scan the other buildings but the darkness kept him from seeing the other men hiding there. He raised his eyes to the windows of the higher buildings that overlooked the long yard. He hoped the Elves were still in their windows but he could see nothing. Then he directed his gaze across the harbor at the huge fortress that was being constructed. Its black walls were outlined against the night sky, and as Angus continued to gaze at it, he felt even more fearful. He raised a hand to shield his eyes. Then, not knowing why he was shielding his eyes, he lowered his hand again.

He studied the dark walls in the distance as closely as he could. He could still see the shadows of moving figures lugging large building blocks up the sides of the walls. It seemed to him that the walls had grown higher even in the short time he had been watching. Then he became aware of a figure standing on the highest point of the walls. It stood in plain sight without any apparent fear of being observed. The figure had its hands propped on its hips and stood with its legs apart: confident, delivering a challenge that Angus could feel in every bone of his body. For as he continued to watch him, gradually he became aware of what that figure was looking at as it gazed across the bay at them. Angus's scars were throbbing with pain, and the burning sensation increased. He placed his hands over his throat. That seemed to help a little.

Was he hearing the thoughts of the Enemy? His fear had spread through every part of him until he was nearly sick with it. He wondered how the Elves were faring, if they too were feeling sick. Or maybe it was only because of his contact with the Enemy through the scars left by the Geketz; maybe they were unaffected.

By gazing away from the fortress, his fear abated somewhat. Then he rose from his seat on the stairs leading into the building and stepped inside, out of the figure's direct line of sight. This eased his pain, but the fear again charged through him, stronger than before. He felt like he was about to lose control of himself.

Suddenly he heard loud noises to the east, toward the city, the clash of metal on metal, metal on stone. He could hear cries of many voices shouting. The clans rose from their hiding places and charged into the yard, then into the streets leading to the yard. Angus was carried along with them. He saw the flash of many Elf Blades in the night and breathless men charging. The mass seemed to be moving toward into the city. He didn't go far before he saw the lightning Bolts, one from farther ahead, then another. He could smell Ogladim, but there was another kind of creature with them. He could see them moving in the streets among smaller bolts of light as arrows rained into their midst from the buildings above. It was Pandemonium.

He became aware that there were Flying Shadows overhead. He didn't know how many, but that would account for the fear he had been feeling. He was too busy swinging his sword with the others to take time to look up to count them. One of the hairy creatures saw him at the same time as he saw it. It charged him. What had the refugees called this thing? Big Mouth--Groessmunden? 'Big Mouth' was good enough for him and it did have a big mouth, bristling with teeth. Its legs seemed longer in back than in front and it was like a human or an Elf, but was neither. It charged him like an angry dog, on all fours, with drool flying from its lips.

Should he cut or thrust? He had very little time to think about it. He thrust his Elf Blade right down its throat. At first the blow didn't seem to faze the creature. Its weight and momentum carried it right into Angus, knocking him off his feet. When they fell together, the creature landed on top of him and it was still alive but Angus' sword was stuck in its throat. Angus still had his grip on its hilt and he thrust again. The creature yelped like a dog and Angus plunged the sword deeper into its throat.

The creature stopped struggling against the blade. Angus pulled his legs out from under it and rose only to see another one charging him. This one was felled by a stream of light from above, an Elf Arrow. He was saved again.

To his horror he saw one of the creatures headed for the door to a building where he knew there were Elves above, firing arrows. He charged the thing with his sword over his head and struck downward over the creature's head as he approached it. It dropped immediately.

Angus turned to see several Ogladim approaching him. A MacDonald cut down one as it passed. An arrow from above took another, and the third reached Angus just in time to be skewered on his blade.

The battle raged on for hours. There must have been hundreds of Ogladim and hundreds more of the BigMouths. Angus lost track of how many he killed and how many he'd seen fall. One of them had landed a blow with its jagged blade and had inflicted a deep cut in Angus's shoulder. He was only half aware of it and ignored the pain. He kept swinging his blade with all his strength until finally he saw the first light of dawn rising over the hills beyond the city. As the sun rose, the Ogladim and the others withdrew, not all at once, but so gradually, Angus wasn't sure if they were withdrawing or if they had simply all been killed.

Ariel's army re-formed in the freight yard where they had previously waited. In the dawn he could see there were no longer as many as before. Their numbers had shrunk considerably. Tristan and MacBain were not among them. When he saw his father he grabbed him in a happy embrace. Ingram was wounded, with blood and dirt splattered in his face that made him look worse off than he actually was. Then Angus realized they were all splattered in the same way. He was thankful to see Marnel, Aelrondel and Star Bright still on their platform, untouched.

Elves leaned out of many windows to watch, while others scoured the streets collecting their arrows. Ariel strode through their midst counting and consoling and encouraging. "He was well chosen," remarked Feshka.

Angus had not seen him approaching and was glad to see that he was alive. "What's to become of us?" asked Angus. "That was a hell of a fight."

"It's just the beginning," answered Feshka. "And nearly half our number are dead or taken. Tonight it may be Geketzim. This last fight was just to loosen us up a little."

Angus and William joined the Elves who were collecting their arrows. They hoped to find Tristan and MacBain. Maybe they were still alive and among the many bodies lying in the streets.

Before the battle, the streets had been immaculate. Most homes had what must have once been beautiful, carefully tended gardens. Now everywhere they encountered dead flesh. The Ogladim stank. The Humans lying in the streets were from all the clans. Their kinsman, like Angus and William, were searching for their own. Every so often someone would be recognized among the dead and a wail would rise up.

So this is war, thought Angus, too overcome with grief to deal with anything more than that single statement that kept repeating itself in his head.

Chapter Twenty-One: Hopelessness and Death

Many more Humans and Dwarves than Elves had been killed. The Elves were in safer places high above the streets where they could shoot their arrows at their ease. The Humans and Dwarves were in the thick of the danger. Angus was glad the Elves were up there. Their arrows had saved him many times that night, and he said so. He was not surprised that many others agreed with him, so that argument was laid aside for the time being.

Some of the clansmen said they could handle a bow and arrow also and were permitted to try. A large MacDonald was one of the loudest and he was given a turn first. His marksmanship was good but by the time he had two arrows on the mark, the Elf who was competing with him had six in his target. There was no question that the Elves' best and most effective place in the battle was high overhead protecting the rest of them.

Yet even there, the Elves weren't altogether safe. Geketzim had crept in through rear entrances and had managed to take several groups of Elves. They reported a loss of seventeen that had either been killed or taken.

Angus was exhausted, and after several hours of fruitless searching, he went back to his assigned shelter to sleep for the rest of the day, if peace allowed. He could see the fortress better in the daylight, and was surprised to see they had made good progress during the night. The walls had continued to rise while they fought for their lives. The masses of workmen continued as though nothing had happened.

Angus's sleep was restless at first but his fatigue won out. He woke

in mid-afternoon. The army was distributed again in their various places. Most of them were sleeping in anticipation of more fighting to come;
he wondered if he could make his third journey in daylight. His past
sojourns in the place of dreams had all been at night and it somehow
seemed more appropriate for them to be at night. He decided to try.

Relaxing his body wasn't as hard as he thought it would be, since
it was still sluggish from sleep. When Angus awoke in the place of
dreams, he was surprised to find it as misty and dark as when he traveled at night. Was it always shrouded in darkness? He looked around
him to find the army as he had left it when waking. Men and Dwarves
were resting and some were eating as usual. The earlier arguments continued but in a more subdued manner. What surprised him most this
time was that when he looked at the fortress across the water, it was no
longer black. The stones seemed grayer than before and it was easier for
him to see them.

Geemayel was standing in the yard waiting for him; he did not have
to call. Angus was glad to see him. The horse had been a faithful friend
in these endeavors and Angus was growing to trust him as he had never
trusted an animal before. But it seemed to Angus that Geemayel was
much more than an animal. He never needed to be guided or told what
to do; he always knew where he was going and took Angus directly to
that place.

The ride was wilder than before. Geemayel leaped nearly straight
up and continued in that direction as though he had been shot out of a
cannon. The Earth below vanished more quickly than before and Angus imagined he was flying over the Great Abyss that lies between the
physical and non-physical realm. This was where Boer may well still
live. Angus now imagined he could feel within him the heat of Boer's
Cudgel and the glowing fire of the Globe of Sheeawn. The burning he
felt inside seemed to urge him on. Those guiding him in the Castle of
the Setting and Rising Sun had said the third and last Gift for Lurelei
would be the most difficult to make, and the most dangerous.

He had been told that although several had traveled before to the
realms of light, none had survived. When Angus told Feshka of what he
proposed, Feshka looked at Angus as though he thought him crazed--
and crazed he was indeed, with guilt and love for Lurelei. He had not
even allowed himself to think of it directly.

Geemayel entered a layer of thick dark clouds and suddenly Angus
was sprayed with a cold hard driving rain made more so by their speed.
It stung his face and ears and in a matter of minutes his clothes were
soaked. He would have started to shiver if not for the burning inside
that emanated from the glowing power of the magic items he had made.

Now this power was increasing beyond anything he had ever experienced as he prepared for the next feat, that of making the Third Gift, whatever it was.

Soon they passed through the nightmare of clouds and rain, yet when they emerged there were no stars or sun in the sky above him. All was darkness, and he rode for what seemed like several hours. His seat was getting stiff and sore and his legs were tired from hanging over Geemayel's sides. Then Angus noticed a slight change as though the first light of day was beginning to touch the world. He was pleased that he would not have to travel farther in darkness, but... wait! What was this light? It continued to grow brighter and still brighter until it became uncomfortable to his eyes and he had to squint to keep it out.

He felt the heat of the light on his skin, and although his eyes were tightly shut, he could feel it burning through his eyelids. He released one of his hands that had been gripping Geemayel's mane and shielded his eyes with it. *If one didn't die of fear in such a place, he may well go mad,* he thought. All was white light around him.

Angus started to doubt his worthiness. How could he ever have thought he could take on such a mission, and how could the Elves have placed such trust in him? He was sure his was not the image in the weaves. What a cowering fool he was!

His scars again began to throb and the brilliance of the light around him was scorching his skin. His wrist burned so much, he let go of his hold on Geemayel's mane. In the next instant, the wind had unseated him; down he fell, turning in lazy somersaults, tumbling through the air.

Geemayel had sensed his unworthiness and dropped him in the Abyss just as he had dumped Boer! Why had he so trusted this dream horse that had no reins? How could anyone trust a horse to run to places no Human had ever gone? Angus knew death was near, that his body would smash like a bug wherever he landed. Was it water below? Was it rocks? Perhaps he would land on the fortress itself. But it wouldn't matter. He would be smashed all the same. Would GaudarKahn be pleased that the Naver he had tried to capture was dead? And what of the Elves? Now they would know he was not the one in the weave, not the figure of the tapestry. That figure was Ariel! He had tried to tell them.

The light grew dimmer as he fell. He was able to open his eyes slightly, but the intensity of the wind in his face caused his eyes to tear so much, he couldn't see anyway. He closed them again, not wanting to know when the end would come. Now it seemed that the wind was buffeting him with strong up-drafts that hit and shook him. Terrified, he let out a loud scream followed by another, and another. He shouted for

Geemayel to come and save him, but the wind shook him all the harder. Down he fell, down and down and down and down. Finally he imagined Geemayel was near and that the horse was somehow calling his name.

"Angus!" it shouted. "Angus!" And Angus woke up.

William had been shaking him and calling his name. "What a dream you must have been having, boy. You frightened me!"

Angus sat up and looked around at the remaining daylight. He was trembling and soaked with sweat. He leaned back again against the wall where he had fallen asleep. "I failed," he moaned.

"Failed at what?" asked William. "You fell asleep and you were having a bad dream."

"No, it was--" Then Angus remembered he had not shared knowledge of the Gifts with his father. William would laugh at him. He would say that Angus had lost his mind. Believing in Elves was bad enough, but believing in their magic was insanity, childish nonsense. Angus looked at William again and for maybe the first time he saw him as a man instead of as his father. William was fairly old by his standards. He was nearing forty-one, not as old as Ingram and certainly not as old as Migalik or Feshka, but they were different. William was a man of the Glen. In the Glen they usually didn't live that long. There were accidents and incurable illnesses no one understood. But William had had a wife with Elf blood.

Had Laura some special knowledge of the Elves? Was that why William had lived so long and was still in such good health? Maybe that's why Ingram had lived so long, too. His wife was also part Elf. They had knowledge of the herb lore and healing that others perhaps didn't have. Angus now remembered and for the first time placed significance on the fact that many used to come to his mother for medicines and cures she made from herbs gathered in the forest.

William had lines in his face that young men didn't have. His chin was gathering flesh underneath, which was the mark of age and distinction. Some of his hair had flecks of gray. He should be home with his wife enjoying their grandchildren, but instead he was at war. The concern in William's eyes should not be there. He should be feeling pride in his sons, not concern. What had Angus brought him to? Instead of enjoying his grandchildren he was burying his neighbors and risking his life in a fruitless venture.

Angus wondered what would become of his father. If he had not fallen in with the Elves they would all be home. Angus would be choosing a wife perhaps, and making more grandchildren for William to enjoy, if he had not gone beyond the falls.

"Did you find Tristan and MacBain?" Angus asked him.

"Yes," answered William. "MacBain, we buried while you slept. Tristan is sitting right over there with a deep wound in his thigh and another on the back of his head." *Tristan was wounded and MacBain dead.* More burning coals Angus could pour over his head.

Where was Feshka? He was relieved that he hadn't fallen into the Abyss. At the same time he was a bit sorry he hadn't died. Now he was back in this hopeless war. He could well be killed that very night and darkness would be falling the last time for him.

"Ariel sent out scouts this morning," said William. "He wanted to try to find out how many Oglats and others the Enemy has around us."

"What did he find out?"

"We're penned in here. There's an army of them on the east side of the city. Ariel thinks there are many more of them than us. He thinks the situation's hopeless."

Angus looked around the yard and found that the streets had been blocked. Barricades had been erected while he slept. "The Elves did most of it," said William. "They said no Geketz could pass through them because of the grass weaves they laid over them."

Angus saw that the barricades were built from boards and rubble gathered from the buildings. Each one had a grassy cover that at first Angus thought was more weaves when he realized the grass had grown over them. He rose and went to inspect them more carefully. It would take months for grass to grow so high, but then he saw Aelrondel with Marnel and Fierrondel. Each was at a different barricade and seemed to be speaking to the plants.

It struck Angus as strange to see rational looking Elves talking to the grass. But as they did so, the grass continued to grow, and fast enough that Angus could actually see it getting longer. When it was standing so tall that the individual blades of grass would not support themselves, the girls began weaving the blades together. On both sides of the barricades, the living grass weaves became barricades protecting the structures themselves. After a few minutes it appeared there was only grass growing tall in the streets. The barricades were completely concealed.

The main defense now appeared to be the Elves. If they could hold off the Ogladim with their arrows and if the Ogladim and others persisted, they could pick them off at their ease. The street entrances to the buildings were barricaded as well, and guarded now by Dwarves and men. It would be harder for the enemy to get at the bowmen.

If the Enemy's forces were unwilling to attack, then the army would have to go and seek them out; but not yet. Then there was the fortress to worry about. GaudarKahn had obviously constructed it as a place of safety for himself. They would have to somehow cross the water to get to him, but there were no boats.

The Elves seemed unconcerned. There were Sea Elves among them. It was said that Sea Elves could walk across the water as easily as on the land, and Angus believed it. He had seen the Elves walk a foot above the ground. Why not a foot above the water as well? But how would they get the Dwarves and Men across the water? There were no boats anywhere that he could see, except those tied up on the far shore. There were a great many of all sizes over there.

As darkness fell, the army grew quiet. Star Bright and the girls were again on the platform where some foreman had probably stood at one time directing the loading and unloading of the ships and boats that docked there. There were several such platforms along the yard, one for every two piers, it seemed; and now, each held a Trine of Elves.

Angus was deeply disappointed in his failure to make the Third Gift. Maybe it had been vain after all to hope to cure Lurelei. He also wondered when he would have another chance. With the coming battles he would likely be killed, like so many others had been.

They were obviously outnumbered last night, but the Ogladim had withdrawn. Maybe it was because of day coming that they'd pulled back. They had fought with them all night. If Ariel's plan worked, they could be holed up in this freight yard for days--and what if GaudarK-ahn simply sent in reinforcements? Obviously the Enemy had plenty of manpower. Angus could see the many figures still on the wall across the water. How high could it be built, he wondered. It was already towering higher than the highest turret at Castle Urquhart, but that was the only castle Angus had ever seen.

All eyes continued to watch the yard and the barriers that had been set up. Every so often a wary eye would be turned toward the fortress. On this night there was no moon. Clouds had settled in over the area, shrouding everything in almost total darkness. It had rained earlier, but now the heavier downpour had tapered off to gentle drizzle. Everything was wet and damp—and quiet. They no longer heard sounds from across the water, if a building block was dropped, the noise would echo off the walls of the city, or sometimes a shout would be heard in the distance. But all this had stopped.

Angus felt something was about to happen. The fear he had experienced the night before had now settled in the pit of his stomach, and this time it was met with anger. He stood up and turned to face the fortress. There it was again: that one lone figure standing at the highest point facing them, hands on its hips, legs spread apart. Then the Flying Shadows appeared over the fortress, headed toward them.

A whisper went up among the men. Angus was not the only one to see the Shadows. Large groups of men and Dwarves began gathering behind the barricades waiting for the attack, but all remained quiet. They could feel the mounting tension. Angus had never seen a gathering so ready to explode, yet no one uttered a word. In the silence more sounds could be heard coming from the direction of the fortress. All eyes turned in that direction, noting that a large fire was blazing within its courtyard. The shadow of the figure standing on the wall watching them was crisply outlined in the yellowish light of the fire behind him.

Some continued to watch the fortress while others readied themselves again to defend the barricades. No Elf covers tonight. Angus could clearly see which among the men were Elfkin and which had solely Human or Dwarf blood. He had told William about the light that emanated from the Elves but William as a pure Human could not see it. He had retorted that he "was not there to defend light or any other such foolishness." He was there to defend the Glen and avenge the murder of his wife. Angus didn't share any more of such things with his father.

His thoughts turned to Lurelei again. He remembered the feeling of the energy building up inside him as he approached the Regions of Light. As they waited for the attack he tried to focus on that energy again. Yes, there it was, building in his stomach. He closed his eyes and visualized her in his mind's eye just as she was before the attack. The energy increased.

Feshka hurried across the yard to him. "What are you doing, Strath-Naver?"

"Oh just thinking." Angus couldn't hide anything from wise Feshka!

"Well, whatever it was you were thinking, that must be what an Elf is thinking before casting the Bolt! You were glowing around your middle. You've stopped now. Try it again. Think about whatever it was and let me watch you."

Angus closed his eyes and once more began thinking of Lurelei. He visualized the energy rising in his stomach, then into his chest, as it had on his journey. As he focused on the vision of Lurelei that he had created in his mind, he could feel the energy move into his arms and legs.

"Are you feeling the energy around you, StrathNaver?" Feshka asked.

"Yes," Angus breathed deeply and tried to not lose his concentration.

"Imagine that the energy is moving into your arms and hands. Can you try to visualize that?"

Angus tried the image and as he concentrated on what Feshka suggested, in his mind's eye the energy that rose in him at the thought of Lurelei, centered on his arms and hands.

"That's good," encouraged Feshka. "Now you need a target. How about the figure standing on the fortress wall? Aim the energy at that figure and release the energy toward it."

There was a flash of light but no Bolt. Angus was disappointed for a brief fraction of a second. In that short time, the light created by his release of energy revealed a number of Ogladim and Geketzim climbing over the sea wall by the piers. The Humans had no idea what he was doing and paid him no attention, but the Elfkin and Elves had been watching him with great interest. Most of them still thought of him as Human or Elfkin, but few Elfkin had any real powers like those of the Elves. It was remarkable to them that any Elfkin had the ability to direct his light. Feshka could do it, but he was an exception, and after all, half Elf. Angus probably had less than a quarter Elf blood.

What they saw in the light terrified them. Geketzim and Ogladim had been expected from the land side but not from the water. How had they gotten there? But that was a moot point. For the moment the main focus was on stopping them, not on figuring out how they got there.

From the platforms Bolts burst forth enough to temporarily blind Angus, but for a moment before the brightness blotted out everything, he was able to see the boats that had crept in under the darkness. So that was why the attack had not come earlier! The Enemy had waited until darkness to conceal the boats moving across the water. Now the Geketzim and Ogladim were crawling over the wall like ants.

Elves had been placed in some of the buildings beyond the barricades to present additional defenses and to fire on the Enemy's backs if necessary. They had chosen only stone buildings so they could not be driven out of them by fire. Dwarves had assisted in barricading the doors with stone so they seemed to join with the walls in one solid mass. The Elves in the outbuildings were safe and presented a serious problem for the creatures that were trying to scale the barricades.

The Geketzim coming over the wall were another matter. They were not expected to be attacking from the sea. Many Elves had stayed with the Humans and Dwarves this time, more as a political gesture than for any other reason; but now some of them ran to the towers to offer additional support for those casting the Bolts. Others stayed back and fired arrows into the approaching creatures. Swords swinging, Humans and Dwarves rushed toward the waterfront.

Feshka joined them. Angus could see the fireballs flying at the invaders. Some of them would strike two Ogladim at once, knocking them back into the water, but then Feshka changed his tactic and began throwing his balls of flame at the wooden boats that had not reached the shore. This created havoc in the boats. The Enemy either had to take to the water or burn. The Groessmunden were the worst affected because their hair was set on fire.

It wasn't long before the Elves on the platforms joined Feshka in aiming their Bolts. The Men and Dwarves could probably handle the creatures that were already on shore. Stopping the rest of them from arriving seemed to be a better idea than just holding them off.

Soon the harbor was filled with burning boats and screaming or drowning Ogladim and Groessmunden. Angus had never before thought of using the water as a weapon until they had sunk the black ship in Loch Ness in the Great Glen. Now he watched as many boats were set on fire, trapping the Enemy on board.

Many of the creatures escaping from the boats made it to the shore; the water wasn't deep enough to drown them. Angus watched them wading toward the wall.

He couldn't decide whether he should be at the barricades or the sea wall. A large crowd of Men and Dwarves were at both. Maybe he should stay somewhere between. But then he saw two Geketzim coming his way. He ran toward the nearest platform, hoping for Bolts and getting none. More Geketzim were racing at him from the waterside. Angus headed toward Star Bright's Trine, and as he approached them he glanced over his shoulder. The Geketzim were difficult to see in the darkness but he saw two of them with arrows sticking out of their backs and chests. The injuries had slowed them down but they were still approaching him with great speed.

Star Bright was no longer on the platform. Her group had been replaced by Elves who were strangers to Angus, three males. Angus finally turned to fight the Geketz when he was directly in front of the Elves. The first Geketz to reach him came on immediately. Angus swung his sword hard at its throat. The creature blocked Angus's swing with its severely injured arm. The creature screamed and lunged for him but Angus had drawn back his sword quickly enough to now thrust point first. As the creature came down at him, Angus stepped aside, guiding it with his sword's point, clean through the creature. But now Angus had more problems: the other two, coming at him.

Angus darted between them, hacking one across the knees with his sword as he passed. Another scream and the two turned toward him. Angus now darted past them again on the right side, slashing at the other one as he passed it. His sword caught it across the stomach and slashed it open wide enough for the creature's insides to begin snaking out. It fell to the ground trying to stuff its guts back into its stomach.

The last one hobbled toward him, favoring its left leg where Angus's sword had done its worst damage. Several more arrows had appeared in its chest and back. Angus noticed it also had one in its right leg in the upper thigh. Without waiting another second, he lunged at it, feint-ing to the right, slashing with his sword again, this time at its stomach. He was hoping for another success like the last one, but the creature blocked his sword with its paw. That was not a good idea. The gash that the sword made in its lower arm caused the creature to scream again, and in rage it charged toward Angus.

Angus was too close to dodge it. Grabbing his left arm, the creature started pulling him. Angus drew his right arm out as far as he could and jammed the point of his sword into the creature's throat, breaking its hold on him. It fell. Angus noticed then that the first one that he had stabbed through the stomach was hobbling toward him again. This time Angus did his best to decapitate it with one swing of his sword. He didn't hit target but still he hit. The creature fell.

Angrily Angus glanced toward the platform. Where were the Elves when he was in such danger? The three on the platform were watching him gleefully and now they let out a yell. "You didn't need any help," one of them shouted over the noise of the battle. "Look out!" he then shouted to Angus.

Angus whirled around to discover he was being charged by two Ogladim. One of them fell, an arrow in its back. The other one Angus discharged himself.

The battle raged on. Angus lost track of time and space. He just kept moving and swinging his sword. Rage and blood lust filled his mind and spirit. When he killed an Oglat, he quickly turned to look for another one only to find a Geketz or BigMouth after him. The Groessmunden were faster than the others. One had gotten hold of him by the leg and he couldn't get his sword positioned right to get at it, so he started stabbing it with the Sky Dhu, his black-handled dagger whose blade was just under six inches. That freed him of the BigMouth; after that, he was more careful of them.

Suddenly he realized he was running out of things to kill. He looked around and in dawn's first light he saw a few boats on the water headed back toward the fortress. He looked toward the barricades and saw that they were unattended. No more of the Enemy's creatures were trying to get over it or to climb the sea wall. Anxiously he searched the area for his father, mentally estimating how many of the army had made it through the night. Quite a few, it seemed. Then he returned to the warehouse wall, sat down and fell asleep, wondering which of the realities he had experienced that day, was the authentic one.

Chapter Twenty-Two: GaudarKahn Closes His Trap

As the sun rose, gradually they became aware that the streets beyond the barricades were still full of Ogladim and BigMouths. It seemed they had stopped fighting to rest and dispose of their dead and eat, while they kept the army bottled up in the sea yard.

Elves were still posted beyond the barricades in the upper floors of buildings, where they had a clear view of the streets. From there they had killed many Ogladim and even Geketzim. Their arrows had rained in the streets like mosquitoes in a swamp. The only reason the enemy still persisted in the streets was that the Elves had nearly run out of arrows. Now they were lying low, trying to be as invisible as possible. But the Ogladim were working at getting into the houses. They had begun by searching for doors, then for secret doors. The stonework of the Dwarves was excellent. The enemy could not even find where there had been once been openings to the buildings.

The Elves hoped the enemy would eventually forget which buildings they thought the Elves had been in, but that was too much to hope for. It had been wise to choose only stone buildings. The Ogladim had set fire to many of the wooden ones. Burning houses filled the air with hot black and white smoke and the wind off the sea sent the smoke billowing inland and away from the army.

Arikin, the son of the Rebeck Ariel was in one of the stone buildings and AriMa, his brother, in another. Mishishel the Rebeck of the Wesheshicans was in yet another, the tallest one. Now these buildings were surrounded by Ogladim and Big Mouths, searching for an access. By midmorning the searchers had given up and were working at knocking down the stones, trying to find weak spots through which they could enter.

With the waterfront clear of any attackers, Ariel was organizing several attack forces of his own. They would simultaneously charge over the barricades into certain streets and provide cover under which the trapped Elves could retreat to relative safety.

When Angus awoke it was around midmorning. Ariel had assigned him a place with his father and many others on one of the designated streets. The rest of the army was divided between the other street accesses.

Fire from several of the burning wooden houses had now spread to the roofs of the stone houses where the Elves were hiding. Angus could see Elves emerging onto these burning roofs, frantically tearing up shingles, burning boards and throwing them into the streets.

This was causing a great deal of confusion on the ground. Some of the burning boards and shingles struck Ogladim below. Many who were not even hit were set on fire. Raging and screaming, the creatures started to fight among themselves. There was no water readily available to put out burning clothing, burning hair. Many tried rolling in the dirt. Others tried to tear off their burning clothing. Some fled in terror, the flames of their clothing leaving a smoke trail behind them.

Ariel took advantage of this situation by ordering his attack forces to charge. Swords drawn, Men and Dwarves poured over the barricades into the streets, shouting their individual cries. Running through the streets, slashing as they went, they drove the Ogladim and BigMouths back while the Elves began descending from second and third floor windows of the buildings. Their only weapons were their bows, and with the few arrows they had left, they shot the occasional Enemies that appeared before them, and snatched the fired arrows back from their fallen bodies as they passed.

The fighting was fierce. Streets were lined with burning buildings and filled with the fallen bodies of Humans and Ogladim. The stench of death and burning flesh was as sickening as the sight of those burned. The bodies of BigMouths and Ogladim littered the streets. Bits of cloth or hair stuck to their blackened skin. Some of them were still alive and obviously in horrible pain. The army fought on, steadily driving back the Enemy. Although they had retreated beyond the city, Ariel ordered that they return to the barricaded area for rest. "The City is too big for us to watch every street and path coming in. If we try to guard its many entrances we will be too divided. The little fortress we built can easily be held."

No one argued the point. They were exhausted from fighting all-night and then into the day as well. Angus's limbs felt heavy and his eyes were dry with fatigue. He could hardly keep them open. When he awoke again, it was nearly nightfall.

"We can't stay here very long," VelMud informed Angus. "There's a well beside one of the buildings so we have fresh water, but the food won't last more than a few more days."

"What then?" asked Angus.

"If we can't resolve this soon, we'll be taken. An army needs food."

"Ariel sent scouts into the forest," said Feshka. "They'll be able to tell us if the enemy is still near. They came back with enough food to last us an extra day."

"An extra day isn't enough," said VelMud. "We could be here for weeks."

"Ariel thinks we broke their main force last night," said Feshka. "We'll be finding out if that's true soon."

Angus was tired of being in this place. He had walked every foot of it many times. This game of waiting and fighting was boring when it wasn't terrifying. He watched the walls of the buildings around them that hadn't burned. He watched the black walls beyond the water and the creatures working on them. He watched the barricades wondering when the next attack would come, and he thought about Lurelei. Where was she now? What was she eating? Had she lost control yet? Was she attacking Elves?

He thought about those soft warm lips that had kissed him. Her voice was still fresh in his ear. The memory of the touch of her hand in his brought back the feelings he'd had at that time. He longed for that reality with only the two of them in the forest under the moon and stars. He longed for the sight of those wise wide eyes that had looked at him with amusement and happiness. Where was Lurelei of the forest, Lurelei of the Grays?

It had been only yesterday that he'd tried to find the Third Gift and failed. What good would it do him now? What good would it do for her, even if he found it or made it--whichever--if he was trapped in Bung-Feddor, the capital city of Wesheshica, surrounded by Ogladim and GaudarKahn's legions? Lurelei was in the Valley of the Naver and he would probably never see her or the River Naver ever again. But still, he had to try. He could not give up.

It was dark again and no sound could be heard from the streets beyond. This time they kept close watch on the water, expecting more boats and Geketzim. But none came. Torches had been set at the ends of the piers to cast light on the water, but in their light, nothing could be seen except the water itself. Star Bright and her crew had been resting all day. Angus had wondered how they could cast Bolt after Bolt, especially when the force required for making only two of them had nearly killed Star Bright before. Feshka had explained they had discovered how to distribute the power by developing the Trines. The more Elves who joined to cast one Bolt, the more powerful the Bolt, and easier it was to form.

"Why not get ten together?" asked Angus, "and blast that castle across the water?"

"To what end?" asked Feshka.

"The Enemy stands on its highest wall to watch his battles," said Angus. "Haven't you seen him there?"

"You have seen GaudarKahn?" asked Feshka in astonishment.

"Well I guess it's him. When they attack again, take a look."

"None have ever seen him!" declared Feshka. "He always stays safely out of sight and away from us."

"He's safe enough over there. It must be five miles across the water."

"At least that," Feshka agreed thoughtfully.

The night continued without incident. Angus stopped his pacing and took his eyes off the fortress. The image had not appeared again.

∽∾

GaudarKahn was happily inspecting his new quarters. The fortress was nearly complete, at least complete enough for him to move in. His suite was large, comprising the entire west wing of the building. He could walk alone through its halls and rooms undisturbed by his minions, alone with his thoughts, entertaining himself.

"Plucky little things, aren't they?" he chuckled to himself. His anger had faded somewhat, for he was confident any attack by the Elves would be thwarted. They didn't stand a chance against his legion. He hated to waste the Elves by killing them when their Light was so valuable to him. He was astonished that he'd lost so many Geketzim the previous night, but it really didn't matter. He had plenty more and could easily create however many he needed.

No Elves ever stood up to him before. Dwarves had done that, but he had no use for Dwarves. Humans had done that, but he had no use for Humans either, except for those with Elf blood.

The defeat was of little interest to him. He had lost many of his creatures, but it was inconsequential. He had plenty more. His only concern was the Light. The little band of insolent Elves and Humans would soon be captured. No need for any more major attacks. They'd weaken when their food ran out; they couldn't have brought that much with them.

It was just a matter of time, as it was with the Geketz that called her-self Lurelei. The first snows would come in only a few weeks and what would she do then?

The Naver was among them. While they were in the midst of battle, before they'd died, his Geketzim had seen him. GaudarKahn knew vic-tory was nearly at his feet. The Naver was hardly more than a boy. How much fight could a boy put up? How much leadership could be expected from him? Not much. The prophecy was a farce.

But he did know if StrathNaver or any of the others realized The Key, he would be lost. This idea infuriated him. The idea of failure was unthinkable, unacceptable, impossible.

✖✖

When Angus looked toward the fortress now, he was no longer gripped by terror. He knew he was still afraid and he still felt anxiety rise in his throat when he looked at its black walls rising in the distance. But now that fear was more related to uncertainty than failure or de-feat. When they'd first arrived in BungFeddor he'd felt it was certain he would die here, but now he wasn't so sure. They were still trapped, still surrounded by the enemy. And no doubt they were still substan-tially outnumbered. They'd killed great many, but it seemed as they killed Ogladim, more simply turned up. As they killed Geketzim, more crawled over the wall and raced toward them.

He had seen Bolt after Bolt lighting the night's sky. In those light flashes he could see what seemed to be hundreds of boats in the water, filled with Geketzim and Ogladim. Where could they be coming from? The question that now troubled him the most was, where were they right now? They had attacked at night and it was now night. *Why were they not attacking?*

Feshka approached. He seemed tired and his sky-blue clothing ap-peared dark, almost black in the light from the stars. "Where are the attackers tonight?" Angus asked him when he was close enough.

"It looks like they're going to try to starve us out," was the reply. Feshka took a seat on the stone steps beside Angus. He wiped his fore-head with his sleeve and took a deep breath. "Have you found the Third Gift yet?" He turned to face Angus.

"No," admitted Angus.

"We're running out of time. You must do this. Can you do it now? There is no way of knowing how long this little peace will last."

"I'll try." More than anything, Angus wanted to succeed, to honor Feshka's request. "Can you watch over me while I go, so no one tries to pull me back before I'm ready?"

"I'll stay right here with you," Feshka promised.

Angus was more fearful this time. He had never before ridden a living flesh and blood horse, much less a high spirited, free-willed stallion like Geemayel. His first rides had been in innocence. He had been fearful of the night and of the creatures that might live in it. He had been fearful of failure. He had feared Boer and the headless creature he had seen on the plain. But now he had a more realistic and physical fear, that of falling off the horse. He had no idea where he might have landed had he not been called back to his body, if his father hadn't been shaking him and trying to wake him.

But Angus wasn't sure if he was saved by being shaken awake or if he'd fallen off the horse *because* he had been shaken awake. He was now frightened of what might happen around his sleeping body while he was out and about. With fear in his heart, his legs trembling, he mounted Geemayel.

This time he was ready with a light scarf when the light became too intense for his eyes. He had covered his skin and his face and he wore gloves over his hands to protect them from the heat. Yet with all this covering, the light's intensity was too great for him. It seemed that his skin was burning right through the cloth. Even under the scarf, he kept his eyes tightly shut against the brightness. With both hands he gripped Geemayel's mane.

Whenever his fear started to overwhelm him, Angus called up a picture of Lurelei's face, focusing his full attention on her eyes, her lips, and the softness of her hair. In his mind's eye he wanted to reach out and touch her cheek, and he almost did, letting go of Geemayel's mane with one hand for just a second. Then he caught himself and grabbed another handful of horse hair to hang onto. The moment of panic passed. It now seemed that the burning sensation was easing. Maybe he was just getting used to it, but it seemed to burn less. He opened his eyes under the scarf and felt no pain from the light.

The thundering of Geemayel's hoofs had stopped. Angus pulled the scarf down from his eyes and looked around. It seemed to him that they were suspended in nothingness but surrounded with brilliant white light. All he could see was white. He had the strange sensation of weightlessness, as if he were falling, but his seat on Geemayel remained firm. He gripped the horse with his knees and held tightly to the hair of its mane, but the sensation of drifting upward persisted. Finally his knees and legs grew tired and he relaxed them. He could feel no weight from his body resting on the horse's back. He felt himself drifting above the horse.

Geemayel turned his head, casting a look of pity at Angus, and let out a snort. Angus let go of the horse's mane and drifted upward and away from the horse. He knew he had arrived at where he was supposed to be and that Geemayel would return for him when it was time. Angus continued to focus on the slowly disappearing horse; it was the only point of reference available. Everything else around him was brilliant white light.

Angus closed his eyes. It was confusing to try to keep them open after Geemayel disappeared, since there was no "thing" on which they could focus. He was amazed and dazzled by the brilliant nothingness and the way he seemed to just hang there in the air, or light. *This place would drive a man mad in only moments*, he thought. Without any point of reference, he was nowhere and everywhere, neither falling nor rising. He couldn't move his body if he tried. His arms and legs still functioned but there was nothing to push off of, or stand on.

Finally he began to grieve. So this was the end - where he would stop existing! He still existed in this bland nothingness, but he knew that time was limited. Lurelei's last hope was lost in the Realm of Light. Again Angus called forth the remembered image of Lurelei. He needed something to be able to see, and there she was before him. The image was so real to him, he opened his eyes; and... there she was...floating only a short distance away!

Angus' first reaction was fear for her. How had she come to this place? Was she now also imprisoned in this constant feeling of falling? He reached out to touch her and as he did so, she vanished. He closed his eyes again, trying to hold the image of her.

Then it seemed he was again beside the River Naver and Lurelei stood beside him. He could hear the rushing of the water nearby. He opened his eyes and in shocked amazement he could see that he was indeed beside the Naver, every detail rich and livid. The grass was green and the sky blue. Angus gasped and it all vanished. Again he was floating in the blank white light with the constant feeling of falling.

He closed his eyes in grief and self-pity. He could feel tears beginning to form under his eyelids and he thought to himself that no one was near and it didn't matter if a tear found its way down his cheek.

In the distance it seemed to him he could hear thunder. It was a new point of reference for him and he opened his eyes again, hoping to see dark clouds, lightning, something for his eyes to rest upon. There it was again, distant thunder, but all was light as before. The thunder sounded again. This time it seemed to form words. Was this a voice? More thunder. He squeezed his eyes shut tightly, trying not to see any more light. He longed for the darkness of natural nighttime. There it was again, and fear welled up inside.

Then the thunder sounded again, and it formed words that said, *"Fear me not, Human, for in such is madness."*

Angus opened his eyes. Before him was a place brighter than the white that had surrounded him before. He tried to focus on it but his eyes were denied that satisfaction. The shimmering glow could not be experienced in detail with his merely Human eyes. He closed his eyes again.

"The only other of Human flesh who entered this place," the voice rumbled," *quaked with fear at our approach and lost his grip on awareness. Let it not be the same with you."*

Angus did his best to stop trembling. He straightened his shoulders and back and held up his head as best as he could while still floating in the light with no place to stand upright. He opened his eyes again and eyed the thing directly. "I will not fear you," he struggled to gather his wits about him. "What are you?"

"I am what I am," the voice rumbled. *"I am something that you cannot understand so there is no point in trying to make you do so. It is better that I ask you some things. Are you the Human sent to us by Forest Old?"*

"I think you know that I am, Sir," answered Angus.

"Yes. We do know," said the voice. *"But it is better for the moment that we make sure that* you *know. Why are you here, Human?"*

"I am here seeking the Third Gift of healing for the Gray Elf Lurelei," replied Angus.

"Such foolish things you Humans do for love," said the voice. *"We have watched wars begun and fought for such. Foolish feats have been won and lost. Lives have been sacrificed for such foolishness. Is your love equal to that of Paris, Agamemnon, or even Jason that you would dare to come here?"*

"I do not know those men, but I believe it must be so, Sir," responded Angus, "or I would not be here."

"Prepare him for the final trial," Angus heard another voice say.

Angus floated silently, staring at the glimmering light before him. The heat around him intensified. At first he began to sweat under his clothing. Then the heat became so intense, the sweat on his face dried as soon as it appeared. The light around him grew even brighter but Angus refused to close his eyes. He glared unwaveringly at the being before him. His skin felt as though it was burning. His beard and hair started to smolder and in a flash it seemed they had burned right off his face and head. His eyebrows were gone and his clothing was smoldering, yet he refused to cry out.

He knew he could call for Geemayel to come and rescue him and he almost did, but the image of Lurelei waiting alone by the Naver held him fast. It was his life or hers. He would stay until he burned to a crisp before he backed down. He believed the creatures around him were only testing his metal and that he would not really be harmed. How could creatures that dwelled in the light murder a guest? How could they be so cruel? He believed it to be a bluff, but it was a good one. His skin seemed to be on fire. The flesh of his hands and face was cooking. He could smell it. His determination began to waver but he held fast to the image of Lurelei. He could not let her down. All this was about Lurelei. *Did he love her or not? Would he really sacrifice his life for her or not?*

The wounds on his neck were throbbing again. It was the first time in days since he'd felt any pain from them. The scars from the Geketz were making themselves felt. His wrists started throbbing and the pain from his throat was beginning to move toward his chest, and his heart.

His clothing was on fire. He could smell the smoke of burning wool around his face. With his lips tight and his breath coming in gasps from the smoke around him he cried out, *"I will never yield!"*

"Yes," said the voice. *"He is more resolute than the other, and more foolish. Let us gather and help him."*

Now it seemed to Angus that his flesh felt whole and cool. He had been right. It was a feint, a bluff. He was uninjured and thankful for the moment that he was not standing, but floating in the void. If he had been standing he felt he would have collapsed.

Now it seemed to him there were others, creatures similar to the first, all glowing and shimmering in the light around him. They gathered in a circle before him and began to move together, as had the aged men in white in the castle on the edge of dawn.

Before him there appeared to be what seemed like a pedestal or base for supporting a sculpture. *"The structure before you is constructed purely of Light,"* the voice began. *"In this place, all things of matter and Magic have been constructed. The Earth, your home, had its beginnings in this place, for all things that exist came originally from the Light. Even the Darkness came from the Light.*

The war you are fighting, in fact, began in the very beginning of creation. It is between the Realms of the Dark and The Realms of the Light. Some stolen Light has been preserved in the Earth. The thieves strive to recover it. It will always be so until the portal through which they pass from the darkness is closed. Perhaps you will close the portal. To do that, you must find The Key. This is your third and final lesson. May you learn it well.

The wounds of the Elf, Lurelei that you have been told of, but be-

ing aware only of the whole, are three in nature. All three are derived from the Realms of Darkness only. This is why, Earth being caught between the two realms, they are very difficult for those of the Earth to cure. But you have friends who love you truly and for whose cause you fight. They have the knowledge to send you to us."

Another voice began, "The first wound is Betrayal. With this type of wound, the victim is robbed of the ability to love. Love generates light. With this wound comes vulnerability to the Demons of Darkness, for the Love and light within is the only shield or protection against these assaults. Its warmth keeps the Darkness away, for the Darkness fears the warmth of Love above all other things."

A third voice entered with, "The second Wound is Separation from all entities of Light, for in them is Love, and the Darkness fears their warmth. It therefore kills them immediately on contact."

A fourth voice began, "And the third wound is the Gift of the Darkness. There are four of us, of the Light, to help you assemble the Crystal, because the number four means 'a passage' and represents the hidden Name of Power. It is the passage through which one may come into the Light and in our number the doorway and Name of Power are present in our midst. You are the fifth party, or the first, and you make us five together. Five means 'a window'. Through this window passes the Light of understanding. With this understanding, you will create the Third Gift for the Lady Lurelei. When you understand The Key behind the creation of these gifts, your power to heal or harm will be nearly unlimited. This is why your integrity has been so tested. Within your creation of this gift lies understanding of The Key, so carefully hidden from Elves and men alike from the beginning.

"We do this," said the first voice, "for those who live on the Earth who are the Children of Light, and in them there is no more darkness than only the darkness of night to hide their brilliance. They are the Elf Folk and they have made you their friend. We help you for their daughter, the Gray Elf, Lurelei and to give you the means to end the war between the Darkness and the Light. It is forbidden that we give you The Key, but it is not forbidden that we give you the tools to find it."

"The Crystal that you shall make here is the most important and most powerful of the Gifts," began the third voice. "Just as a chemical dissolved in water crystallizes when the water becomes too cold to hold it in solution, or the water held in the air condenses on glass or steel when the air cools, this Love Crystal will be condensed into a single mass from your own Love for your Lady. The Wyrm of the Geketz cannot exist in the presence of such spiritual heat. Now we shall see if you bear her such Love."

"*The Love Crystal is pure White as the Light you see around us here,*" the first voice continued. "*It must be formed of the three primary colors that are within you and for of such is Love comprised.*"

"*The highest of these is Blue, the color of Peace,*" one of them continued. "*You must now focus that part of your Love above the platform before you. This is the color of her power and represents that power. Let it be that Peace you feel in her presence, that your Love for her brings to you.*"

Angus focused on the space above the platform and to his amazement a faint blue light began to form in the air. But as he watched, it faded again.

"*You must put aside your disbelief,*" instructed the first voice. "*This is the place where matter is created from thought. Your disbelief unmakes the image. 'Disbelief' is the belief that a thing does not exist. Faith is the power. Do you not remember the things you created by accident before we made our presence known to you?*"

He tried again. This time he released his tenseness and relaxed into the exercise. In his mind's eye, he formed the brightest bluest spark of light he could imagine, and placed it above the platform. He opened his eyes and saw the peace he imagined he could find in Lurelei crystallized in brilliant blue, suspended above the pedestal. As he watched it glowing, he gave it all the energy of Love that he could generate, and it grew in brilliance.

"*Now that you have completed the first part,*" one of them began again, "*the second part of the Love Crystal is the Love you have for her Wisdom, or her mind. This is represented by the color Yellow and it is the brilliance of sunlight in the brightest part of day. Create now the crystal of your Love for her Wisdom.*"

Angus closed his eyes again and visualized the brilliance of the sunlight in the brightest part of day, focused onto one small crystal. He opened his eyes and was dazzled by its brilliance. It hung suspended just below the blue one. The area between, where the two colors overlapped, was filled with a beautiful green glow.

"*Now for the easiest part,*" said the first voice. "*It is the Red of your Passion.*"

He closed his eyes once more. In his mind's eye he could see Lurelei's lips waiting for his kiss. He could feel the warmth of her hand in his and he could see her beautiful eyes waiting to receive him. He then focused all that passion into one brilliant red crystal, in every manner equal to the others. Opening his eyes, he was delighted to behold the brilliance of his passion for her, crystallized into one bright red form. The area between the red and yellow, for the red crystal hung beneath the yellow, was brilliant orange, like a sunset over a blue gulf.

"*Now,*" said the first voice, "*stretch out your hand, above the blue crystal and press it downward into the other two. Press them together to form the One Love Crystal.*"

He did as instructed and could feel the coolness of the blue against his hand. He pressed them downward, the rising warmth of the red with the brilliance of the day between. As he watched, the colors combined to form a Crystal of Pure White, more brilliant than any of the others... more than three times their brilliance, in fact; for the synergy produced was three times more intense than their individual abilities. He withdrew his hand and beheld a thing of beauty greater than could exist in mortal realms. He took the jewel and placed it against his heart as he had done with the others. It disappeared as though absorbed by his being.

"*The Sheeawn within, has made this possible for you,*" said one of them. "*Its creative power, combined with your Love has created the cure for the Gray Elf's affliction.*"

"*Once the gifts are delivered, the Globe of Sheeawn will be her armor against future invasion. The Cudgel of Boer will ward off even the severest attack. And the Love Crystal will fill her now cold Life Center with your Love. Most important of all, remember this. These Three Gifts represent Wisdom, Power and Harmony, for Wisdom generates Power and when Power is wielded by Wisdom, it manifests Harmony.*"

"*Be warned, Human,*" said another. "*For once this gift is delivered, your Love will always be hers, for it is the real Crystallization of what you already hold for her that has made this Jewel a reality.*"

"*It must be placed in her heart while she sleeps, for at such a time, the Wyrm is least active,*" said the first voice.

Chapter Twenty-Three: The Final Battle

The night was as Angus left it, but darker. Clouds had moved over the area, blocking out the stars. The moon had not yet risen, so the sky was totally black. Feshka was still beside him. No others were near.

"Did you get it?" asked Feshka as Angus opened his eyes.

"Yes," Angus grinned broadly. "It's a LOVE CRYSTAL."

He related to Feshka the entire experience and then Feshka in turn brought Angus up to date on their situation. "The Ogladim are back. The streets are full of them. We can't see beyond the buildings but from what we can see of the streets, it seems there are as many as there ever were."

"I'd have thought we'd made a pretty good dent in them. We've killed many."

"Not enough," Feshka shook his head. "Look over there. Can you see the wood piles that were set up along the water's edge?"

Angus tried to see in the darkness, but all he could make out were shadows. "No. What's been done?"

"Along the water's edge they've prepared to build huge fires to keep the Geketzim from climbing over the sea wall. If we see so much as one boat coming this way, those fires will light the night around us."

"What else is going on?"

"I mentioned your idea to Ariel," said Feshka. "They are experimenting with using as many as ten to cast the Bolt. They started by joining two Trines. With six they cast a Bolt at the fortress, but it didn't carry that far. Then they tried three Trines. With nine of them gathered around, the one in the center who actually aimed the Bolt was nearly killed from the concentrated power. Now they are trying it again, this time with three joined to aim the Bolt. It was a good idea, StrathNaver!"

Angus looked out across the water toward the fortress. "Do you see him? There he is right now, watching us!" The lone figure was standing on the highest wall of the fortress, watching.

"They haven't figured out how to send a Bolt that far, but they're working on it. What do you plan to do with the gifts now that you have them?"

"I don't know. Any suggestions?"

"What did they tell you?"

"They said to deliver them when she was sleeping, but how could I find her when she's sleeping?"

"You can join her dream, can you not?"

"She said she cannot enter the place of dreams as a Geketz," declared Angus.

"Then you must find out where she sleeps, but first we have to get out of this place."

"It really doesn't look like we will, does it now?" Angus grimaced.

"You can never guess what the future holds, StrathNaver. The darkest night is always followed by day."

"Or death," finished Angus bitterly.

Angus stalked off to be alone with his thoughts. How would he be able to deliver anything to anyone, penned in as they were? The Enemy obviously far outnumbered them. The only way to freedom was past their encampment in the streets of BungFeddor. They would run out of food probably by tomorrow. If not death by the sword or from a Geketz, it would be by starvation. The Ogladim seemed to know that. As yet there was no attack.

But then why, thought Angus, would the Ogladim attack when they had already won? All they needed to do was sit out there and wait. What did Ariel have in mind for them now? They had to fight their way out. They had to. They would die in the yard anyway.

The Elves had again gathered on the foremen's platforms by the piers. The Trines were formed, just in case. Angus could just make out the forms of the Elves standing in them. He looked out across the water again and could just barely see the outline of the fortress against the night sky. The lone figure was not there. There was a loud crash.

The Ogladim had apparently figured out how to get into the warehouses through their back doors. Those doors had been barricaded and even closed with stone, but now the creatures poured through them effortlessly.

The first alarm Angus heard after the crashing was a shout from within. Then there was the clash of metal on metal and a scream from an Ogladim. Those who were not in the warehouses and not guarding the street barricades rushed toward the sound with Elf Blades gleaming in the night, Angus among them.

At first there was too much of a crowd inside the buildings to get to the fighting. Men, Elves and the few Dwarves who were with the army jammed into the broken warehouse to drive back the invader, but Ariel's voice could be heard warning them to watch the other buildings as well. There were many warehouses fronting on the yard and everyone was crowding into only this one. Those in the back turned and quickly left.

The attack had come at the barricades as well. A dozen or more Ogladim and BigMouths had managed to enter and were attacking anyone near, while still more of the creatures followed. Angus began swinging his Elf Steel as before. His passions rose at first but the fighting was becoming almost mechanical. Swing here. Duck there. Side step now, then again. Dodge. Thrust. It was just like the night past. He killed a Geketz, then another Ogladim.

It amused him that the only a few weeks ago the thought that a Geketz could be killed amazed the Elves. They had thought that Geketzim were invulnerable. Even with the weapons they had developed, the Bolt, the Elf Steel, and with all their other skills, they had thought themselves sheep waiting for the slaughter. What incredible courage it must have taken for them to decide to stand and fight, even though they believed they had no chance.

Angus had changed considerably in those weeks. He had still been only a boy of eighteen when he'd first unsheathed a sword, when he'd first drawn blood from another, with its cutting edge and its point. Now his eyes were no longer innocent. He no longer looked so trustfully at strangers. He watched for the knife in the hidden hand, the cunning of the Enemy behind every door and bush. He expected treachery instead of adventure from the unknown. This new Angus would not have gone beyond the falls that day, fishing with his friend.

They had not found Tristan. MacBain was there among the dead, but his boyhood friend Tristan was nowhere to be found. Angus knew there was no time for grieving. The Enemy was here, bristling with death. It was all around him with weapons, and creatures with teeth. It seemed stronger tonight. There were more Geketzim in the yard and Flying Shadows than Angus had seen before. Was this to be the final battle?

Angus stole a glance at the fortress to see if the lone figure was still watching. There he was. It seemed to Angus that the figure was GaudarKahn himself, overseeing his battle to capture the Elves. His arm was tired of swinging the sword, but worse, his mind was tired of it. Yet he had to continue. He had to survive. If he failed, Lurelei would fail. She would be lost to him and to her family forever. What fate could be worse?

He glanced at the nearest barricade, seeing more Ogladim coming over it. Then with horror and disbelief, he watched as it fell over, pushed from behind. Ogladim flooded through the newly opened gate. More of the army turned their attention to stemming this new flood. Men and Elves converged on the opening, desperately trying to hold back the attackers, but soon they were dispersed over the grounds and fighting individually instead of in a single large group.

Angus moved back toward the northern warehouse, where his clan had been stationed. It was an unconscious move, but he noticed most of his group doing the same thing. They were trying to find a line to hold and the warehouse was the closest thing to home for them. Indeed, it had been their home for several days, so it was the chosen place. Before long most of the army had been driven back into the buildings. They were now fighting a closer holding battle than before. Angus glanced at the platforms from which the Elves had been casting Bolts, but no one was there. What had happened to Star Bright? Where was Marnel?

Angus began to feel a sick emptiness in the pit of his stomach but he didn't have time to think about grief. His attention was demanded for the saving of his life. But wait--there they were! They had retreated down the piers. The Elves had moved. The Bolts still lighted the sky and they still fought on.

With new energy fueled by his relief, Angus killed another Oglat and drove back two more, but the situation seemed hopeless. As they fought, Angus could see still more of them pouring through the open barricades. Some stopped as they entered, and looked around laughing. A few had gathered here and there and were talking. A Geketz had seated itself on the ground not far from him and was waiting for the Ogladim to finish their task before moving in to harvest the available light.

Angus could see fireballs coming from the southern warehouse and knew Feshka was still alive. Another Bolt struck near him and felled four Ogladim at once. Angus had never understood the Bolts. Although the Elves said they came from their life force, when Angus saw them they appeared from the sky like lightning, and a clap of thunder accompanied each one. It was so similar to an electrical storm, Angus was always surprised no rain followed them. Whatever the Bolts' source and nature, he was thankful for them. They had saved him many times during these weeks. He hoped they would save him again.

It seemed the attack was abating again, but dawn had not come.

The Ogladim were withdrawing, not all at once as at first light, but little by little. Then he noticed many were fleeing back down the streets from where they had come, pursued by the army.

Now Angus saw the reason for the retreat. The Dwarves of the Southerlands had arrived. There was another army entering the city, much larger than the first, consisting of Dwarves of every shape and size. Some were lightly clothed and had deep tans, as if they'd come from a warmer climate. Others were heavily clad with coats of wool and other materials that Angus didn't recognize. Still others wore strange hats that Angus had never seen before on Dwarves.

One Human in the army of dwarfs seemed out of place. He was tall, gray and deeply lined. His animal skin clothing was ragged and dirty and his wavy white hair seemed wild and wind-blown. Now he spotted Angus. As Angus grew near, the man declared: "Looks like a Williamson to me!"

"Grandfather!" Angus bellowed out, delight rushing through every part of his being. "We had about given up on you! Not even the Elves knew where you had gone!"

"I told you there was trouble in the south, didn't I now? When I got here I could see that more help was needed than could come out of Alba, so I went farther south to find some."

VeratNonn was beside them. "King BroeNann has arrived," he reported. "I also see subjects of our kinsmen KaarNonn of The Black Mountains, and BereeshNonn of Iberia. When we return to the ocean yard I believe we will see ships approaching from the Bird Islands, from King ValNonn. They have all answered our plea for help. The war is nearly over, StrathNaver, and we've won!"

VeratNonn was right. When the army returned to its former place of rest, Angus could see black sails on the horizon. The clouds had thinned and the moon was about to rise. To the south one could now see a forest of masts rising over black ships swiftly approaching.

Between the two armies the Enemy had been crushed on the mainland. Parties of Ogladim were hunted down and killed. Although the Geketzim had disappeared, the Dwarves were searching for a few that may still be hiding among them. The newly arrived Dwarves were fresh and eager for more fighting. They were a much larger army than the first, by at least triple. Some of them disbanded from the others and went searching for the Enemy in the forests around the city, while others searched all the buildings, trying to find those who may have taken refuge and were hiding. The ships from the Bird Islands carefully docked at the piers in the sea yard with many of the Dwarves boarding them. It was their intention to cross the water and attack the Enemy in his lair.

Angus noticed the lone figure on the fortress walls was gone.

He returned to the building on the north where he had slept and fought. The ground was littered with bodies of men and Ogladim. Very few Elves had been killed, but the clansmen had not fared so well.

Angus's first thought was of William, his father. He hadn't seen him since early evening. First he and Old Will went back into the streets looking among those who were gathered and talking. Then they began searching among those who were gathering arrows and other weapons from the street. William was nowhere to be found. There was Feshka with Aelrondel and Marnel, who were among those collecting spent arrows.

Just after the first daylight, they found William under two Ogladim that had fallen on top of him. He was covered with foul-smelling blood and gore; his clothing was torn and there was a gaping hole in his throat with the jagged blade of a dead Oglat still in it.

Old Will was quiet with a dangerous looking glint of anger in his eyes. Angus was numb.

First it was his mother, then his friend Tristan, and kinsman James MacBain and now William. "My father is dead," Angus muttered to himself. He didn't know whether to sit down and sob, or release his rage with killing. He stood there for a while watching his father's lifeless face in stunned disbelief. The air had grown cold but he didn't notice it. He didn't notice there was frost on the ground where none had stepped, and on the frames of the buildings. Winter was near. The snows were near. The fighting was over. William was dead.

Numb from the pain of his loss, Angus walked over to the well by the edge of the grounds and filled a pan with water that he brought back to his father's body. Carefully he washed the blood from William's face and hands. He combed the clots from his beard and hair and wrapped a scarf around the gaping hole in William's throat. Memory of his father's smile, the way his lips moved when he spoke, the way his hands had caressed his family, his sons and his beloved wife, was too much for Angus.

Removing William's coat, he covered his face with it. Then he walked to the water's edge and sat down, letting his legs dangle over the sea wall as he watched the ships being loaded up with heavily armed Dwarves. One at a time the ships were poled out of their moorings and replaced with another loaded with Dwarves, Elves and Men. He tried to not think about what had just happened. It was a war, after all. People were killed in wars. He himself had killed many. There was blood on his hands and clothes. He still had blood splattered on his face and in his hair and beard. He was alive. He was not even injured, except for the wounds he bore in his heart. Now there was only Lurelei, and of course the final battle. Old Will took a seat beside his grandson and stretched an arm across his shoulders.

"Let's get this done and go home."

Of the original party, besides Angus, only Scobie, Hender and Ingram were left. They helped Angus dig the grave on the north side of BungFeddor in Wesheshica among the graves of many, while Old Will sat nearby watching. It was an ancient burial ground, Angus thought, probably the city's first one. Its graves stretched far and wide under large old trees. The grave markers were mostly wooden, many rotted and unrecognizable. Tristan would have tried to count them, but Angus thought he would have given up before he'd finished. There were simply too many. Even the new graves being dug this day were too many to count. Parties of Humans were everywhere with shovels and spades.

The Dwarves preferred to carry their dead home with them to be buried in deep caves and caverns, as was their custom. The Elves burned the bodies of their dead, and in the sea yard was a huge fire. Aelrondel was there watching the blaze, as were Fierrondel and the others from the Naver. Migalik had fallen that night and with him, Ariel. Star Bright remained alive and while VelMud deeply mourned the passing of his friend, he was near her.

Marnel and Feshka had gone with Angus. There was need for more than one hole and they helped him dig. MacBain was to be buried next to his cousin William. Tristan's body had been found later in the morning. He was to be with them. The burial ground overlooked the sea. From that place Angus could see the black fortress in the full light of day. The perspective was different, since the graves were on the north side of the city. He could see the side of the building, amazed at how large it was. Its wall stretched to the west away from the coastline farther than he thought. It was a monstrous structure.

The Dwarf ships were nearing it, and as they drew closer, Angus stopped digging and took a few steps toward the water, Marnel with him. Beside the north wall of the fortress was a small harbor, out of sight of the approaching black ships. A large dark boat was slipping out of it, turning west. The boat stayed close in near the shore so that the approaching Dwarf ships could not see it. The height of the fortress itself concealed the escaping vessel from them.

"He's going to escape," Marnel muttered.

"What can be done?" Angus said to Feshka who was watching with him.

"We have lost," he said. "When he comes back he will be stronger."

Chapter Twenty-Four: The Gate Keeper's Key

The trek back to the Naver was more difficult, since there was snow on the ground in the mountains. The steep paths were slippery, but at least they were in no hurry. The victory had been hollow and in vain. GaudarKahn had escaped. All these deaths had been fruitless. All the fear and pain and sweat had been wasted.

Angus was anxious to reach Lurelei but first he went to see Robert, his brother to tell him of the death of their father and cousins. The clouds over the Glen were thick, promising snow, but none had fallen yet. The grass in the meadows was lying down, as it did in its wait for the winter sleep. The squirrels had finished their gathering but scurried in the leaves of the forest looking for that last bite of fresh food, whatever they could find before the first hard freeze came to the Glen.

Old Will had gone into Glen Williamson to see the rest of his family. Interested in Lurelei's cure and what could be learned from it, Feshka stayed with him. The half Elf did not expect to live long enough to see the return of GaudarKahn, but he knew he had a duty to pass to those who would need it, whatever could be learned today, from StrathNaver.

Before heading upstream, Angus stopped at his father's house. He cleared away cobwebs and tidied up the place, hoping to return with Lurelei. He wondered at himself as he did it. Oh how he had anticipated this night when he would venture south of the falls again! Since winter was near, the vegetation would not be so thick and he would be able to get through the forest more easily.

The people of the Glen who had gathered to greet him were astonished at the sight of his Elf companions. No more Geketzim had come to the village and no word of the war had reached them since the group had left. Old Will stayed to tell the stories while Angus disappeared again into the forest with Feshka and the others.

Angus and his group picked their way slowly up the river. Its water was not as deep now in the fall, but it was still a torrent of icy water from the mountains in the south. It was still strong enough to easily sweep him off his feet, just as before, thought Angus. He feared the water now more than ever. Remembering his fall into the Haven that turned out to be cavern, he again experienced the terror of almost-drowning. In his mind's eye he could see his breath bubble toward the surface, and the water over his head. He remembered the feel of sinking into it while it soaked through his clothing.

When they reached the falls, Feshka stopped and turned to Angus. "We will stay here, StrathNaver, and wait for you." As their eyes met, they exchanged knowing looks. Then Feshka gripped Angus's hand and squeezed it tightly.

The falls were as he remembered them, but the vegetation was less plush. Tall weeds grew along the water's edge with flowers of red mixed with white, the last to bloom before the snows fell. The climb over the steep hillsides was easier than he thought it would be, but this time he stayed well away from the river. If he slipped he would easily be able to grab hold of a sapling to keep from falling into the water.

He remembered the distance to the level clearing as being greater than it actually was--only a few hundred yards. There was a place for a fire in the center as though Elves had been there, but no fire was lighted, with no evidence of ashes. Wood was stacked neatly beside it, with twigs for tinder and two rocks, one hard and one softer for striking a spark.

Angus understood immediately that Lurelei had left these for him, that when he lit the fire it would be her signal to come to him. Darkness was close. The sun had descended behind the ridge before him. The only light remaining reflected off the clouds. He lit the fire and when it was blazing well, he settled back into the shadows to wait.

As he waited for her, his eyes wandered to study the trees. How bare their limbs had become! The leaves on the ground crackled under his footsteps. A few brown and yellowed ones still clung stubbornly to the branches; he watched them moving in the gentle night breeze.

When Lurelei arrived he didn't hear or see her, but felt a creeping fear move over him as her darkness approached. He studied the darkness, trying to see her form outlined in the shadows; she eluded him completely.

"I'm very hungry, Angus. You're late."

His hand moved to his Elf blade, still sheathed against his thigh, but he did not draw it. From her voice he judged that she was close, only about six feet to his right, and out of the fire's light.

"I'm glad you saw the fire, Lurelei," he responded.

"I am a hungry Geketz and I am about to take your life." Her Geketz voice was harsh and confrontational.

"I have found your cure, Lurelei," Angus did not allow himself to enter into the Geketz's hostile energy. "I'm told by those in the Realm of Light that it can be delivered only while you sleep, for then the darkness is least active."

"The Darkness? What Darkness?!!" Lurelei shrieked. "I am nearly complete! I have chosen my first meal of real light. It lies beyond the falls, and it will be a good meal."

"And if you wait for me, you will be whole again," Angus's voice was strong and firm. He gathered courage. "You will be Lurel of the Gray Elves. You will be a lovely Elfen creature again. There is a cave," Angus continued. "It lies below the falls on the western side of the river. There is a path."

"I know the cave. What of it?"

"Sleep there tomorrow. You will be out of the sun's light and I will be able to find you."

"Do you think to conquer me, Angus? Are you going to try to take me as I am? 'A cure!!' What kind of cure??!!!"

"Enough, Geketz," Angus commanded. "Sleep in the cave and your cure is assured. If you wish to be the Elf you were, be there. If you don't, pursue meals of Light and die like the rest of your kind died at Bung-Feddor in Wesheshica."

Angus felt strong and sure of himself, no longer afraid of the Geketz poison that was blocking Lurelei from him. Had he not killed many of these creatures over the past several days of the war? No Geketz who tried to attack him would ever get away with it again! His Elf blade was stained with the black blood of Geketzim.

"Go now and await me," he commanded Lurelei/Geketz. "When the sun's first light brightens the valley I will be with you." Then he turned and walked away, speedily racing down the hillside below the falls to where Feshka was waiting.

The two talked through the night and when first light approached, they headed toward the cave. Feshka waited at the entrance with Marnel and Arikin.

The cave was as he remembered it. He and Tristan had spent many happy hours exploring it years before. Its deep moist walls had been their hideaway. Inside was a wooden cot, its aging straw mattress falling apart. And there was the rabbit's skin that Tristan had planned to tan for Agnes. Poor Tristan. He was now in the ground near BungFeddor with William and MacBain.

The cave was dark. He had waited till he could see the sun before entering it. The sudden change from light to dark blinded him for a moment and he couldn't see beyond the cave's entrance. As his eyes adjusted, he became aware of the dark form of the Geketz near the rear of the underground room. It was lying on the ground on its back, snoring loudly.

Angus knew what he had to do. He seated himself on the floor of the cave and began to relax his body. Ever since he had made the Crystal he had been able to feel its heat inside him. It brought his memories of Lurelei more freshly to his mind than ever before. As he felt his body drifting into its relaxed and sleeping state, he visualized her once again by the river's edge, her arms around his neck. He could feel her lips on his again, slightly moist and warm.

Suddenly his concentration was broken by the feeling of tight burning hands on his arms and the weight of a crushing burden on his chest. Angus jerked himself back to consciousness barely in time to witness the Geketz seated on his chest, leaning closer to administer the kiss of death. "I thought I would be able to take you before you awoke," it said to him in its grotto-gravel voice. No trace of the Elf's tones remained. "Your friend has been gone for some time, but I waited for you anyway. The Master wants you, Naver. You are now his."

Angus struggled to free himself but he was completely pinned by the Geketz. In the dim light of the cave he could see it fairly well as it bent lower over him. Its black teeth and gaping mouth were open to receive his life. He was about to scream in protest when the impossible happened. Suddenly there was a blinding flash of light and it was as though a hundred clansmen were at his side. A blade of light flashed and his arms were released but he lay still, watching. Some unseen force had attacked the Geketz. It was being driven away from him. It fled deeper into the cave and disappeared from view.

Angus left the cave, still in possession of the gifts.

✥ ✥

Later that day, Angus, sick with rage and disappointment sat by the Strath Naver, just below the falls. Feshka was by his side.

"Marnel and her parents are going to be taking this pretty hard I'm afraid," said Feshka.

Not pleased at the reminder, Angus shrugged. "Many died in these battles.

We all suffered losses. I did all that I could conceivably do. Both my parents were killed. My best friend is buried in BungFeddor and it wasn't even a clear victory."

"Don't be too hard on yourself," replied Feshka. "You learned more secrets than any other Human ever has and this is only a beginning. By the time the Enemy returns, it will be too late for him. You are still in possession of the copies of Boer's weapons. I think it was the Cudgel that drove the thing off of you. And the quest to save Lurelei isn't over until you are ready to give up. Are you ready?"

"No" replied Angus fiercely. "In fact, if you are willing, come with me now. The Geketz sleeps."

In spirit, Angus led Feshka high above the Earth. "Watch below," Angus said to him. The Geketz, Lurelei, will appear to us as a light. There. See it? It's still in the cave?"

"How did you do this?" asked Feshka. "You have made her appear as light when she has none."

"Watch farther," replied Angus. "Those in the Realm of Light said that in the making of the gifts lies the knowledge of a Key understanding. I believe I am at the beginning of that understanding. Let's join her in the cave."

The Geketz had retreated to the deepest part of the cavern. She was half hidden behind a large rock and sleeping through the day on top of the ground. "In The City of The Vision," began Angus. "It was said that the Enemy perverted his creatures by depriving them of self memory. I believe he also deprives them of Light and fills them with Darkness and his own rage.

"One understanding lying in the making of the gifts is this one. There are probably others as well, but listen to this. I made the gifts for Lurelei, just as I made the battering ram that opened the door in the Adytum. I had plenty of help with the gifts, but that help was instructive guidance. I think that the Key understanding is that, I am only limited by my faith and by my imagination.

"Let's try this."

They were standing together, in spirit, in the cave near the sleeping Geketz. Angus stretched out his hands over the Geketz and he visualized a cloud. Giving it the power of his faith and passion, he said to Feshka, "Can you see the cloud I have made?"

"Yes," replied Feshka, "but why have you done this?"

"Let us name this cloud, 'Remembrance,'" said Angus. "Please join me in its creation. Gather your energy and do this with me and help me fill it with the power of remembrance."

Feshka's countenance darkened as he focused his strength. "Now," said Angus, "Let's fill this cloud of Remembrance with Light - our Light, that Light that is Love. Let's allow the Light filled cloud of Remembrance to sink onto the Geketz and see what happens."

As the shining cloud sunk over the sleeping form of the Geketz, they watched in satisfaction, while the darkness of its form evaporated, leaving the sleeping figure of a young Elf whose name would shortly be changed back to Lurel. Angus watched as her eyes opened and a smile appeared on her face.

"When GaudarKahn returns," said Feshka grimly, "he will find a whole new world awaiting him."

∽✦✦⟩

Fall again. Two years had passed since the battle of BungFeddor. Angus had gained some weight and a new daughter - Elskida. With his new plumpness and happiness had come the danger of complacency. Safety seemed easy to take for granted with the Ogladim and Gaudarkahn no more than distant memories. The Elves were content in their forest retreats. Feshka was back in the City of The Vision and the Elf scholars had returned to debating the hidden meaning in the Weaves. No more had been learned of GaudarKahn's departure or fate, but no more fell creatures had been seen in the forests. The Elves were satisfied with their victory and now appeared openly to humans in the light of day.

Angus and Lurel had chosen to live in the cottage Angus secretly built in the seclusion of the mountain. It was far up the hillside, away from the community in Glen Williamson and the protection of society of family and friends. It was a comfortable cottage near a stream. The crystal water fell contentedly down the hillside over rock and mountain contour toward the River Naver. The sound of the falling water lulled Angus to sleep nights in the arms of his beloved lady. He took great joy in watching his new daughter, the very image of Lurel, growing rapidly in the dearly bought safety of the Highland forests. Food was plentiful. The sheep were healthy. The MacDonalds had gone back to their Isles and all was well with the world, or so it seemed.

On this day, Angus went into the forest to search for herbs Lurelei requested that he find. The search was longer than he expected, but he found the desired plants and was making his way back through the trees toward the cottage when he heard the loud crack; the sound that always follows the making of the Bolt.

He stopped in his tracks, recognizing the sound but not immediately registering its significance. "Strange to hear that noise again," he considered. He continued his walk toward home. Gradually, then more quickly his expression changed and suddenly he dropped the pack he had been carrying, containing the herbs. He broke into a frantic run toward his cottage, toward his Lurel and Elskida of the bright red hair and smiling Elf eyes; Elskida of the tiny hands that grasped his fingers one at a time in their year old grip. Terror now seized at his heart, and rage that a new danger may have appeared. Slowing, he grabbed a fallen limb for a club and withdrew his ever present, black handled dagger, the Skyn Dhu, now enhanced with Elf magic. His speed was redoubled. Leaping over fallen wood and rocks, he sailed through the forest toward home with agility enhanced by hysteria and fear.

Finally he could see the outline of his home through the trees but the fall foliage of many colors still concealed the entrance and foreground. He thought he could hear a distant moaning over the crashing sounds of his racing footsteps. The seconds it took to clear the last of the trees seemed to take an eternity of pain, fear and rage. He stopped to survey the yard. He found Lurel seated on the top step before their door with Elskida standing unsteadily before her, hanging on to the side of a basket. Angus could see tiny sparks leaping from Elskida's fingers and hair. She seemed enraged. Her eyes were flashing.

Angus approached, cautiously eyeing the trees. "It's over there," said Lurel, pointing. Angus followed her gaze. It was still changing, when he found it. The head and shoulders of some ancient Elf victim were beginning to take shape, reforming from the monstrosity it had become in the service of the enemy. The Geketz was undone and its former self, emerging.

Lurel rose from her seat, lifting Elskida. She met Angus halfway to the beast. "It tried to take Elskida," she told him. "It tried to take our daughter; a Geketz in broad daylight! I was trying to make the Bolt, but our daughter did it. Elskida made a Bolt, but it wasn't like our Bolts - the Bolt of the Gray Elves. She's only a year old! How could she..."

Angus heard a sound at the edge of the forest and in alarm turned to see Old Will, his grandfather, standing there watching the scene unfold, seeing his great granddaughter for the first time. Old Will was watching the baby with stunned amazement showing in his face. Angus turned his head to follow Old Will's gaze and in surprise discovered Elskida glaring back at the old man. It was Old Will that broke the silence with "So. It's the Morrigan. You've come back."

To Angus's complete surprise, Elskida spit on the ground in the direction of her Great Grandfather, Old Will Roy Williamson of Glen Williamson of the Valley Naver.

Glossary

Aelronde

Aelrondel

Aelrondenne
  The daughter of Migalik. The different forms of the name represent
  the stature of the individual. *See* **Suffixes**

Aeser gods
  This humanoid species lived for a time on the frozen tundras of the
  far north. No one knows for sure where they came from or where
  they went when they vanished, but Norse legend is filled with stories
  of their feats and adventures. Some think that their existence on
  Earth coincided with the events at Sumer, 10,000 to 490,000 years
  ago. It has been theorized that they were refugees from a nearby
  planet, like Mars, which underwent dramatic climatic changes,
  about half a million years ago, making survival on that world impossible. Other ancient sources allude to Giants in the Earth, Nephe-
  lim (literally 'those from above' or 'those who have come down from
  above'), the Anunnaki peoples (remembered as a giant, middle eastern race) and others.

Aesers
  Legendary gods of the Vikings - See "Aeser gods," above

Agri-ifone
  Leader of a Kaduetza of the Ogladim, an OeberKaduetza

Alba
Ancient name for part of Scotland

Albright
Family name in Glen Williamson, i.e. Steely Albright

Angeline
Migalik's Grandmother, the maker of the weaves

Anglesheel
An island in Wesheshica

AriMa
[Accent on the second syllable] Younger son of Ariel, the Rebeck of the Firthlands

Ariel
[Accent on the first syllable] Rebeck of the Firthlands, father of Ari-Ma and Arikin

Arikin
[Accent on the first syllable] Older son of Ariel the Rebeck of the Firthlands

Asgard
The name of the home of Odnir, an Aeser god

Baelrog
A genuinely fell creature

Baerns
[Bay-Airn] Arcaic word for "babies"

Baine
A Family name in Glen Williamson

Banneall
A descendant of the line of Barreal

BarDoschel
[Glottal fricative on the 'osch'] An ancient and respected King of Kings of the Elves of Yeephrawaine, A Grand Sovereign

BarNeesh
A servant or page of VeratNonn

BarNockel
Rebeck of the Southerlands

Bareall
Ancient leader of a race of intelligent canines

BarrenNock
Migalik's father-in-law, the father of Star Bright

Barteel
A young Elf/Human halfling who fought in "The War Between Friends," a.k.a. "The Dwarf Wars"

BaynYamen
An ancient hero of the Elves of Yeephrawaine

Be'erMagrel
One of Angus Williamson's conductors at his initiation

BereeshNonn
King of the Dwarfs of the Iberian Mountains

BooGraTom
OeberKaduetza of a Kaduetza of Ogladim - like a sergeant

Booreetza
The name of an Oglat

Brenna
Mother of Tristan

Brith Gar-Nunsum
An ancient secret order among the Elves

BroeNann
King of the Dwarfs of the Southerlands

Bruda
Wife of Robert Williamson, Angus's Sister-in-law

Brude
Ancient Pictish King, builder of Castle Urquhart on Loch Ness

BungFeddor
A major city in Wesheshica of the Westerlands

Caleel
The servant of Boer

Carly
Wife of Ian Williamson

City of the Vision
Home of the weaves, located in the eastern most Firthlands.

Cosgrove
A family name in Glen Williamson

Drumnadrachit
A beautiful village located in the Great Glen

Easterlands
The European mainland, north of the Iberian Peninsula

Elf
This word is a human corruption which combines the true and ancient form, Eaolofiin, pronounced [aye oh low fee un] with the primary accents on the 'aye' and the 'low.' The Elves were the first peoples in Alba, by far predating even the Aesers who later came to be regarded as gods. Also Eaolofiinen (plural) (Old High Elf)

Elfkin
Any person having some portion of Elf Ancestry

Elskin
Ancient Viking word for "beloved"

Elvehim
Old High Elf for the plural form of "Elf"

Eonomel
Ancient hero of YeePhraWaine

Feshka
Half Elf, half Human and raised among the Elves. He was once the Rebeck of the Southerlands, under the name, Barteel, an honor seldom bestowed upon any who were not pure blooded. He later specialized in the study of light manipulation among the Brith Gar-Nunsum.

Fierronde

Fierrondel

Fierrondenne
One of Migalik's daughters. See *Suffixes* for an explanation of the inflexions

Firthlands
The lands to the west of Alba, bordering the sea

GarMawk
The name of a young male Elf, a friend of Silver Leaf

GaudarKahn
[Gau-oo-der-Kahn] The head bad guy.
Warning: It is unlucky to enunciate this name outloud.

Geemayel
The name of a very special horse

Geketz
Generic name for a type of Servant of GaudarKahn

Geketzim
Plural form of the word "Geketz"

Glowamel
Mother of AriMa and Arikin, wife of Ariel

GreYen
An order of human traders of YeePhraWaine

GroessMunden
A type of servant of GaudarKahn

GroessMundenen
Plural form of "GroessMunden"

GulDockel
A friend and neighbor of Migalik

Gunn
The family name of a neighboring Clan to Glen Williamson

Hadrian's Dyke
A massive wall built across southern Scotland by the Roman militarist of that name. Its purpose was to hold back the Wild Highlanders from raiding the Roman encampments.

Halfling
A person whose mother and father belonged to different races

Hender
A family name in Glen Williamson

Hendersons
A family name in Glen Williamson; Sept name of Clan Gunn

Ingram
Name of a man living in Glen Williamson - Ingram Williamson

Islemen
Generic name for people who live on islands off the coast of Alba/Scotland

KaarNonn
The name of the King of the Mountain Dwarfs

Kaduetza
A group of Oglats or Ogladim 10 or more in number

Kareem
Wife of Guldockel - friends of Migalik

Laura (Williamson)
Mother of Angus, 3rd cousin to Migalik

Lee-eesh
Wife of MarNosh, mother of Lurelei

Lura

Lurel

Lurelei

Lurenne
See *Suffixes* - Daughter of MarNosh and Lee-Eesh, sister to Mar-nel

MacAodh
The children or descendents of Aodh. "Aodh" is thought to be derived from "Ian." The "D" is silent.

MacBain
A family name in Glen Williamson and Sept name belonging to Clan MacAodh

MacCleod
The name of a neighboring Clan

MacDonald
The name of a neighboring Clan

MacDonell
The name of a neighboring Clan

MacFall
The name of a neighboring Clan

MacIntosh
The name of a neighboring Clan

MacKinnon
The name of a neighboring Clan

MacMillan
The name of a neighboring Clan

MacNicols
The name of a neighboring Clan

MarNosh
Father of Lurelei, husband of Lee-eesh

Marnel
Sister of Lurelei. Daughter of MarNosh and Lee-eesh

Migalik
King of the Naver Gray Elves, Dream Maker for the greater Naver Region

Morrigan
A.K.A. Brigid, Brighid, Bride, Minerva, Athena, Hecate and The Morrigan. Morrigan's involvement in the ancient affairs of Clan MacKay, explain why the clan is also sometimes referred to as Clan Morgan. The Morrigan was one of the major, ancient Deities of Great Britain.

Mishishel
Rebeck of Wesheshica of the Westerlands

Napjerking
The act of dropping one's head when falling asleep in a sitting position, then jerking it up again, resisting sleep

Naver
The name of the river, or Strath, flowing through Glen Williamson

Odnir
The name of an ancient Aeser god

OeberKaduetza
The leader of a kaduetza of Ogladim

OeberKaduetzim
Plural form of OeberKaduetza

Offa's Dyke
Same as Hadrian's Dyke but built across Wesheshica to keep the Wesheshicans from raiding Roman encampments. Named for King Offa, a Human king in the Westerlands, also known in the modern-day as Wales.

Ogladim
Plural form of "Oglat"

Oglat
A Human, Elf, Dwarf or other race after its capture and processing by GaudarKahn

Pictish
Being of the race of Picts of ancient Alba

PoleeShimel
Companion and servant of the Rebeck Mishishel

Rebeck
A title of leadership which includes spiritual as well as military qualities. A Rebeck is the most powerful of the Elves, answerable only to the kings.

Rohendrel
One of Angus Williamson's conductors at his initiation

Rhune
An ancient lettering system

Scobie
A family name in Glen Williamson and sept name of Clan MacAodh

Shashiel
Rebeck of the Easterlands

Sheeawn
An ancient high Elf of the order of the Brith Gar-Nunsum, who lived during the days prior to the Elves' residence at YeePhraWaine. It was Sheeawn who studied the nature of light, learning that it is neither wave nor particle, but the very essence of the Divine.

Skyn Dhu
The Black-Handled dagger carried concealed by all worthy Scots

Southerlands
Lands lying to the south of the Highlands; also refers to a clan of low degree who later in history proved themselves evil and brigands to the children of Clan MacKay and others. (Reference "The Highland Clearances" 1814)

Southlands
See Southerland

Strath

Ancient Scottish Gaelic for "River"

Strath Naver

"The River Naver." Not to be confused with StrathNaver which refers to Angus Williamson

Suffixes

...*el* is earned, indicating special valor, or courage, or intelligence
...*a* indicates a child
...*enne* indicates a student, older than a child but less than an adult
...*lei* ndicates tragedy.
As a footnote to these comments: Feshka chose the child ending to indicate his acceptance of his own limitations. It is an acknowledgment of his humanity that he regarded as making him inferior to either pure Elves or pure Humans.

Trined

Anything gathered in threes. Derivative of Tri- Trine or three

Tris

Nick name for Tristan Cosgrove Williamson

Tristan

As in Tristan Cosgrove Williamson - A friend of Angus Williamson MacAodh

Urquhart

The name of a castle thought to have been constructed in the fifth century C.E. by one King Brude, a Pict. The remains of Castle Urquhart lie in ruins in modern-day on the north side of the Great Glen in which lies Lock Ness. Modern archeologists believe that the hidden chambers of Castle Urquhart contain materials contaminated by the Black Death, and so its Haven remains protected by superstition. Castle Urquhart is first mentioned in history in Saint Columba's letters to the Pope concerning his missionary activities in the region, dated 7th Century.

ValNonn

King of the Dwarfs of the Bird Islands

VelMud

Friend of Migalik and Star Bright, one time rival with Migalik for the hand of Star Bright

VeratNonn

Representative of the Dwarf King BroeNonn

VishNaronn
King of the Wood Elves of the Easterlands

WarNock
King of the Sea Elves who live in the far north

Wesheshica
An area in the southern Westerlands-Modern-day Wales

Wesheshican
A person who is native to Wesheshica

Westerlands
See Wesheshica

Wicke
A magnificent city on the northeast tip of Scotland

Williamsons
Descendants of William MacAodh, son of Angus MacAodh, a fair and bright family, indeed, especially in modern day, as illustrated to all who know them by Joel, Jill and Janet.

Will Robert Williamson
Father of Angus

Will Roy Williamson
A.K.A. Old Will - Grandfather of Angus

Wyrm
Old High Elf for "Virus" or "Illness"

YeePhraWaine
See Foreward

YeePhraese
Someone who is a native of YeePhraWaine

ZarFusim
GaudarKahn's word for Groessmundenen

About the Author

Robert G. Makin found his life paths growing up on Laurel Mountain. There he became friends with Elves and Flying Squirrels, did spelunking at Wild Cat Rocks and listened at the feet of his grandfathers to the stories of the Railroad, the Steel Mills and the Old Country. Bits and pieces of Old German and ancient Scottish Gaelic still creep into his conversation from those days gone by. A degree in Fanciful Literature from Indiana University of Pennsylvania fueled his drive to learn more about Elven History and their social structure. He sought fulfillment at Lancaster Theological Seminary of the United Church of Christ where he discovered Essenism, some of the precursors of Biblical History and the stories told to Abraham as Abraham sat at the feet of his grandfathers. They were stories of Nanna, Ningur, Inanna, Ya and Enlil, at the birth of Human Kind. Makin found that there is no history quite like oral history, nor quite as honest. Some truths have been politically incorrect for millennia and forbidden from written histories. Some truths have been corrected and updated to fit what's popular. Makin has found them hidden in Social Artifacts and takes pleasure in their unraveling and revelation.

Makin earned his bread for many years by selling opinions. Today he spends his time, sharing his love for and the history of St. Augustine, Florida with visitors from all over the world who come to hear his tales. In StrathNaver Legends, Makin expresses the exuberant mysticism of the unknown, the what-if's, the maybe's and the things that very well may have been, like friendships with Flying Squirrels and Elves.

www.ingramcontent.com/pod-product-compliance
Lightning Source LLC
Chambersburg PA
CBHW070210030726

47505CB00006B/1631